# EVIL BOYS

# EVIL BOYS

CLARISSA WILD

Clarissa Wild Books

# Author's Note

Evil Boys is an extremely dark bully romance, and with such material comes a warning. Please note that this book is not for everyone. The main girl is incredibly cutthroat and ruthless, as are the boys she's up against, and they will spare no mercy. Not on her or on you.

This book will devour your soul and leave you wondering how on earth it stole your heart. But you will fall in love with these evil boys, just like I did.

Because you're a good fucking girl.

And good fucking girls deserve all the boys who would burn down the world for them.

TW/CW can be found here:

https://www.clarissawild.com/evilboys-tw/

To all the book sluts who go feral over masked strangers
that fuck like they kill ...
I got you.

# Prologue

### LANA

"Look at me," he says, gripping my chin. "Look at the man who owns this fucking pussy."

His pierced shaft stretches me, pushing me to my limits while his fingers slowly tighten around my neck. I can't breathe. I can't fucking breathe. And through all of that ... my pussy throbs with a need I've never felt before.

A need only *they* manage to coax out of me.

Kai Torres, Nathan Reed, Milo Fletcher. Names I was told were forbidden, unspeakable. Names I would soon moan from my lips.

Nathan and Milo each grasp a breast, twisting my nipples until I squeal, the sound making their dicks throb in their hands. And all it does is make me want to beg.

These boys from the Phantom Society have tainted me beyond repair. I'm a fighter, but I'm defenseless against their obsession.

"Yes, give me everything," Kai groans, burying himself inside me to the hilt. "Even your fucking breath."

But I couldn't possibly give something I no longer possess.

Because all I am, all I've ever been ...

Was always theirs for the taking.

# I

## LANA

I stare at the list of names hastily scribbled on the paper Felix stuffs into my hand.

"I don't want you hanging out with any of these people. Got it?" he says, staring me down. "You've been here a couple of months now, so I hope for your sake you haven't talked to any of them."

My eyes transfix on the names.

At the top in bold are two names, Nathan Reed and Kai Torres, and beneath that, practically all the guys from the same fraternity ... Phantom Society.

"I don't even know who these people are," I mutter, annoyed he's making my life more difficult, as usual.

"Good, keep it that way," he says, stuffing his hands into his pocket.

I lower the paper and raise my brow at him. "You for real?"

He squints. "It's your first real fucking year here, and you don't know this university like I do. Those fucking Phantoms can't be trusted."

"Why?" I ask.

Felix's eyes narrow. "Doesn't matter. Don't even think about them." He looks around the campus at the people walking and sitting in the grass, nervously biting the inside of his cheek. His eyes settle on three boys smoking near the fountain.

One of them hides his face beneath a black hoodie like he doesn't want to be spotted, dark streaks of wavy hair peeking out, and both hands stuck in pockets of his track pants. Tattoos can be seen under his sleeves.

Another one with light blond hair and a side sweep, along with sharp, piercing blue eyes, has his hand tightly tucked into his expensive jeans like he's clutching a knife. A bunch of tattoos peeks out from underneath the white shirt covered by a leather jacket.

The third is tall and thin but muscular looking in a lean way, with short red-dyed hair in a side part. He's wearing an actual white button-up shirt and tie. How odd. His thin lips crack a mischievous smile as he toys with the end of his tie.

All of them stare at Felix.

Or us both.

I can't tell.

"You don't know who else is listening," Felix grits.

I laugh. "Oh please. Like anyone cares."

He makes a big fuss out of everything. Dad already said he had enough of all the fighting on this campus. And now that he's taken over this school as dean, I don't see a reason Felix should continue to be so vigilant, especially regarding me.

"Stop worrying so much," I add.

He flicks my forehead so hard I wince. "What the fuck did you do that for?"

"Because I fucking care about you," he retorts. "And so should you."

"I'm gonna chop off your finger if you ever do that again," I retort, threatening him with a finger equally deadly.

He snorts. "Remember what Dad said; no fighting on campus." And he rubs my beautifully combed hair so wildly it pisses me off to the point of screaming out loud.

"Felix! My hair!"

Now I've gotta spend another fifteen minutes brushing out all the tangles to make it perfect and smooth again.

"Looks lovely. Catch you later," he says before he walks off, leaving me fuming and ready to rip him a new asshole.

Suddenly, someone throws their arm around my shoulders. "Hey! Who was that handsome guy?"

It's Brooke, one of my fellow Beta Pi sorority girls who has a room right across from mine. She casually throws her long, wavy blond hair over her shoulder and side-eyes Felix. "Friend of yours?"

The thought that she'd be even remotely interested in him makes me want to puke.

"My brother," I reply.

"Oh ..." She licks her lips. "Well, if he's avail—"

"No. He has a girlfriend."

And besides, I would never, *ever* introduce one of my friends to Felix.

In fact, I would rather swallow one of those dead rats he feeds his snake than see him kiss one of my friends. Gross.

"Aw ... Well, if they break up, tell me first, 'kay?" She winks.

*No thanks.*

"Oh, what have you got there?" she asks, and she rips the paper from my hand before I can tuck it into my pocket.

"Just some stupid list my brother gave me," I reply. "It's no big deal."

I try to steal it back, but she won't let me.

"These names. These are all Phantom guys," she mutters. "And some from Tartarus too."

I frown. "You know these guys?"

"Yeah, of course I know the Phantom Society and Tartarus. They're only the biggest frat houses on this entire campus." She snorts. "Everyone knows about them."

Well, I didn't. I've been far too busy with my studies.

"Can I have it back now?" I ask and snatch it away.

"Why did your brother give you this?" she asks.

"I don't know. He just told me not to ever talk to any of these people." I shrug. "Whatever. It's not like it matters."

She makes a face. "Wow, your brother sounds really obsessed. And protective. Which is kinda hot."

I give her a playful punch on the shoulder. "Oh my God, stop. You're embarrassing me."

"Well, this is more like a grocery shopping list than anything else."

I laugh, and she hooks her arm through mine as we walk across campus, headed straight toward the boys my brother told me not to interact with. "Look. Some of the boys from your list are over there."

Brooke winks at the dudes near the fountain.

"Phantom Society boys are notorious heartbreakers ... and rich," Brooke adds, gloating. "So I'm definitely gonna try my shot."

"I'm not stopping you," I muse.

It's not like I haven't noticed them, but I really don't want to go over there. They give me the creeps. The way they're looking at us. At me.

As if they want to eat me alive.

I throw my hair over my shoulder, determined not to let them get to me. But we're steadily closing the distance, and Brooke's heading straight toward them.

Right as we pass them, Irina, my other Beta Pi sorority housemate, suddenly runs up to me and squashes me into a hug. "Lana!"

"Whoa, whoa!" I mutter as my feet cave under the added unexpected weight, and I fall backward into the fountain.

Midway, I'm stopped.

A firm hand presses into the small of my back.

A chill runs up my spine.

When I slowly turn my head, I stare straight into the face of the guy hiding in his hoodie. But he has only one green eye and one icy white one covered by a gnarly-looking scar from his brow to his cheek.

And I can't stop fucking staring at the one functional eye, sparkling and filled with regret. Hauntingly beautiful. Like he's looked death in the eyes and returned from hell itself.

"Sorry!" Irina drags me away, pulling me out of the spell. "I got too excited."

I don't even know how to respond. I can still feel his fingers even though they're no longer pushed into my flesh. Like a memory imprinted straight into my skin.

"Thanks," I mutter over my shoulder at the guy who saved me from a dirty birdbath.

"Sure," he replies, tucking his hand into his pocket.

But the glimmer in his eye makes it hard to look away.

Especially with the other guys staring at me over his shoulder. It's like they're deciding whether to let me walk or drown me in the fountain.

Fuck.

"Don't look too long ..." the one with the blond hair murmurs. "Or you might lose one too."

My eyes widen.

*Does he mean ... my eye?*

"It's our first day. I'm so freaking excited!" Irina squeals in my ear. "C'mon, c'mon! Let's go!"

She hooks her arm into mine and hauls me away from the boys until finally, I stop looking and focus on what's in front of me. Irina and Brooke drag me toward the school, but I can't stop thinking about those damn boys.

I take another glance at the fountain, too curious why that one guy tried to save me from wet clothes. But they've already turned their backs to us and continue talking to each other like nothing ever happened.

*Why am I even thinking about this?*

"Who are those dudes?" Irina suddenly asks. "I saw the way he looked at you, and damn, it was eerie as hell."

Another chill creeps up my spine.

"Phantom Society," Brooke tells her, and she pulls a can of Coke from her bag and takes a sip. "Sneaky fuckers they are. They're not at the top of the class; those are usually Skull & Serpent Society guys, but if you ask me, the Phantom guys are much more of a threat to most girls."

"Why?" Irina asks.

"They have connections to some grimy and dangerous businesses. And none of it is out in the open. Underground stuff you really don't want to get involved in."

"Like what? Drugs?" Irina asks.

"Oh much, much more from what I've heard," Brooke replies, taking another big sip. "Gambling, shady deals involving blood money ... trafficking."

"The list goes on," I say.

"Exactly."

"So my brother was right?" I ask.

"Well, maybe about some, but not all of them are like that." Brooke shrugs.

"You just never know which one is the bad apple," Irina says.

"Exactly," Brooke replies, winking, but then Irina steals her Coke and takes a sip. "Hey!"

"What? I'm thirsty," Irina mutters, shoving it back into Brooke's hand.

"Not as thirsty as Brooke," I muse.

Brooke snorts. "True."

A smirk spreads on my face. "Anyway, enough boy talk. Let's go inside and find our classes."

*\*\**

# NATHAN

I stare at the girl chatting with her friends near the door to the main building. The girl with the long, straight black hair neatly combed over her shoulders, bangs at the front, and a red ribbon at the top waving in the wind, drawing attention away from her bright-red dress and black pantyhose. The girl so blissfully unaware of all the fucked-up things I could've done to her if she'd stared at Kai for even a second longer.

I know that girl ...

She has those same hollow eyes as Felix, only with a much bigger smile on her face.

A smile I'd happily crush in my hands just to get a glimpse at his rage.

I take another drag of my smoke and chuck it into the fountain.

"Should've just let her fall in," I say.

"And risk getting chewed up and spit out by her brother?" Kai responds, pulling his hoodie farther over his head. "No thanks."

"We've been nice enough not to butcher him and his friends on sight after what they did to us. If it were up to me, I would've dunked her in myself for having the balls to fall into my lap."

"Lucky it wasn't your lap she fell into, then," Kai says.

My eyes narrow, and I stare him down for a moment. "You ... wanted that to happen, didn't you?"

"Oh, do I hear a twinge of jealousy?" Milo taunts, but I ignore him.

Kai snorts. "Of course not." He fishes a small metal flask from his pocket and takes a sip. "But I won't pass up the opportunity to score some points with those fuckers. Keep them from attacking us when we're weak."

"Weak?" I snatch the flask from his hand. "Phantoms aren't weak. Those Skull & Serpent Boys will get what they deserve and you'd better be ready." I take a big sip and shove it back against his chest. "Now are you on my side or theirs?"

He tilts his head and grins. "Do you really have to ask?"

Milo rubs his hands together. "I can't fucking wait."

My eyes land on that girl again. The girl Felix called Lana ... His sister. "Maybe she can be our way in to that fucking snake den."

\*\*\*

## LANA

After our first classes are over, we eat dinner together and chat about our day. Irina and Brooke are good company, and I can definitely see myself hanging out with them during the coming months. They seem very loyal, and I need that type of friend going to this school as a Rivera. Everyone both reveres our family name and despises it in the same breath.

We're a family with a lot of power. A dozen brands under my father's belt like the Rivera clubs make it hard for people to look beyond our wealth and influence. Besides, now that my father is also dean of Spine Ridge University, it makes it really hard for me to walk around anywhere without getting eyeballed from a million different directions.

I'm so glad Irina and Brooke don't seem the least bit scared of all of that. Too bad they can't follow me everywhere.

When the night falls, and all the Beta Pi sorority girls are fast asleep, I'm still scrolling on the web, determined to find my next target. The kind of place I want to go to is not one to look for during the day, and especially not on any regular website. This Tor Browser allows me to search through directories, watching, lurking, and waiting for bait.

And when I finally have it, a wicked smile forms on my lips.

I type out the words I know will cause a ripple in the pond and press send.

Now it's time to move.

I open my closet and take out my bag that I keep for special occasions such as this one. I check if I've got all my gear before I sling it over my shoulder and walk to my mirror. I put on the red ribbon and tie it firmly into my hair, along with some red lipstick and the highest laced booty heels I can find in my closet. Then I grab the black kitten mask and tuck it into my bag.

I'm so glad my dad got me a room without any roommates. The privilege of being rich sure comes in handy when you have nefarious plans.

I smile at myself in the mirror before I strut out the door, putting my bag over both shoulders. I head straight out the back door, worried someone might still be awake. My motorcycle is out front, and I jump on and put on my helmet and gloves, and insert my earbuds, then race off into oblivion.

Violent music blasts through the earpieces as I veer left and right across the road and head for the gates that lead off the compound. My mind goes a million miles an hour, and the bike can't keep up. I need to go faster, harder, louder.

Where I'm going, there are no tears of happiness, no smiles of bliss, not even an inkling of emotion except rage.

Straight into hell's mouth.

Down, down, down, I go along the mountain and into the bustling city, where white collar business and crime go hand in hand. But I'm not looking for a butt-clenching crook, nor have I hooked a big fish. I'm headed into the outskirts of Crescent Vale City, going for the lowest of the lows. Where pure scum live in houses not even a roach would touch.

I park my motorcycle outside the most repugnant house I've ever seen, barely staying upright with crooked wooden beams and taped-off windows. The stench of drugs meets my nostrils halfway across the street.

Taking off my helmet, I fish my kitten mask from my bag and slip it on.

I clutch my bag close to my shoulder as I head into the house without a second thought.

The putrid smell of pot makes me recoil, but I continue through the narrow hallway littered with fast-food packages. In the far back, a loud television blasts, the sounds of squealing women faking orgasms drawing me closer.

In front of the screen is a big red chair covered in stains, inside a man with a potbelly, wearing only a pair of underpants and a shirt that's too small to cover his body.

The floor creaks under my foot with my next step, and I freeze.

The man turns around and looks at me over his chair.

"Oh, you're here," he says.

I don't respond.

He gets up and pats down his chest, crumbs of old pizza falling to the floor. I look around at his miserable life, wondering how a person can live like this and be content.

But the smile on his face gets me the most.

"Can I get you a drink?" he asks.

"No, thanks," I reply, staying put.

"C'mon, c'mon," he says, beckoning me to a couch to the left. "Let's sit over here and chat."

I swallow and stare him down as he flops down and pats the fabric, seemingly oblivious to my revulsion.

He grins at me with bits and pieces of food still stuck to his gums. "I won't bite."

*Doubtful.*

"You ... are the girl I spoke to, right?" he asks, frowning when I don't come near.

I nod silently.

"Then there's no need to hesitate," he says, rubbing his thigh.

In my high heels, I step closer and lower my bag.

"How often do you do this?" I ask.

"With other girls? Never," he replies.

"Don't lie to me," I say.

He sighs. "If I answer, will you sit down?"

I nod.

"Sometimes," he says after a while.

"Same age as me?" I ask, tilting my head as I zip open my bag.

"Of course," he replies, and he puts his hand on my leg to pull me closer. "I like my girls young ... beautiful, like you." He smirks. "You didn't tell me you were into masks."

"Young ..." I repeat, my eyes twitching. "Too young to say no."

And I pull my hammer out of my bag and jam it into his face.

He groans and grips his nose as blood pours out. "Fu—What the fuck are you doing?"

"Giving you what you asked for," I answer, taking my knife from my bag and ramming it straight into his hand.

He squeals like a pig, tearing his hand away from my thigh, but I grab him and twist his arm so badly he's forced down onto the floor.

"Please, don't hurt me!"

"Is that what those other girls screamed?" I retort, twisting his hand some more.

"No, please, they wanted it—"

"They were kids!" I hiss.

He sinks onto the floor, groaning in pain.

I grip his hair and pull back, pointing the knife at his face. "You thought I was one of them, didn't you? Young, innocent, easy to use." My lip hitches up into a tentative smile. "I blend in easy, don't you think?"

"You ... you trapped me?" He coughs up a tooth and spits it out onto the floor.

"I lured you into your own fucking trap," I retort, the knife glinting in my hand.

"Please, don't do this, I'll give you anything you want." His eyes flick back and forth between me and the knife.

"I don't want your money," I reply.

"Then what do you want?" he yelps. "Take it, anything I have."

"I don't want anything but your fucking life."

"Wait, wait, wait," he begs as I inch closer with the knife. "Are you a cop?"

I snort. "Worse."

I jam my knife straight into his abdomen.

He gurgles up blood. "Oh God! Please! Who are you?!" he cries out. "Have mercy!"

But I ignore his pleas and shove another knife straight into his neck.

He gurgles, and a single tear rolls down his cheek.

"I'm retribution."

I tear out the knife, and blood spurts out as the body falls to the floor.

Now this ... this is ecstasy.

Nothing compares to the sounds of perverts dying a painful death.

I wipe the knife on his couch and tuck it into my bag.

*CRACK!*

My ears perk up, and I stop moving entirely. Whispers from the hallway near the front door have me on edge.

*Someone's here.*

*Another victim he tried to lure with his disgusting chats?*

I swiftly grab my bag and put everything back inside, then make my way to the back of the house. There's no way out, no other door outside, just rooms and more rooms. One of them is covered in mattresses, ropes and all, and the view makes me sick to my stomach.

I close the door and head into another. A bathroom with blood stains on the sink, but it'll have to do.

Beyond the room, I can hear more rustling, more footsteps. One, two, three? I don't know how many different ones, I can't keep them apart. But it's more than one person. And they're definitely guys.

The sound of laughter comes to an abrupt halt.

"Yo, check this out," one of them says.

"Holy shit," another one says. "Is he ...?"

"Dead," a new voice says.

"Fuck, someone beat us to it."

*To what? Murder?*

I clutch the door handle tightly, my heart beating in my throat as I try to listen to their conversation. I'm too intrigued to step away, despite knowing it's dangerous. One misstep and I'm going down as a killer or worse ... I'll end up dead right beside that pervert.

"God-fucking-dammit," the second guy says. "I was looking forward to this."

*Wow. Did I just hear that right?*

I can't stop myself from opening the door and leaning in so the door opens to a sliver, allowing me to peek through.

Three guys wearing eerily similar white masks hover over the body. One of them, a scrawny one, grabs his hand and lifts it.

"Yup, definitely dead."

That was the first guy, I recognize the voice.

I push the door open farther to get a good look at all three of them. They're all in hoodies and covered up to the point that I can't recognize a single thing.

"Well, no point in hanging around this stench then," the second guy says. "Let's go."

I lean in farther to see if I can catch a glimpse of their faces because I'm invested now, and I can't say no to my own curiosity, despite knowing the risks.

Suddenly, the third guy puts his finger against his lips. "Shh. Quiet."
He looks around.
My heart stops.
"We're not alone."
Suddenly, their eyes all move around the room.
And one of them, the scrawny one, connects with mine.

# 2

## LANA

"There!"

I throw open the door and rush through the hallway just as they're about to come at me. I chuck a knife in their direction and jump into the kitchen, narrowly avoiding the first guy from grasping ahold of my leg as he throws himself at me.

The third guy jumps over the counter, but I sidestep and throw my bag into his knee, causing him to buck.

"Fuck! Come here, you little—!"

I bolt off toward the front door, but halfway through, my hair is grabbed, and I'm tugged back.

"Fuck off!" I yell.

The ribbon is ripped out of my hair, and I kick the guy behind me in the nuts.

He stumbles and grasps for his crotch with my ribbon still clutched firmly in his hand.

*Fuck. The ribbon.*

*No time to get it back.*

I sprint toward the exit as fast as I can.

But my legs force me to run out the door and into the breathable air.

"Motherfucker, she's getting away!" one of them yells behind me.

I rush to my motorcycle and jump on without putting on my helmet. The three guys run out the door and chase after me.

But right before they catch me, I hit the gas as hard as I can.

I peer over my shoulder as one of them kicks a trash can, and all the contents spill out.

But I made it out.

I fucking made it out alive.

But not without a scratch and more questions than I dare to ask.

\*\*\*

# NATHAN

"Jesus fucking Christ," I say, staring at the body gutted on several sides. I kick him so that he rolls over. There were crumbs all over him, and he didn't have time to get properly dressed, which meant it was a surprise attack. Yet there's not a single trace of a fight taking place. No scratches, no bruising, no broken bones.

My eyes narrow. It's almost as if he let this happen.

"Can't believe someone actually lived like this," Kai says, picking up a ragged shirt covered in gunk. "It smells like shit and death combined."

Milo's whole body shivers, and he makes a gagging noise. "Fuck, please put that down. I'm gonna puke."

"What? From this?" Kai dangles the shirt in front of him, and he almost flips over.

"God, fuck!" Milo retches.

Kai throws it away and laughs. "A butchered body? Fine. But some dirty laundry? That's where you draw the line?"

Milo closes his eyes and pinches his nose. "It's the idea."

I fish inside the guy's pocket and take out his phone, then push his floppy finger against it to unlock it. "Let's have a look at what you're hiding."

Milo sighs out loud. "When are we finished? There's no fun if the job's already been done."

"I have to say, I was quite looking forward to slaughtering this one," Kai says, throwing his knife into the air and catching it again. "Too bad someone beat us to it."

I scroll through the DMs on his phone, looking for clues, but all I find are girls... so many fucking girls and all so fucking young. Disgusting.

Worst of all, he was about to meet one of those girls right before he got killed. I hope she got away and wasn't here to see him die.

And in the most brutal way too ...

I check out the wounds on his hand, the blood staining his nose and lip, and the obvious hole in his neck. But what surprises me the most is the knife still stuck in his abdomen.

One would think a killer would cover their tracks, instead of leaving behind souvenirs. How reckless.

I tear out the blade and inspect the handle, but there are no prints.

"What did you find?" Kai asks me.

"We found our guy, that's for sure," I reply, looking at the dead body. "He's been chatting with girls nonstop for months. But that last one may have become fatal."

Milo's eyes widen. "Wait ... you think the killer was one of the women?"

Kai fishes something from his pocket. "I snatched this off her hair when I chased her out the door. Nearly caught her, but she slipped out of my grip because of this."

He holds up a single red ribbon, which curls around in the air like it's performing a rhythmic dance.

I glare at it and step closer, but the second I try to snatch it from his hand, he pulls back.

"Ah-ah. Finders keepers," he says, smirking.

My nose twitches. "It could be our only clue, and your only thought is playing games with me?"

"I'm not playing games. And this won't lead us to anything," he says, clutching it firmly. "Even if you could get fingerprints from it, you still wouldn't know who barged in here and stole our kill."

"At least it'd be a start," I reply. "And you're not fucking helping."

"Face it. We lost. End of story. Better luck next time." He shrugs.

"Luck's never been on my side, and you know that," I grit. "Someone stole this kill from us, and I'm gonna fucking find out who it was."

"What does it even matter?" Milo shrugs. "This was one time."

"You think?" I frown back. "She was onto the same fucker, which means she's searching the same sites we are."

Milo's face turns white. "Fuck."

"Exactly," I say, chucking the knife back on the ground. "That woman is a threat. She's seen us now."

Milo gazes at the body with narrowed eyes. "By the looks of those wounds, that woman's got a lot of pent-up anger."

Kai smirks, and I throw him a look.

"What's so funny?"

"I'm impressed." Kai holds up the ribbon, inspecting every fiber like he's trying to find a clue. "And something tells me this won't be the last time."

I pull out my phone and take a picture of the ribbon with the dead body in the background.

"What'd you do that for?" Kai asks.

"Keepsake," I reply, a smile tugging at my lips. "You never know when we might need some proof she was here."

\*\*\*

## LANA

I showered and slept well last night, despite the murder that took place, but I can't get rid of this aching feeling in my underbelly that something bad is going to happen.

All because of three fucking dudes who ruined my fun.

I close my eyes and let out a sigh, then take another sip from my breakfast smoothie.

"What's wrong?" Irina asks, squinting at me as she's baking in the midday sun.

"Hmm?" I look her way.

"That sigh was huge," she says.

"Oh, just some shit with some dudes ..." I mutter, taking another sip. "Nothing important."

"Shit with dudes?" Brooke sticks her head out from behind Irina. "You were out last night?"

"Only for a few minutes," I respond when they both eagle-eye me. "It was just some casual drinks. No biggie." I change the subject before things get out of hand. "So what classes do you girls still have left for the day?"

"Ummm..." Irina checks her schedule. "I know there's economics, but I could've sworn I have another one right after."

I adjust the red ribbon in my hair and look at the people in the grass while I wait. But my eyes land on a particular set of eyes, one pure white, the other as green as an emerald.

He stands near the fountain, just like yesterday, this time alone. He has a cigarette between two fingers, eyes smoldering as fiercely as the cigarette's bud while they stare me down.

A creeping chill runs up my spine ... because no matter how hard I try, I can't look away.

\*\*\*

## KAI

*That girl ...*

My eyes home in on her gorgeous oval face, those killer cat-lined eyes, her narrow jawline, and sharp cheekbones as cutthroat as her soul. Her beautiful full, red lips make my tongue dart out to wet mine, her skin so pale not even that black dress she's wearing could hide the fact that she rarely comes out into the sun.

A protected princess, hidden away by her father until even he could no longer contain her.

And now she's here to study, pretending to be a part of the masses.

But now we both know that's only a farce, a mask she puts on to make the people she loves believe she's capable of more than the violence they've all inherited.

Fucking Lana Rivera ...

I take the red ribbon out of my pocket and look at it once more.

A smirk slowly spreads on my face as I gaze up at the girl laughing her worries away, the wind softly breezing through the ribbon in her hair.

Looks like apples don't fall far from the tree after all.

I clutch the ribbon tighter, wondering if I should tell Milo and Nathan.

If I should give them the opportunity to interrogate her ... or if I should do it myself.

All alone, just the two of us.

Killer to killer.

*Oh, little violent kitty ... I found you.*

*You can run all you want ... but I'm gonna find a way to lure you out of your den.*

*And when I do, I'm going to have so much fucking fun with you.*

# 3

NATHAN

**Weeks ago**

"Wait, wait, wait, don't take our car!" I yell at the people filtering through my parents' mansion.

"Sorry, dude, I'm just doing my job," the guy says as he hops inside and starts the engine like he owns it.

I dial our family lawyer. "What are you doing? My family paid you to fix this, and they're still coming for more!"

"You know I can't fix what your parents destroyed," our lawyer says. "They should've taken better care of their finances."

*Finances.*

Like there were any.

It was always fraud and bribery, and now that it's come out to the public, my family is done for. My parents are in jail, possibly forever, and my name is tarnished for eternity.

Panic rises in my body, filling my throat with screams. "But you were supposed to get them out of this mess! You have to do something! Anything!"

"My hands are tied, Nathan. The higher-ups want your parents to go down."

"What?" My eyes widen.

*They're ... using them as an example?*

Fuck this. First, the police take our bribes, and now, all of a sudden, they've grown a conscience just because it's gone public?

"This is wrong and you know it," I growl into the phone. "We need money to survive."

"Look, I'd love to help you, but you know as well as I do your parents' money problems weren't just in their official business," our lawyer says. "This goes way beyond what I was paid to do, and I'm not going to take the fall with them. Risking my job is one thing, but this? This is way over my head."

My hand trembles around the phone. "But they're leaving us with nothing. Not a dime. Not even the house..."

"I know kid. I'm sorry. It's only gonna get worse."

I swallow but my throat is too dry and scratchy for it to matter.

"And if you're smart, you'll gather whatever cash you've got left, take your sister, and leave." His voice darkens. "Leave that godforsaken city, Nathan, before it consumes you too."

And he hangs up before I can even say another word.

\*\*\*

**Present**

I wake up drenched in sweat and with eyes wide open. My heart races a million miles an hour.

*Fuck.*

I get up and rub my forehead, trying to get the nightmare to dissipate, but nothing works. The memory will never leave me.

I check my phone and the texts I've received.

*Romeo: Bring the cash to the parking lot at the base of Spine Ridge Mountain, nine PM. You know the date. And if you're not there with the money... we know where to find you, boy.*

My hand squeezes the phone tight, and I throw it aside before I break it.

Fuck, how am I gonna get out of this mess I didn't even fucking create?

I should've listened to our lawyer and ran with Rory.

God, I fucking hope she's not too mad at me for leaving her with our aunt. But what else was I supposed to do?

I sigh out loud. I can't sleep like this.

I get out of bed and look out the window, staring at the moon, like I always do when I'm on edge. But lately, nothing has calmed me down. It's as if everywhere I look, everywhere I go, the jaws of fate are slowly catching up with me.

Groaning out loud, I walk out of my room and roam across the hallway until I find my way into Milo's room. He's snoring loudly, arms wide and legs splayed across his bed.

Without a care in the world.

I smirk. Like he needs any of the space in that giant king-sized bed with his stick-figure ass.

But I don't want to wake him either.

Suddenly, my eyes land on a piece of paper lying on his desk. I pick it up and read through it. It's a party at the Skull & Serpent Society with a date from ages ago.

*Why does he have this? Did he go there? Or is he keeping it for some other reason?*

I pull out my phone and take a pic, immediately opening my files so I can send it to the server, but then I see the picture I took with Rory mere days ago during our weekly get-together, making me stop and stare.

I wish I could've prevented this from happening.

That I could've stopped my parents and whisked her away before it was too late.

"Trouble sleeping?"

Kai's voice makes me turn around.

"Nightmares," I reply, lowering my phone.

He leans against the doorjamb, arms folded. "You do this often?"

"Only when I need it," I reply, unfazed by his questioning. "But I don't want to wake him."

"Interesting ..." Kai muses with a smile, and his eyes land on my phone. "How's Ro doing?"

*Shit. He noticed.*

"Fine," I reply, clearing my throat. "I'm doing what I can to keep her safe."

"That's good to hear," he says. He steps forward and snatches the paper from my hand. "Hmm... well, this is even more interesting. A party from long ago, but I remember it like it was yesterday."

"You went there with Milo?" I ask.

"Only to check out the chicks. Wild night," Kai replies, folding his arms again. "But now that I'm thinking about it ... a party like this could prove useful."

I frown. "Why?"

"Lots of booze, lots of people," he says. "That's a toxic combination."

My eyes narrow. "Get to the point."

He leans in, grinning like a motherfucker. "This entire school is filled with rich kids. Think about all the bags left unchecked ... bags we could rifle through for cash."

Now he's talking my language. "Go on."

"People who are too drunk to care won't notice some missing jewelry or cards," he says, staring at the paper with a glimmer in his eyes. "It's perfect."

"So you want to throw a party? Where?"

He shoves the paper into my chest. "Right. Here."

\*\*\*

# LANA

I sling my bag over my shoulder and make my way out of class. I'm so glad economics is done for this week. I head toward the cafeteria, where Irina and Brooke wait for me. I sit beside them with my iced coffee and take a much-needed sip.

"Hey, baby." Jason sits beside me and wraps his arm around my shoulders, but I move it off.

"Don't call me that," I reply.

"Why not? I like it," he says, winking, and he leans in to kiss me on the cheek. "When are we going to have another cuddle?"

I'm really not in the mood for whatever he's thinking. We only hooked up a couple of times, but we never made it official, and I'm glad we didn't.

"Fine, never mind," Jason says when I don't reply, and he walks off again.

"Awkward," Irina muses, rolling her eyes.

I sigh loudly. "Tell me about it."

"Done with classes today?" Brooke asks. "I still have one more."

"Yup," I reply. "Sorry, girl."

"Don't be, I love marketing." She takes a sip of her own coffee. "I get to design lots of fun stuff."

"Nice, I wish I could use those programs, but I'm completely lost every time I open them," Irina says. "In fact, I feel lost with most of my classes."

I frown. "You sure you're at the right school, then?"

She shrugs. "My parents wanted me to go here. But I just want to marry a rich tech dude and live a stress-free life." She grins and puts on her shades, making me laugh.

"Oh, what are you even talking about?" Brooke shoves her. "You don't even need that. Your parents are loaded, and you're their only kid. You don't have to do shit, and you're still set for life."

"What about you?" I ask. "You've got any plans for the future?"

Brooke shrugs. "I just wanna work for Wall Street finance."

"Wow. Aiming big," I reply.

"Yup," she says, opening her bag of chips. "I'm not settling for lower than the fucking top. The only shitty thing is the men there."

I snort. "Aren't they everywhere?"

"No. I'm convinced there must be at least one submissive dude out there ready to bow at my feet," she muses, taking a bite.

"Ambitious," Irina says with a nod. "I like it."

Brooke raises her hand, and Irina gives her a high five.

I take the opportunity to steal a few chips from her and shove them in my mouth. That's when I notice one of the guys from the Phantom Society hanging posters all over the cafeteria, his semi-crooked walk on one side of his body making me focus on him. It's the guy with the blond hair, and every time he raises his hand, the obvious stump on his hand draws my attention. What kind of violence is he involved in that would make someone lose a finger?

"Oh look at that, Lana's got a crush on Nathan?"

I almost choke on my chips as I swallow them down. "What?"

Brooke points at the corner where he's hanging more posters, oblivious to my stares. "You were looking at him for quite some time, L."

"She already has a boyfriend," Irina says with a cheeky voice.

"Wait, really?" Brooke frowns. "How come you never told me about him?"

"I mean, not really," I say, shrugging. "It's more of a friends-with-benefits thing." I laugh it off like it's no big deal. "Anyway, I was just interested in the posters."

"Well, in that case ..." Irina jumps up from her seat and runs off before I can stop her.

And fuck me, she's headed straight for him.

I don't enjoy listening to my brother, but he wouldn't warn me about those Phantom guys if it wasn't serious. He knows me. He knows what I'm capable of. But those boys ... they're danger incarnate.

Irina grabs his arm, and he turns around to look at her. They talk for a while, but it's impossible to hear from this distance. He hands her one of the posters, and she gleefully nods ... then points at me.

Blood drains from my face when Nathan's piercing blue eyes lock with mine, the penetrative stare almost drags my soul out of my body. He runs his fingers through his hair, a casual smug smile following suit. And with just that single stare, he's gotten my blood to go cold like snow.

He knows.

He knows who I am.

I can tell from the way he looks at me.

Like all he wants is to hurt my brother and his friends where it hurts the most ... by taking my fucking body and using it any way he desires.

Or killing me.

My nostrils flare, and I turn around, keeping my head held high as I take a big gulp of coffee.

"I wonder what they're talking about," Brooke mutters.

"Don't know, don't care," I reply.

Irina comes running back and sits down like a happy kid on steroids. "Look. It's a party."

"Ooooh, let me see," Brooke says, stealing the poster. "*Everyone* will be there."

"I am soooo going," Irina says. "Wanna go together?"

"Definitely, I could use a little pick-me-up after all these classes," Brooke replies.

"If I'm going to find a rich dude to marry, it's gonna be here," Irina says.

Brooke throws her arm around my shoulders. "You're coming too, right, Lana?"

I grumble. "If those guys are there too ..."

"Who cares? The whole school is gonna be there. You can just ignore them and have fun." She grabs my cup and holds it in front of my mouth. "Take another sip. Or twenty. Then say yes. And let's get wasted."

\*\*\*

On the evening of the party, I slip on my red lace dress that fits my body to a T. After I stick on some fake lashes and swipe on mascara, I use eyeliner to create the perfect cat eye. I tie my hair into a high ponytail, leaving out my bangs, and put my ribbon in along with some spray to seal the deal.

I look like Catwoman but in red instead of black, and I love this look.

"Wow, looking hot there!" Irina says, winking as she leans against my doorframe. "Ready, bitch?"

"Ready to destroy some hearts of guys who think they stand a chance," I muse, walking out the door.

"Aw ..." Irina throws her arm around me. "I almost feel pity for them. Almost."

"Looking good, girls," Brooke says as she approaches us from the hallway in a shimmery light-blue dress. "Let's go party!"

"Where is this party anyway?" I ask.

"You'll see." Irina winks.

We walk out the door and head across campus toward the building teeming with people. Music blasts far beyond the house, and purple and red lights filter through the night sky as they flicker to the beat, drawing in people like moths to a flame.

Several guards at the door hold people back to check bags and make sure no one is trying to surprise shank anyone. I'm starting to wonder what kind of party we're headed into.

"C'mon, up here. I know that guy," Brooke says, and she pulls us both up the stairs, skipping the line. "Hi, Leo."

"Brooke ... I see you finally made it," one of the guys at the entrance says.

"Only because you're here," she muses, pushing up her tits like a pro.

"Looking fly as always," Leo says, winking. "Bags, please."

We all show our purses, and he checks them one by one. I'm smart enough not to carry my knives where people can find them.

"All good. Just the three of you?" he asks.

"Yup, this is it," she replies.

He fishes something out of a duffel bag near the door and brings it over to us. "There you go."

He hands us all a white mask that covers the eyes and nose.

My lungs feel like they cave in, oxygen refusing to enter.

It's an exact replica of the masks I saw the night of the murder.

*Is this freely available in the stores or something?*

"What is this?" Irina asks.

"It's required," Leo responds. "Party rules. Everyone must wear a mask." He leans in to whisper. "Makes it more mysterious."

"Ooh ... I love it," Irina says, clutching the wine bottle Brooke brought. "Can we take this inside too?"

"Of course. The more booze, the better," he says with a big smile.

Both girls put on the mask like it's no big deal, and they head beyond the door with smiles, beckoning me to come too. I eventually cave and put on the mask, wondering who the hell would throw a party with a dress code on campus while I follow them inside.

The place is gorgeous, like an old-school Victorian castle, complete with dark wood panels and intricate designs on the many staircases. Paintings cover every corner, and a delicate statue towers beside each door. The floors are made of pure marble, and the ceiling of the giant hallway is one big glass dome. The spectacular view makes me do a double take.

But then I see the black banners hanging down from the top of the stairs, all of them labeled with the Phantom logo. A white mask covers half of the face of a skull.

Those three guys wore the same kind of mask the night I took someone's life.

And it slowly begins to dawn on me that I just made a dangerous mistake.

"The Phantom Society," I mutter to myself.

*Oh God.*

They're on this campus.

I should've known. I should've realized the second that Nathan dude was hanging those posters on the wall, but at the time, I thought he was helping someone.

How stupid of me.

This is a Phantom party, and the guys who were at that house when I killed that fucker belong to the Phantom Society too.

*Fuck.*

Sweat drops roll down my back as I try not to act unhinged. I clutch my purse tightly as I walk up the steps and follow Irina and Brooke into the Phantom Society mansion, the one place my brother told me never to step foot in.

God, if I'd known the party was here, I never would've said yes.

Not because I'm scared, but because I really don't want to find those three fuckers, nor do I want them to find me. And on top of that, I don't want to deal with Felix's rage the second he finds out I was here.

I touch the mask with two fingers, sighing into my hand. Let's fucking hope this mask does enough to hide my identity while I'm here.

"Lana! Lana!" Irina waves at me from the middle of the hallway.

*Well, that was a great success.*

"What are you waiting for? C'mon, everyone's in here." She points at two wide-open doors that lead into what looks like a grand ballroom.

But on the floor above her, a suited-up guy catches my attention. Even from a distance, the muscles on his body are clearly visible through the seam of his suit, tight at the waist, a red tie clutching the thick strand of neck muscles. A mask hides the stranger underneath, but the broad jawline and subtle stubble still peek out to play, and the slightest tension of his downturned lips makes me suck in a breath. He clutches the banister with one hand while he holds a plastic cup in the other as he stares right down at me. Dark streaks of half-long wavy hair cover half of the white mask, but on the other side, a freakishly green eye connects with mine.

And something about the way it sparkles, almost as if a hint of a smile forms, makes all the hairs on the back of my neck stand up.

I suck in a breath.

I'm torn between sticking up a big middle finger to my brother and father and following Irina and Brooke or running like hell.

Brooke runs back to me and hooks her arm around mine. "You okay?"

"I'm fine. I just had a thought."

"Save the thinking for class," she muses. "C'mon, let's go dance!" Brooke tugs me along onto the dance floor in the ballroom until there's no way back.

# 4

⚛

## KAI

When I spot that red ribbon, I know it's her.

*My little vicious kitty.*

*Lana Rivera, you've finally come to my fucking domain.*

I knew she'd take the bait. Those friends of hers were so easily persuaded to come to a party of ours, and of course they'd drag her along.

A dark grin spreads as I clutch the banister and home in on her. My gaze sweeps over her red lace dress, her body fitting neatly in the fabric like hard candy waiting to be unwrapped and sucked whole. I can't fucking wait to sink my teeth into her sweetness.

Her eyes finally find mine from down below, and fuck me, the fear slowly settling in her eyes is nothing short of pure magic.

*Yes, little kitty ... I know all your dirty little secrets.*

*But do you even know it's me?*

*Do you realize all the things you've unchained in me?*

Her friend suddenly comes running toward her, breaking the spell, but I don't mind. I can easily tell her apart in a crowd of a thousand people.

My tongue trails along my teeth, wishing she could look into my mind and see all the ways I'm going to make her scream.

She's dragged into the ballroom by her friend, but not before a final glance, emboldening the predator lurking within.

I knew it when I first saw her that I'd found the one thing I was looking for—a challenge. Something to conquer. Something to tame.

My fists tighten around the banister.

Ever since I lost my eye, I've been struggling to fit in, constantly confronted with my disfigurement and its effect on my peers. I can't go anywhere without people looking at me, and it makes me want to hole up in this mansion until the end of time.

But these masks ... they even the playground.

They allow me to live the life I remember I used to have.

And I crave it so badly that it feels like I'm starving, hungering for a simple taste, a touch of a girl I'm not supposed to have. A girl I'm not supposed to take.

"What are you cosplaying at? *The Phantom of the Opera*?"

I sigh out loud at the snort that follows. "Thanks for your amazing compliment, Milo."

"Well, what is this fit even?" He grabs his suit and tugs at the fabric like he wants to tear it off and strut around butt naked, and honestly, it wouldn't surprise me if he did. If not now, then at least by the end of the night.

"I feel like an owl in a suit, hoot hoot!" He does a weird little dance, sticking his fingers above his head like he's trying to summon owls from outer space. "Look at this fucking mask. It's ridiculous."

"I think they look nice," I say, crossing my arms as I lean against the thick wooden beam supporting the banisters. "Besides, we're not called the Phantoms for nothing."

"True," he responds, placing his hand on my shoulder. "But that's not what you made them mandatory for, is it?"

I frown as my heart rate picks up. *Has he found out the truth? Or is he just playing me to pry information from my head?*

"Relax," he muses. "I know you don't like it when people see your face. So you made everyone hide. Big deal."

I breathe a sigh of relief. "Yeah. It definitely helps."

"Then why are you still up here?" He grins. "Go and have fun, enjoy your party. Mingle. Dance. Get some donations. Empty some pockets. Get drunk." I shake my cup, which his eyes follow, and he leans in to smell. "That ain't liquor."

"Coke mix," I reply.

"Mixed with what? Apple juice?"

He snorts, so I shove his face into the cup and force it down his throat.

"There. Now you know."

He coughs and heaves, throwing the cup aside as he licks the droplets from his chin. "Fuck. That actually tasted good. Strawberry?"

"Told you," I retort, walking off with my hands tucked in my pockets. "Black cherry vodka and grenadine, if you must know."

"Wait, you're just gonna leave me with a drenched face?" he asks. "Who's gonna clean it up?"

"You can beg Nathan," I muse, winking at him. "I know he likes it when you do."

He rolls his eyes, but I make my way downstairs, determined to find the girl I've set my target on. She's gotta be in the ballroom, dancing away the night with her friends, having the time of her life as though nothing could go wrong. But I know she saw the pure and utter chaos waiting to swallow her whole in those few seconds our eyes connected.

I walk into the ballroom and stalk around the dance floor from the sidelines. The music blasts in my ear, but I pay no attention to it as I scour the room looking for her. It's not hard to spot the ribbon among the crowd. It stands out like a red flag, luring me in.

Until I spot the one thing I didn't take into account.

Her dancing with another man ... And it makes me wild with rage.

He's clutched her waist, and he's getting so close, rubbing himself against her that my blood begins to boil.

His hands are all over *my* woman.

And if he doesn't take them off swiftly, I'll personally cut them off tonight.

***

## LANA

I'm dancing between Irina and Brooke, with Jason humping me from the back. I don't care as long as I can numb my brain while dancing to the music, getting slowly drunker and drunker.

I'm surprised Jason found me among the crowd. Then again, he knows how to recognize me by my clumsy dancing skills, especially now that I'm getting tipsy.

In one hand, I clutch a red cup with only a few drops of champagne left in it. But I won't let my lack of alcohol spoil the fun. With a big grin, I twirl around Jason and smack his bum before proceeding to dance with Irina. Brooke's alternating between two boys on the dance floor, and I can't blame her for doing it. If Jason wasn't sticking to me like a bear on honey, I would too.

Everyone's having an amazing time, but when I slurp up the last bit of liquor in my cup, I'm getting thirsty for more, and I know just the thing to finally get some time to dance alone.

"Jason," I mutter as he grinds up against me.

"What's up, baby?"

"Can you fill this cup for me?" I ask. "I'm thirsty."

"Of course." He grabs the cup from my hand. "Champagne?"

"You know me," I reply, and he waltzes off, but not before slapping me on the butt so hard I nearly squeal. "Asshole," I growl, and Irina and Brooke laugh.

The room suddenly darkens, and we all stop and look around until the laser lights appear and everyone begins dancing like crazy. It's a song with a deep bass, and the techno beat is killing it, so much that I'm vibing on my own without Irina and Brooke, who've gone on to dance with some guys in a corner.

Suddenly, someone snakes their hand around my waist and pulls me in for a dance. I glance over my shoulder and see a mask, but in the dark it's hard to tell who. But their moves ...

Sultry, smoking hot, like our bodies are entwined, dancing in rhythm to the music.

And I just can't step away, no matter how many times my brain tells me I should.

I don't know who this is; it could be anyone, or it could be Jason. Judging from the calloused hands that grip me tightly, it's definitely a guy.

But Jason never danced with me like this, like he doesn't just want to entertain me but move my soul. And as his hand snakes up my belly and my hips move closer to his, my breathing picks up, and my heart rate becomes unsteady.

Unhinged, in fact, as a set of lips breathe hot air right underneath my ear, lingering near my skin like an intention to kiss but without the touch. And fuck me, I'm almost ready to lean in and let him.

"Jason?" I whisper over my shoulder.

"Try again ..."

The voice is so low and gruff, my breath falters while my body continues to sway around in his arms. "Who are you?"

A delectable grin spreads against my skin. "Whoever you want me to be."

He spins me around, and his arm locks around my body. But the darkness in the room still won't allow me to see even a glimpse of his face, let alone his eyes.

*Goddammit.*

"What do you want?" I grit, wondering if I should pry myself away from him before those hands turn into bones. Because when Jason comes back, he's definitely not going to be happy.

The strobe lights reveal a dangerous smirk spreading on the stranger's face. "Dance with me."

Before I can get a closer look, he spins me around again, dancing hip to hip, mixing sultry moves with sexy footwork that would put Jason to shame. I'm so glad he isn't here to see me being whisked around.

"Wait, I have a boyfriend," I mutter.

It can't hurt to lie occasionally if it keeps me safe, and at least then Jason will be good for something.

Suddenly, the stranger pushes me over, and I nearly fall, but his hand cups the small of my back to keep me steady. And at that moment, I'm acutely aware of how each of his fingers gently press into me. He leans in, wolf-like teeth getting dangerously close to my neck as he whispers, "Not anymore."

My jaw drops from the sheer arrogance in his voice.

Until his tongue dips out to lick my skin, and by God, I almost moan.

Just the tip, dragged from my clavicles all the way to my chin. Just that one lick and it's already enough to make me yield.

*What the fuck?*

He pulls me back up again, holding me close to his body as we softly sway to the music, his hand interlocked with mine, and I don't know if I could let go if I wanted to.

His face is right beside mine, and I can feel his body against me—thick thighs, hard abs, trained but lean, built for the kill.

His lips hover close to my ear, whispering deadly words.

"I know what you are ... kitty. A killer."

My eyes widen.

I pull back, desperate to see who it is, but these damn dark lights aren't helping. But the second I do, his hand releases mine, and he disappears into the crowd like a ghost. And I'm left with a thrumming heart and a throbbing pussy.

*Kitty.*

*Killer.*

Two things I was that night I came face-to-face with those three guys.

*They're here.*

# 5

## LANA

The nerve in my neck twitches as I glare around at all the people dancing, wondering where he is, and without a second thought, I start tearing off people's masks in an effort to reveal him. Everyone looks at me like I've gone insane, but I don't care.

"Where are you?" I say to the next dude as I rip off his mask. "Is it you?"

"Hey, get your hands off me—"

"Lana!" Irina calls from across the room as she makes her way toward me. "What's going on?"

My gaze flickers between the random dude in front of me, who was just trying to dance with his girlfriend, and Irina, who seems unaware of what went down on the dance floor between me and the handsome killer.

But I know.

I know what kind of man had his hands all over me, and I'm not about to let him get away with it.

I storm out of the ballroom, seething and scared to death. Whoever he was, that guy who spun me around his finger and tongue with ease knows my darkest secret.

I have no choice but to kill him now.

I gaze around the room, searching for him amidst the chatting people and near the liquor table, but I don't see him there. I do see someone in a suit bolting upstairs. And his pace looks suspiciously irate.

I go for the pursuit, pushing my way through people, keeping a keen eye on the guy, but he's slipping away fast, and I can't catch up. I accidentally bump into someone while peering at the top banister.

"Lana?" Jason's familiar voice makes me turn my head away from the guy.

"Sorry," I mutter.

"You okay? You seem upset," he asks. "Did someone rob you too?"

I frown. "*Too?*"

"I just went to the wardrobe section, and my Valentino bag's gone," he says. "I figured someone might've taken it."

"Should've carried it with you then," I tell him. "Look, I gotta go." I walk past him.

"Where are you going?" he asks. "Don't you want your drink?"

"Later," I reply, but I'm gone before he can say anything else. "Sorry. Excuse me," I mutter as I wade through the people and head for the stairs.

I skip a couple of steps and make my way to the top. There's an extended hallway all around with doors every other step, as well as more hallways up ahead. Where could he have gone? The whole place feels like a maze, and the more time I waste walking around, the easier it is for him to get away.

*Goddammit.*

I'm sure I saw him slip into this hallway. I rummage the nearest door but it's locked, same for the next one. The third gives way, and I open it up. It's a small pool room with bookcases lining the walls and a fireplace in the back along with green satin chairs. The whole place looks like it came straight out of a gentleman's club.

I look around, but no one is in the room except me. But the sounds ... it's nothing like the party downstairs. Almost as if something is going on in the room next door. I follow the sound and approach the wall, putting my ear to it.

*WHACK!*

I lean away and frown.

*What the hell was that?*

Another whack follows along with a sharp yelp, and I touch the wall looking for a way in, but all I find is a hole. A hole large enough for at least one eye to peek through. And I can't fucking help myself as I lean in closer, wondering if it's him.

The room is filled to the brim with metal clasps, wooden benches, and racks filled with whips, canes, floggers, ropes, and constriction devices.

I gasp.

In the corner is a cage, a human-sized cage, and inside, one suited-up guy is whipping another guy who is on his knees with his shirt off. Red streaks mark his back.

My eyes widen.

*What is happening?*

"Having a little sneak peek?"

The voice behind me makes me spin on my heels.

A guy in a mask stares me down, his eyes hidden by a drape of dark brown hair, but the suit, and that voice ... it's definitely him.

I reach for my heels and fish my knife out of the side, unfolding it with one click.

I throw it right when the light is turned off.

*CLING!*

The metal of the blade clatters against a frame.

*Fuck. I missed.*

*I never fucking miss.*

But it's impossible to aim in the dark.

"Show yourself!" I growl. "Who are you?"

"You still have two guesses left." His low voice is commanding and chill-inducing.

My nostrils flare, and I reach for the second knife in my heels. My last weapon. My last shot to get him before he gets me.

I hold it close, ready to strike.

"Answer me!" I yell.

"You're just as violent as I remember," he muses from across the room.

So he is one of the three guys I met at that fucker's house.

I want to throw my knife so badly, but if I do, I'll have forfeited my last shot to get him. And if I miss ... I'm fair game.

"I'm gonna fucking kill you," I growl.

"Oh, now you're talking my love language. C'mon, then. Give me your best shot," he taunts, bolting at me fast.

But as I attempt to throw, he comes out of nowhere and grips my wrist. Within a second, he's got me pinned, and he pries the knife from my hand.

Enraged, I punch him, but he avoids my first hit like an expert.

So I lift my knee and kick him right in the stomach.

He groans and bucks, so I try to throw in another punch, but he grips my throat out of nowhere and pushes me up against the wall. His hand snakes around my neck so tightly I can barely breathe. I scratch at his fingers, desperate to get loose.

"Third try, kitty," he murmurs near my ear. "Who do you think I am? Think fast."

I groan from the sheer force applied to my neck. "Fuck you."

A faint, rumbling laugh emanates from deep within his chest. "I get the sense that you don't want to admit that you were there ..." His fingers dig into my skin as he leans in to whisper. "That you killed that disgusting man."

"You following me around?" I hiss.

He smiles against my skin. "You make it so easy to find you ... when you wear that ribbon."

He plucks it from my hair, and I suck in a breath as it drops to the floor.

So he's the one who stole my ribbon that night. And that means those three definitely go to school here too.

Fuck. Just my luck.

"What do you want?" I rasp.

"You stole our kill." He pronounces each word deliberately like he's trying to make me feel guilty. But I don't feel remorseful at all.

"*Your* kill?" I scoff. "Sorry, I didn't know I had to get in line."

He leans in and whispers, "Jokes won't get you far, Lana."

*Lana.*

My eyes widen, and my heart skips a beat. "How the fuck do you know my name?"

"That's not the question you should be asking," he murmurs. "What you should be asking is 'how can I stop this man from telling the world about my murderous habits'?"

"Fuck off!" I try to break free from his grasp, but he's much stronger than I am.

"Ah, ah ... you won't get away this time," he murmurs.

"You think I want to get away?" I muse. "I came looking to kill you."

He smiles against my skin. "God, I love your tenacity." He slowly invades my space, pushing his body up against me until I can feel his thick thighs rub up against mine, his bulge growing harder and harder. "Your desire to kill me only gets me hard."

"Fuck you," she growls.

"Oh, I will fuck you, all right," he says, and his tongue dips out to lick the rim of my ear. "And you will definitely moan when I bore my way through that wet little pussy of yours."

"You wish." I can feel my pussy throbbing between my legs, but I ignore it.

"I know violence gets you going," he whispers. "I can feel your heartbeat pick up, Lana."

"Don't—"

"Don't what? Call you by your name?" He leans away. "I think you know as well as I do that we're well past introductions now."

God-fucking-dammit, I wish I could see him more than anything.

"You know my name. Now give me yours," I say.

He snorts. "I'll give it to you ..." Suddenly, I feel something cold underneath my chin. A blade. Mine. "After you come for me."

*What? Did he just...?*

*Oh my fucking God, the arrogance!*

"Fuck you, I would never—"

He removes his hand from my wrist, the knife still at my throat like an imminent and very clear threat. If I move, I die.

But his hand slowly lowers down my arm, smoothing along my body, and every single one of my senses is awakened against my wishes. A rumbling groan escapes his mouth as he cups my breast, the sound so low and gravelly it brings goose bumps to my body.

And I don't understand why my body has this reaction.

Why I feel the need to lean into his touch.

*Fuck, what is wrong with me?*

*Don't let him do this.*

But the second my muscles twitch, the blade pushes farther into my skin.

"Don't even think about it," he says, his voice so dark it makes me gulp.

He moves farther down my dress until his hand is right between my legs, making me feel needy, twisted, and debased.

"You like that, don't you?"

"You're a—"

The knife pushes even farther into my skin until I'm forced to tilt my head back. "Don't insult me when the fun is just about to begin, kitty."

"Don't call me that," I say through gritted teeth.

But his finger pushes down on my slit, and I'm having a hard time staying put.

"Don't call you what?" he murmurs, rubbing me through my dress. "A violent little kitty?"

"Ridiculous," I scoff, but his fingers keep working me, and it's hard not to breathe puffy breaths. I hate to even think about how damp I'm already becoming.

*Stop it, Lana, don't even think about getting wet.*

"No, what's ridiculous was thinking that cat mask would protect you from being found," he says, his hand slipping down farther until he reaches the bottom of the dress near my thighs, and his fingers creep underneath. "But I found you. And now I'm going to have so much fun with you."

"Get your hands—"

*RIP!*

My panties are torn apart, ripped at the seam, and he chucks them aside.

"On this needy pussy?" He cups my pussy like he owns it, and I suck in a breath.

With the knife, he forces me to tilt my head and leans in to whisper into my ear, "What would your brother say if he found you here, Lana?"

*What?*

*How does he know who my brother is?*

*Who is this guy?*

"Would he berate you for coming to one of our parties?" I'm acutely aware of the sharp blade traveling down my neck until the point of the knife stops near my heart. "Would he still love you if he knew what you truly are? A cold-hearted murderer."

My pupils dilate at the thought of my brother discovering what I've been doing in my spare time. And not only that but also for him to hear it from this fucker's mouth. "You wouldn't."

*Felix doesn't know, and there's no way this guy—*

"You don't have proof," I blurt out, trying to ignore his fingers as they press against my slit again, slowly swirling around as if to lull me into submission.

"Don't I?" He smiles against my ear while he plays with me. And even though I don't want his fingers there, I'm slowly getting wetter and wetter. "Are you willing to take that chance, kitty?"

I swallow as the blade reaches the top of my dress, my nipples peaking against the fabric.

"*Don't*. Don't involve my brother," I grit.

"Maybe your father, then?"

I hold my breath. Fuck. Not him.

"No."

"What are you willing to sacrifice?" His low voice and breath linger in my ear. "How far are you willing to go to keep your dirty little secret?"

His voice is maliciously dark and laced with desire, and I can't help but moan when he circles around achingly slow. And the knife slowly pushes down the lace dress over my breasts until they spill out of their cups, exposing me. A low, humming groan emanates from his body as the tip of the knife circles across my nipples. *My* knife. And for some reason, I feel like he wants me to know that.

"How much are you willing to bleed?"

I suck in a breath when he punctures my skin right above, warm blood oozing down across my nipples.

*I shouldn't let him do this, but what fucking choice do I have?*

*I'm out of weapons, and he stops me whenever I try to move.*

*Not to mention the disgraceful amount of desire pooling between my legs, distracting me from what I was supposed to do.*

"Now make your choice, little kitty. What's it going to be?" he whispers. "Keep your secret or your body?"

It feels like electricity sparks between us, magnetizing every inch of my skin that touches his.

"Secret."

It's out before I know it, but the choice can't be undone, and I know full well what it will cost me.

A hint of a smile tugs at his lips. I can't see it, but I can feel it against my skin. "Good choice."

# 6

⸎

## LANA

Suddenly, his finger shoves into me, and as I gasp, his mouth covers the wound he just created, sucking the blood. He thrusts into me with greed, and my fingernails dig into the wall. But when his tongue dips out to lick my nipples, I feel lost in the darkness surrounding us.

"Wet already, kitty? You were waiting for this, weren't you? Waiting for someone to take you and claim you without remorse," he says between thrusts. "Well, don't fucking worry, I intend to take *everything* you have to give and more."

His voice comes out in a dark, breathy groan as he pushes in another finger, swirling around inside me and feeling me up. I'm helpless against the onslaught of lust building inside me.

A part of me is eager to fight, eager to form a fist and punch him in the gut, but another part of me doesn't want to disappoint my brother. And that part ... damn that part of me is strong as hell.

"So willing to do whatever it takes," he murmurs, and the knife comes down right underneath my breast again, making me squeal with equal parts delight and anger as his lips cover that wound too.

Fuck me, he's a sadistic motherfucker, all right.

"No wonder you were there to kill that son of a bitch," I growl. "You enjoy blood."

*WHACK!*

The knife rams into the wall right beside my head.

"I don't enjoy anyone's blood ... except yours."

He slams his lips onto mine and kisses me so hard I feel dizzy. I'm shocked, and not just from the electrifying current jolting between us. His mouth is scorching hot and tantalizing and everything I shouldn't ever want or crave. And for a moment, I'm just frozen to the wall as his mouth explores mine, too stunned to bite back.

I can't see, yet my mind explodes like a bundle of stars igniting and going out all at once. All while his fingers are still pounding into me to the point where it makes my whole body quake with need.

When his lips briefly unlatch, the groans that follow set my body on fire. "That's it, gyrate all over my finger like a good fucking slut."

"Fuck you," I growl, trying to ignore the growing arousal he's building in my body.

"If you beg for it, maybe I will," he retorts.

"Dream on."

"What do you dream about, Lana?" he murmurs, grasping my breast, only to cover it with his mouth, licking my nipple until it grows taut, after which he tugs at it to elicit a moan. "Do you dream of monsters to slay? Bodies to bury? Or being fucked so good you wouldn't care about either?"

Fuck, I can't believe he's asking me about this. Is he trying to distract me from his fingers with his words or vice versa?

"What I dream about is none of your concern."

But it's so hard to even speak the words without soft moans escaping my lips. So I shut them tightly and push my arousal to the back of my mind, forcing myself to ignore the onslaught of my senses as he curls his fingers inside me.

"Oh, on the contrary, kitty ... Your dreams are mine to turn into reality."

He pulls his fingers out, and I'm surprised to feel bereft. Until he starts to flick my clit with my juices like he wants me to feel how wet I got for him.

"Do you want to know what I dream about?" he murmurs so close to my lips I can almost taste him. And fuck me, it almost, *almost* makes me want to lean in so I can.

"Revenge on the people who stole from me what wasn't theirs to steal ... and after I kill them, I will celebrate my victory with your little violent, wet pussy wrapped around my hard, pierced cock while you mewl and beg me for more cum."

Fuck. It's hard not to feel my pussy contract, and I don't know if it's from his fingers or his words.

Because I keep hearing that one word repeated in my mind.

*Pierced.*

"I didn't ask, just get this over wi—"

*WHACK!*

The sudden smack to my tit interrupts me and makes me yelp.

"I will take my time, and you will learn to love it."

"Learn?" I snort. The amount of audacity this guy has astounds me.

"Yes, you'll need to learn how to satisfy me if we're going to play this game."

*Game? I'm a game to him?*

"What game? I don't intend to do this again. Ever."

But with every syllable that falls off my lips, he applies more slick twists, rolling around until I'm writhing against the wall, wishing I could ignore the obvious arousal building deep inside my core.

"Oh, you will definitely open these sweet pussy lips for me again"— he swirls around my clit—"and again"—another swirl—"and again"—another flick—"and again"—another one has my mind reeling—"until you can't take it anymore, and even then ..." He thrusts in with full fervor, making me gasp for air. "Again."

His mouth covers mine in an instant, devouring me whole. And his lips are so persuasive that I can't stop, even if I wanted to. I hate how he's so easily made me a willful participant in this dirty game. The kiss is all-consuming and mouthwatering to the point that even my tongue wants to join in as he swirls around inside my mouth like he already owns me. And fuck me, I've never been this turned on in my life.

What is wrong with me? I'm not supposed to be enjoying any of this.

He's holding my worst secret over my head like it's some kind of fun game, and all I can do is stay pinned to the wall and let him kiss me.

*Fuck.*

When his lips unlatch, I almost lean in for more.

"You've been dying for someone to come and take control of your wicked desires, haven't you?" he murmurs, hovering close. Too close.

"Fuck you. You don't know me," I bite.

"By the time I finish with you ..." He rips the knife out of the wall. "I will know..." He slides the knife down my chest and breasts to my hips. "Every..." He pushes the hilt between my thighs and nudges it against my clit until it thumps with greed. "Inch ..." Suddenly, he thrusts the knife's handle into me. "Of your body."

Fuck, he's insane.

He's fucking me with the handle of the knife.

"What the—"

Before I can say another word, his tongue is already in my mouth again, twisting around the same way the knife twists inside my pussy. I feel overwhelmed by both seething rage and insatiable lust.

How dare he fuck me with that ... that ...

My hands brace against the wall, but his fingers instantly curl around my throat.

"Don't even think about it. You want me to keep your secret? Then you will take your own goddamn knife up your pussy like the bad girl you are and make it soaking wet."

"You're a sick fucker, you know that?" I say through gritted teeth.

"You've merely caught a glimpse of all the fucked-up shit I want to do to you." I can't see him, but I can tell he's smiling just from his twisted voice. "Now part those legs like a good fucking slut."

I spit in his face.

He asked for it.

But instead of wiping it away, his fingers tighten around my neck like a noose. "Bad little kitty needs to learn her fucking place."

I can barely breathe as he shoves the handle in and out of me until it's slippery wet, and I feel my heartbeat slow to the point when I'm about to black out.

"I can't ..." I mutter.

"Breathe?" he whispers.

I nod as he pulls out the handle and rubs it along my slit, making me dizzy with desire. "Good."

*Fucking asshole.*

How dare he get me so turned on and spiteful at the same time?

These emotions are not supposed to exist together, yet the way he's been manhandling me has made me soaking wet.

The blade handle circles my slit as he leans in to whisper, "I like your tenacity, kitty. I like how you thought you could outsmart me, but you will come on this fucking knife as a punishment for trying to hurt me."

"F-fuck y-you," I whisper, desperate not to faint.

"So desperate for a cock in your wet, aching pussy, little kitty? Don't worry, I will fuck all that rage out of you soon enough. But first, you'll need to learn how to behave."

He flicks the handle back and forth until I'm starting to lose control.

"That's it, be a fucking slut and come all over this fucking knife like a bad girl," he groans.

His fingers tighten around my throat even more, and my vision slowly turns black. But my clit is thumping and almost there, even when I don't want to be.

"F-Fuck!" I groan as my legs quake, and my defenses cave in on me.

A wave of ecstasy washes over my body, and my eyes almost roll into the back of my head before he finally releases my veins and lets the blood course back through. But all I feel is the mounting orgasm rolling over me, consuming me whole, and a long-drawn-out moan escapes my lips.

He pulls the handle away, and a low, rumbling laugh emanates from his chest. My knees cave in on me, and I drop to the floor, completely wasted on that orgasm.

When I look up, he brings the knife to his mouth and actually licks the fucking handle, the groan that follows igniting my soul. "Hmm ... I will definitely lick your pussy soon."

Fuck him and that fucking delicious and arrogant voice.

"You wish," I retort. "I'll fucking kill you if you try."

He grabs my face and lifts my chin, shoving the blade underneath. "Kill me then, because so help me God, I will fucking have a taste of you." I can hear him pull down a zipper in the darkness. "But first you will have a taste of me."

Warm flesh pushes up against my lips, and I can tell from the hardness it's definitely his dick.

Fuck.

"Open your mouth and show me what you can do with that tongue," he says, his voice laced with desire.

"And if I don't?"

The knife pushes against my chin, and I can feel it cut into my skin as a warm droplet of blood rolls down. "Then your brother will know exactly what you've been up to here at school."

Fuck. If Felix finds out, it's game over for my freedom.

Not to mention the fact that he'd probably tell Dad... and then I'll never see the light of day again.

I know what's at stake, so I part my lips and let him push into my mouth.

The salty taste of his dick as it slowly slips farther and farther across my tongue makes me want to gag. But the second I feel his piercings, I look up at the masked stranger fucking me.

"Noticed my jewelry?" He grips my face with his thumb and index finger. "It's a Jacob's ladder." He pushes in even farther, letting me feel the metal as it slides down my throat. "Do you know why it has that name?"

I gently shake my head, but he holds me steady.

"Every piercing is a step ..." He pushes in farther until he hits the back of my throat and my eyes begin to water. In the darkness, his size is unknown to my eyes, but by God, I can feel its throbbing, thick length. "Ascending into fucking heaven."

He groans out loud when he's in completely, and I struggle to breathe again, choking on his length. He can easily reach far beyond my uvula, where I can't even swallow anymore, and I can feel each one of his piercings scraping against my insides.

"Just like you will be when I come down your fucking throat."

*What?*

*I didn't sign up for this.*

I gag as he pulls out. "Wait, I didn't say—"

He thrusts back in again with no remorse. "Swallow those words along with my cock. I don't want or need to hear them for you to do what you're told. Now suck on this dick like your life depends on it because it fucking does."

He coats his shaft with my saliva, making me choke on his length before he pulls out each time so I can heave and suck in a breath, only to dive right back in again. It's as if he has no desire to hold back. Every inch of him is buried in my mouth, and I can feel his balls slapping against my chin.

"That's it, kitty. Let me hear you choke on my cock."

I cough as he pushes in so far that the tears roll down my face. So many piercings I can't even count them all, but I know there are many. And when he grips my throat and buries himself to the base, I can feel them all.

"Good girl, now lick," he groans.

I swipe my tongue along his length, touching every ridge and barbell as he thrusts in and out of me like a madman who's never felt anything better. More low, gravelly groans from deep within his chest awaken a hidden desire inside me, but I push it away. His length swells with arousal, balls tightening as his moans grow heavier, greedier.

"Now gulp down my cum like a hungry little kitty."

When he explodes inside me, I can feel the salty spurts jet into the back of my throat, again and again, as his dick pulses on my tongue. I've never been this debased in my life, but my pussy throbs with a need I didn't know I had.

The knife pushes underneath my chin, forcing my head up. "Don't even think about spitting."

My eyes widen as it just keeps dripping down my throat.

"Swallow. All of it."

Fuck.

I can't move, even think or speak, so I do what he says and gulp it all down until he's finally spent and pulls out again, making me cough.

"Good fucking kitty. See? You can learn."

"Fuck you," I grit.

The knife pushes deeper into my flesh and forces me to look at him, but I can barely see him in the darkness. Only a faded outline of his figure, and a glimmering eye behind the mask, promises more corruption.

"This was just the tip," he muses.

"I gave you what you wanted."

"You did, Lana ... but I've not nearly had my fill."

My nostrils flare, annoyance getting the best of me. When he pushes his dick back inside his pants, I brace myself against the wall and punch him in the nuts so hard he bends over. I knock his hand away, and the knife clatters to the floor.

I bolt away as fast as I can.

"You little—running off again?" He turns to follow me, but I knock over a chair so he can't catch up. "You know I'll never stop chasing you."

*Fuck, why do I get the feeling he means it?*

I dash out the door and slam it shut. As I run, I swiftly rub my arm against my face to clean up any residue, and I pull my dress back over my breasts, then rush down the stairs.

By the time he's exited the room, I'm long gone, chased out of the building with a racing heart.

But it's not just from the sprint I just did to get halfway across campus and as far away from him as possible.

It's also because my pussy continues to throb between my legs, and my legs still quake from the vile amount of arousal I just felt.

God, I can't believe I just let that happen.

That I not only failed to kill him but also let him ... touch me.

Kiss me.

Degrade me.

Fuck my mouth.

Grope me until I came moaning out loud.

I bite my bottom lip until I feel a pang of pain and touch it. Blood.
Motherfucker. He made me bleed too.
Next time I see him, I'll find out who he really is.
And then I'll finish him off.

# 7

MILO

I listen to the breathy sounds and moans coming from the other room.

Someone in there is having a hell of an amazing time.

*WHACK!*

The whip comes down so hard I moan out loud. It burns and stings my skin and makes my cock burst with need. Fuck.

But my body ... God, my body can't take it anymore.

"Enough," I mutter, breathing out heavy breaths.

"I'm not done yet," Nathan barks.

My knees almost cave in on me. "I can't ... Banana."

Nathan growls but throws the whip aside anyway.

I sink to the floor and lie in a puddle of my own sweat, blood, and tears. A smile slowly erupts on my face. Every inch of my body is doused in tingles and happiness, like lightning zinging through my pores.

"Even now ... you're still smiling?" he asks.

"You know I love it."

Nathan scoops me up from the floor and takes me out of the cage, settling me down on the couch. He grabs some ointment from the top shelf and rubs it into my skin. I hiss from the pain.

"Does it hurt a lot?" he asks.

"It's fine," I answer. "I can handle it."

"You were too late calling out the stop word," he says.

"I know," I reply, smiling.

He sits down beside me on the black velvet couch. "Then why didn't you?"

"I know you needed it." I rub my lips together. "You needed the release more than I needed to quit."

He suddenly pulls me close and wraps his arms around me, hugging me tight.

And it's all I need to pull through.

I know his pain, this need to hurt, the anguish in his heart, and I'm willing to take all of it.

"I can take your pain," I say. "What I can't take is your regret."

He pushes me away again and tips up my chin. "Thank you."

His forehead leans against mine, and honestly, it's moments like these that make it all worth it.

Suddenly, someone unlocks our door and steps inside.

There's only one guy here with a key to this room.

"I hate to break up the private party you guys have going on in here," Kai says, "but you know there's a hole in the wall, right?"

Nathan just stares at him, indifferent. "So?"

Kai leans against the doorframe. "Someone was watching."

Nathan shrugs. "Let them. I don't care. Do you?" he asks me.

I smirk. "Fuck no. Maybe they got off on the violence."

When I think about it, I already get hard, and looking at Nathan, so does he.

"O...kay." Kai swallows away the lump in his throat. "And you don't want to know who it was?"

"Why? Is it important?" Nathan throws him a glare.

"Um..." Kai pauses, and my brow rises from how he fumbles with his words. He never fumbles. "No, not particularly. Anyway, did you guys find enough goods?"

Grinning, I get up, but Nathan grabs my wrist. "Whoa, you're not nearly steady enough to walk yet."

"I know my limits," I reply, and he releases me. "It's fine." I walk off to the closet and shove my key inside, opening it up as Kai walks closer. "Ta-daaa! I present to you the loot."

Kai rolls his eyes. "It's not an online game, Milo."

"Felt like raiding to me," I retort, grasping a stack of the credit cards I stole from the wardrobe section. "This has to be worth at least a couple of thousand. And we've got stacks."

"They're gonna ask questions downstairs, you know," Nathan says.

"While they just got wasted?" Kai scoffs. "I doubt it."

Nathan gets up from the couch. "Eventually. If not tonight, then tomorrow."

"Hey ... we're doing this for you," Kai says, eyeing him.

"I know," he replies, swallowing his pride. "Thank you."

"Yeah, you don't have to worry," I say, throwing my arm around his neck. "We've got you. You're our boy."

"Not my boy," Kai says, winking. "But he can sleep here."

"So are we done for tonight then, or do we need to collect more?" I ask.

Nathan turns to me. "You've done enough."

"Fuck no," I say. "I'd rather stay ahead of those threats."

"I think this will be just enough to ward them off," Kai says, counting the money. "For now."

Nathan breathes a sigh of relief.

"Go enjoy the party before everyone finds out their cash is gone," he adds, and he stuffs it all back into the closet and closes it, tucking the key into his pocket. "I'll see you all later."

"Where are you going?" I ask as he casually strolls out the door.

He lowers his mask over his eyes again. "I've got a ... rendezvous with a particularly interesting friend."

\*\*\*

# LANA

"Lana, I've been looking all over for you," Irina says.

I pull my pillow away from my face and look at her, but her words doesn't really register.

"Have you been here the entire night while we were out partying?" she asks, leaning against the doorjamb.

Well ... yes. After what happened, I didn't know where else to go, so I came straight to the sorority and hopped under the shower. But no amount of rinsing can get rid of this taste in my mouth.

"Sorry, I had to leave. Felt dizzy so I came back to my room to crash," I lie.

But I don't want her to know that someone on this campus knows I'm a killer.

And that he used me in exchange for his silence.

"You feeling okay?" she asks, sounding concerned.

"Yeah," I reply, smiling as I tuck my hair behind my ear. My hand briefly lingers near the missing ribbon, and I swallow away the lump in my throat. That fucker has two of them now.

I wonder if she'll notice.

"I can fix you something to drink if you want," she says. "Or get you an ibuprofen."

"I just need some rest," I say. "I had a good time, though. Thank you." I clear my throat. "Did you dance with a lot of guys? Snatch some hot dude to make out with?"

"Oh yeah, some hot guy started dancing with me halfway through the night." She kicks off her heels and holds them with two fingers. "He was so fucking ripped that I had a hard time keeping my hands to myself."

I smirk. "A successful night, then."

"*God*, it was so good. I'm just missing my fur coat, but I don't care. I'll see if I can get it tomorrow. I'm way too drunk to care." She giggles. "All I can think of is that dude with his hot suit."

*Suit.*

My veins grow icy cold.

"Well, anyway, good night!" She sashays off, stumbling through the hallway as I turn around and face the ceiling, hearing my own heartbeat in my ears.

*Fuck.*

It must've been one of them. A suited-up guy is too much of a co-incidence. No way any of the other students here at Spine Ridge would show up to an informal party wearing one. Was it one of his friends, or was it him? Did he see me dancing with Irina and Brooke and decide to go after them instead to get information about me?

"Fuck," I mutter, punching the bed, but it doesn't reduce my anger by even a little, so I grab my pillow and scream into it.

Some fucker out there knows exactly who I am and that I kill people for fun. And not only that, he fucking used it against me and turned me into a wet puddle with my own fucking knife.

It feels like the entire ceiling is caving in on me.

*Why? Fucking why?*

All I wanted was an outlet. I'm the princess of the family, the one who needs to excel, the one who's supposed to take over my father's grand business because he deems my brother irresponsible. He chose this college, not me. I was just here to study and be steamrolled into the company.

I just needed the release.

This one part of me that no one has to know about.

And now they do.

Sighing, I get out of bed and march downstairs toward the kitchen to grab a chocolate bar, munching on it until it's all gone.

"Wow, and I thought you wanted to lose weight," Jason says.

I frown when he steps into the kitchen, still wearing that white mask he got at the party. I threw mine in the trash immediately when I got home.

"How'd you get in here?" I ask.

"Hey, Lana!" Brooke waves from the hallway, her lipstick smeared and one of her broken heels in her hand.

"Well, that explains it," I mutter, and I take another bite.

"Where were you? You disappeared on us out of nowhere," Jason says, lifting the mask so it's on top of his head.

"I'm gonna go upstairs and crash. G'night!" Brooke yells from the hallway.

"I was exploring the Phantom building," I say.

"And? Did you find something interesting?"

"Nope," I lie.

Not gonna bother him with the nitty-gritty details, especially not when I'm still trying to keep up that good-princess persona I have going for me.

"Bummer. I'd hoped skipping out on more dancing with me would've been worth your trouble," he muses as he plants his hands on the counter beside me, trapping me. "Because I definitely missed you."

"Did you, now?" I muse, raising a brow as I put my hands around his waist.

"We don't need a party or the music to dance." He lowers his mask again.

I snort. "Why are you still wearing that?"

"I like it," he replies. "Doesn't it make me look sexy?" I giggle as he puts my hair behind my ear, his hand lingering to cup my face. "And I don't need to dance at a party to know I want to kiss you."

As his lips touch mine, a memory flashes through my mind of the guy in the suit licking the rim of my ear, making me turn away. God, that fucker has already invaded my mind.

"Something wrong?" Jason asks.

I pick up a wineglass and take out the bottle of wine from the cupboard. "It's just that I realized I haven't even gotten drunk tonight. And I don't want to be the only sober person on campus right now." I pour in the entire glass and chug it down.

"Well, pour me some too, then." Jason grins as he slides a glass across the counter. I fill it up and hand it back.

"There you go."

"Thanks," he says, and he takes a sip.

I chug mine down in one go. "Another one."

"You're really going for it, aren't you?" he muses.

"Yup," I reply, feeling miserable.

I grab my chocolate bar and take another big bite to ease the tension. "I ... Let's just go upstairs."

"Your bed? No way I'm gonna say no to that." He puts down his glass, grabs me, and drags me away so fast I drop the chocolate on the counter.

"No! My chocolate."

"I'll give you something better." He winks.

Oh boy.

# 8

## KAI

It's stupidly easy to find Lana's sorority house. I guess those friends of hers really don't mind spilling all the beans if it gets them a dance or two with a guy they think is horny for them. Lucky for me, I play the part right to ease them into telling more than they should have while I danced with them for just a few minutes. All I had to do was convince them I'd come visit them sometime. Which wasn't an entire lie, but they won't need to know that.

I walk into the back alley, trying to be as inconspicuous as I can when I jump up to catch the emergency fire exit and pull it down to the ground. I jump on and climb toward the top, where her room is, and I make my way across the narrow metal until I find her window. It's opened slightly, and I push my fingers through to release the lock and push it open so I can crawl through.

I close the window behind me so no one outside will be alerted to my presence before I head farther inside. I lift my mask over my head to look around. The room has a regal blue tint and gold foil lining the walls, and lots of expensive clothing brands like Gucci and bags from Hermes lie scattered around the room. The closet is stuffed with clothes and shoes practically falling out.

On the wall is a shelf with a ton of books, some of which haven't been touched in ages, judging from the dust collecting on them. A ton of homework is piled on her desk, all neatly assorted, pens with pink fluff balls on them, just like I expected from a rich Mafia princess who's been sheltered all her life.

But nothing like I'd expect from the vicious killer I met that night.

I smirk to myself.

*Interesting.*

After I'm done looking around, I zip open my bag and pull out the mini camera, then push it between the dusty books, making sure it's not visible to the naked eye. Then I check my phone to see if it's turned on and ensure I can access it from my account.

*Perfect.*

I go ahead and shuffle through her stuff to see if I can find something interesting, like proof that she was going to that guy's house to kill him, or future targets, careful not to misplace anything so she'll never know I was here. Her laptop sits closed on her desk, so I open it, but it's protected with a password.

Of course.

*What could it be?*

I type in some things that come to mind. She said she had a boyfriend, his name was ...

"Jason," I mutter as I type it in.

**Error.**

*What then?*

I try the brands in her room next, but none of them work. Maybe her full name? Or birthday? Which I don't know, but I can ask Brooke or Irina next time I see them. If I can't get into the laptop today, then maybe the next time I sneak into her room.

Suddenly, I hear someone come up the stairs.

I swiftly lower my mask again and rush toward the window, but when I try to pry it open, it won't budge.

*Fuck! Why the fuck won't it open?! C'mon, you stupid piece of shit!*

I groan in frustration, but the noise is getting closer and closer.

There's no more time.

I turn around and make a run for the bed, sliding to my knees before I crawl underneath ... just as the door opens.

"Hmm ..."

I hear some smacking sounds.

Two, no, four feet.

I stay under the bed as they come closer while making what sounds like kissing noises.

"C'mon, it's been too long," a guy mumbles.

"You know I have so much homework to do tomorrow. I need to sleep."

I'd recognize that voice anywhere. A smile erupts on my face. Lana. My little vicious kitty.

But the smile quickly dissipates as the guy's feet hit the side of the bed.

"I can't wait any longer. I need you," the guy says.

"Jason ..."

*So it is him.*

"But you're still wearing that mask," she murmurs.

"Doesn't it make it extra spicy?" Jason replies. "Pretend I'm a handsome stranger whisking you away."

They approach fast, and sweat drops roll down my face as they fall onto the bed.

*Fuck. Too late to run now.*

I can hear the smooches and feel the moans reverberate through the bed.

It's almost like I'm ... a part of it.

Clothes fly off left and right. Shoes first, hers clattering to the floor right beside my head. His shirt comes off next, then a pair of pants and a belt.

My teeth grind into each other so harshly I can hear it. Because above me, I can definitely hear them going at it.

Then a pair of panties drop to the floor. Newly worn panties that I didn't rip apart.

Sick thoughts fill my mind with obsession as they kiss and roll around on the mattress. The filling of the bed dents downward, almost into me. My hand instinctively rises to feel the mattress bump, wondering if it's her body. If I can feel her indirectly, touch her the way I did when I danced with her or when I cornered her in our pool room. When I made her come on her own goddamn blade.

But then the mattress begins to thump.

*Fuck.*

My hand inches toward my pocket, where I've grown increasingly aware of the knife poking into my body. I pull it out as the mattress dips and dips, and his grunts become more obvious with every passing second.

I take out my knife and point it at the mattress, my heart rate picking up as I'm hovering dangerously close to ripping everyone to shreds.

I would kill that motherfucker if we were alone.

But I don't know who I'd hit first if I strike now. If my blade would penetrate his body ... or hers.

And for some reason, the thought of my knife being thrust into her stomach is worse than his dick penetrating her pussy as we speak, the same pussy I fucked with a knife mere hours ago.

That fucker ... he's still wearing one of our masks like he's fucking one of us, and that doesn't sit right with me.

Suddenly, Lana groans. "Are you finished yet?"

"Not yet," Jason murmurs, teetering on the edge, and fuck me, I could gut him for even suggesting he's going to burst inside her.

Lana sighs. "Hurry."

"Ahhh, almost," Jason says.

"Can you be a little more ...?"

"More what?"

She sighs again. "I don't know. More aggressive?"

*More aggressive?*

My eyes narrow, and a hint of a smile tugs at my lips.

*Now why would she suggest that?*

It's quiet for some time while he's pounding away like some lumberjack without giving a second thought to her needs and wants. But I don't think that's what she meant by aggressive.

"Fuck, I'm so tired," Lana says.

"Just a minute more," the fucker moans.

And the tip of the knife hovers so close to the mattress I've almost severed a strand.

It's taking every ounce of self-control not to burst out and kill that motherfucker for trying. For making her sit through this mediocre, yawn-inducing self-absorbed meat slapping.

Jason sighs out loud too now, and the mattress dips less, then I see his feet appear next to the bed. "You know what, never mind. I'm gonna go take a shower. You go rest," he says, and he marches off, socks and all.

*Fuck that motherfucking leech.*

I swallow away the rage and focus on her. She's still in the bed, doesn't move, doesn't make a single sound. One single sigh follows before it goes quiet.

I retract my knife slowly.

*Has she gone to sleep?*

Color me surprised.

I would've expected her to get angry when he just made a mad dash for the shower after not getting his fill. Even though I didn't hear her moan, didn't hear even a semblance of pleasure coming from her. But maybe she was too tired to care.

Or maybe he just couldn't fulfill her needs.

I suck in a breath and touch the mattress, which is far less bent than before, and I can almost feel her through the fabric, her movement, hear every small sound and every breath she takes. And for a second, I can't even do anything but feel, wondering if she can feel me too in her dreams, if she's thought of me the way I've thought of her. Because this little killer kitty has invaded every corner of my mind.

I slowly crawl out from underneath the bed, carefully checking if anyone is in the room before I get up. I can hear the shower running down the hallway, which means that fucker is still here.

I look at her lying in her bed, one hand above her head, her legs parted, hair splayed, as though the last bit of energy was siphoned away by a guy intent on solely meeting his own needs.

Fishing my knife from my pocket, I hover over her, trailing the knife across her skin.

I could kill her right now. Stop both our secrets from getting out. Puncture her skin and end this game of cat and mouse we've got going on.

But this is the first time I can finally have a good look at my pretty little killer, and now that I've finally gotten close enough without her trying to kill me, I want more.

With the knife, I push away some of her neatly combed black hair, and she moans, rubbing her pretty plump lips together before she turns her head sideways into the blade, almost like an invitation to cut her again and make her bleed. But that skin is so pristine. I can see her veins pulsing with heat, throbbing with an unquenched desire.

A desire that makes me lick my lips and swallow as the animal within me comes alive.

She looks gorgeous up close. Too perfect to even break through her skin, no matter how tempted I am. Like a pretty little doll waiting to be petted and owned.

I lean in to listen to her breathing. It picks up. Maybe she's dreaming ... dreaming about the party and our dance... dreaming about me laying waste to her mouth and her pussy ...

Dreaming about how that fucker just left her high and dry to go jerk off in the shower.

My nostrils flare as I trail the knife down her sharp jawline and neck.

"I could give you so much more ..." I whisper as the knife travels down her chest, across her ample breasts and peaked nipples underneath the fabric, all the way down to her belly.

Half her body hides underneath a blanket, but I won't let that get in my way as I pull it off. Her legs are partially over the edge of the bed, her dress is scooted up a little, and her pussy is on full display, panties still on the floor. And fuck me, with the moonlight finally allowing me a glimpse of what she has to offer, I can't stop looking at it.

Mouthwatering.

I swallow away the lump in my throat as I let the knife travel down her thighs, which clench with lingering arousal. Even in her sleep, her legs fall apart as though they're inviting me.

And I can't help but sink to my knees behind the bed where she lies and lean in, the knife still firmly lodged in my hand. But instead of driving it into her skin, I grasp ahold of her thighs, and sniff.

*The smell. God, the fucking smell ...*

My cock hardens in my pants as I bring my mouth to her pussy.

The first lick is divine.

She tastes exactly like I imagined she would. Like innocence and sin combined into perfection. A perfect girl for a wicked sinner like me.

So I continue licking, lapping her up until she squirms in her sleep. A soft moan leaves her mouth, and her cheeks become pink as I circle my tongue around and around. Her pussy is slowly becoming wetter and wetter, much wetter than it was before that fucker left, I'm sure.

Has he ever even touched her?

Made her feel good?

Licked her the way I'm licking her now?

I groan with both frustration and excitement as I kiss her sensitive spot, the knife still clutched firmly against the side of her thigh while I wonder if I should end it all.

But this killer pussy ... it tastes so good, and I can't fucking get enough.

She moans out loud and suddenly stretches her arms, her eyes fluttering open, slowly homing in on the guy perched between her legs. But even that won't stop me from eating her out.

# 9

## LANA

My body feels hot and heavy as I wake up panting in bed, breathing heavy breaths.

*Did I have a sex dream?*

*About Jason?*

No, that can't be it, I've never pictured him as anything other than an okay kisser, and someone to get a quick and easy fix.

But this ... what I'm feeling right now is pure and utter lust.

My eyes open slowly, wondering what's going on, but as my eyelids flutter they home in on something—or someone—perched between my legs at the bottom of the bed with a mask on. Someone whose tongue dips into me, causing shivers all across my body.

*Oh God.*

*Jason? I thought he said he went to shower.*

Arousal builds and builds in my body as he swivels his tongue around, leaving me wet and breathless, and fuck me, I've never been licked like this before. That, or I'm too drunk from the wine to care. But I didn't have that many glasses, right? Or maybe they just hit harder than I assumed they would.

I rub my forehead to try to make sense of things, but the relentless assault on my senses overcomes me.

When I look between my legs, there's a guy ... licking my pussy.

And he's wearing a mask.

I instantly squeeze my legs together, but fingernails dig into my skin.

"Stay."

The voice is possessive and over-the-top demanding.

Jason's never used that kind of voice before.

But good God, I have never heard anything more attractive.

*Is he pretending to be bossy now?*

I lie back and enjoy the feeling because I wouldn't be able to move even if I wanted to. It's as if he took my comment about being more aggressive very literally. I like it.

His tongue swivels back and forth across my most sensitive spot while his hands make sure I don't move an inch.

"Oh God ..." I murmur. "I didn't know you could do that."

He grins against my skin. Arrogant fucker.

"Is this your way of making up?" I muse, writhing away on the bed. "Because you know I like it rough."

"Do you now?"

*Hmm ... why is his voice so much deeper than before? Did he drink too much too? Or does he always sound like that, and are my ears just fucked from the loud music at the party?*

I groan, pushing the thoughts away. As long as his tongue continues doing that. I'm too drunk to care.

Good God, I would've jumped his bones much sooner if I knew he could lick like this.

His mouth is rugged and buried between my legs, tongue expertly diving in.

"Oh yes, do it like that," I mewl.

"You like that?" he asks.

Again, that low voice. God, I must really be drunk. Drunk on this fucking lust coursing through my veins, yeah, because if he keeps going like this, I'm going to come. Maybe even scream. And I rarely come when Jason does it instead of me and my toys. But fuck me, the way he's using his tongue tonight might just do it.

My pussy zings with need, just like earlier when that knife thrust inside.

My eyes burst open, and I force the image to disappear from my mind.

I have to stop thinking about that asshole and focus on the here and now. Maybe his licking can replace the memory.

As he drives his tongue inside, I gasp. "F-fuck." My voice is high pitched, unlike usual, and I almost feel embarrassed, but this feels so fucking good.

His tongue bores into me with a frenzy I've never felt before. He twists his tongue around and around my swollen nub until I'm so aroused I begin to squirm and scrunch up the blanket underneath me.

"Oh, I was so mad at you before, but not anymore," I murmur. "Is this why you went to shower? I thought you were jerking off in there."

He pauses momentarily, and for a second there, I wish I hadn't said anything.

"Focus, Lana."

There's that stern voice again, ready to swoop me off my feet. He's never been this dominant before, and I kind of like it.

"So greedy," I murmur as he laps me up like he's dying for more.

"Do you get licked often?" he asks.

What a strange question to ask. I snort. "You should know. You never do."

A low, grumbling sound emanates from his chest. "I'll lick this pussy every fucking day from now on if you want me to ..."

I don't even know what he's saying. All I feel is that tongue driving me insane.

"Have you ever come so hard you screamed out to God, begging for mercy?"

Wow. Did he really just say that? Or did my drunk mind just make that up?

A slap to the thighs wakes me up. "Answer me."

"No." I don't know what he wants to hear. I just don't want him to stop whatever he's doing with that crazy tongue of his.

"Then you'll start tonight."

I'm delirious with need, consumed by the need to come that I just scream, "Yes! Fuck yes, make me come."

"Come all over my tongue, Lana," he murmurs, his tongue flicking the tip.

And I do. I come so hard I'm moaning out loud. "Fuck! God, that feels good, Jason."

He pulls his tongue back, leaving me feeling bereft, wishing he'd continue so I could come again and again and again. But at the same time, I can't even keep my eyes open, too tired from the party, too wasted from the wine to care.

\*\*\*

## KAI

She called his name.

Not mine.

*His.*

For a second, I almost forgot we're supposed to be enemies.

I was overtaken by the need to give her pleasure, pleasure he wasn't even able to give her, pleasure that never even crossed his mind.

Until she called out for him instead of me.

Something about that made me want to tear off this mask and show her the real person behind all the gratification she just received.

The only thing that kept me from doing that is that she'd probably murder me on sight. And now that she's awake ... it would definitely be risky.

But good God, did that pussy taste divine.

I lick my lips and wipe my mouth, licking off my fingers too. It's rare for me to be so attracted to someone that I can't help myself ... but it's too late. I've already crossed that line.

What do I do now? I was supposed to find out information about her. That, or kill her. Neither of these two plans succeeded because of my unquenched thirst for her pussy.

And fuck me, if I could, I would have another lick.

If it wasn't for the fact that that fucker whose name she just called out could come back any minute now.

Well, at least I'll have my fucking camera taping her in the background, watching her every move.

I lean over her wasted body, her eyes barely staying open. Drowning in ecstasy looks good on her. I grab her face and kiss her full on the lips with everything I have, staking my claim.

Even if she still thinks she belongs to him ...

She's mine now.

She doesn't push me away. In fact, she kisses me back like a drunk having the first taste of liquor. And Lord have fucking mercy on my soul, these lips will be the end of me.

But time is not on my side.

As our mouths unlatch, I stare at her swollen pink lips, begging for more.

*Oh, you'll get more soon enough, Lana. Don't you worry.*

"Sleep," I say.

"Hmm ..." she groans, dropping her head back into the pillow. "Yeah ... I'd like that."

Within seconds, she's already turned away, dress still pulled up, panties still on the floor. She doesn't seem to care since she's exhausted from orgasmic satisfaction.

I smirk to myself. I finished that girl in a way that fucker Jason could never.

And best of all ... I can do it again and again and again. Now that I've had a taste of her, there's no way in hell I've had enough. One single lick was enough to turn me into an addict.

Her phone buzzes right beside her on the nightstand, and I pick it up. Her friend sent her a picture of the party where she's dancing with me. A hint of a memory now deeply latched onto both our brains. I won't forget this night any time soon.

I take a picture with my phone so I have a copy of my own, then open her contacts and swipe her phone number. I put the phone back on the nightstand and look at her gorgeous little face dreaming away of a sexy night.

*Sleep well, little kitty of mine. You'll need the rest for all the filthy things I plan to do to you soon.*

Suddenly, a door in the hallway opens, and I can hear someone walking, so I race toward the window and shove a pen into the crack, wriggling it around until it finally gives way. I jump through and crawl down right as the door to her room opens.

*Too late, fucker.*

I already gave her everything she needed, everything she could never get from you.

That girl is no longer yours.

She'll soon come crawling to me.

And when she does ... my hard cock will be ready.

I head back to the Phantom Society building in the middle of the night, making sure no one saw me walk around the Beta Pi sorority. Can't have gossip fill these grounds and reach Lana's ears just when I'm having so much fun with her. Although I have to say, it would be fun to see the look on her face once she realizes it wasn't her boyfriend who gave her that amazing orgasm.

With a broad smirk, I enter the hallway and close the door behind me, careful not to make a sound. I don't want anyone to wake up because of me even though I am the president of this fucking society. All of those fuckers sleeping in this house are my responsibility, and their achievements at school matter.

If we can't be the richest anymore, we'll be the smartest, goddammit.

I make my way to the kitchen and pour myself a glass of juice, but as I close the fridge, the freaky smile and big eyes appearing behind make me literally shriek. "Ah!" After my heart stops pounding, I add, "What the fuck, Milo?"

His tall and lanky frame almost made me do a double take to check if he wasn't a ghost. "Where were you?" he asks, a mischievous glint in his eyes.

Oh boy.

"Nowhere." I turn around and gulp down my juice as fast as I can.

"Nowhere is a big place," he jests. "Sure is an important place to be in the middle of the night."

"Does it matter?" I retort.

He's right behind me, and I can literally feel his stare on my back.

"Yes, it's the middle of the night, and I want to know where you went."

*He's not going to let this go, is he?*

"Don't you have a party to clean up or something?" I reply, and I take my last big gulp.

"No, we've got cleaners for that. You're avoiding the question," he says. "So that means you found her."

I almost choke on my juice, and I lower the glass and cough out loud.

He hovers around me with that broad grin of his. "You did, didn't you?"

I frown. "How? When?"

He places his hand on the counter right beside me. "At the party. Something about you seemed off. I couldn't put my finger on it earlier, but now ..."

I tilt my brow. "Now what?"

A smirk forms on his face. "Now you're not denying it. And why else would you be out so late at night?"

I roll my eyes. "A stroll."

He laughs. Suddenly, he leans in and brings his nose to my mouth, sniffing, and I feel put off.

I lean back and push him away before snapping at him, "Dude ..."

"You smell like pussy," he says, voice dripping with judgment, his eyes twinkling. "I knew it. You found her!"

My face tightens, and my eyes can't hide the annoyance.

But fuck me, the grin spreading on his face is the trigger.

"How the fuck would you even know how her pussy smelled?"

"So it is *her*? You're not denying it, so it's true."

I sigh out loud and slam my glass on the counter. I should've drunk the whiskey instead.

"Who is she?" he asks. "Where does she live? Did you actually fuck her? Wait, did she wear another ribbon? Is that how you found out?" He fishes it from his pocket and holds it up like a treasure.

My eyes widen. "What the—Where'd you get that?" I snatch it from his hand.

"Underneath your pillow." He bites his bottom lip, withholding a wicked smile that's too obvious to hide.

*That little shit.*

He went snooping through my room while I was away.

He's too close for comfort, but I don't know how to fucking react. "So what's her name?"

My mind races as emotions swirl inside me because this was supposed to be my secret. My fucking treasure.

And now the secret is out.

"Wait, I saw you dancing with a girl tonight ... was it her?" His eyes narrow. "But she was with those other two girls." He snaps his fingers as he thinks. "What was it ... Irene? Iris?"

"Irina and Brooke," I say, annoyed he's still fishing.

His jaw drops. "Holy shit ..."

My hand slowly turns into a fist on the counter.

I don't like where this is going.

"It's Lana? As in Lana R—"

Before he can spit out her name, I slam my hand over his mouth. "Don't even think about it."

But the excitement on his face tells me it's too late to put the genie back into the bottle. Fuck.

"I swear to God, I'll fucking sew these lips together if you say her name out loud."

"Fine, fine," he mumbles through my fingers.

When I lower my hand, he doesn't relent. "Oh my God, *that* girl?" He cups his chin. "Though it makes sense, considering who her brother is."

"Exactly, so keep your mouth shut," I say.

His face contorts. "Does she know it's you?"

I shake my head. "Not yet."

He blows out a breath. "Phew. I was almost scared she was gonna come after us—Wait..." He pauses. "But your mouth smelled like pussy. You gave her head?"

I grab his shirt and pull him up close. "Don't tell anyone. Especially not Nathan. Got it?"

He holds up his hands. "All right, all right." He snorts. "Though, if you ask me, great taste in girls, dude." He makes a pursed fingers gesture with both hands, brings them to his mouth, and kisses the air between them like an Italian. "Perfection. But just one problem. Wasn't she also there to kill that dude? And we caught her in the act?" He's counting the questions on his long, bony fingers. "And doesn't that mean, technically, she wants to kill us?"

"Maybe," I reply.

He smiles. "Can you put me down now?"

I slowly lower him to the floor, and he pats himself, straightening his clothes.

"Thanks."

"So ... the girl we've been looking for, you not only found her but gave her a lick like a goddamn lollypop..." He sniggers to himself. "And here I was thinking that party was just meant to gather money." His eyes home in on mine, and they're suddenly much less happy and much more riddled with savagery. "You were luring her in."

A devilish smirk forms on my lips.

"You already knew it was her, didn't you? How long?"

I fish the ribbon from my pocket to look at it for a moment, the memory of when I first saw that little violent kitty still etched into my brain. "I saw her walk around on campus with a red ribbon in her hair a few days ago."

"Wow ..." He taps his foot on the floor. "You know this will not go down well with Nathan, right? You, falling for the one girl who could destroy our reputation if she finds out who we are."

I clutch the ribbon tightly. "Just as we can destroy hers."

"Hmm ..." His eyes begin to twinkle again. "You want to extort her."

"I haven't decided what I'm going to do with her yet," I reply, and

I tuck the ribbon back into my pocket. "But you ... you'll keep quiet about this. Tell *no one*." I point my finger at his chest. "That includes Nathan, okay?"

"You know I'm terrible at keeping secrets from him," Milo muses.

"Try," I rebuke as I march off toward the hallway. "Or your reputation will be on the line too."

# 10

## LANA

"Oh my God, I feel terrible," Brooke says as she pops another pill.

"You sure you wanna be here?" I ask. "You could go lie in bed."

"No, I've got a test today," she replies, groaning in pain.

"Still hungover?" Irina muses as she sits down on the picnic bench.

"I thought this shit would be over in a day, but I guess that's only for people whose bodies are normal," Brooke laments, huddled over her bottle of water. "Remind me not to drink that much ever again."

I giggle and take a bite out of my sandwich. "I'm sorry. If I'd stayed around, I could've plucked the drinks out of your hand."

"You missed out on a whole lot of fun, Lana," Irina says. "Some dude even came to ask us about you."

I can barely swallow my sandwich. "What?"

"Yeah, I mean, I don't know what his name was, but man, he looked sexy in that suit of his. And my hands were all over that." Brooke holds her hand up high for Irina to clap. "Fuck yeah. I should've gotten his number."

"What did he ask you?" I casually take another bite from my sandwich to avoid appearing too invested.

"Oh, just if we were friends, if we were from the same sorority, and if he could see me more often," Brooke muses, smiling like crazy.

But I know better.

That guy was trying to find out where I lived.

"What did you tell him?" I ask.

"Well, the truth, what else?" She shrugs.

"But what if he's a Phantom guy?" I ask.

"So?" She takes a sip of her drink. "I don't care as long as he's hot."

"He was hot, though," Irina concurs.

"Hey, babe." A kiss on the hair alerts me to Jason's presence. "How have your classes been going?"

"Fine," I reply as he sits down beside me. "Yours?"

"Fantastic. Couldn't be better."

"Sounds sarcastic," Irina says.

"You got any extra sandwiches?" Jason asks, avoiding the topic entirely. "I'm starving."

"So are you two dating now?" Brooke says, pointing at us both.

"Dating?" Jason snorts. "Well, I mean, I would, but ..." He tilts his head in my direction.

"What?" I scoff. "Don't look at me. I wasn't the one sucking off this clitty the other day." I point at my crotch.

Brooke and Irina burst out into high shrieks and laughter.

"Oh my God!" Brooke cheers.

"What?" Jason's brows furrow as he looks at me like I've lost my mind. "When?"

Now I make a face too. "After the party, when you tried to kiss me, half drunk, and we went upstairs."

He keeps eyeing me like he has no clue what I'm talking about.

"After you finished your shower," I mutter.

Everyone's looking at me like they're waiting for the clue, but there is none.

"Whatever." I take another bite of my sandwich. "You were too drunk to remember anyway."

"Well, if I got some pussy ... I consider that a win regardless," Jason says, throwing out an arrogant laugh. "Friends with benefits is cool too."

I finish my sandwich and get up. "Time for more classes. See you guys later."

"Bye, Lana!" Irina waves as I walk off.

I wave at everyone too, but when I turn around, the smile instantly disappears off my face. Something about that whole exchange just doesn't sit right with me. Why wouldn't Jason remember how he finally didn't just think of his own pleasure but mine too? He's always been a sex-obsessed maniac, and now he suddenly denies eating me out right after the party?

I shiver as a cold draft flows across campus, and I tie my scarf tighter around my neck.

But it's not just the chill of the looming winter that makes me feel frigid.

Because I feel like, wherever I go, I'm being watched.

\*\*\*

## MILO

I clutch the tree and glance at the girl walking closer and closer. My heart rate picks up with each step she takes.

God, if she is really that girl we met in that dirty house ...

That vicious murderer ...

This is going to be out-of-this-world amazing.

A grin spreads from ear to ear.

I can't believe it's really her, that she's here out of all places. Crescent Vale City is huge, and to have her be a student here at Spine Ridge University is almost too good to be true.

But it is true.

She's wearing that same red ribbon that girl was, and she walks with the same kind of swagger. Like she knows no one can touch her. And that kind of arrogance only comes with being a killer.

How many men has she destroyed before we met?

It's the kind of violence unusual in a girl, and it's riling me up to no end.

"So ... that's the girl who's been keeping you busy, huh?"

I glance over my shoulder. "Blaine ... Sneaking up on me again, I see."

He folds his arms, a wicked smirk forming on his perfectly chiseled face. "I'm just doing the Lord's work by keeping an eye on you."

"I already regret telling you about her," I say, rolling my eyes.

"Too late to take it back, Milo," he says.

"How do you always rope me into spilling all my secrets every time we drink?" I groan in dismay.

"Tartarus trade secret," he muses, planting a firm hand on my shoulder. "But don't be a creep."

"Me? A creep?" I laugh.

But he just stares at me with a lifted brow. "We both know how you latch onto things."

I frown. "Nah, I never stalk people. That's Kai's thing."

"I'm not talking about stalking. I mean, clamping down on something and becoming thoroughly fixated." He suddenly reaches into my pocket and fishes out my nunchucks. "Like these, for example."

"Hey, give those back!"

I try to snatch them away, but he holds them up high. That motherfucker is using his height against me.

"You learn how to use nunchucks, and now you're carrying them around everywhere," he muses. "You latch onto things ... only now it's a girl."

"You're the one who taught me," I retort, and I jump up to steal back my nunchucks. "And this girl is not just a fun side project."

"All I'm saying is ... be careful." He grabs both my shoulders, leaning down to look me in the eyes. "I'm not your enemy, Milo. I'm a friend who cares. Don't forget that."

I nod. "Don't tell anyone."

"What kind of a friend would tattle?" He winks. "Anyway, I have to go to class. Talk to you later?"

"Yeah," I say.

"And if you really want her that badly, why not just go talk to her?"

He turns and walks away with a casual wave, always with that same flair that makes me snort.

Well, if he gave me the go-ahead, maybe I should go for it.

The cold, crispy air waving through the leaves above me is my signal. But right as I step out from behind the tree, my shirt is pulled up to my neck. My fingers scratch at my neck as the fabric is choking me.

"Are you out of your goddamn mind?"

Kai pulls me behind the tree and shoves me into the trunk, and I groan with both pain and excitement. Because good God, he knows how to pack a punch. Too bad for him he doesn't swing that way, or I would've let him get some.

"You almost got me hard," I groan, laughing.

He smacks the bark behind me. "This isn't a joke, Milo."

"I wasn't joking," I muse.

He looks around for a moment to check if anyone is watching us.

"What were you thinking?" he asks. "Heading right for her?"

I shrug. That's my problem. I usually don't think. At all.

Sometimes it's a curse; sometimes it's a blessing.

"What was your plan, anyway?" he scoffs, pointing at her. "Just walk up to her and be like 'I know what you did'?"

I smile. "You make it sound like that movie. What was that name again...?" I snap my fingers when it hits me. "*I Know What You Did Las—*"

"Shut up." He grabs me by my collar and plants a hand over my mouth as his eyes leer beyond the tree at the girl walking by.

"You're already in that deep?" I muse when he finally removes his hand.

Kai rarely crushes on anyone. He normally shies away from human contact unless it's to beat someone up for messing with his friends. Especially since the incident where he lost part of his sight.

"Look, she already knows we found her. It'd be stupid to out ourselves now that we have the upper hand," Kai says.

My brows furrow. "You told her about us?"

"No, she doesn't know our names."

"But she knows we're on this campus," I say.

"Doesn't matter," he replies.

"Yes, it does. And if she's a killer just like us, I want to get to know her."

His face contorts. "What? Why? Fuck no."

"What else do you want to do?" I ask, raising a brow. "Kill her?"

"I've thought about it," he says through gritted teeth.

"But instead, you licked her pussy raw. Got it."

"Hey, what I do is none of your business," he says, pointing at me like it adds weight to his words.

But I see through him right away. "Wrong. She's seen all three of us there, and if she finds out you're the one who's been paying her visits, she'll know about me and Nathan. We're all in this together."

He seems pissed that I mention it, but we both know I'm right.

"You want her," I say. "And if you're going to get some killer pussy, I want some too."

His nostrils flare, rage firing up in his eyes. "Fuck no."

"What?"

He shakes his head. "You can't have her."

I snort. "She's not yours either. She has a boyfriend. I just saw him sit on that same bench."

He squints, annoyed I'd point it out. "Like I don't fucking know that."

"I'm just saying ... if you're gonna enjoy something that ain't yours, then let me feast too. Otherwise, what's the point? Where's the fun in me keeping a secret without having the benefits too?"

He mulls it over for a second as if it finally dawns on him that he's put himself in a difficult position before he releases me again. "Fine."

I pat his chest. "Good choice, partner in crime." A broad smile forms on my face. "So when are you planning on ravaging her again?"

"What are you guys talking about?"

Kai's eyes widen at Nathan's voice, and he casually tucks his hands into his pocket before turning around to face him. "Class. Money. The usual."

"Speaking of money ..." he repeats, tucking his hands into his pockets. "We still don't have enough."

"What do you mean? We stole loads of stuff," I say.

Kai smacks his hand in front of my mouth. "Do you have to be so loud all the time?"

Nathan lifts his mobile phone and shows us another text he got.

"Another threat?" Kai asks.

"They want more," Nathan replies, the nerves on his face bulging. "It's never gonna be enough." He runs his fingers through his crisp blond hair. "What the fuck am I going to do?"

"We'll fix this," Kai says. "Don't give up."

"You know, we're here for you," I say.

"If my fucking parents could have just done their job correctly," Nathan grits, "I wouldn't be in this shit." His fist balls. "I have to protect her. I don't fucking care what it takes. If I have to shoot a million more men, I'll do it."

"Okay, let's do it, then," I say.

Kai sighs, but he eventually agrees and nods.

"You got any more of those targets from that site you were on?" Nathan asks.

"Let's talk about it after class," Kai replies. "We might be able to do another hit tonight."

"Oh yeah, that's what I'm talking about," I say, grinning from ear to ear.

# 11

## LANA

*Yawning, I stumble through the hallway looking for the bathroom. It's the middle of the night, and my throat is dry. But the darkness makes it hard to see, so I touch the walls, looking around for the door. Light spills from the room to the left a few feet ahead of me.*

*My brother's room.*

*But it's so late at night. He can't still be awake, right?*

*I creep up to the door, yawning into my hand. I wonder what he's doing.*

*Some squeaky noises and a definite groaning sound are coming from up ahead.*

*What is it?*

*When I push the door open and peek inside, I notice a big lump on his bed. Like a monster growing inside the blanket, pushing, shoving, moving around.*

*But I don't believe in monsters.*

*I frown and call out my brother's name. "Felix?"*

*The lump abruptly stops and then moves up, the blanket slowly lowering. Two eyes connect with mine.*

*But they aren't my brother's.*

*Even though I can definitely tell two people are in that bed.*

*I swallow, but the dryness in my throat doesn't go away.*

*"Mom?"*

Shrieking, I sit straight up while drenched in sweat, breathing heavily.

I gather my bearings for a moment and check the time. 1:00 a.m.

Jesus Christ. I haven't even slept two hours and already that fucking nightmare came to visit me again.

I throw myself back on the bed and relax on the pillow, trying to get the memory out of my head, but nothing I do works.

Nothing ever works to quell the rage inside my heart.

*Mother.*

A word I despise so much even though I used to love it so much.

Before I knew how twisted that word could become.

Now all that's left is a remnant of my family.

Broken. Shattered into pieces.

I turn around in bed, squeezing my pillow like I'm choking someone, but nothing will eliminate this anger.

So I throw my blanket off, groaning with annoyance, and get up.

Sleep is not going to work tonight, and only one other thing can calm my raging heart.

Violence.

So I go on to the laptop and check the same website as before, the one I've visited so many times, to see if I've got my next bait.

A smile forms on my face when I find out multiple people have replied to my posts.

All of those people are abhorrent, vicious monsters who deserve to die.

Just like my mother did.

I grab my outfit and my bag filled with tools and weapons, and I make my way out of the door and the sorority building, ready for my knives to meet my next victim's blood.

\*\*\*

When I finally get to the shoddy place in the middle of the city, I park my motorcycle out front and check out the neighborhood before I put on my mask and head toward the house. A big yard in front is filled with all kinds of bushes and trees tightly cramped together like a mini jungle. It looks like a pretty piece of nature, but a wretched monster hides within this place.

I head toward the door clutching my backpack filled with tools and weapons.

My heart's racing in my throat because I know what's about to happen—the thrill of the chase, the hunt, the kill.

It drives me, pushing me to go beyond my limits.

And to me, it's a moment of bliss.

A little sliver of heaven as evil people are punished and cut from this world for their crimes.

As I walk onto the porch, I hear noise inside.

My ears perk up as I listen.

Two—no, three voices. And they sound awfully young.

But my target isn't young at all. He told me he was fifty, so who the fuck are these people?

I'm definitely not alone even though the message the man sent me clearly said he would be.

*What the fuck is going on?*

I creep up to the window and look through.

Three guys wearing white masks just like the ones at the Phantom Society party are beating a dude with a bat and a pair of nunchucks. The hits are slow and painful, and I can't help but focus on their faces hidden behind those damn masks. All that's visible are their smiles and tongues as they dip out to lick the seam of their lips as they torture him.

My heart skips a beat.

I'm fascinated by their obvious delight in violence.

I'm watching way too long, but I can't look away.

That was supposed to be my victim. Instead, he's become theirs.

And I find myself oddly mesmerized by how they seem to enjoy dishing out pain just as much as I do.

One of them grabs his shoulder, pulls him close, and whispers something into his ear.

With a trembling hand, the man points at the closet to the left, and the guy storms at it, opening it up to find a safe, which he easily unlocks.

*So they were beating him to make him say the code?*

The guy pulls money from the safe and stuffs it into a bag. But when he turns, his piercing blue eyes suddenly flick to the window, and I duck. I crawl across the porch and hear footsteps coming toward the door.

*Fuck.*

I inhale a sharp breath and run back to the biggest tree to hide behind just as the door opens up, and three guys come barging out.

*CLING CLANG!*

Some coins drop to the stone pavement below the steps.

"Hey, don't drop any. We need all of it," someone says.

*That voice ... It sounds so, so familiar, but I can't place it.*

"Sorry, it's just a lot. Man, that dude was so happy to part ways with that fucking cash," another guy says, snorting.

Again, a voice I can't place but definitely recognize from somewhere.

*Could it be them? Are these the same guys who I met before in that grimy house?*

*Are they following me, or is it another coincidence?*

I swallow away the nerves as they approach. I don't dare to look.

"Hold on," the first guy says. "We forgot some equipment. Let's go back inside."

"You go up ahead to start the car."

"Okay, okay," the guy says.

The door opens up again, and I can hear two guys walk back in again.

Now it's just me and that one dude who's going to the car.

His whole face hides underneath a hoodie, so I can't tell who it is. He casually strolls down the pavement, whistling a happy tune, but I can smell the stench of fresh blood, like an odor drifting through the wind. Right as he passed the tree, I make myself as small as possible, hoping he doesn't see me. But I know they'll find the motorcycle outside eventually.

*What do I do?*

I lean in to see where he's going, but suddenly, I'm face-to-face with him.

"Well, hello there," he says. "Nice to see you again."

*What the fuck? How did he find me here?*

I immediately go for the attack, and I punch him in the face, but he catches my hand with ease.

"Now, that's not very nice of you."

I try to punch him again from the side, but he dodges that too expertly, along with all my other swings. It's almost as if he can see every one of my attacks coming before it lands.

*Who the fuck is this guy?*

"That's not gonna work," he says.

"How the fuck did you find me here?" I growl back, and I kick him in the nuts.

He groans in pain but swiftly recuperates and knocks me to the ground with a swift body grab and slam. The air is knocked out of my lungs.

"I already saw you the second you tried to make a beeline for this tree," he says. "Lana."

My eyes widen.

*How does he know my name?*

I slam my arm into his neck, making him choke, and I spin him around until I'm right on top of him.

"You have some moves," he muses. "I'm impressed."

"I'll give you something to be impressed about," I growl back, and I punch him in the gut so hard he groans out loud. But the groan is immediately followed by a smile. "Fuck. That almost hit the spot."

My brows furrow, confused as to why he'd say that, but then he suddenly wraps his legs around my body and flips me over with ease as though he's done this plenty of times before. And now I've lost the upper hand.

"My friends will be here any second now," he says. "And I can't wait to show them the kitty I caught."

"Over my dead body." I lean in and bite his arm until it bleeds.

He yelps and retracts his arm far enough for me to slip out underneath him. My hands curl around the mask around his face, and I rip it up as I crawl to my feet.

I kick him and stomp on his chest with my sharp heels, staring down at the face of one of the three men who have haunted my life ever since I came in contact with them.

I know this dude.

He's one of the Phantom Society guys.

The scrawny one with the lanky frame, the long hands, an upside-down cross dangling from his ear, short curtain red hair, obviously dyed. And that wretched grin is still on his face.

Yeah, it's definitely one of them.

*Didn't Brooke say his name was ... Milo?*

I grasp his collar and make him look at me. "Did you follow me?"

His hands lock around my ankle. "No. Did you?"

I flick my knife out of my pocket and hold it over his throat.

My nostrils flare. "If you know what's good for you, you'll leave my name out of your fucking mouth, and you won't show your face to me again. Got it?"

He practically melts underneath my hand. "Oh ..."

I don't know what's wrong with this dude, so I quickly release him from my grip, pouncing onto his chest once more for good measure. But it only makes him groan with a slight hint of arousal.

*What the fu—*

The door opens up again, and my head rises to meet the gaze of the other two hidden behind the same familiar white masks.

*Shit.*

I push him aside and bolt off through the yard, running back to my motorcycle, and hop on without putting on my helmet. It rolls off the passenger's seat and falls to the street as I race off, the two remaining guys chasing me down the road.

Too late.

\*\*\*

## MILO

"Goddammit, that was her, wasn't it?" Nathan yells as he and Kai come back into the yard.

"Yup," I say as I lean up.

"Fuck, she got away again," Nathan growls, and he kicks the tree. "Fuck, fuck, fuck!" He turns toward me, grabs me by the collar, and lifts me off the ground. "Tell me you saw her. Who is she?"

Kai stares me down, the look on his face murderous.

I don't like choosing between the two of them.

"I don't know," I reply. "But she knows who I am now." I can still feel her feet prodding me in the chest, and fuck me, the mere memory already makes me want to touch myself where she pounced on me. "But she clearly knew how to throw some punches."

Nathan furrows his brows, clearly confused.

But I'm not.

That woman was violent and deranged.

Blood still drips from the bite mark in my arm onto the pavement, and all I can think of is ...

*Wow. What a woman.*

Now I definitely understand what Kai sees in her.

Kai snorts. "You're trained in jujitsu, and you let a random girl beat your ass?"

"You're the one to talk," I spit back.

"You'd let that girl walk all over you," he retorts.

A smirk forms on my face. "I'd fucking beg her to."

"Jesus." Nathan grunts in frustration and releases me. "She is *not* your accomplice. She's a liability we can't afford."

"What is she going to do? Tell on us?" I say as I get up from the ground and pat down my shirt. "Expose herself in the process?"

Nathan throws the bag at me. "Fuck, never mind. We're done here anyway." He turns around and walks off.

"If she saw Milo, she'll know within no time we're part of the Phantom Society," Kai says.

Nathan stops in his tracks.

"She'll probably come after us."

Nathan glances at us over his shoulder. "Then we'll give her a warm welcome."

# 12

## LANA

I throw off my kitty mask and gear and chuck everything into my closet before putting on a white silk nightgown. Then I sit down at my desk to silently rage in the darkness. Goddammit, why were they there? They must be using the same site I am. There's no question about that. But it almost feels like this is too much of a coincidence to be real.

I get up and pace around the room without even bothering to turn on the lights while I try to make sense of things.

*Milo... was he the guy who danced with me at that Phantom Society party?*

I close my eyes and picture what the guy looked like, how his hands felt on my body, that voice ... no, Milo didn't sound or feel anything like him.

This means he must've been one of the other two who returned to the house to get their stuff. Two out of three from the Phantom Society, that's definitely not a fluke. They're doing this together as a fraternity.

My hand slowly moves to my mouth.

Like a gang of serial killers.

*CREAK!*

I immediately spin on my heels from the noise.

Someone stands in the middle of my room, right next to my bed.

Someone wearing a white mask, just like those three were.

My eyes narrow.

It's not the lanky dude, that's for sure. This guy is much broader, taller, very much like Jason.

My brows draw together. "Jason? Why would you come in through the window?"

There's an arrogant smirk on his face as he murmurs, "Element of surprise."

I snort.

*He's never wanted to make it exciting. Why start now?*

"Are you still wearing that mask?"

"Close your eyes."

Wow. There's that deep voice again, the commanding one I remember from when he ate me out, and fuck me, just the memory of that makes my pussy thump instantly.

*Is that voice going to be a new thing of his?*

"Is this some kind of new game you made up?" I ask. "You really enjoy that mask, don't you?"

He steps closer until he's right in front of me, and I can feel his breath on my skin. He whispers the word so closely to my lips that they begin to tingle. "Yes."

Suddenly, his hand latches around my throat, and he pushes me back until I hit the door with a thud.

I don't have a second to process before his lips land on mine.

And fuck me, the way he kisses me is all-consuming, mouthwatering madness. Like he wants to not only claim my mouth but own it too, licking the seam of my lips until his greed forces them apart.

And I'm overtaken by desire as he shoves his knee between my thighs, kissing me like I've never been kissed.

*Good God, who is this man, and where did he leave Jason behind?*

*Can he stay forever?*

When his lips momentarily unlatch from mine, I suck in a much-needed breath. "Fuck, I didn't know you could kiss like that, J—"

He puts a finger on my lips, preventing me from saying any more. "I kiss the girl I want any fucking way I want."

His other hand still has a firm hold on my throat as he rubs his knee against my most sensitive parts. And fuck me, I could come just from the pressure he applies to my neck alone.

He's never been this direct, this ... domineering.

"What are you doing?" I mutter.

"You wanted aggressive?" he groans. "You got it."

*Fuck. So he did listen. Oh God, there's nothing sexier than this.*

He pins me to the door and rubs his knee against me until my panties begin to soak through, and I find it hard to keep the moans from slipping out. He smiles wickedly against my skin.

"Are you my dirty little slut?" he whispers in a gravelly voice.

His free hand slides all the way down my silk nightgown until he reaches my breasts, and he circles my peaked nipples without touching the tip, edging me to insanity. I just want to lean in and make him touch me.

"Fuck," I whisper.

I've never been treated in such a debasing way before. It's turning me on like nothing he's ever done before.

"Come on this knee then," he whispers. "You don't deserve my fingers. Earn them."

Fuck, this is so hot.

My hand instinctively reaches down his abs, which are much firmer today. Maybe he's been training? I ignore it because I'm too excited as I make my way down to the bulge in his pants. God, it's much bigger than I remember, but I'm not complaining.

I rub him right through the fabric of his pants, his hard-on growing against my fingers, but the second I try to pull his shaft from his pants, he grips my wrist and pins it back against the door.

"I didn't give you permission to touch me," he whispers, pressing a sultry kiss right below my ear. "You will quiver for me first before your pussy enjoys this cock."

His knee swivels around until my body instinctively begins to gyrate against him.

"That's it, rub yourself against me like a filthy fucking slut would."

Jason's never called me a slut before.

I love it.

A smirk forms on my face as I roll my hips against his knee, but his fingers tighten around my neck like a noose slowly suffocating the life out of me.

"You will come for me and lose your fucking breath while you do," he whispers.

The dirtiness in his words practically sends me over the edge.

God, I can't fucking breathe.

"Not. Yet."

Even his breathy whispers are so controlling, so direct, that my eyes practically roll into the back of my head. I'm normally never like this, but he's pulled something out of me that I want to embrace so badly, I just let it happen.

*Where did he learn all of this? And in such a short amount of time too.*

He pushes my veins so deep my heart rate slows down, and my legs crumple underneath me. I can feel myself slipping away.

His lips linger near my ear, right before I grow too weak to stand. "Now."

\*\*\*

## MILO

I watch the video and play it back over and over again. Lana, pushed up against the door, Kai wrapping his hand around her throat, her legs quaking as he shoves his knee into her pussy and whispers words into her ear.

Fuck, I don't think I've ever seen anything sexier than this.

My hand instinctively reaches down into my pants, and I jerk myself off to them kissing. The way she moves, gyrating against his knee while he tells her she's a slut ... fuck.

I wish Nathan would call me that.

I pinch my nipples and moan a little as the pre-cum begins to flow, and I rub it all over my hard-on, ready to blow my load all over my pants.

Fuck me, if I could, I would go over to that fucking psycho bitch right now and lick that pussy myself. But something tells me she'd stab my eyes out if I tried.

I smirk to myself. I'll make do with the video Kai secretly taped for now.

I'm sure this won't be the last time they play together.

And if she was the one who watched me and Nathan have fun, then there's no reason I shouldn't get to watch her too.

*\*\*\**

## LANA

His knee pushes up against my slit, and a rush of oxytocin enters my body as I find my release. His fingers unlatch from my throat, and as I suck in the biggest breath I've ever taken, an intense moan escapes my lips.

"And what do good little fucking sluts do when they've been given an orgasm?" he whispers, his hand snaking down my breasts, feeling me up.

"Fall apart?" I murmur.

He pinches my nipple until a squeal is pushed out of my mouth.

"They say please and thank you."

God, I don't know whether to slap him for his arrogance or go to my knees and pull out his hard-on. That's how horny he's made me.

I snort. "You're such a bastard."

"Hmm ... and you're such a depraved ... kitty."

My eyes widen.

*Kitty.*

I gasp for air, but there is none.

That's what that Phantom guy called me.

*Is it him?*

I jump away and make a beeline for the light switch, smacking it on. But as I turn around, he's nowhere to be seen.

"Where are you?!" I scream and march to my closet to grasp the knife out of my bag.

There's no response, so I run to the window and look outside, but he's not there either.

*Where the fuck could he be?*

I open the door, but no one's in the hallway.

The door to the common bathroom is open, though ... and the light is on.

I storm inside with a knife firmly lodged in my hand, ready to strike.

There he is, half-naked, wearing nothing but a pair of shorts while he stares at himself through the mirror, and I approach him with the knife.

"You thought you could get away with that?" I growl.

I jump on him and rip the mask off his face.

"What the—"

The knife clatters to the floor.

It's not him.

It's Jason.

And he looks at me like I've gone insane.

"What are you doing?" Jason asks, incensed. "I was just getting my shit together, and now you've ruined it."

I stare at him for a moment with confusion lacing my face, but my whole body begins to shake.

"Lana? Talk to me," he says. "Are you okay?" He clutches my arms.

"Yeah, yeah ... I think so," I mutter.

But all I can think of is that word he just spoke.

*Kitty.*

Could it be that he heard it somewhere? Or from someone?

A cold shiver runs up and down my spine, but at the same time, my pussy thumps at the memory of his knee, eliciting an orgasm out of me.

Jason frowns at me. "You don't look fine."

"I ... can we just hug for tonight?"

He takes off his mask and puts it on the sink. "Without ...?"

"Yeah, just ... cuddling."

He makes a face, clearly disappointed. "Aw. Well, if you really want to."

"Never mind," I say, and I leave the bathroom. "I'll go sleep in Irina's room."

"Wait!" he calls after me, but I ignore him.

# I3

NATHAN

**The next day**

After a long day of school, I head upstairs and open my safe to check the money we still have left. Twenty thousand. And only one day left.

I sigh out loud and shut the door of the safe, pounding it with my fist.

*God-fucking-dammit. How am I gonna keep this up? There's gotta be a better solution.*

Suddenly, I hear some giggling from farther down the hallway, and the sound makes all the hairs on the back of my neck stand up. That definitely sounded like Milo ... but he's not laughing because of me, which means he's found a new obsession.

Grinding my teeth, I stalk through the hallways, approaching his room with rage flooding my bones. But I come to a grinding halt in the doorway.

He's watching some video on his laptop of a girl being knee-fucked by someone in her room. Someone wearing a Phantom mask.

And he's jerking off to it.

My nails dig into the wood. "What are you doing?"

His hand stops moving, and his head slowly tilts, eyes looking like he sees a ghost.

"Uh ..."

My eyes narrow. "Are you looking at a woman?"

"Well ..." He shrugs. "You know I swing both ways."

Approaching him, I place my hand on his shoulder and clasp his cheeks with one hand to turn his head and make him face the screen.

"Who. Is. That?"

"I don't know. Kai's crush," he says, swallowing.

My eyes twitch. "Since when does Kai have a crush?"

He's still holding his dick. "Does it matter?"

"How did you get this video?"

"Kai put a camera in her room when she was sleeping," he answers. "I just stole access to the feed. It was easy enough because he put her name as the password." He sniggers like it's funny, but nothing about this is funny to me.

"That ..." I look closer. "That's Felix's sister."

The sight of her makes me want to ram my fist into his screen. But that wouldn't help us now.

Milo smirks. "I guess. Is that bad?"

This is a recording from a couple of days ago. Both of them are somewhere else now, doing God knows what.

"Is he with her now?"

"I don't know. He could be."

"Hmm ..."

The thought of one of our own fornicating with the sister of the enemy is making me want to gouge some eyes out. But maybe ... just maybe ... we can use this to our advantage.

"He's really going for it," I murmur, looking at the video.

The way he's touching her is quite sexy, actually. Violent, even for him. Almost like he hates her as much as he wants her. No wonder Milo can't help himself.

"Wanna watch with me?" he says, licking his lips, and he brings his hand back down to his hard dick, pre-cum glistening at the tip.

I slap his hand away and grip his dick myself.

"You watch ... And after you're done, you're gonna tell me everything you've seen, every inch of detail, anything and everything we might be able to use against her."

He moans when I slide my hand up and down his length, rubbing the pre-cum all over until he's wet and hard.

"It's no fun if Kai's the only one having fun ... so why not fucking join him?"

"Fuck, I love this," Milo groans as I keep going, but he's about to drift, and I won't let him.

I grip his chin and force him to look. "Look at them. Look at them fuck around. Do you want a taste of her too?"

He nods, his dick bobbing up and down. He thrusts into my hand, whimpering like he always does, and I love the sound.

"Are you willing to do anything for it?" I whisper into his ear.

"Yes, fuck yes," he moans, already on the edge.

"Then you'll help me, whatever it costs," I say.

"What's going on in that violent mind of yours?" he murmurs, breathing heavy breaths as I increase the pace.

"Sex, money, and death," I whisper, and as he begins to throb, I point his tip at his face.

"Fuck, I'm coming," he mewls, and he releases all over his own face.

I pinch his cheeks together and make him look at her. "Make him do more with her, tape it all ..."

"And then?" he says with ragged breaths, still delirious from his orgasm.

But all I can do is smile like the deviant I am. "We extort her."

I turn his chair around and rip down my zipper. Pulling out my hard-on, I shove it into his wide-open mouth. "Now suck like your life depends on it."

\*\*\*

# LANA

I walk around school, eyeing everyone I see to make sure they won't try to jump me from behind. I don't trust anyone. Not anywhere, and definitely not on this campus. All of these students could be Phantoms.

Maybe they're not a part of the fraternity, but they could definitely be working for them.

I feel antsy and on edge.

I haven't slept properly in days, and I can't get the feeling out of my mind that someone is messing with me.

Right in front of the biggest building are Brooke and Irina, chatting away with Crystal, another girl I recognize from Felix's group. I don't know her well, but she often hangs out with Felix's girlfriend, Penelope. Well, he shares her with his friends Dylan and Alistair, so technically, she's the girlfriend of all three.

Complicated, that's for sure.

I walk in their direction, hoping they can take my mind off things, but before I can make it there, someone beats me to it.

And the sight of him runs my blood cold.

Milo.

I'd recognize that long figure and his red-dyed hair anywhere.

My feet freeze to the ground when he begins to talk with them.

What the ...?

He *smiles*.

He's actually fucking smiling at them.

This has to be either a joke or a trap.

My hands ball into fists. I march over, determined to make him eat my boot, but the moment our eyes connect, lightning practically crackles between us.

"Hey, Lana!" Irina says.

"Oh hey, Lana, didn't see you there," Brooke says.

But I grab them by the arms and drag them away from Milo. "Don't talk to him."

"What? Why?" Irina asks.

"Yeah, Lana, why can't they talk to me?"

His voice grates on me already, and he's right behind me too.

"I'm nice."

*Sure you are, Mr. "Nice guy" Killer.*

"He's a Phantom; they can't be trusted," I hiss. "You said it yourself."

"But he's only talking with us," Brooke responds.

"Hey, what's going on?" Crystal asks, approaching us.

"Just ... don't interact with any of them," I tell my friends. "They're ... not good people."

"You seem to know an awful lot about someone you don't know," Milo butts in.

I turn around to face him and shove my finger into his chest. "Stay away from them."

"Or what?" He tilts his head, and that same wicked smile appears on his face again, his eyes glinting with excitement. "You gonna puncture me with that heel?"

"Don't tempt me," I growl.

He leans in. "You're turning me on."

One more word out of that mouth, and I swear to God I will personally castrate him.

"Go on ... do it," he eggs me on.

"What did you say to them?" I hiss.

"Afraid?" he muses.

*Fuck. Is he going to tell them about what I did that night?*

*Or did he already fill them in, and are they all pretending they don't know?*

"Guys, guys," Crystal says, pushing us apart. "Don't fight. Can't we all just be friends?"

"No," I bark back.

"What's going on here?"

A voice behind me makes chills run up and down my spine.

*I know that voice.*

"Oh hey, Nathan," Crystal says, and she immediately runs to give him a big hug. "We haven't talked in such a long time. How are you feeling? Is your leg better yet?"

"Much better," he replies, and he crushes the can of Coke in his hands and shows off with a trick to punt it into the bin. "Almost back to normal."

"Except for the finger," Brooke mutters, but the glare he throws her makes her voice squeak. "Sorry."

Nathan tucks his hand into his pocket. "You done here?" he asks Milo.

"Yeah ... I'm finished." Milo winks at me.

He actually fucking winks. That bastard.

But as they walk off, he throws me another glance over his shoulder.

The words that follow tilt me off my axis completely.

"If I were you, I'd get myself another knee to the pussy."

*\*\**

I stare at my lunch, but whenever I think of swallowing a bite, I feel sick to my stomach.

*Another knee to the pussy ...*

*How did Milo know?*

"Are you gonna eat that?" Jason asks, glaring at my sandwich like he wants to devour it.

I blink a couple of times, trying to process what he just said. Then I shake my head. "Take it. I'm not hungry."

"Don't mind if I do," he says, and he's already stuffed all of it into his mouth like it's all disappearing into a black hole.

I gaze at him and his knees, and I can't help but wonder if he really did all of those amazing things while wearing that mask... or if it was someone else.

Someone like Milo.

As Jason swallows it down, he turns his head and grins. "What are you looking at?"

I shrug. "Uhhh ..."

I'm not sure I want to tell him.

But I *have* to know.

"Can you do something for me?" I ask.

"Depends on what," he replies, snorting.

"Kiss me like you did the other night."

His brows furrow even more, his mouth still open, but then he shrugs and says, "You don't have to ask me twice."

He leans in without grabbing me and presses a soft kiss onto my lips.

*His lips ...*

My eyes widen as his mouth is still on mine, tingles spreading throughout my body.

The bad kind of tingles that make your skin feel icy cold.

This wasn't *the* kiss.

Not that night he licked me, nor the night he choked me.

It wasn't *him*.

I pull back, staring at him while fear and fire settle in my bones.

"What's wrong?" Jason asks.

I scoot back my chair and get up.

"Lana?" he calls as I walk off, but I can't say a word. I wouldn't know what to say even if I could.

I head straight for the first bathroom I come across and shove open a stall, locking myself inside.

My mind spins around in circles like the water in this toilet bowl, and I feel like the world is flushing me down with it.

Until I get a text message.

I fish my phone from my pocket and check.

**Unknown: Do you like it when he kisses you? Does he take your breath away like I would?**

My manicured nails dig into the phone so far I can hear the screen protector crack.

*It has to be him.*

*The dude who kissed and fucked with me that night ...*

*He's watching me.*

Bursting out of the stall, I rush out of the bathroom and storm around campus until I find Milo hanging outside near the fountain on his own, smoking a joint.

That motherfucker ...

Is dead.

\*\*\*

## MILO

I'm enjoying the sun after a long day of schoolwork when a bull comes charging at me. And by bull, I mean the angriest black-haired beauty I've ever laid eyes on. Magnificent.

As I take another drag, the joint is ripped from my hands.

"You sent this, didn't you?"

She holds up a phone, and I read the text.

*Oh … interesting. Very interesting.*

"Nope." I steal the joint back out of her hand.

"Liar," she says through gritted teeth and grabs my collar, dragging me toward her. "You're the one who's been climbing in my window to fuck with me, aren't you?"

I snort. "What?"

"Don't pretend you don't know," she hisses. "I know it wasn't Jason."

"It was most definitely not me either," I reply, amused she'd accuse me.

But good God, the way she grips my shirt is beyond exciting.

"Bullshit," she growls right up in my face. "You're the only one who knows…"

Oh … is she really going there in broad daylight? Now, it's gotten even more interesting. "Knows *what*?"

I dare her to finish that sentence.

Her nostrils flare in the cutest, most violent kind of way. "I swear to God, I will pummel you right into the fountain."

I smile. "We getting wet already? Oh, baby, I'm ready." I run my fingers through my hair.

"Stop," she hisses. "Just admit that it was you."

"Except it wasn't."

"This text. You sent it," she growls.

I take another drag, then chuck it in the fountain behind me. "Nope. Don't believe me? I can put my number in your phone, and you can check."

Her face changes with emotions every second, but she eventually releases me. Too bad, I liked how she kept me in a chokehold.

I hold out my hand until she finally gives me her phone, and I swiftly add my number to her contact list before she snatches it back again.

"Call the number," I say.

When she does, my phone rings in my pocket.

And now she doesn't just have my number ... I have hers too.

I smirk when she checks the text message for the number.

"See?" My shoulders rise. "Not me."

"Then who is it?" she barks. "I know it's one of your Phantom buddies."

"I don't know," I reply. "Could be anyone if you ask me."

She grinds her teeth. "Stop lying to me. Who is it? Nathan?"

"I have no clue if you ask me," I lie. "Though, judging from what they sent, they sound awfully ... jealous."

The rage in her eyes makes her look gorgeous.

She raises a fist and threatens me, but all I can do is smile. "Do it."

Her brow furrows and she swallows.

"Hit me," I say, licking my lips at the thought.

But instead, she releases me and shoves me away. "Fuck off. Don't ever get in my way again."

"Too bad, Lana ... I was having so much fun with you," I muse as she waltzes off.

But all she does is raise her middle finger.

And fuck me ... What I wouldn't give for her to stick it in my mouth so I can suck it.

# 14

## LANA

It's already evening, and I've barely done any schoolwork at all, let alone eaten dinner. I've been attempting to send something back all day, but a part of me wonders if I'm prepared to open Pandora's box. I stare at the text, reading the words over and over until I almost want to throw the phone out the window.

Fuck it.

*Me: Who is this? How did you get my number?*

I hit send before I can stop myself again.

Fuck. No going back now.

I lie back on my pillow and wait and wait, my heart going a million miles an hour.

My phone buzzes, and I anxiously check it, only to see Jason's face.

*Jason: Wanna hang out tonight?*

Sighing, I text back.

*Me: No, thanks. Got some things to take care of first.*

*Jason: Like what? Getting hungover?*

*Me: Ha. Ha. Not after last time.*

*Jason: What? We only cuddled.*

*Me: Right ...*

*Jason: What did I do wrong this time?*

*Me: Nothing...*

I roll my eyes. Of course, he thinks we only cuddled.

Suddenly, my phone buzzes again.

*Unknown: Someone with hands you want around your throat.*

Wow.

Why did that make my pussy thump?

*Fuck.*

I hastily type back.

*Me: So it is you. I fucking knew it.*

*Unknown: Who? Can you even say my name without getting drenched, kitty?*

I sit up straight, all the hairs on my arms and legs standing up.

*Kitty.*

It definitely is him. And now that he's called me that twice, it's no longer a coincidence, either.

*Me: Do you take pleasure in pretending to be someone's boyfriend?*

*Unknown: You don't have a boyfriend.*

*Me: How would you know?*

*Unknown: Because if you did, he'd no longer be alive.*

Goose bumps cover my whole body.

*Me: If you touch Jason, you're going to pay.*

*Unknown: Why do you even care? Does he care about you?*

I grind my teeth, angered he'd involve Jason in this.

*Unknown: Does he even know how to make you scream with his tongue alone?*

*Me: Stop. Which one of those Phantom fuckers are you? Tell me now, and we'll settle this today.*

*Unknown: I'll give you what you want ... if you dare to come and get it. You know where to find me.*

I stare at the texts for a few more seconds before I tuck my phone back into my pocket and get up from my bed, storming straight out the door. I don't fucking care that I still have one more class today. I'll catch up later. I need to deal with this ... problem first.

One of those Phantom guys has been stalking me, using me, playing with me, making me do things I never thought I would ... and I need to know who and why.

\*\*\*

## KAI

*BANG!*

I hear the ruckus beyond the door before it slams open. A guard's body is flung inside and slides across the door, and the clicking of a gun follows.

"Move, and I put a bullet through your brain."

Her voice ...

God, her fucking voice alone awakens my cock.

I get up from my seat in the game room and march out the door to lean over the banister and witness her destruction. A big vase flies through the hallway, crashing into the wall, the shards almost like a swath of glitter to announce her entry.

"Where are you? I know it's one of you Phantom fuckers," she yells. "Show yourself!"

My God, does she look appetizing in that dark red woolen turtle-neck dress and thigh-high black boots. Her black hair, tucked in by a cute white hairband, sways from left to right as she walks in like a goddess set on destruction.

I have been waiting for this moment for so long my dick is already hard just from the thought of getting my hands on her again.

"What the fuck do you want?" the guard on the floor yelps as she points her gun at him. "Get the fuck out of here!"

"Tell me where he is," she grits.

"Who?" He raises his hands when she approaches. "I don't know what you're talking about."

"I do."

I turn my head as Milo stands beside me.

I thought he was busy jerking off in his room. Guess not.

"You've been stoking the fire," he muses as another guard runs in from the side entrance, attacking her with a knife, but I'm not worried. I know she's capable and able to defend herself.

"What do you want?" I ask Milo, ignoring the obvious fight going on downstairs.

"You've been toying with her, and she doesn't know it's you," he says. "She came to me the other day and accused me of sending her texts."

I smirk right through the gunfire. "Did she now ..."

"You like this, don't you?" he asks, peering at her while she throws the knife the guard threw right back at him. "I have to say ... she has moves." He licks his lips, biting the bottom one, and I narrow my eyes. "I get why you didn't kill her and made her come hard instead."

I pull my gun and point it right at Milo's face. "You've been watching me?"

He merely smiles into the barrel. "You should be glad I didn't tell her you hung a camera in her room."

"You broke into my laptop," I say.

*CLICK.*

The safety is off now, along with my sanity.

"Did you tell Nathan?"

Milo tilts his head at me. "I haven't told him. He found out by himself."

My nostrils flare.

"Relax. He doesn't know she's the killer kitty," he muses, walking closer and closer until his cheek rests on the barrel. "That's our little secret."

I lower my gun. "I get how you're able to spin Nathan around your finger now."

He grins. "I just want what you want."

"And what's that?"

He turns to look over the wooden banister at Lana bashing the guard's head in with her heels. He's lost quite a lot of blood, but it seems he's still breathing and groaning.

"Her. But you knew that already."

"Two guys using one girl?" I scoff. I thought he was joking before, but I guess I was wrong.

"She can take it," he muses, gripping the banister like watching her fight gives him life.

Suddenly, her eyes jerk up to meet mine, and I know she's spotted us.

Her face is an eclectic combination of rage and passion, the kind I'd kill for.

*BANG!*

I lean away, and Milo and I look at the bullet that just penetrated the wall behind us.

*BANG! BANG! BANG!*

"Wow ..." he murmurs. "I love her already."

Her gun goes off but misses, and the bullet fires into the pillar beside us.

I lick my top lip. "You'll love her even more after you've had a taste."

She aims again, so we both sidestep and hide behind the pillar until she finishes shooting her rounds. When it's gone quiet, Milo pulls out his knife and jumps down the banister, sticking the knife into the thick curtains to the side to slide down, cutting through the fabric when he gets to the floor.

"Well, hello there, Lana ..." Milo muses.

I watch from above, curious about what he's going to do.

"Was it you after all?" she asks, pointing her gun at him like it will do anything. "Did you give me a fake phone number?"

He tilts his head. "Does it matter what I say?"

"You know my fucking name," she growls. "So no."

She pulls the trigger, but the bullets are all gone.

Guess she forgot to keep count.

Lucky for her, we didn't.

She throws the gun aside and approaches him. "Guess I'll have to do this the old-fashioned way."

\*\*\*

## LANA

I spin around and kick him in the face, but he narrowly avoids my kick. I'm lightning quick, with barely split seconds between Milo and me moving away from each other. But I just can't seem to fucking hit him, and fuck me, it's annoying the hell out of me.

"Stand. Still. Worm," I growl.

He suddenly grips my ankle, twisting me midair.

I drop to the floor with a thud, groaning from the air leaving my lungs.

"I love it when you call me names," he says, leaning over me. "Really gets me going."

*That fucker ... even now, he's turned on?*

I flip over and punch him in the face, and he takes it with a smile. "Fuck, you hit so good."

"What is wrong with you?"

I try to kick him, but he sits on top of me and plants both hands on my wrists. "What can I say?" His upside-down cross earring dangles, catching my attention. "I'm a sucker for pain."

I look down at his pants, which definitely have a bulge. Right on top of me.

*Fuck.*

*He's getting hard?*

"Admit you sent the text!" I growl at him.

"How would you know it was me? It could be anyone here," he replies, leaning in too close for comfort.

"You're the only one stalking my friends," I retort.

"The only one?" His brow rises. "You sound so sure, yet ..."

My eyes widen.

*Someone else from the Phantom Society has been chatting with Irina and Brooke?*

*Fuck. They've been working together. Of course they have.*

"Who is it, then?" I growl. "Tell me!"

I fight against his grip, but even with his lanky frame, he's too strong for me.

His length hides more power than I imagined. I guess I really misjudged his physique.

"Hmm ... I could tell you ... or you could figure it out by yourself," he muses.

He flips me over with ease.

He's on top of me now, my arms pinned to my back, and for the life of me, I can't fight him off.

"Is it that fucker up there?" I ask, lifting my head so I can look at the guy with the one green eye. The gnarly scar running from his eyebrow to the bottom of his cheek makes all the hairs on my neck stand up. He has those same eyes that I saw before at the party, one white underneath his scar, the other sparkling green as they bore a hole into my chest.

*Is that him?*

*Or is it one of the guards I just pummeled to the floor?*

Fuck, it could be anyone here. Felix warned me all of these Phantoms are evil.

"Pull her up," the guy at the top of the stairs says as he waltzes down the steps.

Milo rips off his tie and makes a knot with his teeth, then wraps it around my wrists, sealing them tightly.

"That won't stop me," I growl.

"No ..." He inches down, sliding across my body with his hard-on as he rips out his belt, and I turn my head to watch while he loops it through the holes slowly, eyes on mine like he enjoys it when I watch. For a second, I almost think he's going to pull down his zipper, but then he turns around and tightly wraps the belt around my ankles, preventing me from using them.

"But this will."

"Get off me," I growl.

"Of course, my queen," he muses as he gets up, only to hoist me up too, holding my arms so I can't go anywhere.

I struggle against him and spin around, but then I come face-to-face with the guy with the scar.

He stares me down, tongue dipping out to wet his lips while his eyes sweep over my body, lingering on my peaked nipples before his gaze settles back on my eyes again.

"Bring her to the chapter room."

*That voice...*

Milo drags me away before I can even react, and I can't fight him off, despite trying my best to get rid of these binds. "I'm gonna fucking kill you, you know that, right?"

He groans as he pulls me into a room underneath the stairs. "Oh, please, do try. I'm begging you."

My brows furrow. "What the ...?"

*Why does he sound like he's begging me to do it?*

"Try it. Go on." The new voice makes me turn my head. Milo stops in his tracks too and swishes me around so we both face him.

A lean guy wearing a pair of beige khakis and a black shirt with light blond hair casually styled to the side, radiant blue eyes, and thick lashes stands before me, his naturally pointy lips drawing attention as he rubs them together when he spots me.

He's the kind of beautiful that would make people turn after walking past him.

Even the guy with the scar turns his head when he spots him, his wavy hair casually falling over his face. "Nathan. I thought you were with—"

"That got cut short by an alert on my phone," Nathan replies, taking off his sunglasses as he stands in the door opening to the chapter room. "Someone broke into the building." He folds his arms and leans against the doorjamb as he eyes me up and down. "And that someone was wrecking everything in sight. A certain ... Rivera girl."

*So he knows who I am.*

"Darryl!" the guy with the scar calls through the building, and a guy rushes into the room.

"Someone got shot in the hallway, and there's another guy on the floor with a knife wound in his stomach," Darryl says.

A proud smile forms on my lips. I fucking did that, and I'm not fucking sorry.

The scarred guy narrows his eyes at Darryl. "Get Tom and Waylon. Bring the wounded to the school clinic. The nurse will know how to handle this. It's not like she hasn't seen worse."

"Yes, sir," he replies, and Darryl bolts right past Nathan again.

*Sir ... The scarred guy is in charge?*

Nathan walks toward me. "And now I wanna know why you're here."

"Like you don't fucking know exactly why," I say, spitting on the floor in front of his feet.

"Enlighten me," he muses.

"Because one of you fuckers came into my room and—" Milo smacks his hand in front of my mouth before I can finish.

"She claims one of us has been sending her dubious texts," the scarred guy behind me says.

He casually sits down on the couch behind me, legs spread open as he gawks at my ass which is barely covered by my dress. Fucker.

"One of us? Dubious?" Nathan snorts. "Interesting. And now you want to know who? Why does it matter?"

I bite Milo's hand until his skin bleeds.

He pulls away his hand. "Fuck."

"I warned you," I hiss, but he's already licking the blood off his hand when I look at him over my shoulder.

*Fuck.*

"One of you fucking came into my room and kissed me," I say, swallowing my pride.

Nathan's eyes narrow even further, and a twinge of hate settles on his face.

He turns and glares at the guy behind me and then Milo. Without words, the looks they exchange speak volumes.

*One of them did this.*

*But do the other two even know?*

Nathan's head slowly turns to me again, the intrigued look on his face anything but soothing. "Interesting ... Do you even know what you've gotten yourself into?"

"I don't fucking care. One of you did it, and I want to know why," I bark.

There's a long pause as he looks me up and down, his eyes slowly swooping over my body like he's taking it all in and then some.

"All right then, I'll play along." Nathan flicks his fingers.

Milo moves away from me and sits on the table to the side, legs crossed.

Nathan approaches me, circling me like a hawk, but when he steps close enough, I'll bite his fucking head off.

"So how do you want to go about proving it was one of us?"

My nostrils flare as I look around at each one of them, my hands twitching against the tie cutting into my flesh. I have to get out of here. After I've figured out who to kill, of course.

I'm acutely aware of the knife in my boot, but how do I reach it when I can't even bend over without falling?

*Fuck. Think, Lana, think.*

"Ticktock, Lana," Nathan says, tapping his watch in front of me before sitting in a thick leather chair next to the dude with the scar. "You want to punish us? Tell us who kissed you, then, and maybe we'll let you." He leans forward with his elbow on his knee. "But if you guess wrong ... you'll be the one punished."

A terrifyingly wicked smile forms on his lips.

Fuck.

I glance at the scarred guy and then Milo, who seem to be exchanging looks.

*Are these actually the three guys who have been getting in the way of my kills?*

I swallow away the lump in my throat. If I ask now, they might kill me on the spot. Maybe they don't know that I know. Yet.

Are they all in on this scheme?

None of them will tell me the truth, even if I force them.

There's only one way I'll find out who entered my room and toyed with me.

"Fine, then. Kiss me, and I'll tell you."

# 15

NATHAN

Lana fucking Rivera, sister of that fucked-up asshole Felix, is in the fucking building. A beauty who prances around these school grounds with her seductive looks, red lipstick killer smile, sharp catlike eyeliner, and black hair swaying back and forth like she owns the fucking campus.

And the first thing she demands while under our roof is that we kiss her?

*This has to be an elaborate prank ... or a suicide mission.*

"Kiss *you*?" I repeat.

I turn to look at Kai and Milo, but neither seems even mildly amused. Or surprised. Neither does she.

*Interesting indeed.*

"I'll recognize the lips," she says.

Milo snorts. "This couldn't get any juicier."

"Shut up," I bark at him.

*What is she trying to do here?*

"Are you afraid?" she muses, tilting her head.

My eyes narrow, and my muscles tense. She definitely hit the spot when she said those words.

Fuck me.

Afraid? Me?

It'll take more than a violent little bitch to shake fear into my soul.

"Fine," I say, leaning back. "Milo." I beckon him. "You first."

She frowns as Milo jumps off the table and struts toward her with a confident smile and a giant hard-on in his pants. And fuck me, it makes me want to slap him, but that would probably only make him harder.

"Don't have to tell me twice," he says, grabbing her face and smashing his lips on hers.

He's rough with her, hasty too, like he wants to pull everything out of this one kiss. It's definitely wild as fuck, and his tongue dips out to lick the seam of her mouth.

When he leans back, he whispers, "Fuck, no wonder ..."

*No wonder ... what?*

"Your lips are amazing." Milo blinks a couple of times. "I could definitely do this again. Milo Fletcher, at your service."

"In your dreams," she hisses, fighting against the tie tightly wrapped around her wrists like she intends to pummel him into the next room.

Kai and I laugh our asses off. "Hear that? That's the sound of a heart being stomped on."

"You've got a big mouth for someone who didn't even want to try," Milo rebukes, glaring at me. "Go on, then."

Fuck, I hate it when he challenges me because I don't fucking back away from one. Ever.

But before Milo steps away, he grabs a strand of her hair and coils it around his finger. "Even if I'm not the guy ... I'm definitely available for more, queen."

She jerks away from him and turns her head sideways. "Next."

"Cold," Kai says.

Her eyes settle on his as he swipes his index finger across his top lip. And I don't like it one bit.

I know what he's done with her in secret. Things he doesn't know I've seen with my own goddamn eyes. And I don't think it's fair of him to keep this little plaything all to himself.

I curl my finger up and make her look. "Come."

Her nostrils twitch, but she still moves closer in her petite dress that barely covers her ass. Daring, I have to admit. Especially considering she knew she was going to come and step foot in our Phantom Society ... where everyone's deepest, darkest fears become reality.

And I'm about to turn hers into a wicked nightmare come to life.

\*\*\*

## LANA

It's hard to walk when your ankles and hands are tied, but I do what I have to in order to see this through to the end. Nathan keeps curling his finger until I'm right in front of him, and only then does he stop. He leans back in his chair and runs his fingers through his chilly blond hair, his blue eyes twitching with arrogance. He's obviously handsome without effort, and he knows it.

Fuck him and the high horse he rode in on.

"So ... you want a kiss," he muses. "What are you going to do to get one?"

"You've got some nerve thinking you can demand things from me," I retort.

His brow rises, and his gaze slides over my body dangerously slow. "Yet I'm not the one tied up, helpless and completely at our mercy."

His eyes flick back up to mine with that same tenacity as before, but with an added twinge of sexual energy that catches me off guard.

I look away and check out the exits, one behind me and one to the right behind the couch. Too far to run before they'll catch me. And I'm pretty sure there's a guard behind every door, or a freshman ready to jump me in case I try to make a grand escape.

Not that I had anything in mind. I came here for a reason, and I intend to stick around until I have what I came here for. No matter the cost.

"Don't even try, Lana," he says, eyes darkening. "Not after what you just did to our house. Our men."

"To me," Milo adds.

"Wasn't thinking about it," I retort. "Not until I have what I came for."

"Just give her what she wants," the guy in the back mumbles, annoyed.

Nathan smirks. "A kiss from all of us ..." He leans forward in his chair and tucks a middle finger underneath my dress, brushing my thighs as he pulls me closer until I almost fall into him. "Do you know how many girls would beg for that chance?"

"I doubt it," I spit back, glancing at his index finger, which is merely a stump. "Is that your good hand or your bad one? Poor girls."

"Oh boy," Milo mutters. "Now she's gone and done it."

Nathan's face tightens, and his jaw tenses.

"Fingers are a poor man's choice," he says through gritted teeth as his fingers inch farther up my thighs, setting my senses ablaze. "There are infinite toys to rise beyond what even flesh can't offer. Everything you could ever dream of, I have at my disposal. The way I please would have you screaming and begging for God to make the rolling orgasms stop."

He pauses. "Kneel."

"What?" I frown.

"You heard me." He leans in and comes eye to eye with me, darkness spreading in his grim smile. "Kneel." His gravelly and low voice brings goose bumps to my skin.

"Nathan ... really?" the guy on the couch says, shifting in his seat. "Do we have to do this?"

"Yes, really. Now."

Suddenly, he grips my shoulders, and my knees are forced to cave beneath the weight of his hands.

His middle finger pushes my chin up to meet his gaze. "Now ... you want to know if I kissed you?"

"Yes," I reply.

He leans in with a seductive look on his face. "You'll get your kiss ..." he murmurs. My eyes close, lips puckered, waiting until I finally know if it was him. "After you've begged."

"What?" I lean back, incensed.

But he's already stood up and marched to a boudoir in the back of the room.

Nathan returns carrying what looks like a saddle, along with a kind of rose-shaped item.

*What the ...*

"What is that?" I ask.

He pushes the rose into the saddle and goes to his knees before me, his hand sliding underneath my dress. "A rich man's choice of ecstasy."

*RIP!*

I gasp as he rips my panties away and pushes me down onto the device. He leans in to whisper, "You won't need those anyway. Unless you prefer them completely soaked through."

The smirk when he sees my reaction makes me want to punch him. But these ties still keep me from trying, and he knows.

Fuck.

He pulls a remote control from his pocket, and my eyes follow as his middle finger hovers over a certain button.

The guy on the couch whose name I still don't know sighs out loud.

Nathan turns his head. "You've got a problem *now*?"

They exchange daring looks, but then the guy simply waves his hand. "Fine, go ahead."

"Good choice," Nathan says. "You're gonna love this."

And then the saddle suddenly begins to buzz underneath me.

Good God, it's not just buzzing. The rose inside the hole ... it's sucking at my clit.

My jaw drops as my whole body vibrates with the devices going crazy on me. Nathan tilts his head, looking at me with acute interest as I'm trying my best not to be affected, but fuck me, is it hard.

I slam my lips shut, determined to keep all the sounds inside. Not a single moan will slip out of me. No fucking way am I going to give them that satisfaction.

Nathan stands, towering over me with that devilish grin, and runs his fingers through his blond hair before he brings his hand to his zipper and pulls it down.

My eyes widen as he pulls out a half-hard seven inches—but so goddamn girthy—cock.

"What? That wasn't part of our—"

"You're not in the position to make bargains, slut," he growls back. "You came into our lair demanding our lips ... but you'll get some cum on your face first."

"What?" I gasp.

He pushes the button, kicking the vibration underneath me up a notch. I can't even say a goddamn word without a mewl spilling out. But all my eyes can do is home in on the guy in the back, clutching the couch with both hands, fingers digging into the fabric as Nathan steps closer and begins to rub himself right in front of me.

And fuck me, my eyes are almost drawn to the size of it, along with all the piercings hooked in his shaft. At least three, maybe more. I recognize the prince albert, but I've never seen the rest.

*But this jewelry ... could he be the guy who came into my room? Who danced with me at that party and made me lick him?*

"You came in here thinking you could one-up us without repercussions, Lana?" he muses, stroking his long length. "You should've known we would destroy you."

If this is him, he's just as arrogant as I remember.

"Fuck you," I spit back.

But it only makes him turn the suction device harder.

My clit is throbbing so badly I can't stop the wetness from dripping out of me.

"I'll make you wish you got my cock up your pussy instead," he says, jerking himself off right in front of me as the suction increases its intensity. "You'll come so hard you'll see stars, Lana Rivera."

"Fuck, this is so goddamn hot," Milo says, rubbing himself through the fabric of his pants.

"Don't say my name, you don't deserve it," I say between ragged breaths.

The vibrations are becoming too much.

"Your name belongs to us now," Nathan replies, smirking as he steps closer and tilts my head up, shoving his dick in my face. "Just like this beautiful face after I cover it with cum."

When he attempts to shove it into my mouth, I bite and miss, my teeth clattering with arousal.

"Bad slut," he says, and he spits down right into my face, rubbing it in with his length. "Do you even deserve a kiss after trying to bite my cock?"

Milo snorts. "I can help open her mouth for you."

"No ..." Nathan says, glancing at me as he tilts his head. His thumb reaches for my top lip and slowly drags down the spit along my chin. "She'll open that mouth of hers eventually. Willingly. Greedily."

*CLICK!*

He pushes the button again while studying me intensely, and the sucking on my clit is so intense that I can't stop it any longer. A whale of a moan leaves my tongue as the forced orgasm is pulled out of me. Just like that.

The waves cause my whole body to shiver, all my senses coming alive like a bud of a flower blooming. And the worst part is that the buzzing between my legs never stops driving me insane.

"Beautiful ..." he murmurs, watching my face. "Again."

"What?" I gasp, still trying to recover.

He steps back but doesn't stop the vibrations between my thighs, and I get so annoyed I try to hop forward, to no avail.

"You won't get out from this one," Milo muses, snorting as he comes closer, sporting an obvious hard-on. "And this isn't even the worst the Phantom Society has got in our possession." He glances at Nathan. "Mind if I join in?"

"By all means," Nathan muses, still looking at me like I'm his personal plaything. "Let's make her pay for hurting two of our fellow phantoms... And maybe afterward, we'll give her what she asked for."

"You're sick," I growl.

"Hmm ... you've only seen an inch of what I'm capable of," Nathan says as he coats his dick with my saliva, right out of reach. "But you'll get a taste soon, don't you worry."

Milo joins in, standing beside him as he zips down and pulls out his cock. It's much curvier than Nathan's without a piercing in sight. Instead, it's marked with tattoos that make my jaw drop. It's not just a random pattern, but a swirl of black ink along with the Phantom logo.

Wow. Talk about dedication.

"Like my tattoos?" he says, licking his bottom lip. "I'll let you lick them if you want."

"You wish," I retort, but it's so hard to focus with these vibrations between my leg, spurring me to gyrate on top of the device.

"Oh yes ..." Milo groans, rubbing himself until pre-cum drips out of his tip. "I'd very much beg for the opportunity."

Fuck me, I could just about come again from the suction device alone. But those dirty words of his don't help to keep the orgasms at bay either.

"I told you, I won't stop until you beg," Nathan says.

"Never," I groan, forcing out the ragged breaths.

He steps forward and pushes the button right in front of my face. "Then you'll come again and again until your pussy is red and swollen, and your cries fill these halls. And then you'll come some fucking more just because I like to see you fall apart as my personal whore."

Fuck. It's vibrating so hard I can't stop another orgasm from rolling over my body, consuming me whole. I let out a long-drawn-out moan, and he grins right in my fucking face.

*Motherfucking asshole.*

"That's the face, Lana," he whispers. "Again."

I try my hardest to inch my fingers into my sleeve and fish out the tiny knife I keep hidden there. It's my last shot, my only chance at freeing myself.

But the suction device keeps going until even I can't stop another orgasm from forcing its way through, making my whole body erupt into goose bumps.

"I can't," I mutter. "I can't do it again."

"You can, and you will," Nathan groans.

The vibrations are so strong I can't fight them off, no matter how hard I try, and when the fourth orgasm comes, I feel like every inch of my soul is drawn out of my body. It rolls over me like a tsunami, flushing my body with endorphins and pain; pain because the muscle contractions won't stop as long as the device keeps going.

Fuck ... I can't take it anymore.

My eyes home in on the guy in the back, his nails digging into the couch so harshly I almost wonder if he's going to rip the fabric off. But he stays put, watching me with clenched jaws, his green eye a sparkling beauty among the madness.

So I mutter the only word I can think of while the onslaught of lust and orgasms swirls through my body, "Please ..."

\*\*\*

# KAI

*Please ...*

She looked at me.

Not him.

Me.

Begging. Begging for *me*.

I stand, forced into action by her words.

"That's what I want to hear," Nathan grunts.

Right then, ropes of cum spurt out, and he covers her in filth. And for a second there, I almost want to rip his face off for even putting a speck of dirt on her pretty face and body.

But then I remember he doesn't know the truth.

He doesn't know who she is or what she's done.

If I step in now, he'll definitely find out she's the girl we've been looking for. And he wouldn't ever let her go if he knew.

I swallow down the rage, my hands forming fists at the sight of him covering her with more cum, the groans that follow from his mouth setting my rage ablaze.

I didn't think he'd go this far to make her pay, but I guess I was wrong.

Too fucking late.

Milo moans loudly and squirts his loads all over her too, and it's fucking everywhere—her clothes, her hair, even her legs. Only her lips and eyes were spared.

Nathan releases his hard-on, which dangles between his legs, and he grips her face and kisses her full on the lips, claiming that mouth that once only belonged to me.

And fuck me, it sets something off deep inside me.

I'm halfway across the room on my way to them when his lips unlatch from hers. Her face is riddled with confusion, eyes wide open, lips still parted like she was waiting for more. Like she actually enjoyed that kiss.

"Now you have what you came here for, slut," he whispers, smiling in her face.

And she stammers, "No ..."

Her eyes slowly turn until they finally find me.

And the invisible thread that connected our fate unravels before us.

Suddenly, a flash of light fills the room, coming from Nathan's phone, with which he took a picture of her face covered in his cum.

Fuck. She's not gonna like that.

I march over and push Nathan aside until he almost falls back into the chair. "Hey, what the f—"

But I ignore his protest and rip the buzzing devices that drive her insane out from underneath her, chucking them aside. Then I grasp her face and smash my lips onto hers.

A soft moan escapes her lips as I coyly play with her, forcing her to remember my taste. Her lips are heavenly, just as I remember, sweet, plump, filled with hidden desires she's kept buried all this time ... until my tongue swiping across the roof of her mouth unleashes them.

When our mouths unlatch, I smile against her lips. "Hello again, my violent little kitty. My name is Kai."

Her widened eyes almost bore a hole into my face, and each second feels like an eternity as her eyes search my face for a reason, a meaning behind all of this insanity.

"You ..." she murmurs, her face mesmerizing me. "You're the one who stole my ribbon."

*Her* ribbon.

All the blood instantly drains from my face.

Nathan's low voice rumbles through the room. "What ... what did you just say?"

*He heard.*

*Fuck.*

Suddenly, she rips open the tie around her hands. With a roar, she shoves a knife straight into my thigh.

Fuck. Guess I deserved that.

I groan and fall to the floor in pain while she tears away the belt stuck around her ankles and jumps away.

"You ... you're the girl we've been chasing?" Nathan roars out loud as he bolts at her.

She runs toward the back exit, tucking down her dress while Nathan is on her heels.

And all I can do is lie here in crippling pain. "Fuck!"

"Kai, are you okay?" Milo asks, going to his knees in front of me.

"I'll be fine, go!" I yell, and I rip the knife out of my thigh and chuck it aside.

"Don't you fucking run off now, Lana!" Nathan roars through the building. "Not when we just got to the fun part!"

"Fuck all of you!" she yells back.

I drag myself up by the chair and stumble out the door, but Lana's already near the front door. In her hands is a gun she stole off the floor that belonged to one of our guards she nearly murdered.

"Lana!" I roar.

Her eyes briefly home in on me, her body freezing as I clutch my leg, blood oozing from the wound.

"Fuck this," Nathan growls, seething as he rips one of the ornamental swords off the wall.

"Nathan, you sure that's such a good idea?" Milo rasps, grasping his arm.

"If you're not gonna help me, stay out of my way," Nathan retorts, pushing him aside.

She swallows and throws me that same look she did when they played with her, and dammit, it's making me want to bite through this pain.

But then she points the gun at Nathan. "Stop him," she tells me. "Or I'll kill him."

Nathan's too consumed by rage to care.

"Nathan," I say. "Don't do it."

"She's that goddamn girl with the mask who stole our kill. She *saw* us," he grits. "She knows too much."

"Nathan!" I roar through my pain, forcing him to turn and look at me. "Stop!"

He knows he has no choice.

He might've been the wealthiest and most influential before his parents got ruined, but this place ... this place is mine, and if he wants to live here, he needs to obey the rules.

*My* rules.

His hand tightens around the handle of the sword as he grinds his teeth, but then he drops the blade. "I know your fucking secret now," he growls at her. "You can't run away from this."

Her nostrils flare, but she still pulls back and tucks the gun into her pocket. "Keep your fucking mouths shut about me. All of you. Don't ever mention my name again."

Nathan's back straightens as he slowly creeps closer to her, despite my warnings. "Or what?"

"Fucking try me and find out," she retorts.

"Oooh ..." Milo muses from the side, tickling his own arm to show off his goose bumps. "I love it already. Can't wait."

Her face contorts, and she grunts out loud before she turns around, her black hair flicking over her shoulder. She rushes off, slamming the front door closed behind her like a queen set out on a quest of revenge.

# 16

## LANA

I bolt away from the building as fast as I can to get away from those fuckers. Not only have I found the guy who danced with me at the party, who crept into my room and kissed me ... but all three of the guys were there the night I killed that pervert.

And now they know it was me who thwarted their plans.

Squeals and laughter from farther down the street put me on edge. Any sound, any movement makes me skittish, like a stray cat ready to dart and hide.

I'm never this uneasy, this unsettled. But I can feel in my bones that nothing will ever be the same again after tonight.

Adrenaline forces my feet to keep moving, avoiding the streetlights where I can so no one can see me. Their sticky cum is still in my hair and all over my clothes, and wiping does me no good.

Fuck, I can't believe I let them do that to me.

All because of one fucking kiss.

But a part of me wanted to find out so badly which one of those fuckers invaded my home that I couldn't say no.

The price was high to get an answer to the question burning in the back of my mind.

The boy who tormented me, threatened me, stole my ribbon, snuck into my room to kiss me ...

Kai Torres.

I'll never get that shimmery green eye out of my mind, so vibrant and filled with duplicity.

I swallow down the nerves before I head into my sorority and seal the door behind me, putting on all the locks as if that will keep them out.

I run up the stairs and storm into my room.

Suddenly, another door opens halfway down the hall. "Lana? That you?" It's Irina.

"Yeah, sorry, went for a run," I mutter before I close the door.

I'm still breathing wildly when a knock on my door follows.

"You all right?"

It takes me a while to respond. "Yeah ... I'm fine."

I don't enjoy lying, but for the sake of her safety, I will. I cannot involve my friends in this.

"Just a little tired from all the running, that's all," I add.

"Okay, well, if you're still hungry, I put some leftover pizza in the fridge downstairs."

"Thank you," I reply. "I appreciate it."

"Night," she says, yawning loudly.

"Sleep tight," I reply as she shuffles away.

When her door finally closes, I can breathe again.

My eyes float through my room, wondering if anyone is here. If Kai will come creeping up to me at any moment. I rush to the window and shut it tightly, making sure it's locked. Then I check my laptop and fill in my password to check no one logged in while I was gone. Luckily, everything still seems the same.

The exception being me.

Nothing I do calms my racing heart.

Those boys ...

They don't just have a grip on my biggest secret but now also on my body, and I fucking hate it.

I scoot my chair back and rip off all my clothes, chucking them into the bin before I put on my bathrobe and head to the shower. I turn it on the highest heat, throw off my bathrobe, and jump under, basking in the scalding water to rinse myself of their filth.

But with each wash and each lathering of more and more soap, the dirty memories of them toying with me, kissing me, licking me, making me come become clearer and clearer until my clit thumps again, and my legs quiver against my will.

*Stop it, Lana. Just fucking stop it.*

*They're just three fucking boys trying to bully you into submission, that's all.*

But they're not just three boys.

They're all on my brother's no-go list.

Fuck. Now I understand why.

I should've listened to that fucking list, but now it's too late. If my brother finds out what they've done to me, he'll go after them ... And then they'll tell him what I did.

After which my life as I know it will be over.

I was supposed to be the golden child. The perfect daughter my father raised so she could one day take over his business empire and continue the family legacy.

But now all that dangles on a single red thread.

\*\*\*

## NATHAN

I clutch the red ribbon and stare at it while sitting on the couch in the chapter room.

"This girl ..." I mutter. "*This* is the one you've been visiting?"

I look up at Kai, who's sitting on a chair at the table so Milo can clean his wound.

His eyes narrow in a suspicious manner. "How do you know I've been in her room?"

My jaw tenses. "You first."

"I kissed her, yes, if that's what you want to know," he replies.

My nostrils flare as the ribbon curls around in the air.

This fucking girl ... she's the girl we've been looking for all this time, and he found her.

I slam my fist onto the table. "You knew it was her, didn't you?"

Even Milo stops bandaging him now.

Kai doesn't respond.

"Tell me the truth," I growl.

Kai's stoic face says it all, and I stand and throw the ribbon at him. "Why the fuck didn't you tell me?"

"Because I knew you'd want to hurt her," he replies after a while.

"Hurt her ..." I look away for a second and run my fingers through my hair. "She literally knows what we do. She's a threat, and you knew that. You have a crush on her or something? Is that why you went to her room?"

He frowns. "How did you even find out about me visiting her?"

"I've seen your videos."

The one pupil he still has dilates. "How the fuck—" His gaze darts to Milo, and the anger on his face is fitting, considering it's exactly the kind of betrayal I feel in my bones. Pot meet fucking kettle.

"You *watched* the camera I put up there?"

Milo pauses his work on Kai's leg and looks up at him. "We talked about it."

"I didn't give you permission to go through my fucking laptop and watch my stuff," he growls back.

"Well, technically, I didn't watch it on your laptop." Milo rubs his lips together. "I just hacked into the IP and stole the feed, then watched it on my laptop."

"That's the same fucking thing," Kai retorts.

"Does it even matter? You agreed we'd share her."

*What the ...*

"You were in on it?" I roar.

Now, I really can't contain the fury anymore.

"Oh boy," Milo muses.

I'm fuming, completely out of my mind enraged. "Since when?"

"He saw her walk around campus with that ribbon," Milo fills in, wrapping the bandage around Kai's wound and sealing it tightly. Kai throws him a fierce look, but all Milo does is shrug. "What? He already knows we fucked up."

"Damn right, I do. You both knew that girl was the one, and you never once came to me to tell me about it. Instead, you lied and went to her on your own, to do what? Grope and kiss her?"

"Hey, I didn't fucking lie," Kai responds.

I snort. "Oh, because that makes it any better."

"I don't recall needing permission from you to fuck any girl I wanted," he replies.

"*Wanted*?" I repeat.

"Yes." When Milo finishes, Kai jumps off the table and points his finger at me. "I want her. And judging from the way you just fucking jizzed all over her, so do you."

I scoff. "I was making a point."

His brow rises in a taunting way. "By eagerly kissing her?"

"She begged for it," I retort, stepping forward.

He's right up in my face now. "She wasn't begging you. She was begging *me*."

"Guys, guys," Milo says as he pushes between us. "No need to fight over some pussy."

"She's not *some* pussy," Kai says.

"What, you've got the hots for her now?" I scoff. "Ridiculous. You know who the fuck she is."

"I know damn well—"

"Felix fucking Rivera's sister." I point my finger at his chest. "Don't you fucking forget what he and his friends did to us. That family and the Skull & Serpent Society deserve the worst of our revenge."

"Like I don't fucking know that," he responds, swatting my finger aside.

"Sounds like you're in way over your head," I say.

He makes a tsk sound. "It's none of your business what I do."

"You made it my business the second you decided to hook up with the only girl who could destroy us and our whole fucking society in a heartbeat," he replies. "Do you have any idea how dangerous this is?"

His fist tightens as he pushes Milo out of the way to get closer again. "Do *not* talk to me like that."

"Like what? Like I'm the only one making any sense around here?"

Suddenly, he pulls out a knife and points it right at my chest. "Too far, Nathan. My patience has a limit."

"Kai," Milo says. "Please ..."

"No, Milo, this is between me and Nathan," Kai tells him, still focused on me.

My eyes narrow. "You're making a mistake. She's the one you should be knifing down, not me."

I gulp as the knife pushes farther into my chest.

"I trust you as a friend. But don't mistake my kindness for weakness."

Finally, he retracts the knife and tucks it back into his pocket.

I take in a deep breath. "You owe me your help. After what my family did for years to keep this society up and running—"

"Haven't I given you all my loyalty? My friendship? My blood?" he retorts, pointing his finger at his missing eye. "Haven't I given you enough?"

\*\*\*

# KAI

**Last year**

The girl we cornered and swore at runs off, crying her heart out, and I fight the guilt flooding my veins.

When she's gone, I turn to Nathan. "Do we really have to do this?"

"If there were another way, I would've taken it," he replies. "Trust me. This is the only choice I have."

"What about the rest of your family? Can't they do something?"

He shakes his head. "They've already ignored us. All we've got left is my poor aunt."

"We've already pushed Eve beyond her limit," I say.

"We can't stop," he says, sucking in a breath. "We have to continue. No matter the cost."

"Why? What could be so important that you can't say no to him?"

"Because ..." Nathan hisses, looking around to make sure no one's listening. "My family will be reported to the police if I don't cooperate."

Shit. I didn't think he was in this deep.

"I don't want to lose my family, okay?" he adds. "So, help me out. Please."

I sigh out loud. "Fine." I tap his chest. "But after this is over, you owe me. Big time."

\*\*\*

# NATHAN

I swallow down the guilt. "Yes."

"You know I've sacrificed enough to defend your honor. Your place at this society. Even your goddamn life as you know it."

Even though I hate it more than anything, he's right.

When I needed him, he defended me, and it cost him his sight. On top of that, I never could've stayed at this university, this society he's the leader of, if it wasn't for him and his wealth. All my parents' money is gone, and with it, my life of luxury. I depend on him.

"So let me have this one taste of sin," he responds, placing a hand on my shoulder. "As my friend."

My body grows rigid under his grip. "Fine. But if she tells the world what we do, it's over for us and our society."

"She won't," Milo says, and we both turn to look at him. "You said you had evidence she was there. Use it to make her do what we want." A lopsided smile forms on his face.

I think about it for a moment, but then something clicks in my head. I grab my phone and open my gallery. The picture I took of her is so fucking dirty that it makes me grin, even after the fact. My dick swells again just from the mere memory of watching her squirm on one of my toys.

"Hmm ..." That girl might just prove to be the one thing I needed after all. "You know ... that might not be such a bad idea. In fact, I'm pretty sure a girl with her stature and beauty would do anything to keep her violent little secret hidden from the world."

"What are you thinking?" Kai asks, cracking his knuckles.

Opportunities.

Ripe. Rich. Decadent. Wish-fulfilling opportunities.

I throw my arm around his shoulder. "You know, a girl who's desperate is a girl hungry to please."

There's a glimmer in his eyes. "I've already been using her secret against her to make her mine. And now that she knows who I am, I don't intend to stop."

A wicked smile forms on my face. "Then, as your friends ... let us join in on the fun."

"Oh, fuck yes, I'm in," Milo muses.

At first, a hint of jealousy and anger bursts through Kai's eye, but then his tongue darts out to wet his lips.

"Think about all the filthy things we could do with that girl," I say.

"She's mine," he rasps.

"Of course she is," I reply, not wanting to step on his toes. He's never been this possessive over a girl, but I guess there's a first for everything, and I definitely get it with this one. She's violent as hell. Just the type to drive him mad. "But on your own, it's hard to keep her in check."

"That's where we come in," Milo adds, raising a brow. "Or come in her ..."

"Hmm ..." Kai eyes us both, his body tensing up. "As long as you two remember who she belongs to, maybe we can work together and bring her to her knees."

My grip on his shoulder tightens, and I pull him closer. "Now you're talking."

# 17

LANA

I tap my pen against my notepad as I try to summarize what the professor said. But every time I write down some of the words that pop into my head, I stop at a single word repeated many times in his sentences.

*Come.*

A very normal word for people who haven't spent a single second on a device that forced them to actually come over and over again.

That word is now tarnished forever in my mind.

Each time I hear it, I stop and pause to take a breath, my panties getting wet.

*Don't think about it. Forget it ever happened.*

"Hey, have you got any plans for tonight?" Brooke whispers into my ear.

"No, nothing," I reply.

I wouldn't dare to go out on another hunt right now. Not with those boys watching my every move.

"Wanna come to Club Rivera with me?" she asks, smirking. "I heard all the sexy Skull & Serpent guys will be there."

God, I hope she's not referring to my brother.

"Um, sure," I reply. Maybe it'll be good to get my mind off things. And since it's my dad's club, my safety is guaranteed. And better yet, those Phantoms don't have a chance of stepping one foot inside that establishment. "Yeah, let's do it."

"Awesome," she says, clutching my arm. "I'm so excited. Do you think there's a discount because you're a family member?"

I snort. "Wouldn't count on it. Dad's too busy with the school, so someone else manages the clubs." I smile at her. "But maybe a free drink."

"Aw yeah." She hugs me tight. "That's what I'm talking about. You and I are gonna have so much fucking fun tonight."

"What about Irina?" I ask.

"She's sick in bed," Brooke replies. "But I can ask Crystal."

"My brother's friends?" I frown.

"Yeah, we're friends," she says, like it's the most normal thing ever. "She's really sweet. You'll like her, promise."

"Okay. Crystal, huh? Sure, why not," I mutter, still trying to focus on what the professor is saying.

But then he checks the time and puts his suitcase on the desk. "That was it for today. Make sure to fill out the papers and give them back by Monday."

"Fuck ..." I sigh out loud.

Brooke eyes my notes. "Oh, here." She takes a photo of her own notes and sends them over in a text. "You can have mine."

"Thanks." I smile.

"No worries. Always willing to lend a distracted friend a hand." She winks. "Must be boys, right?"

My eyes widen. "What?"

"It's always boys," she murmurs.

But the hairs on the back of my neck still stand up as she packs her bag and gets up from her seat. "See you tonight, L!" And she throws me an air kiss before she walks out of class.

I'm probably the last to leave as I swiftly tuck my notepad, pen, and book into my bag and throw it over my shoulder.

Suddenly, my phone buzzes, and I pause to check.

**Unknown: You want us to keep your secret?**

My fingers dig into the phone. It's him.

**Me: I know it's you, Kai. Stop the charades.**

*Kai: Yet you seemed to be so enamored by my mask.*

I gulp. Fuck. I can't believe we're talking about this.

Or that he's the guy who snuck into my room and ...

*Kai: Do you remember how my tongue rolled around your wet little pussy?*

My breathing falters.

The night I drank too much wine with Jason, when he couldn't get me off while fucking me and decided to go shower instead ...

Jason didn't come back to my room to lick me off.

It was *him.*

The phone almost slips from my hand.

*Kai: I do. Every single second of the day. I think about how good you tasted. How you hungered for more. How you moaned into my ear as you rubbed yourself on my knee.*

Fuck. I didn't want to think about it, but now the memories flood my brain like a movie come to life, and the mere thought has my pussy throbbing with need.

*Me: Fuck you. Leave me alone.*

My finger hovers over the block button as I waltz toward the exit of the classroom.

*Kai: If you block me, I will tell the world what you've done.*

I pause.

*How does he know I was about to block him?*

My gaze immediately flicks toward the window, but no one is there. God, he's really gotten underneath my skin.

*Me: What do you want?*

*Kai: You know what I want.*

My teeth grind together. I should've never given in at that party and let him have his way with me.

*Me: Enlighten me.*

*Kai: Your mouth wrapped around my cock with that pussy dripping wet while you beg for cum.*

I feel dizzy, light-headed, and I grasp the table beside me to steady myself.

*Me: Stop.*

*Kai: You asked me, and I obliged. Your turn.*

*Me: You already had what you wanted.*

*Kai: What I had was a simple taste ... what I want is every inch.*

*Me: When is it going to be enough?*

*Kai: Do you really want to ask that question?*

*Me: Stop the semantics. I don't have time for games.*

*Kai: You'll make time for me and the copious number of games I intend to play with you.*

*Me: Fuck you.*

I look up from my phone for a moment to take a breath, but my heart is unsteady. Rapid. Unlike my usual cool self, and it's pissing me off.

*Kai: I will ... after you've screamed my name.*

*Me: Kiss my ass.*

*Kai: Come here, and I'll lick it for you.*

My jaw drops. What the f—

*Me: You're a perverted freak.*

*Kai: You don't know half the things I'd do for you.*

Wow. For someone so deranged, he sure has a lot of confidence. And sass, I'll give him that.

*Me: Why? You don't know me.*

*Kai: No ... but I want to. I want to know what you hide in that killer mind of yours.*

I make an annoyed face, but at the same time, I still feel morbidly curious why he'd be so interested in me.

*Kai: Tell me, kitty, what does it take to make you scream?*

*Me: Like I'd ever tell you.*

*Kai: You don't have to. I'll figure it out.*

All the hairs on the back of my neck stand up.

*Me: I won't let you get close enough to even try.*

*Kai: Oh, I won't need to be close to give you all the goose bumps currently scattering across your body.*

I look up and turn around, checking the room, the windows, even the door, but no one is in sight. How does he—

*Kai: I don't need to see you to know exactly how your mind works. How your body feels. How your flesh reacts to my words.*

My pussy thumps without my approval, and I hate it. I hate how he's managed to speak to both the unquenchable rage coiling and twisting around my heart and the unwieldy fire burning deep inside me, yearning to be released.

*Kai: But don't worry, kitty ... I'll give your soul all the surrender it craves soon.*

*Me: Remember that knife in your thigh? If you tell a single person about anything I've done during my time at this school, I will personally come and put a knife in your fucking balls too.*

I turn off the phone before he can send me any more texts and arouse me any more than I already am. Fuck. Fuck him and those dirty fucking words, and fuck that arrogant asshole.

\*\*\*


# NATHAN

**Later that night**

I sit back and silently enjoy my whiskey on the rocks, watching the crowd dance. Considering the current dress code, it's busy in this club, which surprises me. All black, no color, except for a red mask that covers half the face. A mask quite like the ones the Phantoms use, which is peculiar considering this is a club owned by the Rivera family. The family who also owns the Skull & Serpent Society, enemies of the Phantoms, and a thorn to my eye.

My hand clutches around the glass, and I take another sip to quell the rage firing up my heart. An exclusive section is tucked in the corner to the left, but I can take a peek inside from where we're seated. Felix, Dylan, Alistair, and Penelope sit there, having a drink and chatting with their friends, and the second I catch a glimpse of their smiles, the glass I'm holding almost shatters.

Suddenly, a hand snakes around my thigh. "Relax." Milo smiles at me. "They don't know it's you."

"No, but I know it's them," I retort, placing the glass back on the table before I make a scene. Milo gently grabs my face and makes me focus on him. "Remember why we're here."

A smile tugs at my lips. He always knows how to calm me down ... with a promise of violence. And I can't fucking wait.

Because I've just spotted that diamond in the rough walking into the club in her thick five-inch black heels, a skinny pair of white jeans, and a V-cut black crop top with long sleeves, along with some pretty jewelry dangling down from her neck all the way to her belly button. The red mask she was forced to wear doesn't remotely hide her identity. She's dressed like a sweet little snack waiting to be unwrapped.

Perfect to sink my teeth into.

Perfect to unravel and destroy.

But I'll let Kai have his little moment with her first. I'll sit back and enjoy the show while he's busy making her sweat until it's finally my time to shine.

And I can't fucking wait for the fun to begin.

# 18

## LANA

"Don't dance with any of those fuckers out there, got it?" Felix slams his drink down on the table.

I roll my eyes. "I don't need your fucking permission, thanks."

"Lana," he warns. "I mean it."

"Felix, don't be so hard on her," Penelope says.

"Yeah, let her enjoy the dick for once," Dylan muses at him, dodging an immediate sucker punch by jumping up from the couch. "Missed!"

"Come here, you fucker," Felix growls, but Dylan's already run off onto the dance floor before Felix can grab him.

"Jesus," Alistair groans, and he takes a casual sip of his drink. "I really don't want to get involved in whatever this is."

"No, you don't," I reply. "Now, if you'll excuse me, I—"

Felix grabs my wrist before I can turn around. "Is Jason here?"

"I don't know, and I don't care. Don't get close with any guys here," he grits.

"He's worried about you," Penelope adds.

I stare at him, both annoyed and glad that he cares about me so much he'd ruin my dating chances. But I trust Penelope. "I can take care of myself. You don't have to worry about me."

He swallows. "I'm your brother. I always worry about you. The same way you worry about me."

He squeezes my arm, and I know what it means, what it's always meant.

The gravity of his words ... the powerful connection we have ... it can't ever be denied.

"I know," I reply.

He finally releases me. "Go on, then. Have fun with your friends."

"If you see Dylan, tell him he still owes me a drink," Alistair says, clinking his empty glass on the table.

"And if you need me, you know where to find me," Felix says. "If some guy touches you or there is any sign of trouble ..."

"Yeah, yeah, I get it," I say. "See ya."

And I walk off before he can slap on any more rules I'm obliged to follow because Daddy dearest told me to listen to him while studying at Spine Ridge.

I growl under my breath as I put my mask back on.

When I finally spot Brooke and Crystal near the bar, I wave, and a bright smile forms on Brooke's face. "Lana! I already ordered us drinks." She points at the three glasses on the bar.

"Hey, Crystal," I say as I make my way over, and we hug briefly.

"I'm so excited," Crystal muses, and she looks around until she finds Penelope and waves wildly.

Brooke hands me my drink.

"Thanks," I say, pulling my card out of my pristine white pants.

She waves it off. "Nah, this one's on me." Brooke raises her glass, and we toast the three of us. "Let's go party!"

We all chug down a considerable amount of our drinks before we head out onto the dance floor.

The music at the Rivera clubs is always so easy to get into; they always play the best tunes. The only thing I don't like about them is that they have a dress code every once in a while that's completely outrageous, and apparently, that's tonight because masks are everywhere.

And I mean everywhere.

So much for a relaxing evening.

"God, I love this place," Crystal says, boppin' her head to the music. "They've got the sickest beats."

"C'mon, dance with me!" Brooke yells at me through the loud music.

I start rolling my hips against both of them, attracting lustful eyes from the men in the club eagerly looking for their next willing girl to latch onto. But I'm not on the market. I never was, not even when I hooked up with Jason every once in a while. I'm a forever-single girl who dances just far enough from the sun so she doesn't get burned. I don't let them get close, even when they think they have.

I don't trust myself or my heart with anyone, so I keep it to myself. And tonight, I don't plan on involving myself with anyone except my friends.

I check on Felix and his gang of friends, but they're gone, and it makes me pause.

"Hey, did you see where Felix went?" I ask Crystal.

She shrugs. "There's an exclusive backstage area, or so I've been told. No one's allowed in there unless invited by a Rivera. They're probably hanging out there, smoking weed or something."

"Or having sex." Brooke winks.

"Ew," I mutter.

I do not want to imagine my brother having sex.

"Don't you want to be with them?" Brooke asks Crystal.

She shakes her head. "I told you I'd accompany you tonight! Besides, Penelope asked me to keep an eye out for any Phantom boys. She doesn't trust them. But I don't think they're that bad."

I wince at the thought of Phantoms coming here, particularly three of them.

They probably wouldn't dare, though, since this place is infested with Skull & Serpent Society members.

I shrug it off and focus on having a blast. We dance and drink away, hip to hip, vibing to the music while drinking our shots again and again and having an awesome time.

But the more we dance and drink, the more my eyes become hazy, and the colorful lights in the room meld into one.

"Wow," I murmur.

"You all right?" Crystal asks.

"Yeah, yeah, just getting a little tipsy," I muse.

"I'm gonna go to the bathroom. You wanna come?" Brooke yells over the music.

I shake my head. "I'm good. You go ahead."

"I have to pee," Crystal says, adjusting her dress. "I'm coming with you."

They walk off while I continue dancing on the floor by myself, ignoring all the stares from the hungry men in the back desperate for attention. I know I draw them in like bees to flowers, but I can't help the way I look. They wouldn't dare to come close if they only knew the killer monster that hid underneath.

I twirl around and look at the exclusive backstage area, but my brother isn't back yet. When I spot a stranger near the VIP booths staring at me with that obligated mask on, I pause. The blond streaks of hair peeking out behind the red mask and the icy stare have my knees quaking.

I suck in a breath, feeling dizzy, like I'm about to throw up.

*It's just a coincidence. A ton of people are blond and have blue eyes. Get yourself together.*

I turn around and push through the crowd, heading for the other side of the club, but I come to an abrupt halt in the middle of the dance floor.

Near the entrance to the club, a red-masked stranger leans against the thick column, swaying with what looks like a red tie in his hands. A tie that looks just like the one I had wrapped around my wrists at the Phantom Society.

And it feels like my lungs are collapsing, and all the oxygen evaporates.

I spin on my heels but come face-to-face with a guy in a black suit and a red mask, his fingers running through his wavy dark hair. There's a peculiar kind of glimmer in his eyes that's hard to ignore. One green, one white.

I attempt to bolt in the opposite direction, but before I can even try, he's already grabbed ahold of me and pulls me in, fingers splayed across my belly. He closes the distance between us until our bodies are pressed together, and my hips fit neatly into his.

"Hello, little kitty." Kai's low voice near my ear instantly puts me on edge. "Miss me?"

"No," I lie, trying to wring out of his clutch, but it's nearly impossible.

Suddenly, warm, wet lips settle underneath my ear, dragging a line down my neck, and I shudder in place.

He smirks against my skin. "Yet you're quivering from my touch."

His dick swells in the small of my back, poking me and sending shocks up my spine.

"Let me go," I growl.

Instead, he spins me around and pulls me into his embrace. "Dance with me." I can't even say no as he dances around with me like I'm a puppet and he's the master puppeteer.

I step on his foot, but he ignores the pain entirely, clenching his jaw as he leans in. "Do you remember our first dance together? Just you and me, with these same kind of masks."

Kai grins, his hand moving down to my ass ever so slowly, making me painfully aware of how alert my senses have become since he stepped onto the dance floor. "How easily you yielded to me?"

"Stop," I groan with frustration, trying to get away, but he won't release me. So I lie instead. "Jason's here, and if he sees you dance with me, he's gonna punch you into the hospital."

He snorts. "Doubt it. Last I checked, he was still in his dorm room at the Skull & Serpent Society jacking off to some porn."

I gasp.

*How the fuck—*

"You've been spying on him?"

"I have a friend of a friend who keeps track of his movements ..." Kai spins me around and sways me against him once more. "Just in case he gets it in his head that he can still come to the Beta Pi sorority to fuck you..." His lips hover near my ear, and I can feel him bare his teeth. "I'll cut off every single one of his fingers if he tried."

I gasp. He's just as sadistic as my brother, if not worse. "Fuck you. If you hurt him, I'll stab you right back."

We swing around, pretending nothing's going on even though I'm dancing with a killer.

"You think your violence will deter me?" he murmurs, cracking a smile against my skin. "It only makes my cock hard, Lana."

My body heats uncontrollably, and I don't like it one bit.

"My brother's right there. If he sees you, you're dead," I say.

"Let him watch. I'm sure Nathan would love an excuse to kill him if he tries to intervene," he says.

*Kill my brother? That's a step too far.*

Defensive rage floods my veins. "Fuck no, I'd kill you both before you even tried."

"How many jabs would you get in with that little knife of yours before I put a bullet in his brain?" he asks, and my hand instinctively reaches down to his pocket, where I definitely feel something hard, metallic, an outline of a gun.

My jaw tenses. Of course he wouldn't sneak into a Rivera club empty-handed.

And fuck me; I hate admitting he's right. I wouldn't put a dent in these fuckers before they shot up everyone I loved.

"Are you willing to take that risk?" he asks. "To have all these people suffer because of your choices?"

Fuck. When he says it like that, it's impossible for me to run to my brother.

"You sure are confident for someone stepping into enemy territory," I reply, trying to play it off cool.

He swirls me around again until we're face-to-face. "We don't fear people ... people fear us." His finger dips underneath my chin, forcing me to look up into his eyes, which glimmer with a kind of madness I've only ever seen in the mirror. "And your fear is what I crave."

I swallow the lump in my throat, my heartbeat shooting up. "Have you always been this fucked up and depraved?"

"Not until I met you ... and decided I wanted to make your little violent heart mine."

I scoff, "You wish. I don't belong to anyone."

He pulls me so close I can barely breathe, his lips mere inches away from my face. "You already belonged to me the second you came looking for me, yearning to learn who it was that kissed you."

"I was trying to find out who the fucker was that invaded my privacy," I retort.

"The one who made you come on his knee and licked your pussy until you pleaded to God?"

My pussy thumps in response to his filthy words, and I fucking hate how easy it's become for him to get me all riled up. Fuck. I'd hoped he wouldn't bring it up again because I'm still so goddamn embarrassed I let him do all that, thinking it was Jason.

"You pretended to be Jason," I hiss.

"I didn't pretend to be anyone. You made that assumption," he responds.

And fuck me, he's right, I did, but who wouldn't?

"How did you even get into my room?" I ask. "Jason was still—"

"Fucking you," he interjects, making me hold my breath. "And I was already there."

My eyes widen.

*Wait ... what?*

*He was there ... when Jason fucked me?*

"Where?"

A filthy smirk slowly marks his face. "Under your bed, listening to every sound, every breath, every nonexistent moan." He leans in to whisper. "Moans I gave to you the second he left."

My heart stands still for a moment, and even though this place is packed to the brim, it feels as though only the two of us are here.

*Fuck.*

"You're a bastard."

His fingers dig into my skin right where my pants end, and my skin begins. "Call me whatever you want, you can't deny that he wasn't giving you what you craved. What you needed to get off." One hand cups my face, and he squeezes my cheeks together. "I did. And nothing will ever stop me from claiming you."

*Pfft. How would he know what I need?*

"All that, just so you could get some pussy," I spit back. "Pathetic."

*Who even does that? Lie underneath someone's bed while they're getting railed?*

"Not some pussy ..." He cups my ass, squeezing tight right in the nook where my thighs meet. "Yours and yours alone," he whispers. "Because this pussy was *made* for me."

I can't believe he just said that.

"Over my dead body," I say through gritted teeth.

Another spin during our dance has me dizzy.

He sways his body from left to right against mine—hard cock grinding into my ass, one hand on my waist, and the other skirting dangerously close to my neck. "You think you still have a choice, but you already made yours."

"Why? Just because you caught me killing someone?" I retort. "Or were you stalking me before that? Is that why you three were there at that house at the same time?"

"Hmm ... a happenstance. Call it fate, if you want," he responds.

"Lies," I grit.

"Believe what you want, little kitty ... it won't change the fact that you belong to us now."

*Wait...*

My brows furrow. "*Us?*"

Amusement tugs at his lips. "You didn't think I'd come here to drag you out of this serpent's den alone, did you?"

My whole body tenses against his, and an icy chill courses through my veins.

"But I'll play fairly this time and give you a chance to defend your-self ... After all, I like a challenge. And bringing you those goose bumps I promised was already too easy."

*Easy? Me? What a joke.*

But when his hand skitters down my arm, the obvious bumps on my body betray me.

"But that scream you owe me? Now that's a challenge I'll take on."

*Scream?*

Suddenly, it clicks, and I feel like the oxygen is ripped straight from my lungs.

*The texts he sent me.*

"So go on, little kitty ... see if you can stay out of my claws."

*What? Is he for real?*

Part of me wants to pummel him in the face for even calling me that in public and making me feel uneasy, but another part ... hums with desire.

He grabs my shoulders, fingers digging into my skin, as he leans over to whisper, "I won't say it a second time ... Run."

And when he pushes me forward, I immediately turn my head.

He's gone.

Like a ghost, vanishing into thin air.

But I can still smell his scent lingering in my nose. I can still feel the imprint his hands left on my waist, still feel his lips and the mark they left on my skin ... Still hear his voice as it whispers dangerous promises to me.

*Run, little kitty, run.*

So I do.

I run as fast as I can through the crowd beyond the dance floor and head straight for the exit, where Milo waits for me. But he doesn't grab me or even move a muscle except for the slight twitch in his cheeks as a smile is born.

He's not stopping me because we both know what's about to happen.

A chase.

And I'm the prey they'll be hunting.

# 19

## KAI

I watch her voluptuous ass dressed in that scantily-clad pair of white pants and black crop top that sticks to her sweaty body as she rushes out the door, heels click-clacking across the floor. When even the last shadow disappears, a darkness rouses within me, stirring my dick.

"What are you doing? Why'd you just let her walk off?" Nathan barks after he rushes at me through the crowd.

I smirk as he attempts to grab my collar but then quickly regains his senses. He knows better than to taunt me.

"She's gonna get away and—"

"Do what?" I say. "Tell people?"

He knows it'd be foolish of her to expose even an inkling of detail to anyone because it would expose her own violent truth too. The one thing she's been dying to keep hidden.

Anger flashes across Nathan's face, and he marches over to Milo near the entrance. "You let her run right past you."

"Kai told me not to intervene," Milo responds.

I approach both of them with a smug smile on my face.

Nathan slowly turns his head toward me. "You *wanted* her to run?"

I can't help the wickedness from contorting my face because of the depravity to come, and Nathan returns it with an equally filthy shit-eating grin when he finally realizes what I plan to do. "You dirty bastard. You want to hunt her down ..."

"Let's give her a head start," I say, my veins filling with a mixture of adrenaline and lust from the coming chase. "Let her think she's got an advantage. That it's going to be easy to evade us."

"How long?" Milo asks.

"Three ... Two ... One ... "

A wicked grin spreads across my cheeks, unleashing the predator inside me.

I bolt off through the exit, chasing after the girl I almost want to eat alive. I don't know where she's gone, but it won't take us long to find her. There's only one street and only two ways she could've gone. The clouds have cracked open with water, casting darkness over the city, but this rain is like droplets on a hot stone to me. Nothing will cool the blaze burning inside me, an unquenchable need to find my little kitty and break her resolve.

I run to the left while Milo and Nathan each go to the right, one of them checking each alley. With this kind of downpour, the streets are deserted, save from the few people carrying umbrellas and the sparse cars driving past.

But my little kitty doesn't have an umbrella, nor the guts to take her time to hide from the rain when she knows full well it'll only delay the inevitable.

We *will* find her.

And when we do, she'll beg on her knees for mercy.

I hear footsteps ahead in an alley, and my heart picks up. Someone is hiding behind the dumpster, and it makes me tilt my head in excitement.

Because the black hair that curls around the person's shoulder definitely looks like Lana's. I kick a can in her direction, and her eyes flick to meet my gaze, a hint of fear residing behind those beautiful brown orbs.

Fuck.

Suddenly, she bolts off again, shoving a few boxes filled with trash in my way, along with the red mask from Club Rivera.

"Run, little kitty, run," I growl, and she skitters off on those heels, each click of them against the pavement causing a wave of ecstasy. "I'll fucking catch you and make you *mine*."

God, it's been such a fucking long time since I last felt this alive. Not even during my killings do my senses awaken, but this ... this sets my fucking soul on fire.

And I chase after her through the dark into the abyss of my own making.

I pull my phone from my pocket and call Nathan. "Found her. St. Mary's Street headed for St. John's Street."

"Coming," Nathan replies, and I turn off the conversation and focus on the chase.

She rushes across the streets, crisscrossing from alley to alley, but every time her eyes catch mine, I can tell the rage in her body grows impatient, ready for a fight. And when she is, I'll be right there to force her into submission.

\*\*\*

## LANA

I run as fast as I can, my heart racing in my throat as I make my way from street to street. But every time I glance over my shoulder, there he is, in his slick black suit, catching up with me fast.

Fuck.

I never imagined I'd be sprinting in these heels in the middle of the night while getting soaking wet from the rain, but here we are. I wish I'd put on something easier, clothes that didn't stick to my body and heels that didn't make it tough to run.

I cut a corner and speed across the pavement.

*CRACK!*

One of the heels breaks underneath me, and I struggle to stay standing. But when I look back and see it lying on the sidewalk, Kai appears from beneath a shop, his dark figure looming over the heel as he picks it up.

Fuck. I can't run like this, but I have to, so I kick the heels off and carry them in my hands while I rush into the nearest alley. It's a narrow road with high buildings on each side, and there's a turn on the back end. I wonder if it leads to another road.

I know this city, but I don't know each nook and every cranny. I haven't studied the maps enough to know every inch. But what if he does?

My heart races in my throat as I come to an abrupt halt in the middle of the alley.

Because in front of me is a giant wall connecting the two buildings, preventing me from running any farther.

*Shit. Shit. Shit!*

I turn.

Too late.

Through the pouring rain, a figure appears, casually tossing a knife up and catching it. My eyes follow the blade glinting in the only street-light that illuminates the street at the edge of the corner.

I swallow, bundled nerves coaxing out a fear I've never felt.

Is this what my victims feel when I hunt them down to make them bleed?

Will I be the next corpse to litter the streets?

"No more hiding, little kitty ... I've found you now," he murmurs under his breath, a wicked, almost sinful smile appearing underneath that red mask he's still wearing.

The knife in his hand travels along the wall, the screeching sound it creates making all the hairs on my arms and legs stand up.

"What the fuck do you want from me?" I yell.

"You've asked that question so many times before, and the answer will always be the same, Lana."

He says my name like it's never been spoken out loud before.

As though he's the one who fucking gave it to me.

And that alone makes my bones quiver.

"You," he finally answers, the knife creating sparks against the wall.

I walk backward with each step he takes.

"Why? You don't even know me," I retort.

"I've seen enough to know that I want you," he replies, his voice dark and ruffled with messed-up desire. "The way you kill, the way you fight, the way you bleed ..." A tormented groan leaves his lips, and the sound reverberates in my soul. "I want to own *all* of it."

When he lifts the blade from the wall, I suck in a breath. "I'll fucking fight you."

"Good."

God, the confidence in this dude is making me want to sucker punch him and, at the same time, drop to my knees. How is this normal?

I have to stop this. Fuck, I should've brought my knives, but I thought I'd be safe at a Rivera club.

"I'll kill you," I blurt out, hoping it'll keep him at bay.

Suddenly, in the back, two more figures appear wearing red masks, one with short red-dyed hair, the other half-long blond hair, and my boisterous courage wanes quickly.

Milo and Nathan.

Three against one is a tough win, but I can try.

Then Kai says, "Give us your worst."

When the two boys approach from the side, I step back farther until my back hits the wall, and I have nowhere left to go but right at them. Fuck. Guess it was always unavoidable that we'd clash again.

I stare at those haunting eyes, one white, one green, sparkling with so much thirst they make my heart throb, and I fucking hate it so much I feel the need to lash out. "Do you see so little through that eye of yours you have to bring your buddies to a fight to make it even?"

"Oh boy, not the eye ..." Milo mumbles at Nathan. "He's not going to take that lightly."

Kai's face darkens, the smirk dissipating, making place for disgust. "You think insulting me will get you out of this mess?" His fist tightens. "I'll make your mouth pay for that comment."

I snort. "I'd love to see you try."

The confident smirk returns on his face. "Watch me."

Nathan groans. "Fuck, this is getting exciting."

"God, I can't fucking wait for a taste of that pussy," Milo says, getting closer than the others.

"In your fucking nightmares, this pussy has fangs!" I scream.

I charge right at him with my heels held like a knife to hit him in the face, but he avoids my jabs. This time, I'm prepared, and I kick up, kneeing him in the face. An *oompf* sound leaves his mouth after he's tasted my knee, and I shove him back, thrusting my heels right up in his face.

Until Nathan jumps me and holds me down.

"You think you can beat us at our own game?" he murmurs into my ear.

He knocks the heels from my hands and chucks them away.

"I'll beat your fucking ass and spit on your fucking face when I'm done," I growl back, kicking back, hitting him between the legs right where it hurts the most.

He groans, excitement bolstering him as he wraps his arms around my throat and chokes me.

I claw at his fingers, desperate for air.

"You'll pay for that, Lana," he says, squeezing tightly. "You begged us to kiss you, but now that you face the consequences, you regret it."

He's right, I do regret kissing him. Not because of the consequences, but because I can still taste his foul possession of my mouth, and I hate every second of that memory.

Kai's slowly approaching from the back, his looming presence pushing me to knock my elbows back along with all the air from Nathan's lungs.

But the second I try to make a run for it, Milo's on my back, wrapping his whole body around me like a monkey latching on, refusing to let go.

"Get off me!" I shriek, but I'm brought to my knees with his weight bearing down on me.

"I get off on you, yeah." Milo laughs. "Especially that time you got all wet on his knee."

"Oh yeah, that was damn sexy. I gotta admit," Nathan groans.

He eyes Kai, who merely smirks, and I feel so fucking cold. Not from the rain but from the icy reality that both Milo and Nathan know what happened in my room, which means Kai told him ... or they were both watching us.

"Were you two there too?" I grit.

"Physically? No. Mentally, oh yes," Milo groans.

My nostrils flare. "Fucking creep."

I throw him off me and get up to kick him in the stomach and knock off his mask, but it only makes him moan.

"Oh, do it again, baby," he begs, catching me off guard.

Long enough for Nathan to grab my arms and swiftly pin them behind my back.

"I've got you now, little slut," he whispers into my ear.

"Let go of me!" I yell, trying to fight him off.

Suddenly, Kai's blade enters the scene, swooping in like a flick of the wrist, right underneath my chin. My eyes flutter to the side to meet his perpetual gaze, one bright white eye confusing my soul as the green one sucks it out of my body along with my breath.

"Face it ... you lost, little kitty. But you put up a good fight."

Milo gets up from the ground and wipes the rain through his hair before he approaches and looks me up and down. "Got yourself stuck in a dangerous game, baby."

"You think I won't scream?" I grit.

"Oh, by all means, scream," Nathan says, clutching my wrists so tightly my bones might snap. "Scream as loud as you want because the last thing any fucker who tries to intervene will see is my bullet."

*He's carrying a gun too? Shit.*

"Fuck you, I'll fucking bite off your dicks if you try anything on me," I growl. I know it's a lie, but I can't help the fighter in me.

"The only one eating anything here will be me," Kai says, tilting his head as he slightly shifts the blade enough to make me lift my head.

"Is that a threat?" I ask.

"I don't need to threaten anyone," he says, a devilish smile forming on his lips as he removes his mask and chucks it into the rain. His marred, square face almost looks beautiful, with the rivulets of water cascading down his dark hair that sticks to his skin. But I know better than to think of a Phantom as anything but a monster in the making.

"When this night is over, you will be crawling on your knees to us. Begging."

I snort. "Are you high?"

Nathan chucks his mask aside too and leans in to sniff at my wet hair, his lips dangerously close to my ear. "The only thing we're high on is your smell."

"I'm not doing shit for you," I rasp. "So you can shove—"

"Your secret in your brother's face?" Kai interrupts, tilting his head.

I frown. "Again, where's your proof?"

The knife pushes farther into my skin as a dangerous smile tugs at Kai's lip before he pulls something out of his pocket. A soaked piece of paper of my username on a particular site I frequent to find my next target ... a site I have never told anyone about.

My eyes widen.

*How does he know?*

"Sicklittlebitch13? I'm disappointed, Lana. I expected something a little more creative," Kai mumbles, staring at the paper like he can't believe he actually found me.

"How did you find that?" I ask.

"You underestimate his obsession with finding out every *intimate* detail about your life," Nathan murmurs into my ear.

"You went onto my laptop?" I grit.

"I have my ways," Kai responds.

Nathan's hand casually dives into my pocket, and he takes out my phone.

"Hey! Give that back!" I grit.

"Finders keepers," he muses, tucking it into his pocket.

"But why the 13?" Milo asks me. "I'm curious."

If I can't prevent them from knowing everything about my twisted side job, at least I'll keep this secret to myself.

"None of your goddamn business," I growl.

"Maybe she wanted her victims to think she was that age ..." Kai muses.

I swallow away the lump in my throat.

"Smart," Nathan says behind me. "But not smart enough not to get caught."

I twist around in his grip, but it's no use. He's far stronger than I ever will be.

Kai chucks the paper at me. "Smart enough to know not to tell her family ... But we will."

My nostrils twitch. Of course this was always his plan.

Once wasn't enough after he had a taste.

"You sick f—"

The blade suddenly moves to my lips, silencing me. "Ah, ah, think very carefully of your next words, little kitty."

Milo casually folds his arms, watching the spectacle with a smile on his face like he's enjoying this.

"This is your only chance, so make it count," Nathan says.

"We show this to your family, you're done for," Milo says, pointing at the paper lying crumpled on the wet pavement beneath me.

"Is that what you want?" Kai asks.

Of course not. But he already knows that. He just wants me to say it.

My lip curls up into a snarl. "No."

His knife slowly lowers down my neck, and he watches my veins twitch in response. "Now you know how far I'm willing to go ... your turn."

"Fine. Tell me what the fuck you want," I growl.

His green eye glints in the darkness with a kind of evil I've never seen, a promise of what's to come. "Your body. Ours to do with as we please in exchange for our silence."

*Fuck.*

*I knew it was coming, but it doesn't hit any less hard.*

*An impossible offer, completely deranged, yet ...*

The blade reaches the point where my exhales become visible to the naked eye, and it settles there like he means to bury either the blade between my breasts ... or his cock.

His tongue darts out to wet his lips. "So what's it going to be, little kitty?"

"You tell my brother, my father, hell anyone, and I'll cut off your balls and feed them to you," I retort.

Milo lets out a soft moan, and it makes me narrow my eyes at him.

However, the blade puncturing my skin right below my sternum forces me to watch Kai's every move.

"Answer him," Nathan says, twisting my arm until I hiss.

Fine. If I'm gonna do it, I'm gonna look him dead in the eyes and make him witness the unraveling of my soul. Because if I'm going to go down this path to hell ... I'm taking those fuckers with me.

"Yes."

Milo's face immediately erupts into a shit-eating grin and he squeals with delight.

I know what I just said. I know the gravity of that one word. How it ties my twisted soul and binds it to theirs for however long they please. Fucking devils in handsome suits come to steal every last inch of my body in exchange for the last shred of dignity I'll have left.

"Good choice, little kitty ..." Nathan murmurs into my ear. Milo throws him the tie he was holding earlier, and Nathan ties it around my wrists with ease. "And now the fun begins."

*SLICE!*

# 20

## LANA

The knife cuts through my outfit with acute precision, and the long-sleeve black crop top splits apart right in the middle, falling sideways to expose my breasts.

The groans of arousal that emanate from all three of them are something else.

"Feast your eyes, boys," Kai says, the sound of his low voice laced with desire reverberating through my goddamn bones as he steps back to take a good look. His eyes along with Milo's swoop over my naked body, my nipples peaked from both the cold and their hungry gazes.

"Fuck you," I growl.

"Such a potty mouth," Nathan says, pinching my cheeks together with one hand. I can feel his body press up to my back. "It's about time someone fucked that rage out of you. Now kneel."

One hand pushes down onto my shoulder until my knees cave underneath me, and I'm forced onto the cold, wet street in soaked jeans.

Kai smirks and slowly unzips his pants, and I can tell he gets great pleasure in watching me follow his every move. He pulls out a dick so huge and rigid, littered with piercings, I have to swallow away the lump in my throat.

"You remember this cock, don't you?" He tips my chin up with the knife. "When you so desperately licked it after I made you come all over this blade."

*My* blade.

The one he stole from me when I failed to kill him.

"That knife belongs to me," I grit as the tip pushes into my skin.

"You want it back?" He raises a brow. "Earn it."

My nostrils flare as he inches closer, stroking his ample length, each piercing glinting in the dark. "Open your mouth for me, kitty."

Fuck. It's too late to run, too late to kill them, so my only option left is to obey.

My lips slowly part, angered by the mere notion I've been defeated. But that doesn't mean I can't fight.

His tip brushes along my lips, the feel familiar, instantly pushing memories to the forefront of my mind that flood my body with sensations.

My mouth opens wider, my fangs at the ready to chomp down.

"You won't bite ..." he murmurs, as if he can read my thoughts. "If you do, I won't be the only one bleeding over this pavement." He pushes the blade farther into my neck as if to make good on his threat. "Right, kitty?"

I swallow and nod, and he slowly retracts the knife, tucking it into his pocket before he grabs ahold of my face with one hand, his dick in the other, and slips into my mouth. His cock is just like I remember from the first time, slipping easily across my tongue until the piercings touch my throat, and I gag.

"That's a good kitty. Make those sounds for me," he groans.

He feels just like I remember.

"Fuck," Milo groans behind him while fondling himself right through the fabric of his pants.

A growl emanates from deep within my chest because I want nothing more than to claw out his eyes for even looking at me, but my bound wrists force it to be a fantasy.

"Now take it deep," Kai groans before burying himself to the base, and I struggle so hard not to choke on it. He's that big. "Good girl."

Goose bumps scatter across my skin, but I tell myself it's from disgust rather than from the words he just said.

When he pulls out, he says, "Now take your last breath because I'm going to take it with my cock."

"Wha—"

The word can't even leave my lips before he thrusts back again, burying himself even deeper than before. Until I can feel his balls tighten against my chin, and my eyes practically roll into the back of my head.

My clit thumps in response, and I groan with frustration.

Nathan stalks around us, watching Kai with great interest, the bulge in his pants too big not to notice.

"Look at me," Kai says, tipping up my chin, forcing me to focus. "Look at the man who's buried nine inches deep inside that hungry mouth of yours, who can make your pussy throb with just one word. *Mine.*"

His length bulges against the inside of my throat, my eyes watering as I struggle to keep him in. I can't breathe. I can't fucking breathe. And through all that, my pussy throbs with a need I've never felt before.

It's as if the memories of him licking me, kneeing me until I came are mixing with what's happening right now, confusing both my body and my mind.

"That's it, give me everything you have, little kitty," he groans, and he pulls out again for a second, only to thrust back in the next. "Give me your fucking breath."

But I couldn't possibly give something I no longer possess.

He dips in slowly, dragging each of his barbells along my tongue like he enjoys the sight of them disappearing inside me. His hand slides down my chin all the way to my neck, and he squeezes it tightly, preventing much-needed blood from circulating, and my vision slowly starts to blur.

My eyes briefly make contact with Milo's, whose greedy eyes take in my body like he's never seen anything more delectable to eat. His tongue dips out to lick his lips, his hand sliding down to his zipper to pull out his curvy cock covered in tattoos. He strokes it slowly all the way from base to tip, never breaking eye contact. "God, you look so fucking good on your knees, Lana," he says. "I could almost drop down there with you."

But I can't even focus on what he's saying with Kai ramming down my throat.

"I want to test your limits, kitty. How far can I go until you use your sweet voice to beg me again, just like you did last time?" Kai murmurs, pulling out briefly.

"You can wait the rest of your goddamn life," I answer.

Even though I know I'll probably cave before this night is over.

"Then you'll enjoy my cock plundering your mouth for the rest of this goddamn life," he groans, and he slams right back in again to the hilt while clutching my throat, feeling his own dick slip down.

My clit thumps from the sheer size of his length as it chokes me.

"I think she needs some encouragement," Nathan muses as he circles up behind me and says, "Throw me the knife."

Kai fishes it from his pocket with his length still buried deep inside me and chucks it at Nathan like it means nothing. And I can feel Nathan position himself behind me, his hands snaking up my waist. "You like that, don't you? Being used."

When his hands grip my breasts, I choke out a groan, swallowing my pride as he begins to twist my hardened nipples. The onslaught of sensations is almost too much to take.

"Are you ready to receive, little slut?" Kai groans, pulling out for a brief second to slap his shaft onto my tongue.

"I'd rather—"

I can't finish my sentence before he buries himself in my mouth again.

"Every time you think of spewing hate, I want you to remember this moment, Lana. I want you to remember how you went down on your knees for me and let me open this pretty little throat with my cock by your own goddamn volition. Willingly. Like a good, needy little slut begging to be punished."

Fuck.

I can't even process what he's saying because his fingers are so deeply entrenched in my neck, my soul is about to leave my body. It doesn't even register that Nathan's moved his hands away from my sore nipples.

The knife suddenly cuts through my pants in the back, ripping it open at the seam right in the middle. With one single slice, he tears through my panties and rips them to shreds.

I pull away from Kai's dick as Nathan chucks the knife right back at him.

"What are you—"

A loud moan cracks through my throat as Nathan swipes two fingers past my slit. "So fucking wet."

*Fuck.*

Kai grins at him before returning his attention to me. "Wet already, little kitty? I knew you were a dirty little slut who enjoys being chased and pinned down."

I hate them. I hate how they've so easily made me do this. "Fuck yo—"

He squeezes my throat and pushes his dick over my tongue again. "Bad kitty. Take it deep now like a good girl."

He tilts my head up to meet his tip and shoves inside with no remorse. Behind me, three fingers slither across my slit as Nathan rubs my wetness all over. When he pushes his middle finger inside, my whole body tenses, and I have to withhold a moan. All while Kai's piercings scrape along my mouth, swiveling salty pre-cum all over my mouth.

"Roll your tongue around," Kai orders, watching as my tongue dips out to lick his length. "That's it, kitty. Worship this fucking cock that brought you to your knees."

"Fuck, she just clenched around my finger," Nathan groans.

When he pushes in another finger, my whole body begins to writhe.

Fuck. The arousal builds in my core hard and fast.

"Knew you were a filthy one," Milo says, jerking himself off right in front of me. He eyes Nathan. "Show it to me."

Nathan pulls his fingers out, and I almost feel empty. Milo's grin tells me he can see my wetness on his fingers. "Fuck." His groan is long and drawn out, his dick bouncing in his hand.

"Now tell me, Lana, are you my good girl yet?" Kai asks, pulling out for a moment. "Think carefully about your next words."

If I don't tell him what he wants to hear, he'll continue to use me until all my breath is spent.

I suck in a breath, casting my self-worth aside. "Yes," I growl back.

He mercilessly thrusts inside again, making my eyes roll back so hard I see the darkness hiding behind them.

"Say the words. Tell me what you are."

His length swivels across my tongue, a promise for more if I don't give him what he wants. "I'm your good girl," I murmur, seething with hatred at every syllable.

His face contorts with pure pleasure, his lips parting as an almost animalistic groan leaves his mouth before he pulls out and steps away. "Fuck." He sounds like it's taking every ounce of effort not to blow his load right then and there.

He flicks his fingers at Nathan. "Move."

Nathan gets up, leaving my ass exposed to the torrent of rain, but Kai swiftly replaces his body as he perches behind me. His calloused hands shove me down until my face almost rests on the pavement, and they slide down my spine, raw energy crackling between the tips of his fingers and my skin until his hands finally settle on my waist. He lifts me with ease, raising my butt cheeks to the point where I can no longer keep myself up, and my face is pushed to the asphalt. My pussy and ass are on full display, my core being debased into oblivion as I drag in the missed breaths.

But when he bends over and swipes his tongue across my slit, I suddenly become acutely aware of every breath I take.

"Hmm ..." The carnal sounds coming from deep within his chest set my body on fire. "I told you I could lick this pussy every day, Lana. Now let me satisfy you."

His tongue bores into me, but even now that my throat has all the space to suck in a breath, I'm still out of air as a deranged moan spills from my mouth. "Fuck!"

God, this is the tongue I remember from that night. The tongue that could make me beg for more.

"Oh yes, I'll fuck this mouth good." Nathan suddenly kneels before me, his hand coiling through my hair, pulling my head up to meet his glistening cock, piercings dangling from the tip. "Now open wide, slut."

I only do what he says because of the tongue thrusting into me, making it impossible not to mewl.

"Fuck, you taste divine," Kai murmurs against my pussy lips, driving me insane with lust.

Nathan grips my hair tightly as he forces my head over his length and pushes me down. I struggle to fully take him. Even though he's not as big as Kai, he's much thicker and rougher with me. "Coat my cock like you coated his. Show me how much of a slut you'll be for us."

I can't even react because of the tongue swirling around my clit.

"You're so goddamn wet for me. You liked throating my hard cock, didn't you?" Kai groans behind me, his tongue circling around and around, dipping into me whenever Nathan thrusts into my mouth, and I can barely take it.

"Are you gonna come all over my tongue, little kitty?" he muses, the hint of arrogance in his voice so annoying I want to kick him in the face, but this fucking tie and his strong grip won't let me.

"Fuck—"

*You.*

I say the word in my head, but all that spills from my mouth is a choked moan as he drives his fingers inside too, swirling his tongue around my clit until it's swollen and throbbing.

Nathan buries himself inside my mouth to the hilt, groaning wildly as he throws his head back, wet hair flipping hundreds of tiny water beads into the air. "Fuck, I see why he was obsessed with you."

"God, I love watching you two fuck her," Milo moans as he steps forward from the shadows, coaxing out the pre-cum from his tattooed dick.

"Come closer then," Nathan tells him. "Kneel in front of her. Feel that fucking body because you won't ever feel anything better than this."

Milo does what he says, kneeling in front of me, and he reaches for my breasts and squeezes them, his shaft bouncing up and down in his hands.

"Fuck, your tits are so goddamn beautiful," Milo rasps.

Nathan bites his lip, sucking in a droplet of rain as he pulls in and out of me, coating his dick with my saliva, then spreading it all over my face with his length, each barbell scraping across my cheek. "So fucking pretty ... so fucking filthy."

He spits on my face and rubs that in too.

"Fuck you," I grit.

But he pinches my nose and pushes my chin down to thrust right back in. "What did I say about that potty mouth of yours? You want to be fucked so badly?"

I shake my head, but he only dips in deeper.

"I don't believe that ..." Nathan says, a wicked smile making the sides of his lips quirk up. "You're just lying to yourself."

"I can taste your arousal on my tongue, Lana," Kai murmurs, spearing me with his tongue until I feel dizzying amounts of lust coursing through my veins. "Admit that you want it."

When Nathan pulls out again, I rasp, "Fine! Yes, fuck."

"Hmm ..." Kai groans behind me, spearing his tongue into me once more before he pulls out, leaving me feeling bereft. "I can arrange that."

Suddenly, he leans up against me, his strong thighs flexing against mine as he pulls me up farther and swipes his hard-on through my slit.

"You wouldn—"

Another moan rolls off my tongue from his sheer size as he enters me.

"I told you I'd make you moan out loud when I fucked this greedy little pussy," Kai groans, clutching my waist as he buries in so deep I see stars. "Now take my cock like a good girl."

He pulls out and slowly pushes back in again, stretching me, filling me so deep I can almost feel him in my stomach. Fuck. It's so full I can barely breathe, let alone think.

Milo's squeezes turn into nipple twists, and I scream out another moan as I'm being railed on both ends. Nathan grips my wet hair and slams into my mouth each time Kai does the same, and the more Kai begins to bounce inside me, the more I'm forced headfirst into Nathan's dick.

Both my mouth and my pussy have never been wetter.

I hate them, and I've never been more turned on in my life.

Nathan pulls out his dick and says, "Spit."

I spit over his length, only for him to swipe it over my cheeks, and he spits right on top of my face.

"Hey!"

He thrusts right back in again, mixing our spit inside my mouth.

"You'll accept my spit and my cum like a good fucking slut," he groans.

Nathan is more vicious than Kai and far more focused on the emotions riddled on my face as though he enjoys seeing the hateful looks I give. Like he hates me just as much.

"And you..." He turns to Milo. "You're gonna come while you watch me fuck her mouth instead of yours."

"Fuck," Milo rasps, breathing raggedly as his shaft throbs in his hand.

"Focus on her tits. Make yourself on the verge of busting from those nipples alone," Nathan growls at him.

Milo follows his orders almost instantly, twisting both my nipples until I can barely keep the screams inside, but Nathan's shaft is in the way.

"Fuck, your pussy feels so tight around my dick," Kai groans, and he spanks my ass, rain droplets splattering all around. "I could own you with my cock every fucking day for the rest of my life and still not have enough."

Fuck.

He plows into me with full force, not giving me an inch to breathe, let alone move as his forceful grip holds me steady. I've never been fucked like this, so fucking hard and fast while I was so fucking wet I could drip all over the pavement.

*What is wrong with me?*

Hands all over my breasts, my waist, my ass, even my throat as I'm being driven to madness with every inch of my body now belonging to them.

"I want to suck those beautiful tits," Milo groans, lowering himself to the ground, crawling underneath me, and bringing his mouth up to my dangling breast, covering it with his lips. I gasp when his tongue circles my nipple, and his teeth gently tug and bite.

Nathan grips Milo's shaft out of nowhere, and I'm too surprised to even choke out the moan stuck in my throat from the way he just thrust inside me.

"Oh fuck, I'm gonna come," Milo murmurs, his teeth clenching my nipples.

"Fucking come then while you suck on those tits," Nathan grits.

"Fuck!"

Nathan jerks him off so fast, Milo shoots his load, and part of it hits me in the face, cum dripping down my cheek, and it only spurs Nathan to bury himself deeper and deeper. Both of them boring into me drives me insane with greed for more of these devils I'm supposed to hate.

Kai grips my wrists and holds the tie to push in even deeper even though I didn't think that was possible, and fuck me, my entire body begins to quake with need.

"That's it, Lana, come undone for me," Kai groans as my pussy begins to clench around his length. "Beg for me, and I'll give you what you want."

"Fuck, please," I mewl without realizing what I'm doing.

His fingers move to my clit, and with just a few circling touches, he manages to push me over the brink. I moan out loud as the orgasm washes over me, completely drowning out any other noise beyond this single fucking alley and any other feeling but these cocks driving into my body, filling it with a lust I've never known or craved so badly.

"Fuck, such a cumslut," Nathan groans, and I can feel him jet into the back of my throat, his slickness dripping down. "Swallow it all."

I cough, but it does nothing to keep the forced swallows at bay, and I gulp it all down.

Kai groans loudly, the sound so sinful I could almost burst out into bliss again. He thrusts deep, balls clenching against my thighs as warm seed fills me to the brim.

Milo crawls out from beneath me right before both boys pull out.

I'm dripping from both ends, still reeling from the onslaught of desire pooling in my stomach.

Fuck. I never knew sex could be so cold yet so hot that I could barely feel anything but their bodies clashing with mine. That I could want something so badly I would beg for it like it was my last day on earth.

But I did. I fucking did, and he'll never let me forget.

"Jesus Christ ..." I mutter.

Kai bends over me, grasping the tie wrapped around my wrists as he leans in to whisper, "If you must pray to someone to relinquish you of the shame you feel right now..." He pushes some of my wet hair aside and tucks it behind my ear, then adds, "Pray to us."

*SLICE!*

He cuts through the tie with the knife, releasing my wrists before standing up again and moving away from me.

"F-fuck ... you," I stammer after regaining my senses, but my hands still feel too mushy to support my weight.

All those boys do is let out savage laughs as they stand tall and look at my body lying here on the wet gravel. A flash of light emanates from Nathan, and I cover my eyes as he lowers the phone again.

"A perfect image of a perfectly broken doll," he mumbles.

A picture taken with *my* phone.

He taps the screen a few times with a gratified smile. "Sent straight to my stash."

"You motherf—"

"Ah, ah," Nathan interrupts, holding up my phone like a hostage. "I have your number now. So whatever you're thinking ... don't."

I grind my teeth together to keep the insults from rolling off my tongue in a hurry while my body shivers from the rain.

"Cold?" Milo removes his jacket and throws it over me like he's throwing a dog a bone. "Keep it."

Nathan places my phone right in front of me, but just far enough so it's out of reach.

Kai goes to his knees in front of me. "You belong to us now," Kai says, tilting up my chin with the knife. My knife. "And when we call your name ... you *will* come."

He retracts the blade and throws it away, the sound of metal clattering onto the pavement the last thing I hear before they walk off and disappear into the shadows of the night again, leaving my body cold and naked in the pouring rain.

And after just having the most fucked-up, most mind-blowing orgasm of my life, I would almost thank them for it.

Fuck.

# 21

## MILO

"Do you think we were too hard on her?"

Both of them stare at me as we walk back to the car like I just set loose the fucking angel of vengeance or some shit.

"You insane?" Nathan says.

"Some days," I muse.

It's quiet for a moment before Nathan bursts out into laughter and pulls me close, rubbing his fist against my shoulder like he always does. "You're ridiculous. I love it."

"She can handle it. She's a firecracker." Kai pushes the key and opens the door. "Let's get out of here before she comes looking for more."

"Hmm ..." My dick strains in my pants. "Would that be such a bad thing?"

Nathan crawls in first, and I hop in beside him while Kai closes the door and jumps in to the driver's seat.

Nathan swipes his blond hair aside and puts his hand on my knee. "You still didn't have enough?"

"Hey, I wasn't the one shoving my dick into her mouth and pussy," I retort. "All I got was a little jerk-off action and some titty sucking."

His brow rises. "You're eager for a fuck?" His hand slides up my leg. "Because I can give you one. All you have to do is ask."

"Save it for when we get back home, please," Kai says as he starts the car and kicks it into gear.

"I'm always ready for you," I muse as Nathan's fingers tickle my thighs to the point that my hard-on bursts out of the seams of my pants. "I'm just saying ..." I lick my lips. "If you two got to feel that pussy, I want her too."

"Patience, Milo." Kai glares at me through the rearview mirror. "She'll come to us. And when she does, you'll get all the pussy you could ever need from her."

Nathan's fingers thrum against my tip, and ragged breaths spill from my mouth. He pulls his phone from his pocket and shows me the picture he took of her on her knees, in the pouring rain, clothes ripped to shreds, face covered in his cum, pussy dripping with Kai's seed.

*Fuck.*

My shaft bounces up and down against his fingers.

"Take a good look, Milo. Because all of this belongs to us now," Nathan groans, rubbing my dick until I'm all hot and bothered again. "This is just the first of many."

"F-fuck," I groan, my mind torn between the dirty looks he's giving me and the girl in front of me. God, I wish I could lick her right through the phone.

"You want her just as much as he does, don't you?" Nathan asks, biting his lip.

I nod as he keeps coaxing out my cock until it's staining my pants with pre-cum.

"Good. Because I'm gonna need you to throw out your conscience if we're gonna do this." He winks and leans in to whisper into my ear as he rubs me so hard I could come right through my pants. "I need you to be a good boy and stay quiet for me while I use this girl to get what I want. And you're going to help me do it."

"What?" I whisper. "You've thought up some diabolical plan, haven't you?"

"This picture is just one of many more I'll use to make her pay," he whispers as a wicked smile forms on his face.

"Extortion?"

My eyes immediately flick to Kai, who's still glaring at us through the mirror, but he can't hear the words Nathan whispers.

Nathan violently grips my chin, forcing me to focus on his icy-blue eyes. "Shhh ... eyes and ears on me. Always."

"What are you two talking about?" Kai asks.

"His hungry cock," Nathan retorts, briefly glancing at him. "Want some?"

"I'm spent, thanks," Kai replies, rolling his eye, and he focuses on the road again.

Nathan's fingers play me faster and faster until I can barely focus on the words he whispers into my ear like a lullaby. "She wants us to keep her violent secret and this filth to ourselves? We can, for a price."

A grin forms on my face. "You're an evil fucker. You know that, right?"

He smirks against my ear and playfully slaps me on the cheek as he says, "Just the right amount for a Phantom Society fucker. Now, are you going to make me wait, or do I have to wring that cum out of this cock myself?"

And I can't help but obey his every sick whim as he drives me deep into the trenches of hellish lust only a sadistic master like him could.

\*\*\*

## LANA

I drag the jacket over my body, coughing up the salty cum, trying to stay calm.

But my heart ... it's never raged this hard, this loudly, and a scream still manages to burst through my mouth and fill this dark void with a fight for life.

They may have left me like a discarded toy, but I refuse to fucking give up.

They think they can break *me*?

Lana *fucking* Rivera?

Over my dead *fucking* body.

I crawl up from the pavement, still dripping from all exits, still adjusting to the feeling of having been taken from both sides. Now barren. As though my body misses something it never knew it craved so badly.

And it makes me rage so wildly I scream again as I stand, pouring every inch of rage into this one bellow before I swallow it all down, never to be seen again.

I waltz to my knife and phone, picking both up from the ground, wiping the dirt on my clothes before I grasp my heels and put them back on.

My phone still works despite the rain, so I swiftly open the group chat app and text the girls. I find a bunch of texts from them both.

*Brooke: Where R U?*

*Brooke: Hello? Earth to Lana?*

*Brooke: This isn't funny.*

*Crystal: Lana, please RE! Are u OK? You disappeared on us.*

*Brooke: Tell me ur in the bathroom, or I swear to God I'll walk over to your brother and tell him you're missing. I don't want no fuckin trouble.*

*Me: Sry, got sick so I got home on my bike. Don't worry bout me.*

It's so obviously a lie, but I don't want her to worry.

*Brooke: O shit. That sucks.*

*Crystal: Are you sure? I can come. I don't want you to be alone.*

Crystal is always so nice, even when I barely know her. No wonder Penelope's such good friends with her. I could use a little kindness right now.

But I don't want them to worry about me either.

*Me: Yeah, I'm fine. Go party! But also, pls don't tell my brother.*

*Brooke: Don't want him to worry, huh?*

*Me: Yeah. Did he notice something?*

*Brooke: No, they were still in that exclusive area for a good while. I don't even wanna know what they were doing in there. TMI.*

*Me: Pls just don't tell him I was gone.*

*Crystal: We won't tell him, don't worry. As long as you're safe.*

*Me: Thank you.*

*Crystal: DM us if you need us, and we'll be there in a min, OK?*

*Me: GO dance. Don't worry about me.*
*Crystal: OK, get better soon!*
*Brooke: K, feel better!*

I don't know how I'm going to get home yet, but I'll figure it out. I'd rather walk all the way back to Spine Ridge than face any of my friends looking like this.

With a sigh, I tuck my phone back into my pocket. Or at least, what's left of it. Even if my pants and shirt are no longer whole, and my hair is soaked, and my face is covered with a mixture of cum and saliva ... at least I'll walk out of this grimy alley with my head held high.

They may have taken my dignity, but they'll never take my pride.

# 22

## NATHAN

**Days later**

Underneath my desk, I stare at the picture I took days ago, completely enamored by the girl I know should be my enemy.

She's the daughter of the man in charge of Spine Ridge and sister of that obnoxious asshole Felix. Just the thought of seeing his fucking face on this campus makes me want to crush this phone with my bare hands.

I should not be thirsting for a girl who's related to him, yet ... all I can think of is sinking my teeth into her skin and making her moan my name.

Suddenly, my phone buzzes and a text drops.

*Kai: Stop staring at your phone.*

*Me: I'll do whatever I damn well want to.*

*Kai: You want the professor to kick you out? What are you even looking at?*

*Me: Her.*

*Kai: I never asked you to take pictures of her.*

*Me: You don't have to ask. I'll do it for free.*

I smirk. The thought of taking more photos of her in various compromising positions makes my cock twitch.

*Kai: As long as I get to take a peek at them too.*

*Me: Whenever you want. Mi casa es su casa.*

*Kai: Good. Anyway ... Are we still going tonight?*

*Me: Ofc. We need the money.*

*Kai: You. You need the money.*

*Me: But you'll help.*

*Kai: If you ask nicely.*

I roll my eyes. Always the one to make me beg. Milo couldn't do it, but Kai ... damn him.

*Me: Please.*

*Kai: What is it that you told Milo again? Oh right ... good boy.*

*Me: Do you enjoy this?*

*Kai: Very much.*

*Me: I'll give you a test ride if you want.*

*Kai: Maybe I'll take you up on that offer one day.*

I smirk and look up from my phone down to where he's sitting, and he briefly glances over his shoulder and winks at me. Maybe one day, he won't be such a pussy and join Milo and me in the playroom.

*Kai: Enough banter. We'll talk later about our business for tonight. Put your phone away before someone sees.*

*Me: Got it, boss.*

But I merely close the app and open the image right back up so it's centered on my screen. I can't fucking stop staring at her. No wonder he was so hung up on her the second he got ahold of her ribbon.

"Got yourself a new obsession, Nathan?"

I turn my gaze across my shoulder to the fucker who dared to sneak a glimpse at my phone, fuming with fire. A fucker from Tartarus, no less. A society we used to be allied with until they abandoned us when we needed them the most.

"Did I ask you something, Rhett?"

His eyes connect with someone sitting a few rows down, and I don't need to see who he's looking at to know who's sitting there.

Kai.

Still, he shrugs. "Don't need to. You make it obvious as fuck. Didn't peg you to be the type to bring girls to their knees, though, but I dig it," he says, winking. "Boys, girls, anything with a hole is good."

"Get your fucking nose out of my business," I growl. "Before I cut it off."

He raises his hands. "Relax, I'm not. I didn't see much except for some tied hands. I don't give a fuck who you're banging," he says. "I'm just surprised any of them would do you."

My eyes begin to twitch.

The foul smirk on his face makes me home in on him. "You know ... need some fingers to pleasure a girl."

He lifts his hand with one finger lowered.

The same finger missing from my hand.

And he wriggles it around like it's all some big bad joke to him.

Within an instant, I jump out of my seat and grab him by the collar, punching his face with fist after fist until his nose turns bloody and his tooth falls out.

"Mr. Reed! Mr. Reed!" the professor yells from down below, but I ignore his pleas and continue hammering on my opponent.

"Stop, stop, it was just a joke," Rhett splutters, but I don't fucking care.

I don't know when I'll stop.

If I'll ever stop.

My fists have been hungry for blood for so fucking long.

And this fucker just spewed the wrong fucking joke.

I'm halfway across his desk, punching like a madman. I don't give a shit who sees. He messed with the wrong one.

"NATHAN!" Kai's voice calls from down below.

I look up.

Too late.

A fist hits me right in the jaw.

"You don't touch one of our own, you fucker!" It's another one of those Tartarus guys coming to the rescue. Arlo.

"Stay out of this!" I scream back.

*PUNCH!*

Another hit right in my back has me arching, and I crawl off the desk to fight him instead.

The whole class has turned around to watch us fight, each punch drawing out a collective gasp, but I pay them no attention.

Kai jumps up from his seat, running up to me, but not fast enough before this fucker and I have exchanged more punches, taking one in the gut each. Suddenly, Rhett jumps up from behind me and puts me in a chokehold.

"Fucking calm down, pussy bitch," he growls. "It was a fucking joke."

"I'll cut off your fucking head!" I yell, kicking the one in front of me in the nuts.

But he's choking the life out of me, and I can feel myself slipping away.

*SLICE!*

Kai's knife punctures Rhett's arm, and he releases me.

"*Fuck!* Stay out of this!" Rhett hisses at him.

I scramble away and suck in some much-needed breaths.

"You invited me in the moment you attacked my friend," Kai retorts.

"This isn't about you. I made a fucking joke, and he couldn't take it," Rhett says.

"You piece of shit," I growl, grasping him by the collar and dragging him over the desk until his face hits my knee.

"Hey!" Arlo growls, but he can't throw his knife at me because Kai's right up in his face, threatening him with his collection of knives.

"Don't fucking move an inch, or I'll gut you like a fish," Kai growls, his knife pointing at Arlo's stomach.

"You think you can hurt me?" Arlo licks his lips. "Don't tempt me with a good fucking time, Torres."

Suddenly, the fire alarm goes off, drawing our collective attention. The dean's grim look as his hand hovers over the button while he stares me down from the slammed open door to the classroom has me swallowing the lump in my throat ... because I'm immediately reminded of the promise I made to him last year.

No more fighting on campus.

*Fuck.*

\*\*\*

## KAI

"Was it worth it?"

The deadly stare the dean gives us makes me want to look away. I never fucking look away, but damn, this fucker's got a threatening aura. I suppose it's no wonder, considering the name he carries.

I make a tsk sound and turn away, folding my arms. "I did what I had to, to protect my fellow Phantom Society member."

"And you?" Dean Rivera focuses on Nathan now. "Punching students in the middle of a class?"

Nathan lifts his four-fingered hand. "Rhett insulted me. I don't take that lightly."

The dean sighs, rubbing his forehead. "And you think punching and knifing down your fellow students will bring back your finger?"

"No. But they'll think twice before those Tartarus boys talk about me," Nathan says.

"Hey." The dean's eyes darken as they home in on us. "Don't even think about starting more beef with another frat house."

"If they can keep their mouths and hands to themselves, I won't have to intervene," I reply, leaning back in my chair.

"Until you lose another eye," the dean warns.

Damn, that was a low blow.

He chucks his pen down onto the table. "Do I need to put you guys through more community service?" He tilts his head. "Maybe this time I'll include cleaning all the restrooms on campus. Hmm?"

Nathan makes a disgusted face. "Gross."

"No, gross would be months in jail," he says sternly.

And it shuts us both up quickly.

The dean's fists rest on the desk as he leans over it. "Do you think you run this place?"

I shake my head.

"Then tell me ... who does?"

"You, sir," I reply.

"And do you think I need you two boys to put some Tartarus dimwits in their place?"

Wow. Never thought I'd hear a dean speak about his own students like that, but I guess it shouldn't be a surprise, considering the frat house his son belongs to. He's obviously biased toward the Skull & Serpent Society.

"The answer is no," he adds. There's another pause. "You will clean up the yard outside Saturday."

"What?" Nathan stands up from his chair.

"Sit. Down."

Rivera's harshness has him quickly seated again.

"Three hours."

"But those fuckers hit me too!" Nathan growls.

"*They* will get their own punishment," the dean interjects. "And you will *not* associate with them any second longer. Do you hear me?" When we don't respond, he adds, "We've had enough drama surrounding this school in the past two years. I don't need you two adding more fuel to the fire."

"So Rhett gets to insult me, and I don't get to defend myself?" Nathan scoffs, folding his arms.

"You turn the other cheek."

"I did that," Nathan says, his voice quaking with rage. "With your son."

The dean stares at him for a moment.

"I know what my son took from you. And we have made ample reparations to your family."

"My family is in jail," Nathan growls.

"That is from no fault of ours," the dean replies. "And we have done all we can to help you and your family after the feud between you and my son."

"And those damn friends of his," I add, my nostrils flaring.

Suddenly, the door behind us opens, and someone barges in. But by the time I've turned around, the familiar sound of those click-clacking heels, that wave of black hair moving past, along with that sweet succulent scent of prickly roses and passionfruit make me lose all my breath.

And the second our eyes connect, it feels as though all time stands still, and I've forgotten all the reasons to exist except ... her.

*Lana.*

The mere sight of her in her tight black skirt and red sweater, buttons barely holding together those ample breasts, makes my mouth water.

She narrows her eyes at Nathan and me, who's also lost all the words he was going to say the moment she walked in.

She cleaned up nicely after the messed-up state we left her in. It's almost as if none of it ever happened, and she's carried on with daily life.

I wonder if she listened to our conversation.

*How much did she hear?*

She leans in to press a kiss onto Rivera's cheeks, her eyes still homed in on us.

"You called for me?"

Fuck.

That sentence and the way she said it makes me rock-hard. Because it's exactly what I told her we'd do ...

*We call, you come.*

"I'm in the middle of a meeting," the dean says, grinding his teeth.

"Sorry, I assumed you meant *immediately* when you said *now*," she muses, smiling like nothing's going on.

Like we didn't rail her senseless just a couple of days ago.

"It's all right," the dean says. "I just wanted to make sure you were doing okay at school. How are your classes?"

She blinks and throws us both a look before answering, and fuck me, my heart just skipped a beat at the possibility of her spilling all the beans to her father.

*She wouldn't dare ... would she?*

"I'm ... adjusting," she replies. "The first months were quite boring, but now that I've found out where I fit in." Her eyes narrow at me, and the weight her glare carries could make any man fall to their knees and beg for mercy. But I'm not merely any man. Not to her.

"It's become quite the game to get ahead."

"Hmm, don't get yourself too worked up with grades," he says, totally oblivious to the double meaning in her words. "Above average is good enough for the business."

Her face contorts at that last word, and she focuses on him. "Dad, I can be a great asset to the company on my own, unlike Felix."

I glance at Nathan, who seethes from the mere mention of his name.

The dean grips her shoulders. "Felix is doing great, as are you. Now are you still available for tonight's dinner?"

She smiles at him, but I can't tell if it's an actual genuine smile or if she secretly wants to end everyone in this room.

"Sorry, I can't tonight. I have a test tomorrow, and I forgot to study for it, so it's gonna be an all-nighter."

"Aw ... well, I'll move it to tomorrow then."

Her teeth glint in the light. "Perfect. Wouldn't want to miss a second."

But her eyes ... her eyes are all over me, as though each glare is a tiny knife cutting away at my skin. And fuck me, it almost makes me moan right there and then.

"And bring your boy ... What's his name? Jason."

*Her boy?*

The mere mention of his name makes me want to cut out his heart and hand it to them on a silver platter. But if I did that, her father would definitely know I'm involved with her.

And then the Phantom Society would cease to exist.

She kisses him on the cheek again. "Of course. Love you."

But her eyes remain on mine, almost as if she wants to say "you will never hear these words."

But I can wait. I'll wait as long as I have to for a girl like her.

And one day ... she'll say those words to my face while she's on her knees, sucking me dry.

A wicked grin spreads on my lips as she walks away, leaving an air of death and destruction in her wake. "See you tonight."

I don't know if she said that to him ... or us.

*Was that a threat?*

*Fuck.*

"Boys," the dean says, turning to look at us. "You're dismissed."

We hop off our chairs like predators ready for a chase, but the second I open the door, the dean adds, "Don't forget ... no more fighting. Or I will resort to heavier punishments."

"Yes, sir," Nathan replies before he shuts the door behind us.

Down below, the last flicker of her black hair disappears behind the stairs, and I rush after her.

Too late.

She's already disappeared into the crowd of people, leaving me with a roaring heart, desperate for a chase.

# 23

## MILO

**Forty minutes earlier**

I happily chomp away at my apple, not giving a care in the world while I enjoy the shade up here in the tree. It's such a good fucking day that nothing could ever ruin it. Especially not some messages from Kai and Nathan asking me if I'm coming along tonight.

For just a minute, I'd like to pretend we're all just students trying to make it through college without all the serial murdering shit.

Though I have to admit, Nathan does look fucking sexy when he's covered in blood.

My blood would be better, but still.

I take another bite of the apple, but the piece barely makes it down my throat when I spot the girl in high heels waltzing across the pavement, headed straight toward me in that short black skirt and red button-down top that barely keeps her perky tits together.

And I must say, I can never, ever fucking get used to just how good she looks in real life compared to the videos and images Kai collected.

My dick twitches in my pants, still thick and filled with unmet desires from our previous encounter. Especially after Nathan added some tickling on top to make me extra squirmy. He loves seeing me unstable and on the fucking edge.

But I get the feeling she might be just as vindictive, if not more. And that alone makes it worth all of my time to ruin this perfect day.

\*\*\*

## LANA

I check my phone to see what and where my next class is after my break, but the second I walk past the biggest tree on campus, I shriek as something falls out of the branches.

An actual fucking dude.

Dangling upside down.

With an apple in his hand.

And it's not just any guy … it's Milo.

"What the f—"

"Hi, Lana!" he says with a cheerful smile.

I'm too shocked to even take another step. How the fuck is he even here right now?

"Headed somewhere?" he asks like it's totally normal to hang from a tree. Upside down.

Talking to *me*.

The girl he and his friends used in a dark alley and left all alone to deal with the mess.

Rage bubbles up to the surface, and I follow my instinct.

*PUNCH!*

Right in the fucking face.

His eyes roll into the back of his head, and he tumbles out of the tree while I step back to avoid any damage to my expensive Manolo Blahnik shoes. With a loud groan, he falls onto the grass all crooked and fucked up, but I guess he's still alive, considering he's still making sounds.

Too bad.

"Fuck …"

The apple rolls across the ground in front of me, and I kick it away. "Serves you right," I retort, folding my arms.

"God, that felt good."

I frown.

*What is up with him?*

"Are you insane?"

"Maybe. Do you like insane guys?" he muses as he scrambles up from the ground, patting himself down. "Because if so, I'm as crazy as they come."

I roll my eyes and waltz right past him. "Whatever."

"Hey, wait up!" he yells.

"No, thanks," I reply, keeping my head held high while I continue to strut.

But he keeps following me around, to the point that it gets me so fucking pissed I punch him in the face again when he's right behind me.

He groans, but it swiftly turns into a high-pitched moan as he clutches his bloodied nose.

"You made me bleed."

"Maybe you shouldn't keep following me around then," I retort. I fish my small knife from my pocket and point it at his stomach real close-up so no one can see. "I can make you bleed a whole lot more right now if you don't walk away."

"Oohh ..." He practically giggles and presses his body farther into the blade. "Don't tempt me, please."

My brows furrow, and I just stare at him, utterly confused by his reactions to my violent nature. He should be scared, mad, angry, hell, maybe even upset, yet he's the opposite.

I push the knife farther into his stomach and watch him hold his breath.

"For you, I'll happily bleed," he murmurs.

"Is that your way of apologizing for what you and your fucked-up buddies did?"

"I'm not sorry," he says. "But I am sorry you hated it when I loved it ... so fucking much."

"You're sick," I hiss.

"I'm not the only one."

The sparkle in his eyes makes it hard to look away.

*What does he mean with that?*

"Are you insinuating—"

When I attempt to punch him again, he catches my fist midair, and a wicked smile forms on his lips. "Yes. You like to cause pain."

I gasp, too flabbergasted to speak. In a rush, he suddenly pushes me all the way to the wall of the school building, pinning me to it.

"Don't act so surprised. You already knew how sadistic you were. You just never thought others would find out."

"No, I'm not. I don't like—"

"Not the mental pain." He grabs my hand and puts it against his reddened cheek. "Physical pain."

I slap him again, but even my second hand is caught midair, and now I'm truly trapped between him and the wall.

"You stopped me again. Why didn't you stop me earlier?"

The grin on his face only becomes bigger. "Just because I can doesn't mean I want to." He leans in so close I can feel his breath on my skin as his hand slowly lowers from my wrist to my face. "Now are you going to try to slap me again just for saying hi?"

I expected him to hit me back.

What I'm not expecting is the sweetest caress I've ever felt, and it knocks the oxygen out of my lungs.

"Or are you going to let me kiss you?"

His lips are so close I can almost taste them, his eyes on mine as though he wants to see my reaction.

But when his lips connect with mine, I bite.

He inches back and brings his fingers to his lips, showing the blood. "Fuck ... You know that only makes me want you more, right?"

"You enjoy pain," I rasp.

"Only realizing that now?" he jests.

"What do you want from me?" I growl.

He plants his hands beside me on the wall. "I want what you gave them." He tilts his head and whispers into my ear, "I want your body in exchange for the secret to be kept."

Rage boils up inside me. "You're despicable."

He raises his brow. "Is that a no?"

"You were there in that alley too."

His hand slowly slides down my face and across my chest. "I was there ..." He goes all the way down to my nipple and pinches it between his fingers so harshly I almost cry out with a moan. In broad daylight. In front of the entire school.

"But I've not nearly had my fill of you."

"Fuck you," I grit.

"Oh yes ... I would literally let a girl like you fuck me," he groans, lips hovering dangerously close to my neck. "I would be a beggar on his knees praying to your goddamn pussy like I'm going to heaven."

Jesus. I didn't know he was that desperate for me.

But why the fuck did that make my pussy throb?

"You've got balls, I have to give you that," I growl.

"Big blue balls," he jokes. "But I know you're more than willing to help me out with that ..."

Wow. He's really asking for a punch in the dick. "Why in the fucking hell would I?"

His hand covers my boob again, and he groans in my ear. "I can give you information."

Now he's got my attention.

I lean away to look into his playful eyes. "What kind of info?"

He looks around to see if anyone's watching us before he leans in to whisper, "I know where our next kill will be."

I suck in a breath at the thought of catching them in the act again.

If I can get there on time and take pictures, I'll have just as much dirt on them as they do on me. And then I won't be the only one with a secret on the line.

But I don't trust him.

It's too easy.

I narrow my eyes. "Why?"

"Why not?" He shrugs, casually running his fingers through his short red hair. "I mean ... you're just as violent as we are. I say, why not share the fun?"

"You'd betray your friends for me?"

He puts his hand up against the wall and leans in. "Well, it's not really betraying if they don't know you're there because of me."

I take in a deep breath and think about it for a second. "Okay, tell me."

A smirk spreads on his lips. "I will ... for a price."

My nostrils flare. "Fine."

I grab his face and slam my lips on his, putting everything I have into this single kiss. And even though I hate him and his slinky ass with every fiber of my being, I still kiss him like my life depends on it. But when his lips part to kiss me back, his tongue swirls inside and claims mine like he's wanted to kiss me since the day he set his eyes on me, and it catches me off guard.

Suddenly, his hands move away from my breasts, and he grips my face, slamming me into the wall as he kisses me so hard my brain goes numb, and for a moment, I'm too consumed to care I'm kissing one of the three worst boys on campus.

He groans into my mouth, tongue circling as he lavishly licks me, desperate for more. It's as though my mouth is the sole reason for his existence, and something about that makes my heart jump into my throat.

I pull back and stare at him for a second, confused by what just swirled through my body. Was it overpowering rage or something else? Something more dark and disturbing ... a type of hunger only satiated when I thrust a knife into a fucker's heart.

But this kiss ... it was nothing like the one he gave me in the Phantom Society.

"Satisfied?" I ask, wiping my lips to rid myself of the taste of him because I don't want to be reminded of what I just felt.

"Fuck no ... but it's a start." He grins. "I don't just want your lips, Lana." His hand drops down to my red top, and he pops one of the buttons, practically salivating at the mouth. "I want *all* of you."

I frown. "Out here?"

He bites his lip and pops another button. "I'll go naked with you anywhere, anytime, but if you want some privacy, I know a place."

Before I can even say a word, he's grabbed my hand and drags me into the building. "Wait!" His firm hand clutches mine so hard it's impossible to shake him off. I never knew a guy as thin as him could have that much strength. Then again, those fucking veins and that fighting skill do kind of give it away.

He pulls me up the stairs to the second floor, where there's an out-of-order bathroom, and he pulls a key from his pocket and shoves it inside.

"How do you have that?" I ask.

"Stole it from the concierge," he muses with a smile like it's the most normal thing to do on a college campus. "They haven't been able to get in here since I got ahold of it."

"There's only one key?"

"It's one of the older non-renovated bathrooms no one ever uses," he says. "So it's been a perfect place for some potheads to get high and wasted."

"You mean you and your friends."

I roll my eyes, but when he opens the door, he pulls me inside and shuts it behind us, trapping me inside.

There's a bunch of stalls to the right, and a whole room to the left filled with showers that haven't been used in ages. The place is grimy and smells like weed, and the small window in the back is barely large enough to let the fresh air in, let alone to sneak through.

A loud burst of steam exits through a vent in the back, and I shriek from the sudden noise.

Through the fog, he approaches like a stalker in the night, eyes lowered like a predator searching for prey, and my heart begins to race as I step back farther and farther until my butt hits the broken radiator.

And I worry for a moment this is gonna get rough.

A jacket slowly slips off his shoulders and falls to the floor as he loosens his cuffs and rolls them up. He reaches for his tie, a black one this time. The suits he wears are always a distraction to my eye because it makes him look sexy even when he shouldn't. He takes it off slowly, the top button on his white shirt coming undone too, tattoos peeking out from below. I swallow, unable to look away as he stops in the middle of the bathroom, clenching the tie.

"Are you going to tie me up again? Use me like your friends did?" I ask, contempt lacing my voice.

He tilts his head forward and suddenly wraps the tie around his wrists, making me gawk. "No ..." His knees slowly cave in on him, and he sinks to the cold, hard stones right in front of me. His eyes gaze up at me like he wants to worship me like I'm his goddess. "I want to submit. To be punished, to be hurt ... to be used. Command my body. I am yours."

# 24

## MILO

She stares at me in shock, but all I see is the beautiful, violent creature I would give my fucking life to. I barely know her, but I've seen enough to know she's exactly what I've been looking for.

Exactly what I've been searching for in Nathan too, whose callous touch makes me yield so easily. But his grip is harsh, uncaring, and the dynamic we share only exists because of his need to release his pent-up rage.

But this girl ... this girl has all the bottled-up desires, all the fucked-up darkness I crave ... even if she doesn't realize it yet.

But I will coax it out of her.

"Are you joking?" she asks.

I shake my head. "Would I be on my knees for you if I were?"

Her eyes narrow and I love how the confusion on her face is slowly making place for intense curiosity.

She steps away from the radiator, confidence slowly pouring back in. "You want *me* to hurt you?"

I lick my lips. "You've brought your bigger knife, haven't you?"

She snorts and loses the insecurities for arrogance, the kind that makes me hard as a rock without ever being touched. And she pulls it out of her pocket, dangling it in front of me.

"Of course I have. You didn't think I'd go anywhere without it, did you?"

A filthy smirk forms on my face. "Attagirl."

She walks closer and raises the knife, tipping up my chin with the blade. "You talk mighty for someone on his knees." She slips the blade farther and farther until the sharpness cracks my skin open right where my Adam's apple meets the blade.

I swallow. "You seemed like you needed encouragement, so I gave it to you."

"Encouragement?" The blade pushes farther until it breaks me open, and a drop of warm blood rolls across my skin, the heat setting my body on fire. "How's that for encouragement?"

Fuck, I love her disdain, the smugness; it turns me on so much my cock's already bursting at the seam of my pants.

"Yes," I groan. "Whatever you want."

"Anything?" she asks.

"Anything."

The cut becomes deeper.

"What if I cut you until you can no longer breathe?"

I close my eyes and suck in my last breath. "Then I'd be a lucky man to have taken my last breath shared with you."

Her eyes narrow as she stares me down and grips the knife tighter, her body hardening as she stands before me. But then she suddenly retracts the blade and cuts into my shoulder instead. A moan slips from my mouth as the blood stains my shirt.

"Fuck ..."

Another slice to the other shoulder makes my shaft bounce in my pants, stretching the fabric to its limit.

"That's for coming all over my body in that fucking house of yours," she grits.

*SLICE!*

The next one hits me right in the chest, and I groan with excitement and pain as the cut goes deep.

"And that's for tying me up and touching my nipples and coming all over me again in that fucking alley," she says through gritted teeth.

*SLICE!*

She crisscrosses over the previous cut, so there's an X on my chest, and my shirt falls apart. "And that's for letting your fucked-up friends use me!"

"Yes," I groan.

She grips my hair and forcefully jerks my head back. "Apologize to me."

"I'm sorry," I say.

"Do you even fucking mean it?" The blade cuts into my skin, but the pain doesn't faze me.

"I would beg you for forgiveness every fucking day for the rest of my life if you let me."

Her nostrils flare. She looks so fucking gorgeous when she's angry with me and everyone who ever did her wrong. "I never asked you to be in my life."

"Yet I'm here, in the flesh, at your disposal, ready for your every whim."

The knife suddenly hovers over my face right in front of my eye. "Why?"

"Because you're a vicious killer, and when I first saw you, I already knew all you needed was someone who you could take out all your rage on."

Her face contorts, and she mulls it over for a second, the blade still hovering dangerously close to my eye.

"Tell me I'm wrong," I say. "You can't because it'll be a lie. You crave someone to punish, and I'm here."

"I don't want to punish you; I want to punish *them*," she responds. "Kai and Nathan."

"They won't let you," I reply. "But I will."

"Is that why you let Nathan jerk you off in that alley?" she asks. "Does he tell you what to do? Does it get you off?"

Finally, she's beginning to recognize my depravity. "I serve whoever knows how to control me."

Her eyes glitter with interest as though she's finally beginning to understand what I'm offering her.

She leans away and pushes the knife into my chest, only to slip away the fabric, revealing all of my tattoos and the two piercings in my nipples. The tip slides underneath one of the bars, and she tugs at it until I hiss.

"You will obey me."

I moan with delight when she leans in and whispers close to my face, "Say it."

"I will obey you ... my queen."

The lewd smile that briefly tips up the corner of her mouth makes my cock twitch. It disappears as quickly as it came.

But I won't fucking forget.

Not a single second of this entire fucking day. No, scratch that, this entire fucking year.

She slides the knife down my body and slips it into my pants. "Open your zipper. Show me how hard you are."

I do what she asks, even with tied up hands, but I make it work, releasing my cock from its cotton prison. Her eyes slide over my length, her tongue running along her lips like she's enjoying the sight.

"Why the tattoos there?" she asks.

"My cock likes the pain most of all." I groan when she pushes the tip of her knife into my shaft. "Tattoos were the closest thing I could get to heaven."

"Heaven ..." she repeats, pushing it even farther in until the skin cracks, and I hiss when it bleeds. "A heaven like this?"

"F-fuck ..." I can barely contain my arousal as my length bounces up and down in the air just from her touching it with the knife.

"Fine then."

*SLICE!*

She cuts into the skin near my V-line, and blood oozes down across my dick.

"Jerk yourself off," she says.

I bring my hands down to my shaft, rubbing myself as rivulets of blood roll down my length, spreading the blood all over until my dick throbs and oozes with pre-cum.

"You like that?" she muses.

"Fuck, so fucking much," I groan, desperate for more. "Treat me like your fucking slut."

She gazes at my dick, and it springs to life like a celibate man smelling wet pussy.

Fuck.

"You want to be my whore?" she asks, grasping my chin to make me look at her.

"Yes, so fucking badly. I would do anything for you, my queen," I say, jerking off as hard as I can to her pointing that knife at my face.

"All right then. Make your fucking queen happy." She pulls away and sits on the sink beside the radiator, spreading her legs to show off her red-laced panties underneath that black skirt. And fuck me, I'm about to die and go to heaven if she starts playing with herself.

"Come here," she says.

I crawl to her on my knees, my eyes shifting between her face and her pussy, desperate for a taste.

"I see you looking," she mumbles, leaning back. "Take them off."

I lean in and gleefully hook my fingers underneath her panties, slowly slipping them down her creamy thighs, pushing them all the way down to her heels before I chuck them away.

Her legs spread even farther, allowing me to see what I've been missing out on all this time, and fuck me, from the smell alone, I understand why Kai was addicted after the first lick.

"Go on then. Stick out your tongue and lick like your life depends on it."

Fuck, I don't have to be told a second time to dive right in.

My mouth is all over her pussy like I'm a dead man tomorrow, sucking and nibbling at her slit with all I have in me. With my hands tied, it's impossible to grasp the sink to keep steady, and my face is buried deeper and deeper into her. But I don't fucking care for even a second that I might break my neck by leaning into her because if the last thing I tasted was this divine fucking pussy, I would die as a man blessed by the fucking angels themselves.

My tongue circles her slit, hungrily swiveling back and forth to taste all of her and give her every inch of pleasure she could ever wish for.

It's been so long since I last tasted pussy. The women or men who came for me were never harsh enough to bend my twisted soul, so I sought my solace in Nathan's wicked ways. But she ... she pulls out the tramp in me with ease, and it's about time she realized the power she holds over me.

"Fuck, harder," she moans, shoving my face in even deeper.

I groan with delight, smiling against her slit as I dig in and eat her out with all my heart.

When she begins to gyrate against me, I know I hit the right spot.

"That's it," she moans.

"Your clit is all mine," I say between licks. "All mine to enjoy, all mine to lick and suck and feel its explosion all over my mouth."

"You want it?" she asks.

I cover her pussy with my mouth and suck on her clit. "Yes, I want you to come all over my face."

"You think you deserve that?" She clenches my face between her thighs, forcing me to keep licking.

"I'll do anything to make you come for me," I groan, pushing my tongue into her crevice.

God, she tastes so fucking good, even my dick begins to throb along with her, pre-cum dripping out onto the stone floor.

"Keep jerking off then. Bring yourself to the fucking edge, but don't fucking come," she says.

"Fuck yes," I say, rubbing myself with both hands, trying not to fall over as I lick her senseless.

She rubs herself against my mouth, her wetness spilling all over me, making me so goddamn ready to shoot my load. But I persist and force myself to stop before I bust, leaving me with unkempt desire. Drawn-out moans slip from my mouth each time I bring myself to the brink, but her pleasure takes up all my attention as she leans forward and pushes my head in deeper.

Suddenly, the knife cuts along my back, and I whimper from the agony and bliss.

"Keep licking," she says. "Don't fucking stop until I tell you to, slut."

And I do. Despite every cut she gives me, every slice into my back, a little sliver of heaven is handed to me on a platter as I circle her clit. I feel it explode right as she thrusts an inch of the blade into my shoulder.

I howl from the burning sting as a stifled moan leaves her lips, and her pussy gushes into my mouth while warm blood oozes down my back.

"Fuck!" I moan against her slit, licking at her while swallowing down the lust so I don't combust immediately.

When her clit stops thumping, she opens her eyes wide and shoves me away so violently I fall back onto the stones. The oxygen is knocked out of my lungs as she sits on top of me and rips the knife from my shoulder.

I whimper from the wound it left in my flesh.

"You liked that, didn't you?"

"Fuck yes," I say.

"You wanna come?" she asks, placing the tip of the knife against my dick.

"Fuck, I'd give anything," I say.

She bites her lip in such a seductive way that I wish I could sit up and kiss her. "Say please."

It flows off my pussy-whipped tongue with ease. "Please."

She slides the knife along my dick like she's stroking it. "Come then. Just from the touch of this fucking knife that just penetrated your fucking skin."

The tip of the knife caresses my shaft, spreading pre-cum and blood. She slides it along my length, keeping her eyes on me—almost as if tempting me with the idea she could cut me there—and the mere thought sets me off.

I whimper from the pent-up arousal finally pouring out of me and come all over myself. She rolls the blade through the cum on my chest.

"All that cum without ever touching you," she muses.

"Fuck ..." I groan.

An arrogant smirk forms on her lips as she lifts the blade and pushes my chin until my mouth opens. "Now eat it like a good fucking slut would."

She pushes the knife into my mouth and forces me to swallow it, and fuck me, my own cum never tasted this good.

The knife skims across my tongue, but when she retracts it, it's all clean, and something about the twinkle in her eyes tells me she's oddly satisfied with me.

"Hmm ... didn't think you'd do it," she murmurs.

"I told you, you don't know the lengths I'd go to ..." I lick my lips to taste us both together, the closest I'll come to actually fucking her ... for now. "The depth of my fucked-up needs."

She bites her bottom lip and looks at me with confusion.

"Did you enjoy that?" I ask.

She furrows her brows. "What?"

"Hurting me."

She seems flustered and immediately gets off me. "Fuck."

I scramble off the floor and sit, admiring my new soon-to-be scars while she angrily scoops her panties off the floor, puts them back on, then waltzes to the sink and stares at herself in the mirror.

"It's okay if you did," I say.

"I wasn't asking for permission," she bites, glaring at me through the mirror.

A filthy smile spreads on my lips as I try to undo the wraps around my wrists. "But you did enjoy it."

Suddenly, she lunges at me and pushes the knife underneath my chin. "Don't. Don't fucking spin this around and make it look like you did this for me. I did this because you *begged* for it."

"And I'd do it again in a heartbeat," I say with a grin, but it makes her rage out loud.

"We had a deal. Now give me the information."

"I'll give it to you if you help untie me."

She frowns. "You tied it yourself."

I shrug, embarrassed. "A little too tightly from excitement."

She rolls her eyes, then thrusts the knife between my wrists, cutting through my tie.

"Hey!" I hold the two separate parts with a broken heart. "That was one of my good ties. I still wanted to wear that."

"Too bad; should've thought of that before you decided to hit on the violent girl," she retorts, throwing me a wicked glance.

God, I thought I couldn't fucking love her more, but apparently, I was wrong.

The fucking bite of this girl is amazing.

Her hand suddenly dives into my pocket, and she takes out my phone, then grabs my finger and smashes it against the screen.

"Fine, you won't tell me? I'll find out myself."

"Hey!"

I struggle against my own ties as she searches through my phone.

"Interesting text messages," she mumbles. "So your buddies *are* on that same site. I knew it. No wonder we met during a kill. They were already perusing the site, looking for a kill."

"Those messages are private."

"So was my interaction with Kai, yet you and Nathan somehow knew all about that," she says, tilting her head to look down at me while scrolling through my app.

"Hey, I can't help he was spying on you," I say.

But I immediately regret it the moment I say the words out loud.

Because from the way her pupils dilate, this is new info to her.

And I just fucking spilled the beans on the one thing I promised not to tell.

*Fuck.*

"What did you just say?"

"Nothing."

She immediately pushes the knife against my throat again. "Tell me. Right now. Are there cameras in my room?"

Well, if I'm being threatened like this, I'm sure the bros won't mind if I spill the beans. "Yes."

She looks like a motherfucking dragon ready to breathe fire. "FUCK!"

She retracts the knife, only to chuck my phone at my face.

"Wait, don't tell Kai I was the one who told you," I say as she marches toward the door. "He will kill me. Slowly. And it won't be any fun."

"Fuck that," she growls back as she storms out. "He won't because I'm going to fucking kill him."

Wow.

I don't know whether to be scared or deathly turned on.

Probably both.

# 25

LANA

I can't even cope with how fucked up that whole encounter with Milo was and how conflicted it made me because I'm too consumed with rage to even care.

I head straight for my sorority and run upstairs. Halfway across the hall, I bump into Irina.

"Lana? What's up? You seem in a hurry."

"Sorry, have to get to my laptop," I reply.

"School?" she asks.

"No. Boys."

She grins as I pass her. "Oh ... boys. *Multiple*? Nice."

Well, it's anything but nice, but I don't want to involve her in this mess I've created.

"Don't tell anyone." I wink at her before I shut my door and look around.

Rage bubbles up to the surface as I scan the area, trying to compose myself, but the more I think about just how much of an obsessed maniac this fucker must be to put actual fucking cameras in my room, the more I'm beginning to lose my shit.

Grunting, I tear away at my pillows, look under my bed, under my desk, my chair, my notes, all of my books. My shelves come undone as I rip everything apart and check behind each item. Nothing is left unscathed.

Until I finally find it.

A tiny square box with a camera and a wireless transmitter.

"Motherfucker," I mutter, staring straight into the camera.

I crush it in my hand, boiling over with anger.

Suddenly, my phone buzzes, and I almost crush that too in my rage.

**Dad: Come to my office. Now please. I want to speak with you.**

Great. Just when I'm about to set loose my inner demon, my father forces me to behave. Can't explode in front of the entire school.

"Everything okay in there?" It's Irina.

"I'm fine. I'm fine. Just some annoying texts," I reply.

"Those boys again?" she muses.

I throw myself down onto the bed. "Yup."

"Well, if you need someone to talk to, I'm always here," she says.

"I really don't want to talk about it. But thank you for being there," I say.

"Of course. My door's always open," she replies. "Well, I'm gonna go to my next class. See you tonight!"

"See ya!"

But I don't think I'll be here tonight.

Definitely not tonight.

Not when I know exactly where to find those fucking boys, thanks to Milo's info ... and I'll absolutely be there waiting for them.

When Irina's gone, I exit my room and head downstairs and straight out the door, making my way back to the main building where I just fucked with Milo.

Good God, that fucker is insane.

But in a sort of messed-up, arousing way.

I don't know how to explain it, not to me nor anyone else if they ever asked. But that twisted fucker got me off so good while I was able to unleash all of my anger issues onto him, and the release that followed ... fuck. It was unlike anything I ever experienced.

But I have to stop fucking thinking about it, or I'll drive myself insane with lust all over.

Fuck, those boys really pull the worst out of me. And to think I'd actually enjoy it ... No wonder Jason could never get me off.

I run up the three flights of stairs to the dean's office, but I pause in front of the door when I hear familiar voices that make the hairs on the back of my neck stand up.

"My family is in jail."

*Nathan.*

"That is not a fault of ours." That's my father. "And we have done all we can to help you and your family after the feud between you and my son."

"And those damn friends of his."

*Kai.*

My hand rests on the doorknob, sweat drops trickling down my back.

They're in there with my fucking father.

My enemies.

I jerk the handle and throw the door open, but when my eyes connect with theirs, I feel something other than the mere need for vengeance; excitement.

And the thrill on their faces when they see me in the flesh, totally unabashed, unshaken by their destruction of my dignity.

Because I am the motherfucking queen of this campus, and they'll have to rip this crown from my goddamn head after I'm buried six feet under if they want to subdue me.

So I barge in and head straight for my dad, planting a kiss on his cheeks while he's in the middle of berating those boys. "You called for me?"

\*\*\*

# KAI

**Later that evening**

Blowing out smoke from my cig, I check my watch. 11:00 p.m. The exact time Nathan arranged for a meetup with a stranger at the Shack, just beyond the school grounds and a little bit down the road. It's an old, run-down house that hasn't been rented or sold in years and mostly used for illegal parties by students from the school.

A perfect place to commit a crime in the dark of night.

Nathan pretended to be a young kid to lure an old rich fucker into coming here, and I'm antsy to see the shock on his face when he sees all three of us grown-ass men waiting for him.

When a car slowly comes up the hill, I flick my fingers. "Milo. My knives."

He stops sharpening them and throws them over.

I tuck them into my pocket and throw away the cigarette. "Thanks."

I put on my mask, and Milo does the same. Nathan takes a huge drag of the cig until there's only a bud left, and he chucks it onto the ground, then puts on his mask. "I'm so fucking ready for this."

Milo winces as he adjusts his coat as though his shoulders hurt.

"You okay?" Nathan asks, narrowing his eyes.

"Yeah, yeah," Milo says, clearing his throat.

"Hide in the bushes," I tell him. "We'll wait inside and trap him. Make sure he doesn't escape."

"Gotcha," Milo replies, as I follow Nathan into the house, and we each take a side of the hallway; him in the living room, me in the kitchen.

The car stops, and my heart begins to beat in my throat. Not from fear but from excitement because I know what's about to happen, and the bloodthirsty monster in me wants to be set loose.

The door opens and I hold my breath.

"Hello? Anyone there?"

We wait and signal each other.

"Little boy, are you here?" I can hear his old age from his voice alone. "I've brought a candy bar and some cool toys. Wanna see?"

I wink at Nathan, and we both jump him at the same time. The man falls to the floor, screaming.

"Help! Help!"

"No one's coming to help you, old man," Nathan growls.

"Please, don't hurt me," he says.

I throw Nathan the rope. "Don't move," I threaten the old man with my knife, then direct my attention toward Nathan. "Tie him up."

Milo bursts into the front door. "You got him?"

"Help me tie this fucker up," Nathan commands, and Milo immediately springs into action.

Nathan and Milo tie his hands together and then lift him.

"Put him on the chair in the living room," I say.

"Let me go!" the fucker yells, crying. "What are you doing?"

Nathan and Milo place him on the chair, and I'm on his neck with my knife.

"Please, I haven't done anything," the man says.

"You really think so?" Nathan pulls out his phone and shows him the text exchange they had. "Or are you going to pretend this wasn't you, Harvey?"

Harvey's eyes widen. "That ... but that's ..."

"Me." Nathan grins maniacally. "You've been talking with *me*."

"No, no, no," the man stutters. "This is a mistake. I didn't—"

I slam the knife into the chair's armrest. "You tried to get it on with a little boy."

"I didn't have any plans, I swear," Harvey says.

"Sure you didn't." Milo laughs. "And I'm not a fucked-up masochistic bastard."

"Well, I ..." the man stutters. "I don't know what you want. I just want to leave."

I clutch the armrests. "You won't be leaving."

Tears run down his cheeks. "Please. I don't want to die."

"Oh no, you won't get to die ..." Nathan says, licking his lips as he grips the man's shoulders from behind the chair. "We're just going to have some fun with you."

"What? Why?" He desperately shifts his head among all three of us, looking for a sliver of humanity. But he won't find it here. "I haven't done anything."

"I don't believe you."

Nathan snatches my knife from the armrest and slams it into the fucker's thigh, and he yelps out in pain.

"Please, stop!" Harvey cries out.

"How many more boys have you been to, Harvey?" Nathan grits. "How many of them pleaded with you to stop?"

Nathan pulls the knife from his leg only to jam it into the other.

"How many of them did you ignore?"

"Please, don't kill me!" he begs, tears rolling down his cheeks.

I snort. "You're a menace to fucking society. Scum like you don't deserve to live."

"But we might let you ..." Nathan twists the blade in his leg until he screams in agony. "If you tell us your fucking bank account details."

Suddenly, something rustles in the bushes outside, making us all look away from Harvey.

"What the fuck was that?" Nathan growls.

I point at the hall. "Milo. Go. Check the area. I don't want visitors."

"HELP!" Harvey screams, so I punch him in the face to shut him up.

There's some ruckus outside, and I can hear Milo's nunchucks whipping through the air, along with the sound of groans.

Nathan looks at me. "We've got company."

More grunts emanate from outside, and Nathan barges toward the hallway to see what it is.

"Don't."

Nathan stops in the middle of the living room, clenching his fist. But he's not the only one.

I'd recognize that voice anywhere.

*Lana.*

She wasn't joking when she said she'd see us tonight.

Fuck.

She enters the house wearing an actual fucking latex bodice and jeans along with that same kitty mask as the first time I saw her. And fuck me, just the mere sight of her in that outfit makes me want to rip it off and fuck that pussy raw.

Her knife is against Milo's throat, his hands clutched behind his back.

Nathan stares at them in disbelief. "What the f—"

Milo rarely loses a fight.

"On. Your. Knees," she grits at Milo.

And he sinks to the floor, whimpering from her knife against his throat.

Nathan fishes out his own knife, but Lana pushes her blade into Milo's neck even farther.

"One step and I slit his throat," she says.

"You fucking wouldn't," Nathan growls. "Don't you fucking dare!"

"Wanna test me out?" she asks, tilting Milo's head with her blade.

"I'm sorry, Nathan," Milo pleads, looking up at both of us.

"How did you even fucking win against him?" Nathan grits.

"Does it matter?" I say. "She's here now. How the fuck did you even find us?"

The crazy smile that forms on her lips almost makes my cock twitch. "You're not the only one who knows how to stalk someone ..."

Oh fuck. Now that really made my cock bob against the fabric of my pants.

"But I have your fucking friend to thank for the exact details," she adds, glancing at Milo.

"What?" Nathan growls, staring at Milo, who looks up at him with guilt lacing his eyes. "You *told* her?"

"He ratted you out," she muses, proud of her accomplishment. "After I gave him what he wanted."

And fuck me, I thought I couldn't fall any harder, but apparently, I could. What a devious little fucking kitty.

"What *he* wanted?" Nathan parrots, and he glares at Milo.

He looks like he's lost himself. "I'm sorry. She made it impossible to deny her."

She leans in to whisper something into his ear. We can't hear it, but the look on Milo's face as he melts away tells us enough. He's smitten.

Nathan points his blade at her. "You ..."

Fuck.

Lana suddenly shoves Milo face-forward and thrusts her knife mere inches from my face. "You put a fucking camera in my room."

Oh ... now I understand why she's so upset.

She fishes something from her pocket and chucks the debris at me. "Here's what's left of it."

*SLICE!*

I narrowly avoid a cut in the face as I lean back and grasp her arm midair, but she swiftly jerks free and starts to fight me.

Nathan aims, but Milo throws his nunchucks at the knife, which clatters onto the floor.

"What the fuck, Milo?"

"Don't hurt her," he says. "Please."

Nathan storms at him and grips him by the throat. "Are you out of your mind?"

But I'm far too busy fending off Lana's attacks as she strikes left and right with her knife, nearly puncturing my skin like she wants to kill me.

"Is that how you fucking knew my login info?" she yells. "You watched my laptop?"

"That's not all I watched," I muse.

*SLICE!*

She cuts into my arm, the warm blood oozing from my skin.

"You had no fucking right!"

Suddenly, Harvey jumps up from his chair and attempts to run off through the other exit.

"Nathan!" I yell while trying to stop Lana from thrusting her knife into my chest. "Harvey is getting away!"

But he's far too busy with Milo, who's attached himself to his legs like a bunch of bricks.

Lana's eyes follow the man, and right before he exits through the door, she stops fighting me and chucks a knife right at his neck. A whelp follows a thud as he drops to the floor, blood pouring from the wound.

"There. Solved your fucking problem."

"Fuck!" I yell.

"What happened?" Nathan calls, dragging Milo by the arm.

"Harvey is dead," I say.

Lana whips her knife around my face, and we continue to dance around each other, avoiding each other's strikes.

"What?" Nathan growls, incensed as he shoves Milo away and storms at Lana.

I grip her arm right before another strike and say, "No. I'll deal with her."

I push her to the back near Harvey's body and shove her back along with both arms into the wall. An *oompf* leaves her mouth as the knives are knocked from her hands and clatter to the floor.

"You shouldn't have fucking done that," I tell her.

"You talked to him on that site, didn't you? Same old fuckers as I track down. Dying was the only gift he had left for this fucking world."

"That was *our* kill," I reply.

"He was running off, and I took care of it before he had the chance to go and tell the world what you were up to." She gloats. "You're welcome."

The fucking arrogance. God. She's so fucking attractive when she makes that face.

But I shouldn't let myself get distracted.

"You got Milo to reveal our plans?"

"He gave them to me after I played with him a little ..." she muses, glancing at a seething Nathan behind me. "He willingly went to his knees for me."

"Milo ..." Nathan says through gritted teeth, and he grips Milo by the hair and tilts his head back.

"I can't help it. She's just like you. So fucking violent and ... God, amazing."

I'm impressed. Milo never bows to anyone but Nathan, not even me, yet ... she managed to weaken his resolve and subdue him.

Guess I'm not the only one who's become obsessed with this girl.

"You were spying on me," she says.

A smirk forms on my face. "I don't hear a question, kitty."

"Where are you keeping the videos?"

With my hands still firmly lodged around her wrists, I lean in to whisper into her ear, "Safely hidden away on my laptop, where I watch them every fucking day."

Her face ripples with anger.

"I've watched you while you were concocting your plans ... I've watched you while you were talking with your friends ... I've watched you undress." My lips hover closely to her neck, and I brush them along her skin, unable to stop myself any longer. "I've watched you play with yourself under the covers of your bed after your boyfriend failed to satisfy you."

She shudders when I place a soft kiss on her neck.

"And I jerked off along with you, imagining I was touching you instead."

She whimpers when my teeth come out and bite her right below her ear. When the blood rolls, I suck so hard it leaves a hickey on her skin.

"Fuck."

She thinks I didn't hear, but I definitely did.

And I don't believe for a single second I'm the only one who's lost control of their desires. And what I desire more than anything is writhing right in front of me. She's trying to fight me every step of the way even though we both know this will only end one way—with her tight pussy wrapped around my eager cock.

So I release one of her wrists, only to grip her face and smash my lips onto hers.

# 26

## LANA

I'm completely taken aback by his sudden kiss, unable to move, to even process what's happening until it's too late. His lips are on mine, searching, coaxing, tongue dipping out to crack open my mouth and invade it with ease. And when he probes around my mouth, I'm helpless against the lust building inside me, coursing through my body like poison injected straight into my veins.

As his body smashes into mine, my tongue swirls around his with just as much passion. I can't fucking stop. The groan that emanates from his body as he claims my mouth is beyond this world, so fucking possessive that I can't push him away even if I wanted to.

His hand travels down my neck to where he bit me, circling the wound before sliding down my breast, cupping it, rolling my hardened nipples between his fingers, forcing the arousal to take over. He kisses me so hard and fast I'm out of breath and out of the will to resist.

"What the fuck, Kai?"

Nathan's voice makes me pull away, and we glance at Nathan and Milo, who are casually staring at us like we've lost our damn minds.

I most definitely have.

When Kai turns back to me, I slap him. Hard.

He merely stays there, the stain on his cheek growing redder and redder.

He releases my other wrist too, and his hand moves to his face to touch the spot I marked.

I slap his other cheek with my newly freed hand, biting my lip, enraged at the fact that he'd kiss me, but even more enraged by the fact that I'd gleefully go along with it.

*How dare he?*

*How dare he make me feel so fucking hot for him?*

*God, I fucking hate him so much.*

Yet those lips stained with my red lipstick draw me in so much that I hover closer and slam my lips on his again even though I know I shouldn't. And my arms immediately wrap around his neck as his tongue bores into my mouth, his kisses so rough and greedy that I've become addicted.

He shoves me right back into the wall, hand gripping my throat, squeezing tighter and tighter with every passing second as though he's waiting for me to pull back and force him to stop.

But I'm too lost in his possessive kisses to even care about losing my breath.

That's how fucked up he's gotten me.

As my vision grows dark, his fingers release from my neck, allowing the oxygen to flow back to my brain, and I suck in a breath when his lips unlatch from mine.

"I knew you would come to me ..." he murmurs. "Come to offer your lips to me, little kitty?"

*Fuck. What the hell am I even thinking? Kissing him a second time?*

"Fuck off, you trapped me," I respond.

The foul arrogance on his face makes me want to slap him a third time. "Yet you kissed me again out of your own volition."

I spit in his face.

He just makes me that fucking angry.

He wipes it off slowly, his fingers tightening around my throat again. "I warned you the last time ... bad kitties get punished."

"Can't ... breathe," I mutter.

"Good. Your breath belongs to me."

*Oh my God.*

"I want you to remember this feeling. This need creeping up deep inside your chest," he says, his fingertips traipsing my chest. "Submission." He tips down my chin until my lips forcefully part. "You are mine. All of you. That was our deal. And if you're so intent on being a hissy cat ... then you'll swallow it all."

And he shoves his fingers, along with my spit, into my mouth, rubbing them on my tongue in the far back of my throat until I cough.

But all I can think of is that one breath I need.

"Swallow."

I do precisely what he says just so his fingers will unlatch.

"Good girl."

His fingers unfurl, and I struggle to suck in the breaths before I lose it entirely.

"Now tell me why you came here."

"You ruined my life. It's only fair I ruin your kill," I respond.

"*You* ..." Nathan growls behind me as he steps up. It's two against one now. "Do you have any idea what you've done?"

"You lured him here to kill him, no?" I raise a brow. "Job done."

Nathan drives his knife into the wall beside my head, startling me.

"We needed his money!"

"Money?" I frown, snorting. "Why? Aren't you rich?"

His eyes narrow, but he doesn't respond, which tells me everything I need to know.

"*Was.* Was rich," Milo says from the back.

Jesus. And here I was thinking these boys were wealthy as fuck. Must be some fall from grace.

Nathan throws him a damning glance before continuing. "It's none of your concern. You stole what I needed. Twice. And you're going to pay for it."

I snort. "What do you want me to do? I can't bring him back to life."

"Maybe you guys should've told her you wanted to keep him alive?" Milo muses.

"Shut up," Nathan and I say in unison.

Kai steps aside to allow him access, but he's still got his hand around my throat.

Nathan tilts his head, a devious smirk slowly forming on his face. "I know how you can repay us." He pulls the knife from the wall and brings it to my chest, toying with my nipples right through the fabric of my top as he leans in to whisper into my ear, "You're going to fucking offer up your own hard-earned money."

He fishes in my pocket, filtering out all of my belongings, finding only mere change.

"Where do you keep it, Lana?"

"You're out of luck, bud. I don't have what you're looking for," I say. "My father has a tight leash on the money. And I've already spent most of mine this month."

His nostrils flare, rage overflowing behind his eyes.

"Then you'll offer up your beautiful fucking body."

My eyes widen. "What?"

"Or I could show your family all the proof from your killer side business," he says.

Vindictive son of a bitch.

"Oh, you dirty bastard," Milo muses. "You just want her for yourself."

"Fuck off. You already had your turn," Nathan grits at him, but his eyes are still homed in on mine. "If I can't have the money, I'll take the fucking pussy instead."

"No," Kai interjects, his fingers still clasped around my throat like he doesn't want to let go. "I'm going to teach her a lesson first about interfering with our work. And then you can have your way with her."

Suddenly, he pulls me away from the wall and drags me to the shoddy wooden chair in the middle of the room. The one that fucker called Harvey was sitting on moments before I killed him. Blood stains the wood.

"Sit. On your knees."

I frown but still do what he says, perching my knees on top of the seat.

He walks to the front and drags the chair around until I'm facing the dead body on the floor, and my ass points at the dirty couch in the back of what used to be a living room.

Kai's hand softly caresses my ass, setting my senses on fire as it slides farther down. "You belong to me, and you will learn to fucking take it like a good girl."

*RIP!*

He cuts through the fabric of my jeans and panties in one go.

"Now bring your fucking fingers to the back."

"What?"

He moves away, and when I glance at him over my shoulder, he's sat on the couch, legs spread, hard bulge clearly showing, an ominous grin beneath that mask so obvious it makes my pussy clench.

"Touch yourself."

Nathan smirks as he watches my eyes fill with rage, and he folds his arms, waiting to see what I'll do.

So I bring my fingers underneath my body and start to play with myself, glaring at the soulless eyes behind that nefarious mask as I circle my slit.

"You're already wet, aren't you?" Kai muses from behind me.

My teeth grind together as I try to ignore the obvious, but it's hard when my fingers so easily slide up and down my slit.

Nathan's bulge grows, and he adjusts it before saying, "Guess I'll enjoy the show then."

He pushes himself off the wall and walks to the back, and I can hear him flop down onto the couch as well.

"Oh fuck ..." Milo groans as I hear him shuffle around.

"No. You go sit below her ass," Nathan growls. "You haven't earned a front-row seat."

Milo perches behind me, and I can hear him breathing heavily as I circle my pussy.

If I can't fucking escape this deal I made, I'll fucking give them the show of their lives.

"God, yes," Milo moans beneath me, and even though I hate it, his beggary ways turn me on a little as I swirl around my slit.

"That's it, kitty. Make it nice and wet," Kai muses.

Suddenly, I hear a clicking noise, and I stop and glance over my shoulder. Nathan's holding up his phone.

"Don't look at me. Look at that fucker you just killed."

"What?"

"Do it. Or I *will* send this video to your brother."

Grunting, I turn my head around again and look at the bloodied stain on the floor while pleasuring myself. My fingers dip in and out of me, spreading the wetness all over. The excitement to kill another fucked-up soul really gets me going like nothing else.

*Am I really that fucked up?*

"Getting drenched already, kitty?" Kai says. "Then fucking come all over those pretty little fingers and show us how badly you want to be owned."

Kai's voice sets me off, and I feel my pussy contract against my will, an orgasm rolling through me just from the sheer wickedness of this.

"Fuck, she's dripping," Milo says, and his tongue suddenly touches my inner thighs. "God, the fucking taste of you."

"Fuck no," Nathan grunts. He jumps up from the couch and shoves Milo aside, shoving the phone into his hand. "This pussy is mine to taste. Fucking tape it all."

Before I can even protest, he's already gripped my ass and buried his tongue deep inside my crevice.

"Fuck!" I groan as his tongue swirls around inside.

He drives in and out of me, lapping me up, all while Milo videotapes me like I'm some porn star getting her pussy eaten out.

And fuck me, right now, I don't even mind as long as Nathan continues what he's doing.

His tongue expertly rolls around my slit, setting my body on fire. And I can feel another orgasm building while his tongue bores into me.

Suddenly, he pulls away, leaving me bereft. He swiftly spins the chair around with me still on it, forcing me to look at the couch where Kai sits with his hand still down his pants.

"Watch him while I drive you insane and tell me how jealous it makes him that you're mine to use," Nathan grits.

He perches behind me and buries his tongue in my pussy, driving me mad with lust.

The look in Kai's eye as he watches me is nothing short of magical, the kind of rage I almost wish I could've given him myself. And it makes me want to gyrate against Nathan's face just to piss him off.

Judging from the way Kai just ripped all nine inches of his pierced shaft from his pants, I succeeded.

"Fuck," he grunts, slowly jerking off as Nathan's tongue plows into me.

Milo videotapes us from all sides, his hand rubbing his bulge as he watches us too, and I don't even care. I'm too overwhelmed by the sheer lust coursing through my veins as Nathan's tongue circles around, bringing me to the edge.

"God, this fucking pussy tastes so good," Nathan says. "No fucking wonder Kai couldn't control himself."

"Do you get it now?" Milo says, his eyes sparkling behind that mask of his. "That pussy is an addiction in itself."

"This pussy wasn't yours to bow to," Nathan growls. "It's fucking mine."

And he drives his tongue into me so wildly, my eyes roll into the back of my head. "Fuck."

He sucks at my clit and circles his tongue around it so good I don't even know whether I still hate him enough to want to kill him after all this is over. As I clench the chair with every inch of strength, my eyes can't help but find Kai's in the dark. His hungry eyes hidden behind that Phantom mask practically beguile me to tumble off the chair and crawl to him on my knees.

And when his pierced hard-on bounces up and down in his hands, almost ready to burst, I fall apart.

"Yes, come all over my tongue. Let me taste that ecstasy," Nathan mumbles against my skin.

And I do. I come so fucking hard I see stars, all while his tongue dips in and out of me, lapping me up like he's an addict looking for a fix.

And fuck me, I could almost go for another round.

"Good fucking God. Now I understand."

Nathan pulls away from my pussy only to march to my face, grip my cheeks, and smash his lips on mine.

His tongue drives into my mouth, forcefully claiming me, and I'm still too aroused to even care about biting back. Our tastes mingle in my mouth, the sweet and sour mix of sex making me want the kiss even more.

*Fuck, have I gone insane?*

"Enough," Kai says, and Nathan's lips unlatch from mine.

Kai gets up from the couch, stiff and ready to plow into me. "Let me feel just how wet that pink pussy is for us and see how far I can take her."

*Oh fuck.*

With a grin, Nathan wipes my juices from his chin and licks his fingers, then looks up at Kai. "I get why you're addicted."

Kai hooks his fingers underneath his hoodie and tears it off with his shirt. The devilish smirk on his face doesn't prepare me for the number of abs that appear from underneath. He's ripped in all the right places, scars marring his skin. Tribal tattoos decorate his arms and a giant Phantom logo is tattooed onto his chest with a date tattooed right underneath his heart.

*What could it mean? And why do I even care?*

"My turn," Kai says as Nathan steps away, but then he grabs the camera from Milo's hand and forcefully lowers it. "This part of her is all mine."

Milo swallows and moves away from us while Kai approaches me, only to rip my mask off my face.

"Hey!"

He grips my throat, silencing me immediately. "*Nothing* will stand in my way of claiming you."

I swallow as he releases me, and he circles me, only to perch himself behind me.

Nathan sits on the couch, hard-on dripping and on full display, and flicks his fingers. "Milo. Sit."

Milo walks toward him, but instead of sitting on the couch, he sits on Nathan's lap. Nathan zips him down, and now both cocks are dangling freely. And Jesus, is it a sight to behold.

But I can't even focus because of Kai's pierced length pushing against my aching pussy.

"Are you ready for me, Lana?" He grips my hair, forcing me to tilt my head and look at him. "Answer me, kitty."

"Yes. Get it o—"

I can't even finish my sentence as he rips right through my pussy, no-holds-barred, and my mouth turns into an o-shape as a drawn-out moan slips out involuntarily.

"What were you saying again?" Kai muses. "Oh, right ... words become hard when you're impaled by the only cock that could break you."

Fuck. He's such an arrogant asshole.

As Kai thrusts into me, Nathan holds a hand in front of Milo's face and says, "Spit."

Milo drools in his hand, and Nathan brings it down between Milo's ass.

And right as Kai pulls out and drives back inside, so does Nathan ... into Milo.

Holy shit. They're fucking.

I didn't know they were lovers.

"Fuck!" Milo groans as Nathan plows into him with every inch.

"Tight?" Nathan says, holding Milo's legs as he pulls all the way out again. "Good. You betray me, you feel the fucking burn."

And he plunges right back into his ass right in front of me. He raises Milo's body and flops him down on top of his shaft, again and again, railing him from behind. And watching them is kind of a turn-on.

Kai and Nathan move in sync, and Kai grips my hair so tightly I can't look away, even if I wanted to. It's almost as if he wants me to enjoy the same show I just gave them.

"How deep can you take me, Lana?" Kai murmurs into my ear, thrusting into my pussy. And I'm so fucking wet I don't even mind. "How far are you willing to dive into depravity with me?"

Suddenly, I feel his finger near my ass, and I gasp.

"You wouldn't."

"Bet." He spits down and dips his finger inside, using the spit as lube. "It's about time you felt what it's truly like to be owned."

He pushes in deeper and deeper until I can feel him everywhere, taking both holes at once, and the sensation of pleasure and pain mixes until I'm no longer able to differentiate the two. Staring at Nathan fucking Milo in the ass is not helping me conquer this lust either.

"Fuck," I hiss when he pulls out, leaving my pussy aching, needy ...

"Oh yes, you're ready for me," he groans, the sound of his hands sloshing as he spreads my wetness over his length drawing my attention.

"For what?"

"Hold the chair tightly, kitty. You're gonna need it to survive this."

My eyes widen when he pushes the tip against my ass and dips inside. I can feel each and every one of his piercings like a fiery burn as he enters me.

And he says, "Your ass is gonna be filled to the brim with cum as punishment."

# 27

NATHAN

I thrust into Milo's ass, watching Kai play with Lana, but all I can think of is being the one to plow into her.

I know he wants her. He wants to be the first to lay waste to her, but dammit, every time he thrusts inside her, I want to bury myself deeper into this little pretty boy's ass.

When did I become so obsessed with a girl who's been nothing but a thorn in my side?

Grunting, I take him deeper, forcing him to stretch around my girth, his moans only fueling my blazing fire. I'm taking all of my anger, all of my pent-up arousal, out on him, and he takes it like such a fucking good boy.

"Ride me," I command him, lifting his hips.

He does what I say, bouncing on my lap like he's been waiting for this. "Fuck, your cock feels so good in my ass, Nathan."

It's been too long since I last claimed him, yet now that I am, it doesn't feel the same. Not as fulfilling as what I would imagine taking her ass would be. And I keep my gaze fixated on her while I ram into Milo.

Kai buries himself inside her to the hilt and says, "F-fuck."

The faces she makes are nothing short of pure perfection, the pain making her squint. She looks so fucking beautiful while being punished for her crimes.

"God, fuck, it's so tight," she mewls.

The filthy smirk on his face makes me grin. "I'm not even two inches in."

Her eyes almost pop out of her skull. "What?!"

He shoves in even farther, and her body tightens against the chair, legs squeezing tightly, face all scrunched up.

"I'm going to slowly bury myself inside you, and you will feel every fucking inch of my cock stretching your core until your knees begin to cave." Kai grips her hair and forces her to look at us. "And you'll take it all with a smile like the good fucking slut you are, won't you, kitty?"

He pushes in even farther and pulls back her head. "Answer me."

She grinds her teeth but still hisses, "Yes."

I plow even harder into Milo, satisfied she's being punished for sabotaging our plans yet again. "That's it, use her real good."

"Oh, I haven't even fucking started," Kai responds, and he pushes in another inch.

Her pretty little nails dig into the wood. "Asshole."

"Oh yes, your asshole feels so fucking good when it tightens around my dick," he says, and fuck me, now I'm throbbing inside Milo's ass just from how dirty he is with her. "But it's gonna feel even better with my cum as lube so the others can have their turn too."

"WHAT?! I didn't say that—"

He plunges in even farther. "One more word and I will spear this ass down to my balls within one thrust. You understand?"

She swallows and immediately shuts up as he inches deeper and deeper. "F-Fuck ..."

God, she looks so appetizing, and I hate that I'm so turned on just from watching them. Fuck, this was supposed to be a punishment, not some playtime.

So I rip into Milo like there's no tomorrow, wasting all my rage on him. He moans and mewls like a good little boy. "Yes, take all of me up your ass."

"Fuck!" he groans, his noises making even Lana flush.

But then I see the ropes of cum spurting from the tip of his dick.

I snort. "Did you just fucking come?"

When he brings his hand to his shaft, I swat him away. "No. You don't get to finish properly after what you did."

He whimpers and mewls as I continue plowing into him, and I brush some of the cum off his thigh and shove my fingers into his mouth. "Taste your fucking ruin."

"Fuck," Lana moans again, and I can see Kai is almost buried to the hilt inside her.

"Just a little more, kitty ..." he groans. "I know you can take me."

But it's no fucking fun if he's the only one who gets to punish her.

"You know what?" I pull Milo off me, dick still bouncing up and down with need. "I'm not gonna sit here and watch. Milo, take her fucking mouth, but don't you dare fucking come until I say so."

"Oh ... Gladly," he moans, still high on the ecstasy of his ruined orgasm as he approaches her. And he tips up her chin and makes her look at him. "I'll be gentle with your mouth, my queen."

Her nostrils flare, but her lips still part when his dick hovers near her mouth.

"Don't you dare bite," I warn her. "Or I will bite equally hard into your nipples."

"Oh, she can bite. I don't mind," Milo muses as he slowly pushes inside.

"You'd only enjoy it, wouldn't you?" she grits.

Kai finally buries himself fully, and I can see it in her eyes, the simultaneous explosion of both pain and pleasure, like she just ascended to heaven itself.

And fuck me, it's exactly the kind of thing I love to see.

"Now take her mouth," I tell him as I circle up behind him and pinch his nipples.

Overtaken by the arousal I caused, he drives into her mouth, coating his salty cum all over her tongue.

"Fuck, that tongue feels so good," he says.

"Does she now?" I reply, positioning myself behind him. "Then I'm sure you won't fucking mind if I force you to show your fucking *queen* just how far we're willing to go."

And I push my tip against his ass and thrust inside with no remorse.

\*\*\*

## MILO

Fuck. The second her tongue starts to swirl around my shaft, Nathan drives into me, and my eyes nearly pop out of my skull. That's how good it feels. But he ravishes my ass so aggressively, forcing me farther inside her, all the way past her tongue until I hit her uvula, and she heaves.

"I'm s—"

He slaps my cheeks.

"Don't you fucking say it," he growls, grasping my chin to make me look at her. "She needs a good punishing. Now give it to her."

"Fuck," I groan, pushing even farther inside, way beyond her limit.

But I've never felt anything this intoxicating in my life. No amount of head can compare to the way her tongue wraps around my tatted-up shaft, her eyes growing watery from the sheer limits she's being forced to push.

"Fuck, your ass feels almost like it's a virgin," Kai groans, thrusting in and out. "Are you, Lana?"

When I pull out, she gasps for air. "No."

He slaps her ass, and she jolts up and down, but at the same time, Nathan drives into me, forcing me to plunge into her mouth.

"Don't lie to me," Kai growls. "I can feel it from the way your body tenses up. Your fucking boyfriend never did any of this, did he?"

As Nathan retracts, I do too, and she takes another wild gasp. "No. He's not my boyfriend."

*THRUST.* "Focus, Lana."

After another plunge into her throat, I pull out again, my cock throbbing with a need so dire I might defy Nathan's orders and spend it inside her after all.

"Fingers, yes. Cock, no," Lana finally responds.

A devilish grin forms on Kai's face, his eye sparkling with hunger. "Then your ass belongs to *me*."

He pulls out fully only to bury himself to the hilt inside her, making her moan so loudly it sets off all my buttons.

I ram back into her mouth, desperate for that feeling again.

"That's it. Make her regret she ever stepped foot in here," Nathan says as we move in sync.

Every time I pull out, I cover her face with a mixture of her saliva and my cum and then thrust back in again, the sight of her face destroyed so pretty I could come just from looking at her.

But fuck, if he doesn't stop tickling my prostate, I might just burst anyway.

I know he wants to punish me and make me feel bad for what I did, but looking at her now, being fucked by all three of us on that chair, I have zero regrets.

"Oh fuck, I'm gonna come," Nathan groans, plowing into me so fast I can't keep up.

And when I feel him combust inside me, I moan along with him, my balls tightening as they eject right into her throat.

She mewls with both surprise and delight as I coat her throat, coming harder than I ever have in my life.

And fuck ... I don't think I could ever settle for less either.

\*\*\*

## KAI

When both the boys moan, I look up and watch them hit the peak of their arousal. Lana's body tenses beneath me. The sheer force of Nathan shoving Milo farther into her as they both fall apart is too much for her to take.

God, all that fucking cum has gotten me a little too excited as well, and I bury myself to the hilt, howling like a wolf mad on lust as I jet into her ass. "There you fucking go."

"Fuck, it's so full," she mewls as I keep going, coating her insides with my seed.

I pull out of her, my cock still throbbing with need, still not satiated after that amazing sex.

Nathan pulls out of Milo and immediately approaches Lana's backside. "My turn."

"Move," I growl at Milo, and he steps away like he's afraid I'll spit fire if he doesn't.

I waltz to the front and rip my belt through the loops, pulling it out like a whip. Her eyes follow the leather as I wrap it around her neck. I fasten it closely to her skin, holding the long end as a leash. "Open up, kitty. Purr for me."

"Wait, but Nathan—"

Her words are interrupted by a sharp whelp as Nathan plows into her ass.

"Fuck! She's so goddamn tight," he groans, gripping her thighs.

"Motherfucker," she hisses.

I tug the leash, forcing her to look at me. "I told you we were going to fill you to the brim ... and we won't stop until every last one of us has had their fill of you." I push her chin until her lips part, and my cock dips inside her wet, delicious fucking mouth.

God, I worry there will be nothing left of her by the time we finish with her.

Nathan groans, enjoying himself on what belongs to me.

But I don't mind sharing as long as they all know their place.

Milo moves to her backside too, and he crawls beneath her and onto the chair with his head tilted. I can tell from the moans spilling from her mouth that his tongue has started to enjoy her taste.

So I grab the leash tightly and bury myself inside her mouth until the tears spring into her eyes, and her face becomes red. "That's it, kitty. Choke on my cock. Let me take your fucking breath away."

Her eyes practically roll back when I pull out, and I tighten the leash even further, only allowing her small gasps before I thrust right back in.

Every inch of her warped mind belongs to me, every thrust another scar added to her twisted soul until all she'll ever see and want is us.

\*\*\*

## LANA

Holy shit, I'm being railed on both ends and fucked in ways I've never been fucked.

I should hate it. I should hate it with every fiber of my being, yet I can't stop the wetness from dripping down my legs as my clit thumps from the sheer defilement of my body.

Every time Kai pushes my limits even further, I feel like a part of me is about to break.

Yet I don't even mind.

It's as if he's slowly fucking all the resolve out of me, and all that's left is a puddle of wantonness and disdain over how he made me submit so easily.

Fuck.

Milo's tongue swirls around while Nathan bangs my ass, and I'm being bombarded with sensations I can't imagine. Every inch of my body is being used, and I have never been so goddamn aroused in my entire life.

*What the fuck is wrong with me?*

"Fuck, she's dripping all over me," Milo moans, lapping me up.

"I'm not gonna last long if you're gonna lick me too, Milo," Nathan grunts, thrusting into me even harder.

"You both taste so good together," Milo whimpers.

But I can't even focus on what anyone is saying as Kai pushes my limits, his piercings scraping along my throat, making tears well up in my eyes.

"That's it, kitty. Take it deep like a good fucking slut," he groans, tugging at the leash. "Watch me destroy your every fucking resolve."

I can't even look away from that beautiful white eye of his that sparkles in the darkness like a beam of light straight from the depths of hell.

"I told you we would own all of you," Kai says as he pulls out for a moment to allow me a breath. "One more."

"One more what?"

A devilish grin forms on his face, the scar on his face almost striking fear into my heart. "Breath."

My pupils dilate when he pinches my nose and thrusts in deep.

Both of them drive into me at the same time, spearing me on both ends.

"God, your ass feels so good," Nathan groans behind me, and his fingers dig into my thighs as he pushes farther and farther with each thrust.

"Come inside her, fill her up to the brim," Milo eggs him on.

"Oh yes, and you're going to lap it all up like a good boy, aren't you?" Nathan says.

"I want it," Milo moans, his tongue circling my clit. "And I want this queen to come too."

"*Queen*?" Nathan seethes, plowing into me even harder than before. "There is no one you will fucking bow to but me."

Milo squeals, and I can only imagine what Nathan just did. "Ah, my nipples!"

Nathan howls out loud behind me as he jets into my ass, warm rivulets of cum running down my legs, followed by Milo's tongue.

"That's it, lick it all off her."

When I try to turn my head, Kai tugs at the belt, forcing me to look at him. "Eyes on me when I bury my cock inside your pretty little mouth."

I want to spit out *fuck you*, but it's hard with a massive hard-on shoved inside your throat.

Nathan pulls out of me, and I moan out loud from the way it feels. He slaps my ass, and it reverberates all the way to my needy pussy. I fucking hate how much it makes me miss him there.

"Milo. Stand."

Milo slips away from underneath me, and after a few seconds, he moans. "You like it when I touch you?"

"Uh-huh."

"Remember your fucking place," Nathan says.

"I'm sorry."

"Show us how sorry you are. Make her pay."

A new cock pushes up against my ass, teasing me.

"Fuck my cum deeper into her," Nathan says, his roguish voice dark and corrupt.

My eyes nearly jerk away if it wasn't for the fact that Kai's got an ungodly strong grip on my jaw. "I'm gonna fill up this throat too."

I shake my head. "But you already—"

"You will *never* be enough for me," he says, pulling out. "I want so much fucking more of this sinful body. But you're more than willing to give it to me, aren't you?"

He thrusts back in with no remorse and pulls out only to swipe my saliva across my face ... and then force himself right back in.

He leans in to look at me while he's balls deep inside me. "I will ruin you forever."

Right then, Milo slowly pushes inside my ass. I can feel it's him from the curve alone, and fuck me, I can barely take it.

"Stretch her to the limit," Nathan eggs him on.

"Fuck, so tight," Milo moans.

"That won't take long," Nathan muses.

*SLAP!*

My ass stings from his hand.

"Every second it takes, I'll add another slap."

*SLAP!*

"I'll make her bright red if you don't finish soon," Nathan growls.

*SLAP!*

"And if you don't ... I'll start slapping you too."

"Oh fuck, you know that only makes me hornier," Milo says, thrusting in and out of me.

"Good. Maybe if you're a good boy, I'll give you more dick later."

Milo's balls tighten against my ass right when Kai howls out loud. And within seconds of each other, they blow their loads inside me— one in the mouth, the other in the ass—making me clench the chair so hard it nearly breaks beneath my fingers.

"That's it, kitty, gulp down that cum."

I swallow it all down until he's finally spent, and when he pulls out, more cum drips out of my mouth. The belt releases from around my throat, and I can finally breathe normally again.

Milo finally spills out of me, and they all walk away from me like they're admiring their artwork from a distance.

"Perfect."

A bright flash follows.

I wasn't even aware Nathan was holding a phone.

That's how delirious I've become from sheer sexual madness.

"That's what you get for messing with our plans," Nathan muses.

"What are you going to do now? Call the police on me?" I ask.

Kai leans in with his hands on his knees while I can't even fucking move. "No, we're not savages. We'll have our men take care of the body later." The lopsided smile that forms on his face makes me want to chew through this chair I'm holding on to for dear life. "But you *will* be a good girl and do as you're told from now on ... right, Lana?" He tips up my chin and forces me to look into the mask. "Answer me."

"Yes."

A shit-eating grin follows. "That's my girl."

And they all grab their things and walk out the door, leaving me feeling like I just got bulldozed and run over a million times, all for killing that one man still lying in his own puddle of blood.

But fuck me ... it was worth it.

# 28

## KAI

**The next day**

"I'll give you nineteen hundred for that one," the pawnshop owner says as he inspects the Valentino bag.

*Fuck.*

After not being able to swindle that last guy we lured for money because Lana decided to kill him prematurely, this was supposed to be the last-ditch effort. But this ... "That's not enough."

"I'm sorry, kid. It's not worth that much when it's secondhand." He lowers his glasses. "I can add a hundred on top of that if you give me that ring of yours, though."

I lift my hand and stare at the ring my father once gave me after I'd made my first kill.

He was so proud of me.

A Phantom initiation ritual, he called it. My father and all of his friends once ruled this fraternity that I now lead. All of them went on to become some of the wealthiest businessmen in the world—some legitimate, some not so legitimate. None of it changed anything about who they were to each other; friends through thick and thin. Phantoms for life.

All because of the one secret they all carried to the grave.

I slowly push the ring off my finger and place it on the counter, the weight so heavy it feels like a drum is set off in my heart.

"Hundred."

A hundred might just be enough.

The pawnshop owner smiles at me and takes both items below the counter, then starts sifting through his register for the cash, licking each bill as he counts before he smacks them down on top of the counter.

"Two thousand, as promised."

"Thanks." I take the money and turn around to watch my mother freak out over a skeleton in the back of the shop.

"Kai, do we really have to be here?" she asks, barely touching a bone before jolting up and down. "It's so ... musty."

"Nope," I reply, tucking my money into my wallet. "I'm done."

"Wait, where's your ring?" She grabs my hand to inspect it.

I jerk back. "Sold it."

"¡Ay, Dios mío! Kai!" She throws me an insulted look. "You can't be serious. Your father gave you that ring."

"Sí. So it was mine to sell too," I retort, walking right past her as I waltz out of the pawnshop.

The doorbell behind me rings as she steps out. "Kai, wait."

"No, I have to get back to the Phantom house," I reply.

"Why do you need that money?" she asks, walking beside me. "Your father and I give you an abundant allowance every month."

I pause mid stride and look her dead in the eye. "Would you give it to me if I didn't tell you what it's for?"

She frowns. "Well... I mean ... if you need something."

"Not me. Mi amigo."

She licks her lips. "Un amigo ... Please tell me that Nathan boy isn't involved. You know that boy and his parents can't be trusted anymore. They've—"

"Fallen out of grace," I parrot as she's told me so many times before.

"Some things just can't be undone."

I look her dead in the eyes. "Would you give me the money?"

"No. Para nada."

*Of course she wouldn't.*

I walk back to the car.

"Do you know how expensive these last few months have been? Your eye surgery?"

A surgery that didn't work because I still can't fucking see shit through that eye.

"Besides, his family obviously can't be trusted with money."

"What?" I pause while opening the door.

"Well, with his parents being in jail, and everything they've done ..." She swallows and throws me a snooty look. "I honestly believe you should stop associating with him."

My brows furrow, and my nostrils flare. "After everything they did for us—"

"That is in the past." She interjects. "We've already been grateful time and time again. Enough is enough, and with you acting this way, selling your father's ring..." She grabs the door before I can throw it shut again. "Nathan Reed is a threat to our family. I need you to kick him out."

I stare her down just as harshly. "No."

I get inside, and she sits beside me with indignation marring her face. "What don't you understand? His family is dangerous. He keeps asking you for money. If we get involved in that stuff, we'll surely go down—"

"Since when are you afraid of cops?" I growl back.

"Well, I ..." She stammers without giving me an actual answer. "I didn't, I just—"

"Never mind." I hit the gas and turn out of the parking lot. "I'll deal with it on my own. Just like I always have."

"And what about Nathan?" she asks.

"Phantoms stick together," I reply as we race off. "Always."

\*\*\*

# LANA

I stare at my drink and the bubbles fizzing to the surface, but my mind has gone off somewhere else. More specifically, the Shack and all the dirty things that happened there.

I can still see the dead body in front of me, melting away in that pool of blood while those boys pounded into me.

Vicious.

Heinous.

So fucking disgusting.

Yet my pussy still thumps every time a memory of them using me springs into my mind.

I should not be thinking about this. But why can't I stop?

"Want a snack?"

I look up and almost jolt up and down from the sudden question.

Jason holds out a bowl of popcorn from which he's casually taking small bites. "Sweet and salty."

"Where'd you get that?" I ask.

"Stole it from the kitchen," he replies casually like it's the most normal thing to do. "Want some?"

"No thanks."

He shrugs. "Your loss." And he flops down beside me on the couch.

God, why did I have to bring him to my dad's house again?

Oh right, my dad wanted to meet him, thanks to Felix blurting out I was half-assed dating him or something.

Felix busts into the room and watches with keen eyes how Jason throws his arm around my shoulders. "Dad says the cooks will have dinner ready at six."

God, this fucking dinner at my dad's house could not come at a worse time.

Suddenly, Penelope sits between us. "Hi."

"Hey," I reply, shifting in my seat.

I'm happy she jumped between us, though. I really do not want his sweaty armpits all over me.

"Are you okay? You seem a bit off."

"Yeah, I'm fine." I tuck my hair behind my ear. "Just been a bit ... occupied lately."

"Spine Ridge does that, yeah," she jokes. "Though, I have to admit, it's mostly the boys that cause it."

"Yeah, that sounds about right," I reply, glaring at Jason.

She gives me a weird look. "What? I'm just here for the food."

"I don't mean him," I say.

"Oh ..." Her brow rises with piqued interest. "Well, tell me more."

I'm not about to tell my brother's girlfriend what I've been up to lately.

But maybe she knows something I can use against them. It's worth a try.

"Ah, never mind, it's nothing," I say, adjusting my long, glittery purple dress. "I just want to know why Felix would make that list, you know? I don't enjoy him trying to decide who I hang out with."

She frowns. "What list?"

*How does she not know?*

I pull my phone from my pocket and show her a picture I took of the list. "He told me never to talk to any of these people. Why?"

"Wow, interesting," Jason says, but I ignore him.

Penelope scoots uncomfortably in her seat. "Ahh ... those Phantom boys are just ... not a good crowd."

"You say that like the Skull & Serpent Society is any better."

She snorts. "Well, I guess you're right there."

"I just want to know if there's a reason."

"Oh, the Skull & Serpents and the Phantoms have never seen eye to eye from what I've been told. Even back in the day, when your dad was in there, there were always feuds between the different frat houses."

"Interesting," I reply. My father never told me about that.

In fact, I know shockingly little about his time before he met ... *her*.

I shiver at the thought of the woman who birthed me.

"Anyway, is that why Felix and all his friends fought with them?"

Penelope looks around to see if he's listening before she leans in. "Not just once. They fought several times, and those fuckers nearly got me killed."

"Wait, what? You almost died?"

"Well, sort of. We had this whole fight. Felix, Dylan, and Alistair were involved too. It was quite a mess."

"Yup," Jason says, laughing. "I mean, I wasn't there for most of it, but when I was, it always felt like an all-out war between us and them."

*Is that why they hate me so much? Because Felix is my brother, and I'm related to the Skull & Serpent Society? Or is it just because I caught them in their dirty schemes and this is all just a mad coincidence?*

"Don't tell Felix I told you all this," Penelope adds casually like it's nothing.

"Oh no, I would never," I reply.

"It'd only give him more reasons to kill me too," Jason muses, putting his hand on my knee.

"So why do you want to know about those Phantom boys in particular?" she asks.

"Oh, no reason. Felix just seemed to really hammer down on me about not even making eye contact." I laugh.

"Baby, all you ever need to look at is me." Jason flexes, making me gag.

Penelope laughs. "Don't worry about any of it. We settled it all. Those boys are not your problem; they're ours."

If only she knew.

"Those Phantom boys did community service for their crimes."

"But why were they fighting with you guys to begin with?"

She rubs her lips together. "They bullied my sister. We lost her."

"Oh ... I'm so sorry." I take a sip of my drink.

"It was a long time ago," Penelope responds. "We made sure they paid the price for their bullying."

No wonder Felix didn't want me to hang out with them. Now I'm even more conflicted about the fact that I seemed to enjoy the wicked games they play with me.

Someone behind us clears their throat, and we both turn our heads. It's the head chef. "Dinner's served."

We get up and move to the table, where my father is already seated. Felix comes in and sits beside Penelope, pressing a greedy kiss to her cheek before he folds his arms and impatiently starts tapping his foot.

Meanwhile, Jason sits beside me and kisses my cheek to imitate them, but he feels a lot less welcome. I guess I'll just stomach it and sit through this to get it over with. I know my father has wanted to meet him for some time now.

"Jason, right?" my father says when he lays eyes on him.

Jason leans over the table to shake his hand. "Yes, sir, nice to make your acquaintance."

*Oh Jesus.*

I grab my glass of water and take a large sip.

"So ... you're the boy who's got my daughter's heart?"

I almost cough up the entire glass. "No."

My father frowns. "Felix told me you were seeing him."

"Well, we are sort of dating," Jason says.

"No, we're not," I reply.

My father looks at Felix, but he only raises his hands. "You just asked me if she was seeing anyone."

Penelope giggles beside me.

"So which is it?" my father asks.

"It's undefined," I reply.

"She's shagging him," Felix says, folding his arms. "I told her it was a bad idea."

"Hey!" I lean forward to glare at him. "I don't remember asking for your permission."

"Lana, Felix, please, no fighting," my father asks, and I try to simmer down for him, but it's so hard when Felix keeps being all up in my business.

"I was just ... having a good time with Jason, that's it," I mutter under my breath.

He squeezes my leg under the table, making it even more awkward.

"What's up with you lately?" he whispers into my ear. "You haven't dropped by my room in weeks."

"I've been busy," I whisper back.

The chefs enter the room with a ton of plates. "The first course of this evening. Foie gras parfait with port wine reduction and parmesan emulsion." The chef places the plate down in front of me.

I make a face and look up at my dad, who seems elated by the food, but all I can think of is how many geese suffered for this.

"Our next dish will be wagyu beef strip loin with peppers and an array of steamed vegetables. For your dessert, we have selected the finest soft-baked chocolate, creamy caramel, pretzel Rocher, and local ice cream."

"Delicious," my father says.

"Enjoy," the chefs say, and they all walk away.

My stomach is roaring, but I'm not eating that.

Meanwhile, Jason scoops it up like ice cream, making me want to throw up.

"Aren't you going to eat, Lana?" my father asks as he takes a bite.

"I'm on a diet," I reply, picking off a piece of the lettuce beside the foie gras, and I put it in my mouth to pretend I'm enjoying my food. "Saving some space for dessert."

"A diet? With your figure?" Penelope says, equally unamused by the foie gras, as she pokes at it with her fork.

I throw her a look. "I'm waiting for the main course."

"You can just say you don't like liver," Felix says, stabbing the foie gras like it's still alive. "I don't."

My father sighs as he puts down his fork. "Kids ..."

*Kids? Really?*

"I thought you said you wanted one-on-one time together?"

"That was her idea, not mine," Felix balks.

"Hey!" I clench my fork tightly. "That's not fair, and you know it. I didn't say we needed to have dinner. I just said—"

"You wanted to feel more like a family." My father interjects.

A blush creeps onto my cheeks. "Right."

"Well, we're here together now," Penelope says, but her face reveals the situation's awkwardness.

"Yes. My family together as one. Let's not fight over something as petty as food." My father flicks his fingers at the chef waiting in the corner. "Bring my daughter something else."

"Of course, sir."

The chef quickly comes to take my plate.

Felix stares at me like it's my fault they didn't take his too.

"So, Lana, how are your studies coming along?" my father asks as he takes a bite.

"Oh, it's fine. I'm getting good grades, and it's not that hard so far," I lie.

I don't want him to worry about me.

"And have you made friends besides Crystal, and of course Jason?"

"Definitely," I reply.

"Irina and ..." Penelope mutters.

"Brooke," I say.

"Right. I've seen you around with them. At one of the Rivera clubs too, right?" she muses.

My veins grow icy cold, and I put down my fork. "I wasn't feeling well that day."

"That's a shame," my father says. "I mean, you should be able to enjoy your time off at campus while you still have it."

I frown. "What do you mean?"

"Well, once you finish with your studies, much work will be waiting for you. I suppose it'll all depend on how much your future husband will take on so that you'll still have some time—"

"I'm sorry, what?" I say and glance at Jason. "Future husband?"

"Wow ... what?" Jason seems confused.

"Yes. We already talked about this." My father's eyes almost bore a hole into my head. "You carry our name. That comes with certain privilege but also with obligations."

"Obligations ..." I hold the napkin in my hand so I have something to squeeze. "You mean marriage?"

"The Rivera empire must be continued," he says, taking another bite. "You know that. And Felix won't be able to do it on his own."

"That's not fair," Felix barks. "I'm more than capable of—"

"Fighting for our name, yes." My father interrupts. "But we need someone to make alliances as well, someone to barter deals, someone with wit and the balls to hold off when needed."

Penelope snorts and hides her laughter behind her sleeve when Felix throws her a killer glare. And I kind of dig the low-ball insult to his intelligence.

"My point is, you two form a good team," my father continues. "And for a business to be successful, it must be run by a family unit. You're on your own, you need a trusting partner, and I have my connections."

My eyes widen, but I don't even know how to respond.

"Well." Jason clears his throat. "As it stands, my family and their aviation company are well known across America. I intend to take over for them one day, so of course I would be more than happy to join hands with your esteemed family." Jason grabs my hand. "And I am more than willing to marry your daughter."

I have to put a stop to this.

I scoot back my chair and stand. "Look, I have no intentions of marrying anyone, let alone—"

Suddenly, my phone buzzes, and I fish it out of my pocket.

Nathan just sent me a picture.

I frown and open it up, but all it does is bring me more rage.

It's my body on the pavement in that alley, covered in cum.

*Nathan: Two thousand. That's what I need. If you don't bring it before eight o'clock tonight ... this might end up in the wrong hands.*

I almost crush the phone with my bare hands.

*He's blackmailing me?*

"What's wrong?" my father asks.

"I gotta go," I say, right when the chef returns with my newly created dish. A perfect Caesar salad for a hungry soul. But I'll worry about filling this stomach with food later.

As I march out the front door, someone grabs my shoulder and stops me. "Where are you going?" Jason asks.

"I have to meet someone. Now."

"Can't it wait?" he asks. "I thought you said this dinner was important. I want to make a good impression."

"Yeah, well then go back inside and talk with my dad."

"I can't do that if you're not there too," he says. "He thinks you're my girlfriend."

"Girlfriend?!" I parrot. "Look, I don't have time—"

When I take one more step, he grips my wrist and steals my phone straight from my hand.

"Hey!" I try to snatch it back.

His eyes widen.

Too late.

He's seen the picture.

"What ... what is this?" he murmurs, his voice laced with disgust. When he looks up at me with bloodshot eyes, I can barely look away. "Did you take this?"

"No," I reply.

"Then who did?" he asks, swallowing. "You've been ... fucking other guys? Is that why you've been so distant?"

I snatch the phone back from him.

"Why? Tell me why, Lana." His voice fluctuates in tone like his ego is bruised. "Why would you do this to me? I thought we were—"

"They're extorting me," I interject.

"Who is *they*?"

"Does it matter?" I scoff. "I don't want the picture they took to be seen by anyone. I didn't mean for you to see it, but I guess it's too late for that now."

"Yeah, I won't be able to get that filth out of my brain any time soon."

I frown. "Well, you sound very supportive."

"I'm sorry, Lana," he says, sighing. "I mean, what do you expect? I'm seeing my girl completely covered in some other man's cum. Of course I'm upset. I mean, why didn't you tell anyone?"

"Who the fuck should I tell about this, huh?" I scoff. "Felix?"

"No. I don't know." He runs his fingers through his hair. "All I can think of is those fuckers having their hands on you ..." He shakes his head. "I can't. I can't fucking deal with this, man."

"What do you mean?"

"I'm just saying, they must've had a reason. And I know how sexy you are and how that might give people the wrong ideas."

"What?" My jaw drops. "Are you blaming *me* for this?"

"No, that's not what I mean. It's just that ... I don't want people to look at you like this."

"Neither do I!"

"I don't know how to deal with this."

*I can't believe this.*

"So you're just abandoning me?"

"I ... I'm sorry, Lana. I don't ... I can't ... "

He can't even finish his fucking sentence.

*Coward.*

"Fine," I seethe, then turn around and march off.

"I'm sorry!" he yells. "I'll tell your father we ... broke up."

I turn around only to yell at him. "Can't break up if you were *never* my boyfriend!"

I flip him the bird and jump on the bike that I rode here on.

"Hey! How am I supposed to get back home now?" Jason asks, running up to me.

"Fucking figure it out yourself," I growl, and I rev up the bike. Right as I bolt off, I yell, "And by the way, I faked all of my orgasms!"

The shocked look on his face is a small victory on an otherwise sour night.

But I don't want to think about him any longer. With no time to waste, I have a bully to meet up with.

# 29

## LANA

I hop off my bike and march straight toward the Phantom Society building. The two guards outside watch me with keen eyes, but I don't even grant them one look as I barge toward the entrance.

They broaden their shoulders and lift their arms. "You're not allowed entry."

"If you don't let me through, I will personally cut off your fucking arms." I hold my knife up for them to see. "With this fucking knife."

One of them smiles. "I'd love to see you try."

So I hold up my cell phone and show them the text Nathan sent me where he's clearly inviting me over for tea before his untimely demise. "Last chance ... now are you going to let me enter, or do you want to do this the hard way?"

The one that told me off swallows and lowers his arm but still holds out his hand. "Knife."

I narrow my eyes at him.

Do I want to go into this starting a fight again?

Or do I want to approach this in a smarter way and beat them at their own game?

I don't want to risk the chance of Nathan sending that damn photo to anyone.

Grunting, I slam my knife into the fucker's hand. "Keep it fucking safe. If you so much as move from this spot, I will fucking haunt you into your death."

He just throws me a glare as I walk to the door and push past the other guy, knocking him off balance. I enter the building and march across the hallway, my heels click-clacking on the marble floor, determined to give Nathan an earful.

I head straight for the chapter room and shove open the doors.

He's standing there with a bottle of whiskey in one hand and a glass in the other. He looks up at me with a devilish lopsided grin. "Lana ... I'm surprised it took you so long."

"Delete those fucking pictures," I growl at him. "Every single one of them."

He casually pours the drink, taking his time. "No, I don't think I will."

"Why?" I yell. "We had a deal."

Clutching the glass tight, he takes a sip. "And now the deal has changed."

"You can't just change deals one-sided." I get right up in his face, but he's not swayed even a little bit by my rage. "You already took everything I had to give. When is it going to be enough?"

His hand suddenly rises to meet my face, and I freeze when he grabs a strand of my hair, gently tucking it behind my ear. His hand grazes past my cheek, and electricity crackles between us. "I will never have enough of you now."

My teeth grind together, and I slap him.

Hard.

"How dare you?"

When I try to slap him again, he grabs my wrist midair. "You can slap me all you want. It won't change what's going to happen."

"Oh, do fucking enlighten me," I grit.

"You'll be a good girl and give me the money I told you to give me, and I won't release those pictures."

"Fuck you," I say. "Why are you so desperate, huh? Don't you fucking have enough? Your parents are the wealthiest—"

"My parents are in jail," he roars, tears suddenly staining his eyes.

My eyes widen, and he releases my wrist.

"And whether you are willing to give it to me or not, I *need* that money. And I'm going to get it."

"Why?" I ask. "Give me one good reason."

He clutches the glass so tightly I'm almost starting to wonder if it will crack beneath his fingers.

"You can't ... because you don't want to," I scoff. "Penelope was right. You're just a fucking bully."

"Penelope?" he grits. "You think she's telling you the complete truth?"

I shove my finger into his chest. "You bullied her sister. Damn right I know she's telling the truth."

He grips my finger. "You have no fucking clue ..."

"Did you do it or not?"

His face darkens. "I had no fucking choice."

I snort. "No choice ... no choice but to bully someone? Sure."

He roars out loud and smashes his glass against the wall. "I was fucking forced to do it!"

I frown.

*Who would force a guy to bully someone else?*

"Why?"

"Ask your brother, he knows the fucking truth," he grits. "If I didn't oblige, my parents' fraud would be exposed to the police. Did you think I wanted to be responsible for them going to jail?" he says, closing the gap between us. "I did what I had to for *my* family."

"By breaking another family apart ..." I mutter.

His face contorts with regret and guilt. "You don't know the pain I went through for them." His hand rises, the missing finger a thorn in his side. "I paid the price."

"And all that bullying was for nothing because they're still in jail," I say through gritted teeth. I can tell from the look in his eyes my words are like tiny knives jabbed straight into his heart. "Just like you trying to threaten me with pictures will be all for nothing."

"Lana, give me the money," he says, his voice gravelly, too serious to ignore.

"No," I reply, jerking my hand free from his grip. "You won't even give me the reason. You're fucking evil."

"Just give me the fucking money, goddammit! The reason doesn't fucking matter. Just give it to me, and I promise to keep the pictures safe."

I step away from him. "You don't *want* to tell me, do you? You can't even face the girl you're trying to extort."

His face is marred with disgust and hatred, but I don't know if he feels that way because of me or himself.

"It's a matter of life or death," he says through gritted teeth.

I tilt my head and smile wickedly. "Then die."

And I walk off, sticking my middle finger in the air while I glance over my shoulder just to watch him seethe.

\*\*\*

# NATHAN

**Later that day**

I check my watch, the ticking making me anxious. I need to get there on time. If I don't ...

My heart beats in my throat, and I push the thought away.

I grab my bag and count the cash again, but I'm still short. They'll never accept this.

"Damnit!" I slam my fists against the steering wheel.

Someone knocks on my window, and when I look up, Kai's smiling at me. I don't know what he's smiling about.

I lower the window. "What?"

He pushes a wad of cash inside. "Here."

I frown. "Wait ..."

"I sold one of those stolen bags," he says. "Found it in the closet underneath some shoes."

I count it, and it's the exact number I need. But it's more than anyone would've given for that bag we forgot. "You added more. Did your mom give this to you?"

He shrugs. "No, but I figured it out on my own."

My eyes flicker down his body to the hand that just gifted me the money. The ring that usually adorns his finger is missing.

When he sees me looking, he retracts his hand. "Don't worry about it."

"Thanks," I say, tucking the money into the bag.

With this, I'll have just enough to settle the score.

"This means more than—"

"I know." Kai interrupts.

I return his smile and put the bag aside.

He taps the top of the car and then walks away, but within seconds, he's opened the passenger side door and sits down beside me.

"What are you doing?" I don't want him to get the wrong idea. "I don't want you to be in danger."

"I don't care," he says, leaning in. "You know I'd go to war for all of you fuckers, right?"

"It's just a simple deal. In and out. That's it."

"And I'm coming with you," he says while I put the car into reverse. "Now go." His eyes flick to my watch. "It's time."

Not another second goes by before I race off and head out the gates of Spine Ridge U. The road down is long and winding, and with every curve, my heart picks up a beat. I'm anxious, beads of sweat rolling down my back as I make my way toward the city's outskirts.

At the end of the long road, there's a left turn, and instead of heading for the Crescent Vale City, I drive to the small parking lot in the back of the forest, where there's a backpacking trail for adventurers seeking thrills near Spine Ridge.

A seedy-looking car waits for me there, headlights turned toward me as I park my car and turn it off.

"Want me to do it?" Kai asks.

I shake my head. "They want to see it's me."

He clutches the gun in his hand tightly and shows it to me from underneath the dashboard. "I'll be here. If they so much as try anything, I'll back you up."

My heart's racing in my throat, but I ignore it and step out of the vehicle, adjusting my suit before I grab my bag of cash.

Someone steps out too and walks to the front of their car. "Glad to see you showed up. Wouldn't want to barge in unannounced."

Must be that fucker who sent me all those texts.

"Romeo?" I ask.

"Talking to him. You got the cash?"

I hold out the bag like a severed head. "It's all in here."

"Hand it over."

"No." I swallow down the lump in my throat. "Not until you guarantee our safety."

The pause feels eternal.

"That money belongs to us. Your mom and dad owe us."

"I don't give a shit about them. It's not my fault," I retort.

"That may be so, but family is family, and you will pay the price," he barks, his voice low and intimidating. "Now give us the money."

A gun clicking off its safety is all I need to hear to know my life is on the line right this very second.

"You will leave my family alone after this payment," I grit. "Or the next delivery will be a bullet."

The guy in front of me snorts but doesn't say another word, so I throw the bag onto the ground in front of him. "This debt is out of my hands now. Pick it up yourself."

And I march back to my car and slam the door shut before I race off into the night with a steadfast heart.

"Fuck, I can't believe it's done," I mutter.

"You did good." Kai slaps me on the shoulder.

I drive all the way back to the Phantom Society, despite wanting nothing more than to drive to my aunt's house. It wouldn't be safe. I don't want to be the reason that ...

My hands clench around the steering wheel.

*Don't. Don't ever fucking think about it.*

Suddenly, I hear something in the back of the car and immediately hit the brakes. "What was that?"

Kai's eyes follow mine to the back. "Did you hear that too?"

I park the car on the side of the road and get out, slamming the door shut before I march straight for the trunk and open it up.

Inside is none other than fucking Lana Rivera, throwing me a vicious smile. "Surprise, bitches."

# 30

KAI

I hear an *oompf* sound and immediately shut the door and run to help Nathan. But my eyes widen the minute they settle on Lana, crawling out of the trunk.

She kicks him in the stomach, but he swiftly grabs her leg and twists her around. "Let go of me!"

I jump up behind him and grab her other leg, and we both drag her out of the car and shove her to the ground.

"I've got her," Nathan says, and I grasp her by the throat. "What the fuck were you doing in there? Spying on us? Tell me why!"

"I wanted to know what the fuck you two were up to after you tried to extort me for money."

"Extort you?" I growl, and I turn my head to Nathan.

The guilty look on his face tells me everything I need to know.

"Oh, you didn't tell him?" she muses at Nathan.

I tighten my grip around her neck to make her look at me instead. "Tell me what?"

"Nathan tried to shake me for money so he wouldn't send those lewd pictures around."

"You did what?" I growl at him, releasing her from my grip.

As I stand, he lets go of her leg to face me. "I had them already, and I needed the fucking money."

"You've been taking pictures of her all this time just so you could send them to her family?" My hand suddenly wraps around his throat instead, enraged he'd even attempt it.

I pull my gun from my pocket and point it right at his face, angry he'd threaten the girl who belongs to me.

"I needed the money," he mutters through coughs.

Lana crawls away underneath me, catching her breath while I focus on Nathan.

"So that's why you suddenly wanted to become involved with her too," I say through gritted teeth, feeling betrayed.

"No, it's not like that," he replies, his voice weak from my strong grip. "I already liked what I saw. I just saw an opportunity as well."

"An opportunity?" Lana snorts behind me. "That's all I am?"

"No. It's become far more than that, and you know that," Nathan gurgles.

"She was mine to begin with. I only allowed you two to join because I enjoyed it. Not so you could go behind my back and try to ruin what we had by threatening her with the videos and photos we had by using them to extort her!"

Lana stays put even though I'm not keeping her from running. But something tells me this exchange is the exact reason she's staying.

"It's not like that," Nathan hisses.

"Then tell me why!"

"You *know* why!" he grits back.

My eyes widen, and my face contorts because he's right; I do know the reason. I'm just pissed off he'd stoop that low just for ...

I release him from my grip, and he drops to the ground, coughing and heaving up spit.

"You know how much I'm willing to sacrifice," Nathan mutters.

"Even your fucking soul?" I reply.

It doesn't even take him a second to answer, "Yes."

I sigh out loud, and for a moment, it's quiet, so I stare up at the stars above. God, all of this has turned into a giant mess.

I turn to look at Lana, who takes a step back just from my eyes alone. Or maybe it's the gun still in my hand.

"How much did you hear?"

"Everything."

"Tell me."

"Nathan's parents owed some bad fuckers money," she says. "And you paid them off, hoping they won't come back for more."

I swallow.

Her nostrils flare. "Is that why you guys have been fucking with me? For money?"

"No. Never," I answer, throwing a glare at Nathan. "As for him ..."

"I did what I had to. That money I asked you for was the last of what I needed to pay them off."

"Then how come you still had enough?" she asks.

"I gave it to him," I respond, breathing out another sigh.

"Oh right ... because that's all he needed. A reward," she hisses, looking anywhere but at me.

Nathan approaches her. "You don't know what's at stake here."

I'll allow him to have his moment with her.

"Your life," she retorts as he barges right up to her. "Yeah, I got that part."

"No. Not mine," he says through gritted teeth.

"Is that why you kept fucking with me?" Her nostrils flare. "Just for the money so you could bail out your mommy and daddy?"

He grabs her face. "I fucked with you because I enjoyed it, because I like seeing your naked body writhe, because I love to see that lusty face as I bust all over it." He pauses. "The pictures I took of you are just a bonus, the icing on the fucked-up cake."

I push up between them. "Okay, enough."

"No. I want to know why you needed to destroy me," she says, glaring at Nathan and me. "You owe it to me."

I grab her arms and make her look at me. "You went through all that trouble, hiding in the back of the car, just to find out the truth?"

She nods.

I take a deep breath.

"Well, now you know," Nathan says. "I don't regret anything I did. Not for a single second."

"Let's go," I say, and I grab his arm before we start another fight in the middle of the night on an abandoned road. I walk back to the car, and Nathan jumps behind the wheel.

Suddenly, I hear the back seat door open and in crawls Lana. We both look at her, questioning whatever it is she's doing.

"I'm coming with you."

Nathan snorts. "You've got to be kiddi—"

"If she wants to come, let her." I interject.

His nostrils flare, but he doesn't protest and looks out the window instead.

"What did you want to do? Leave me out there by myself so those fuckers you just traded hands with find me?" she asks, raising a brow.

She's got a point there.

I do not want anyone's grabby hands on her ... except mine.

"You sure about this?" Nathan asks.

"Go," I tell him.

So he starts the car and races off.

***

# LANA

I can almost taste the tension between us, the air crackling with the heat of unspoken desires and rage. None of us is willing to speak on the matter, so it just gets churned up a notch.

Nathan's putting all his anger into hitting the gas, and we swerve across the streets to get back to Spine Ridge U. When we drive onto campus, they head straight back to the Phantom Society. The sight of the melancholic building makes me swallow because of all the history I have here, but I'm too far into this to back out now.

Milo's waiting outside for the boys to park the car. "How did it go?"

he asks casually, leaning over Nathan's door as he opens it. "Were they satisfied?"

"I guess so," Nathan replies.

"Found a stray cat on the curb," Kai muses.

Milo's eyes land on mine, and his whole face turns white as snow. "Lana? What is she doing here?"

"I don't know," Nathan says, shutting the door.

I open my door and step out too. "What? Don't act like you don't know why I was there. You wanted to extort me for money, so I came to check why."

"Wait, what?" Milo follows Nathan as he heads up the steps to the building. "She knows?"

"Wait, you knew?" I frown at Milo.

Milo's face reddens, and he focuses on Nathan.

"Doesn't matter," Nathan says. "They probably won't leave us alone now that they know I'm able to pay."

"But you gave them what they asked for, right?" Milo asks. "You paid off your parents' debt. Isn't that enough?"

He shrugs. "I don't want to think about it."

I catch up with them. "That's easy for you to say. Your pictures didn't end up in the wrong hands."

"Did they?" Kai asks, stopping midway up the front steps.

"Yes."

His eyes narrow at me, bolts of lightning almost flickering from his eye. "Who?" He cracks his knuckles. "Who do I need to kill?"

I'm sure he'd try. "Jason saw it by accident. And I don't fucking care. It's too late."

Still, Kai won't let me out of his sight, and he grips my waist, forcing me to stay put. "Does he know we're involved?"

I shake my head. "I didn't tell him anything."

"Good." He leans in so close I can feel his breath against my neck, sparking desire inside my core. "Keep it that way."

"Like I'd ever want to tell anyone you're fucking with me just to keep my kills a secret," I say.

"Oh ... I'm not just doing this to keep your secret, Lana," he whispers, pressing a coy and dangerous kiss right beneath my ear. "Don't you know I've always craved you?"

I suck in a breath, but it's hard, so damn hard to ignore the growing arousal.

"You wanted to come, so come," he says, smiling like he's crazy before whisking me inside.

And why do I have the feeling he meant something else when he said *come*?

"God, I just want to forget about today," Nathan groans as we walk into the mansion.

"Well, I can help you take your mind off it," Milo replies, winking.

"Not now," Nathan responds.

"Aw ... I was so looking forward to the room," Milo says with a frown as he closes the door behind us.

Nathan takes off his coat and slings it over his shoulder. "I'll show you all corners of the wall soon enough, don't worry."

Milo grins with excitement.

Is this why he begged me to use him?

Milo is submissive to Nathan, yet he called me his queen.

"Wait," Milo says, and both Nathan and Kai stop in the middle of the hallway while he runs into the living room and swiftly closes the door behind him.

A few seconds pass before the door opens again. He's holding hands with a little blond-haired, blue-eyed girl, and the rage on Nathan's face practically melts away.

"Rory," he whispers.

"Who's that?" I ask, but Kai merely squeezes my waist and puts a finger to his lips.

"I thought I'd bring you a welcome home gift," Milo says with a gentle smile on his face. "Just for a couple of days."

Nathan immediately drops his coat, runs toward her, and gives her the biggest hug I have ever seen, twirling her in his arms.

"Fuck, Ro, I missed you."

And for a moment, all I can do is stare at their loving embrace.

She giggles like the cutest little girl ever. "You swore! Mommy said we're not allowed to use bad words."

"I'm sorry," he says, pecking her on the cheek. "I won't do it again."

"Pinky promise?" she says.

He holds up his pinky and hooks it around hers. "Swear on my life."

"At least not in front of her," Milo mumbles.

"Is that ...?" I mumble in shock.

And Kai's answer suddenly makes all the sense in the world. "His sister."

# 31

LANA

I swallow the damn rage I'd felt mere hours before.

Kai leans in sideways to whisper, "You wanted to know why he needed the money. Now you know."

No wonder Nathan said it was a matter of life and death.

That trade wasn't just to pay off the debt his mom and dad owed. It was to save her. That tiny little girl hankering for his hugs, looking up to her big brother like he's her entire world.

Everything she has left after the world has crumbled around her.

Rory looks around with awestruck eyes. "Is this your home?"

A proud smile forms on Nathan's face. "Yup."

"Can I live here too?"

"Oh my God, she's so cute." Milo bursts out into *aahs* and *oohs* and the sound almost makes me burst out into laughter too.

"No can do, Ro, sorry. You can stay for a couple of days, but nothing more," Nathan says. "This society is for grown boys only."

"Aw ..." She pouts. "But I like Milo."

She turns her head to look at him, and he winks at her.

"Do you now?" Nathan muses. "Well, you're not the only one."

"He gave me this lollipop," she says, showing Nathan a bright red one.

"Milo keeps those stashed away in the kitchen for when he's got one of his midnight cravings again," Kai whispers into my ear.

And I have to say, I'm not even mad I'm being fed all these details I never knew I needed.

Everything's suddenly starting to make sense.

"I *love* strawberry. It's my favorite!" Rory excitedly waves it around.

"When all of this is over and you're done living with Auntie, I'll take you to an ice cream shop and you can have as many strawberry scoops as you like. Okay?"

Her face lights up like fireworks. The kind that brings joy to even the most fucked-up souls. "Really?"

Her smile is contagious as Nathan begins to grin. "Pinky promise." He hooks his pinky around hers again. "Swear on my life."

"Yay!"

When he puts her down, he momentarily glances at me, and for a moment, all the pain and darkness in his eyes are back.

As though he means to tell me everything there is to know about him with just one single look.

A guy dead set on protecting the only family he has left.

And it breaks all the resolve and hatred I have burning within me.

Rory grabs his hand and drags him with her. "C'mon! I've gotta show you the unicorn in Milo's room!"

"Unicorn?" Nathan narrows his eyes at Milo.

He simply shrugs with a big old smile as we head toward his room upstairs. Sure enough, there's a human-sized stuffed unicorn right in the middle of his room. "Bought it on the way to her place. I figured she might want a friend while she waited here for you."

"You're nuts," Nathan jests, shaking his head at Milo.

We all gaze in wonder at a little girl having the time of her life on an imaginary rainbow ride.

Nathan finally approaches us and looks at Kai first. "Thank you for helping out."

"It was nothing," Kai says.

"Eh, we just stole some shit and sold it for cash, big deal," Milo says.

"I mean it," he adds.

Kai plants a hand on his shoulder. "We've got you."

"Right now, you're the only family I've got left," Nathan says, sighing. "Let's just hope they don't come after the rest of my family too."

"Won't let that happen," Kai says, watching Rory jump off the unicorn's head, only to jump right back onto its back.

"We'll be there to cover you both," Milo says.

They embrace in a sort of bro-hug. "Phantoms stay Phantoms. Even into death."

Suddenly, my stomach roars, and it's the worst timing ever.

Because all three of them are now looking at me like I interrupted their private time together.

Milo smiles and lifts his head. "Hungry?"

I feel gawked at. "Well, I ... haven't eaten in a while."

Milo breaks out of their bro-hug, grabs my hand, and drags me along. "My time to shine."

He pulls me all the way to the lavish kitchen and sets me down on a stool in front of a bar, then goes to the fridge and pulls out all sorts of food. Cucumbers cut into strips, cooked chicken, avocado, and a whole bucket full of rice.

"You like sushi?" he asks, laying it all out on the counter as he grabs a piece of nori.

"Um, sure?" I mutter, still a bit overwhelmed.

Within seconds, he's got the nori layered with rice, then drops on some cucumber and avocado, and slices through the chicken like a seasoned chef. I've never seen someone assemble a sushi roll that swiftly. Then he slices them into small pieces and throws the mayo around like he's putting on a show before dabbling them all with the sauce and a little bit of spice.

"There you go," he says, sliding the plate my way. "Fresh, handmade perfection." He kisses his own lips with his fingers. "For my hungry lady."

"Wow ..." I mutter, impressed. "Thank you."

He winks, and for the first time since I met him, I'm actually blushing. "Enjoy."

It's been a long time since someone personally cooked for me. Jason would never. The last time I tried his homemade sloppy joe, I almost threw up.

But this ... this sushi looks magnificent, and the moment I take a bite, I can't help the moan that slips from my mouth.

"Well, I'm glad you like it," Milo says.

And I swiftly plop another one into my mouth to stop the embarrassing blush from spreading. "Why are you doing this for me?"

"Why not?" He frowns, looking at me like I'm crazy. "You didn't think I'd let you go hungry, right?"

"But we're—"

"Enemies?" Milo leans across the counter. "I told you ... I am yours. I always was. From the moment I laid eyes on you, I knew nothing would please me more than to give myself to you."

Okay, now I can't stop the blush from spilling over my face and chest.

"And if my queen is hungry ..." He grabs my hand and presses a gentle, chivalrous kiss on top. "Then I will satisfy her stomach as thoroughly as I satisfy her pussy."

I swallow down the piece of sushi, but it's hard, so incredibly hard, when someone like him is staring at me like I am a fucking goddess to him just by being in his presence and eating his food.

And something about that feels ... humbling.

No one has ever gotten down on their knees for me. Nor have they worshipped me like this.

He leans in to grab a piece of sushi and tips down my chin to put it on my tongue himself, and he watches each bite I take like I'm taking a bite out of him.

And I don't understand why. All I've done is try to kill these boys.

I've hit him, kicked him, fought with him every step of the way, and here he is, feeding me like he's grateful for it.

"Aren't you mad at me?" I ask after a while.

He runs his fingers through his red hair. "No, why would I be?"

"I hurt you," I say. "And I got you into trouble with Nathan."

He laughs. "Oh yeah, I still owe him a whipping."

My eyes widen, and I grip his wrist. "Whipping? Nathan whips you?"

He pauses his feeding me. "I don't mind."

"So that was you in that chamber," I mutter.

"You ..." His eyes narrow. "You were the one watching us during that party?"

The grin on my face speaks for me.

Milo tilts his head. "Did you enjoy it?"

I release his wrist. "I don't understand. I thought you'd be upset."

"Over someone seeing us? No. I know who I am and what I like. And I more than happily take whatever anger Nathan has to give me." He leans in to caress my face ever so gently, and wherever his fingers touch, my skin comes alive. "Just as I'll take whatever rage you want to release on me."

"I don't have rage," I retort.

A filthy smirk spreads on his lips. "Who are you lying to? Because I don't believe one word."

"I ... I ..."

"You think your rage is something to be hidden," he says, his fingers lingering near my lips, and every fiber of my being fights the urge to lean in to kiss this man who's seen every inch of my fucked-up soul and still wants nothing more than to love it. "But all I see is perfection."

But he is part of their group, part of the three evil boys who have done nothing but use me, and I pull away to stop myself. "I'm just saying, it's wrong."

His brows twitch. "It's not. Who told you that?"

"I don't know." I shift in my seat. "I just ..."

"You don't want your family to know about your secrets," he murmurs. "You enjoy the violence you dish out."

I chomp on another piece of sushi, but it doesn't taste so divine anymore when I'm being interrogated.

"I do what I have to," I reply.

"Just like Nathan does what he has to," he says.

"I don't kill anyone for sport or money."

He cuts through a new sushi roll, the stare he throws me from behind the strands of red hair making it hard to look away. "Then what do you kill for?"

I swallow, but a piece of sushi catches in my throat, and I cough. "Nothing..."

He plants the knife into the board. "No one kills without reason. You can tell me."

"And have you hold it over my head?" I muse. "Add another way to extort me? I'm not stupid."

"Hey, that wasn't my idea," he says, arranging more rice on a nori sheet. "I just do what I'm told."

"You always listen to Nathan, so when he tells you to hurt me, you will."

He glances at me and then plucks the knife from the board again to chop some salmon. "I will never, ever hurt you," he says. "Unless you want me to, of course."

"Then what was all that fucking around you guys did with me? In the alley, and in the Shack, and right here in this house?"

He layers the salmon on top and places them neatly on a plate before presenting it to me. "*That* was pleasure. And I know you felt it too."

The way he looks at me makes it impossible to look away.

"Now eat. I won't have you starving in this house. Not while I can help it."

I frown and pick up some of the sushi. It practically melts on my tongue, so delicious.

"First you fuck with me, then you feed me. You can't expect me not to find this all a bit confusing."

"It doesn't have to be," he says. "We can just enjoy each other's company, and after, you can cut me with your knife if you want." He whips around his knife as a devilish smile appears on his face. "Or mine. Your choice."

The salmon slips down my throat. "You're really weird, you know that?"

"I don't deny that," he says, and he plucks one off the board to eat. "I just don't hide it."

*Why does that feel like a dig toward me?*

"Anyway, please don't be mad at Nathan," he says, catching me off guard. "He only did those things because he needs to protect Rory."

"From what?" I ask.

He looks at the door before returning his attention to me. "His parents are real gamblers. They were rich, but they also couldn't stop spending, and they got involved with the wrong crowd. Kept borrowing money from the wrong people. And when the police caught on to their money laundering schemes, they went down for the crime, leaving Nathan all by himself with his sister."

Wow. No wonder he'd go that far to keep her out of harm's way.

"I know he's done some bad shit, but he did it for the right reasons."

Suddenly, someone clears their throat, and we both stop eating. Nathan's leaning with his arms folded against the doorway, his eyes practically shooting bullets at Milo.

And Milo immediately starts cleaning up the counter, putting all the food away with just as much swiftness as he pulled it out for me.

"What are you doing?" he asks.

"Feeding her," he replies.

His brow lifts. "Why?"

*Why does Nathan make it sound like he thinks Milo had ulterior motives?*

He frowns. "She was hungry. Why else?"

He rolls his eyes and sighs out loud.

"Shouldn't you be with Rory?" Milo asks.

"She's asleep," he retorts. "In your bed."

"Oh ..." Milo responds, but then a wicked smile spreads on his face. "Oh, that means I can sleep with you."

"Not yet," Nathan says and turns his attention toward me. "Come with me."

I just stare at him.

Milo points at both of us. "Who? Me or her?"

"Lana."

I almost want to flip him the bird again, but then I remember the smile on that little girl's face and just how much their hug affected me.

Maybe I owe it to myself to listen to him.

I hop off the stool and follow Nathan, too curious to know what's going on to leave now.

He walks me upstairs, hands casually in the pockets of his pants as he strolls to a room not far ahead in the hallway and opens the door for us. I peek over his shoulder at the beautiful blue-painted walls and portraits hanging from the wall, along with a cozy fireplace in the corner. In the middle is a large king-sized bed. But it's the metal clasps on the wall to the right that draw my attention, along with all the whips, chains, and toys hanging from the hooks.

"What's this?" I ask, stepping inside slowly.

He closes the door behind me. "My bedroom."

I swallow and look around, but it's hard to take everything in with him breathing down my neck. "Now you know why I did what I did."

"To protect your sister."

"Do you hate me?"

The question catches me off guard, and when I open my mouth, I don't know what to say.

Do I hate him? Or do I just hate his attempt at wringing money from me solely to save his family? Could I even stay mad knowing the truth?

When I don't answer, he circles me and stops in front of my face. "You can tell me the truth. I know you do."

"You had no right," I say, shaking my head.

"You would've done the same for your family."

I swallow. I could lie and deny that, but we both know he's right.

"Why did you bring me here?" I ask.

He sighs out loud and sits down on the bed behind him, hands splayed behind him.

"I just ... wanted to talk with you."

I fold my arms. "Okay then, talk."

He looks at me, and the pain in his eyes almost makes me waver. But I have to remember he will always be a Phantom first. An evil boy dead set on making my life miserable just because he knows about my vigilante side job.

He pats the bed. "Come. Sit with me."

After a while, I cave. And I don't know whether it's because I feel forced due to the nature of our arrangement, or because of the way he asks.

"Milo told you about my family," he says. "Didn't he?"

I nod. "They're in jail because of fraud. Something to do with a bad gamble with dangerous people."

He lowers his head between his shoulders. "My parents only cared about making more and more money, no matter what it cost them." He looks around at all the expensive furniture and the paintings on the wall. "But all the money in the world couldn't buy us the safety we need now."

"They're still after you?" I ask.

He shrugs. "I don't know. After my parents were ratted out to the cops, the collectors came for their remaining debts, but they left me with nothing. We scrambled together every bill by stealing ..."

"And killing the people so they wouldn't talk," I fill in.

He nods.

"And I got in your way."

His silence speaks volumes. "I did what I had to." He looks at me, the pain in his eyes so sincere it moves me. "For *her*."

"You should've asked me," I say.

"And say what? Please give me money, but I can't tell you why?" He scoffs. "You think you would've given it to me?"

"You didn't even try."

"I know your family," he grits. "You don't help; you destroy."

I frown. "My family has nothing—"

"Your family has *everything* to do with this. Your brother and his gang of friends kept getting in our way," he interjects. "And when I realized you were his sister, I took pleasure knowing we were about to ravage a Rivera."

My jaw drops, and my hand rises to slap him, but he catches my wrist.

Suddenly, he pulls me down onto the bed, swiftly crawling on top of me in my surprise, and pins both my hands to the blanket.

His sparkling eyes are filled with anger and hurt.

But it's not my fault, and I refuse to bear the burden.

"Why do you hate me so much?" I grit.

"Hate?" His full lips crack open, and he licks the bottom one. "No ... this is obsession. I thought I only wanted to use you, get you to do my bidding so I could get the money I needed, but you ... you beguile everyone who crosses your path." He sucks in a breath through his teeth. "And *that* is what I hate." He leans in, his breath lingering on my skin as he whispers, "I hate how much you make me want you to the point where I can't stand to see you with the only boy who's ever understood my needs."

My eyes widen. *Is he talking about Milo?*

"You're jealous?" I frown. "You can have him."

"I already have him." His hand slides down my arm toward my breast. "But I want you too. I want to hear your moans, your cries as you beg for mercy, as you pray to your goddamn forsaken family to save you from my hard cock."

And suddenly, his lips slam down on mine, and I'm so lost and confused by the sudden affection and obsessive kiss that I let him. I actually let him kiss me.

*Fuck, what is wrong with me?*

I bite down. Hard.

He flinches and leans up, abs visibly protruding through his white shirt as droplets of blood roll down his cheek and stain his shirt. But he doesn't seem to care the slightest bit.

So I hook my legs around his and flip him over, slamming him into the bed before grasping one of his wrists and pinning it above his head. But he doesn't fight me or even flinch as I overpower him and take back control.

"My family has nothing to do with your sadistic needs. And I did *nothing* to deserve your wrath."

He swallows, biting his lip right where the blood seeps out, his eyes ogling my chest almost as if he's enjoying this more than he thought he would.

But instead of pushing me off him, he merely lifts his hand, the one with the missing finger, and says, "You want to know why I get off on hurting you? Because it was *your* brother who did this to me."

# 32

NATHAN

**Last year**

"Look! Look at what he's done to me!" I hold up my finger, the stump so gnarly it hurts to even look at it.

The nerves have been firing off all day, reminding me of the finger that no longer exists, and it's driving me mad.

"Felix did this to me. All because of that fucking girl," I grit at him, but he refuses to even look at me. "You made me do this. This is your fault."

"Boy, I told you what was at stake here," he mutters.

"I didn't agree to lose a fucking finger!" I yell.

"You should've done your job more carefully then."

"Why did you even want me to bully that girl?"

"Not important for you to know," he replies.

"Of course ... you refuse to tell me, yet you still want to use me. Why?" I take a stance. "No. I'm done."

He approaches me slowly. "I paid off a portion of your parents' debt." He grabs ahold of my painful finger, squeezing it. "Do I have to remind you of all the information I own about your parents' ... *hobbies*?"

My eyes twitch, but I don't say a word, despite wanting to spout every swear word in the dictionary.

He towers over with a vindictive look on his face. "I suggest you start obeying. Before I take away more from you than those three fucking boys ever could."

I swallow away the lump in my throat.

He's threatening to put my parents in jail.

Or worse.

Have them killed.

Finally, he releases me. "Now go."

\*\*\*

**Present**

Her face turns pale as snow, her pupils dilating as they witness the depth of the sadism of her own damn brother.

"He cut off a limb ... all because he wanted to make me pay for bullying the girl I was forced to bully or my own family would go to jail."

She swallows, but her fingers slowly unlatch from my wrist as though she no longer has the strength to hold me down. And even though I hate to admit it, I was growing quite fond of her hand latched around my wrist.

"I did what I had to, and I paid the heaviest price of all," I say, the pain of that day still so fresh in my mind that it makes my voice crack. "Do you know he still has it?"

"What?" she replies in shock.

"He keeps it in a jar like a wet specimen. A trophy. Me."

When she tries to move away, I grip her hand with mine, showing the four fingers I have left.

"This is why I *hate*. Why you call me evil." I slowly lower her until her face is mere inches away from mine. "Does it make me evil to love my family to the ends of the earth? To the end of me?"

Her eyes well up with tears, but she swallows them back.

Just like I always do when I know it would be better if I just let them go.

If I just let someone see that part of me ... the part I've always been told was weak.

*Stay strong. You're a Reed. Reeds don't cry. Reeds stick together. Reeds fight for what belongs to them.*

That's what my father always used to say.

Until he vanished and disappeared into the belly of the justice system.

I grab a few loose strands of hair and push them behind her ear. I understand now why Kai was so fixated on that ribbon of hers ... on this picture-perfect face that hides a beautiful lie.

"If I'm evil for killing and using people, then so are you."

She frowns. "I don't kill for—"

"Sport?" My brow rises. "What then? Excitement? To feel powerful?"

"To make sure those fuckers are erased from this goddamn earth," she retorts, still holding me down. "And I won't fucking stop, not even if you threaten me."

"Oh, by all means ... kill as many of them as you like. I won't stop you," I reply, struck by how pretty she is when she's angry and on the verge of yet another murder.

Would she kill me if she had the chance?

Or does she feel the same electricity sparking between us when we touch?

With my hand on her cheek, I pull her close, her lips almost puckering as mine approach, ready to stake my claim.

Suddenly, the door opens from the outside, and our heads rise to look.

Kai's dangling a key around his finger, the amused look on his face making her blush because he's seen her sitting on top of me.

She scrambles off me and pats down her clothes.

"Are you done?" she asks.

"Hardly," I reply.

"If you have nothing else to say to me, then I'm done here," she seethes, and she blows out a breath before she marches toward the door.

"Are you gonna let me pass?" She stares Kai up and down.

A slow smirk spreads on his cheeks before he finally steps aside and lets her go wherever she needs to go.

Home, probably. To wallow in her growing rage over the fact that she almost tried to kiss me back.

"What were you doing with her?" Kai asks.

I flop onto the bed with a massive boner and groan out loud. "She's a handful."

"Oh, I know," he replies. "You can leave her to me if it's too much for you."

"Fuck no," I retort. "I won't let you have all the fun with her."

"Seems like this was more than just fun," he says, leaning against the doorjamb.

"What? Can't I just give her a fucking kiss?"

"Hmm ... you keep telling yourself it was only just a kiss," he muses before he turns around and walks off. "I'm going to bed. See you tomorrow. Good luck sleeping with that boner."

"I'll take care of it," I say.

"I can help you with that."

Milo's voice makes me lift my head, and he closes the door, leaving just us two in my bedroom. I sit up straight, legs spread, hard-on springing right back into action when he licks his lips.

But I don't trust that he's wholly mine anymore.

"You bowed to her," I say as he approaches.

He drops to his knees in front of me. "I would do the same for you."

I grab his hair and make him look at me. "I don't like to share."

"We can make it work," he says.

My nostrils flare, and I rip off his shirt from seam to seam until nothing is left, revealing the marks she left on him. Dozens of slashes and a clear puncture wound in his shoulder.

"Was this from before or after the fight?"

"Before."

The pain he endured hits me like a brick in the stomach. Not because of how much it must've hurt but because I didn't inflict it.

"You want to be hers so badly?" I ask, letting my hand slide over his wounds until I grip his throat. "Or do you prefer being mine?"

"Don't make me choose. Please. I want both," he squeaks. "Can't I have both?"

My nostrils flare, but my rage is not purely his fault. He can't help that I'm a jealous bitch, just as much as I can't help him being such a sucker for someone who can own him. We both have our weaknesses.

All of which now point to *her*.

Lana fucking Rivera.

The girl who's got all three of us vexed.

"Fine. You want to make things right with me?" I ask.

He nods eagerly. "Punish me. Use me. Make me yours."

I zip down and pull out my raging hard-on.

"Open your mouth."

I drag his face over my length and shove him down to the base, feeling his tongue circle my length.

"Earn the fucking right to eat my cum."

And I pull out my knife and stab him right in the shoulder where she hit him.

Moans follow his cries as I thrust deep into his throat again, owning every part of his submissive soul, just like I always do in the pits of these darkened halls.

My parents would die if they knew the truth.

But for now, there's no one here to judge.

No one here to tell us we're wrong for enjoying what we do.

No one here to hear him scream.

# 33

## LANA

**A few days later**

I tap my pen back and forth, but I can't for the life of me focus on my homework. This paper isn't going to fucking write itself, but dammit, my mind is somewhere else.

"I really don't get this part," Brooke says.

"What?" I mutter.

I almost forgot Brooke and Irina were here too.

"Oh nothing, I'm just really wondering why on earth I chose this class."

I laugh. "I can relate to that."

"No shit, what are we even doing here? Why aren't we out there socializing, drinking, and having a fucking party? I thought that was what college was all about."

"College kind of implies studying too," I jest.

"Yeah, who even made that up?" She sighs. "I'm so done with this."

Irina laughs. "You always say that, yet you're still here."

"Exactly. Why don't I just stop?" Brooke whines.

I grab her papers and hand her a bottle of water. "Have a drink first. Take a breath. Try again later."

She groans but still takes the bottle to chug down some water. "You're always so calm and collected. I don't know how you do it."

I snort. "That's just what I want you to see. On the inside, I'm a raging witch."

"Well, that makes two of us," she retorts, laughing. She spots someone behind us, and her eyes almost melt off her face. "Oh my God, don't look. It's those Phantom boys. I think they're coming over here."

"Wait, what?"

She slaps me with a book when I attempt to look over my shoulder. "I said don't look."

"Why not?" I hiss back, frowning. "Are you scared or something?"

"I don't want to look desperate."

My face contorts as I try to keep my laugh together. "Girl, why?"

"We danced, remember? At their party?" she says.

Oh right, I almost forgot Kai danced with them. But he only did that to get information out of them about me.

Brooke taps Irina's shoulder. "Quick, does my lipstick look good?"

"You look fine," Irina replies. "Who is it?"

Brooke whispers, "I think it's Nathan."

*Oh boy.*

And here I was, trying to keep my shit together.

After our altercation in his room the other day, I haven't been able to think about much else. The way he looked at me, almost as if he could want more from me than just my body, still makes me shiver.

Something has changed.

Not just with him ... but with me.

When I saw that little girl jump into his arms, I think it was the first time I saw him for the man he really is. Protective and loving. And that scares me.

I can't help but turn my head, curious if he's really on his way here.

Nathan marches into the place like he owns it in that preppy boy outfit of his, and my eyes instinctively follow wherever he goes. His swagger is unmistakable as he looks around, searching for something. I look up, almost wondering if it's me he's after. His eyes briefly connect with mine, and the pen in my hand stops moving. I can't look away even though I know I should.

These fucking boys aren't right for me.

They're a foul distraction, nothing more than devils in disguise looking for trouble.

Yet I can't seem to stop thinking about every dirty fucking thing they did to my body. Especially now that I know *why*.

It doesn't excuse what they did, but for some reason, it feels like it all suddenly makes sense.

*But they're actively extorting you, Lana.*

Nathan sets his eyes on Milo, who's chatting on the couch with a guy I've never seen before. A guy with long black hair and a charming smile. Nathan talks to the guy like he knows him, and I wonder how many more friends those two have outside of the Phantom Society. If they told anyone about me.

*That'd be ridiculous. You don't want anyone to know about you. What if they find out what you really enjoy?*

I bite my lip and focus on the paper again, but Brooke can't stop staring at me, and it's such a distraction.

"What?" I bark.

She smirks. "You've got the hots for him."

I scowl. "No, I do *not*."

Suddenly, someone throws a bunch of books on the table, and I look up to see Crystal standing in front of us. "Hey guys!" She tucks a strand of her hair behind her ear, revealing a rose adorning her hair. "Mind if I join you with to study? Sitting by myself is much less fun."

We all look at her like we've seen a ghost.

"What? Am I not welcome?"

"Of course you are," Brooke says, scooting back a chair for her.

Crystal narrows her eyes at us. "What are y'all talking about?"

"Nothing," we say in unison.

She looks at us like we've lost our marbles. Maybe we have, I'm not sure.

"Ooookay," she mutters. "That sounds like a mutual secret. Am I butting in to something?"

"Oh no, it's no secret Lana's got the hots for Nathan," Brooke muses.

Crystal's eyes widen. "Nathan?"

I slap Brooke's arm with her own book. "The hell I do."

"Your mouth says that, but your eyes tell a different story." Brooke laughs.

"Oh my God, Brooke, you can't just throw people's secret crushes around," Irina tells her.

"Too late," Brooke muses, proud of herself.

Crystal sits down. "Well, tell me all about it."

"No," I reply staunchly.

"Why not?" Crystal asks, putting down her books. "Nathan's a friend of mine. I want to know what he's up to. And with Felix's sister, no less."

"There's nothing to tell," I say, fighting the blush on my cheeks with everything I've got.

*Nothing I could ever tell them anyway.*

Brooke swivels around on her chair and circles her pom-pom pen at me. "Oooh ... she's getting flushed. She's totally kissed him already."

Irina gasps. "Wow, is that true? He didn't even tell me."

"I never said anything—"

"You don't have to. I can see it from the way you look at him," Brooke interrupts.

"*How* do I look at him?" I'm getting a little aggressive now, but I don't want anyone to know anything about anyone.

"Like you want to eat him up and then some." She smirks.

*Fuck.*

"The sister of a Skull & Serpent Society member with a Phantom Society member?" Brooke says. Like it would be such a scandal.

I raise a finger. "Don't. Say. That. Out. Loud."

"Why?" Brooke muses. "Your brother isn't here."

"No, but those Skull & Serpent guys are everywhere, and I don't know all of those fuckers who join that frat, so can you please keep your voice down?"

Her brow rises. "So you admit you hooked up?"

"No," I retort.

Crystal smashes her lips together to hide a grin. "Lana?"

"What?" I still can't help the blush from spreading on my cheeks. "I plead the Fifth."

"What's this heated discussion about?"

We all look up to see Milo casually swaying a bottle of water back and forth.

"Oh, don't mind me, I'm just here for the tea."

"What tea? There is none. Why are you here?" I ask.

"Nathan asked me to check on you. See if you need anything."

My eyes widen, and they immediately connect with Nathan, who winks at me.

He actually fucking winks at me.

*What the hell is going on here?*

All three girls stare at me with blown-up cheeks before they burst out into laughter. "Oh my God, so it's true!"

"Milo!" I stand. "Can you not?"

"What? You know I always do what I'm told." He winks. "Do you need some water to cool down?"

"Since when do you two even care what I need?" I bark back.

"Oh ... oh boy, this is getting hot," Brooke mumbles to Crystal.

"Wait a minute, you know both of them?" Crystal asks me.

"Oh, she knows me all right," Milo muses, licking his lips. "And she knows I'm always at her service."

He grabs my hand and presses a kiss on top, and the girls practically swoon with excitement.

Good God.

I did not want this public display.

Not in a million years.

Yet I can't even move as he layers it on extra thick and says, "My lady."

# 34

LANA

"Oh my *Goooooood*," Irina exclaims, practically falling off her chair.

My entire face turns red, and I retract my hand. "Okay, that's enough."

"Lana, I did not expect this from you," Crystal muses.

"Me neither, and there's nothing to expect," I say, turning to face them. "There is nothing between us."

"Excuse me, I beg to differ," Milo muses behind me.

"Swear to God, Milo, I will smack you into the fucking hospital," I grit, trying to keep my cool so I don't blow up in front of everyone in this goddamn library.

"Don't threaten me with a good time," he retorts.

"Wow," Crystal mutters, her eyes widening.

So I whisper to all three of the girls, "Please don't tell my brother. Or anyone for that matter. They've been stalking me."

"Stalking you?" Milo scoffs. "You're the one who—"

I smack my hand in front of his lips so he doesn't blurt out more. "You. Come with me. Now."

I grasp his arm and drag him out of the library. Everyone's looking at us, but I don't care. I'm just taking him for a walk and talk.

"Where are we going?" he asks.

"Somewhere private," I mutter.

The smug grin on his face is insufferable. "Oh, I like the sound of that."

I drag him all the way to the underground swimming pool that I know no one attends right now because the doors are locked.

"Wait, this is locked."

"Not for me." I fish out a key and shove it in to open the door.

"How'd you get that?" he asks.

"My father's the dean," I reply.

His eyes narrow, and a wicked smile forms on his face. "You stole it. You're not so different from us after all."

"*Borrowed.* And I'm nothing like you guys."

"Sure, you keep pretending you're better than us."

I push him inside and shut the door behind us, then corner him against the wall. "What were you trying to do there? Out us all?"

He holds up his hands like he wants to make peace. "Nothing. Nathan just asked me to go check on you."

"Why? Why does he care?"

"You say it like it's surprising that he could," he says.

"Of course it is, he's never once shown interest in my safety or well-being."

"Just because we use you for sex doesn't mean we don't care," he says.

Grumbling, I push myself off him and pace around near the edge of the water. "I don't understand. Ever since he paid off those fuckers and saw his sister, something about him has just ... changed."

"His sister is important to him. And now that the load of stress is off him ... you're just seeing him for who he really is," Milo says.

"Whatever." I sigh out loud. "Still ... that doesn't mean you can just walk up to me and my friends."

He pouts. "Why not?"

"Well, you literally just outed me to my friends. What if they tell Felix, huh?"

His brow rises. "Would that be such a bad thing?"

I just stare at him with my jaw dropped. "Felix *hates* you guys. Like,

I'm not kidding. He'd actually cut out your eye and feed it to you for touching me."

"Oh ... fuck, that just made me hard."

I slap him in the face. "Focus!"

"Present!"

"Don't talk to me in public," I say, trying to ignore his obvious hard-on. "Not in front of anyone. I don't want this to get out."

His eyes narrow, and he tilts his head. "Are you embarrassed to be seen with me?"

My cheeks flush, but I roll my eyes and turn away so he won't see. "Embarrassed is a strong word."

There's a pause. "You like me."

My eyes widen, and I turn my head to glance at him. Big mistake because that stupid shit-eating grin of his only makes my blush worse.

"No, I don't."

"Yes, you do." He pushes himself off the wall and approaches me, and when I try to move away, he grabs my arm. "Don't run away from this."

"I'm not running anywhere."

"You don't like to be confronted with the truth," he says.

He pushes my hair behind my ear, his fingers lingering near my neck, every touch sending delicious shocks up my spine.

*Fuck, stop this, Lana.*

"Fine, you want the truth? We made a deal. My body for your silence. You're not being silent right now."

"I'll be quiet for my queen whenever she demands ..."

*Oh, there he goes again.*

"Don't," I grit.

"Don't what?" He tips up my chin. "Treat you like you deserve to be treated?"

I gulp at the intensity with which he says those words. "I never asked—"

"You don't have to ask. Like I said ... I'm at your service ... I don't want this to be just about some deal," he says, pulling me closer.

My eyes narrow. Fine. He wants to play this game? I'll play. "Then tell me who that guy was you were talking to."

"A friend."

"What kind of friend?"

He smiles slyly. "I'll tell you about mine if you tell me about yours."

Of course he's going to play hard to get.

I sigh out loud. "Milo ..."

"What? I want to get to know you." He wraps an arm around my waist. "But you won't let me."

"We're enemies."

He cups my cheek as he leans in. "What if I don't want to be?"

When he presses the softest of kisses to my lips, I almost, almost forget he's supposed to be an enemy. His lips eagerly roam mine, his fingers coiling through my hair like he adores every strand, and it's a kind of love I haven't felt before.

No number of kisses Jason ever gave me could come close to the kind of adoration Milo pours into them. He pecks me on each corner of my lips like he's leaving tiny little trails of infatuation. Each kiss is followed by a glance, a glimmer of excitement in his eyes as he leans in to kiss me again and again, until my mind can't even tell if I hate him or adore him.

*Fuck.*

I try to push him away, but instead, I lose my balance and slip. "Whoa, whoa, whoa!"

I fall backward, clutching his shirt ... and we tumble into the pool.

# 35

## LANA

Spluttering, I come up for air, wiping the water from my eyes. "Fuck! We fell in the fucking pool! All my clothes are wet!"

He's laughing like he doesn't give a shit. "Who cares?"

"I do! Look at me!" I show him my wet red dress and headband.

Goddammit, I did not want this today. I have studying to do.

He cups my face again, looking me dead in the eyes as he says, "I am."

And I'm suddenly at a loss of words, feeling like I'm floating in space instead of a pool.

Why do those words feel like they have so much more weight behind them than there should be?

He corners me against the pool, placing both hands behind me on the edge, and leans in to press another kiss right below my ear. "We're already wet now ... would it matter if I made you a little wetter?"

*Fuck. That made my pussy thump.*

He leans up, forehead pressed against mine, as his eyes command me to look into his. Dark, beautiful haunted brown eyes stare back at me filled with complete and utter devotion that leaves me breathless.

"I'll give you anything you want ... Anything you ask for, I'll do it for you," he whispers, his fingers coiling through my hair again as he slowly lowers his lips. "All you have to do is ask."

I shudder when a droplet of water from his lips lands on mine.

"Kiss me then."

A deadly smirk forms on his lips before he tips up my face. When our lips collide, it's impossible for me to ignore the thrumming of my heart. He explores my mouth like it's the first time we ever kissed even though I burst into the Phantom Society building to demand each of their lips to know which one of them it was that was stalking me.

This time it isn't just to learn the truth, and instead, I'm discovering a whole new side of me filled with longing for a guy who knows exactly what I need and doesn't shy away from offering his soul on a fucking platter to me.

"We have to stop," I mutter between kisses.

His lips unlatch, and he presses sultry kisses to my chin, leaving a trail of fire in his wake. I almost melt into a puddle right then and there just from the softness of his lips as they caress my skin along my jawline. "Do we? Or are you just saying that because you don't think you deserve my kisses?"

He presses more and more to my neck until I'm delirious with need, and his hands slide across my body underneath the water. Each brush as he skitters past my nipples is an even bigger turn-on.

Suddenly, he lifts me in his arms and sets me down on the edge, parting my legs.

"Your body deserves to be worshipped," he murmurs, pushing my dress up with his lips until my panties are exposed, and even those he slips aside. "So let me worship this fucking pussy."

And when his mouth lands on my pussy, I can't say no anymore.

\*\*\*

## MILO

I kiss and suck with everything I have to give, applying ample pressure to her slit until she's writhing with pleasure. Watching her from down below like this while she's enjoying my tongue is a dream come true for me. If I could give this to her every day of the week, I would. She deserves nothing less than everything she wants, everything she ever needs, and then some.

God, she tastes so fucking good.

"My tongue is yours to use," I murmur, lapping her up. "Yours to command."

"Fuck, lick harder," she moans, and I do exactly what she says, rubbing my whole mouth against her like I'm eating my last fucking meal.

In fact, I'd probably die happy if she'd drown me after.

Every second was worth it.

Groaning, I bury my face between her legs, licking and sucking like a madman. I grip her ass to pull her closer as her legs begin to quiver, so I steady her with my palms. Her fingers find their way to my hair, and she pushes me down even farther, making my cock throb.

Fuck, she's so fucking hot when she lets me do this for her.

"Faster," she moans. "Fuck, I hate that you make me want this so much."

"Do you want me to apologize?" I mutter between licks.

"No, don't stop," she murmurs.

I smile. "Do you want to strangle me for making you enjoy my tongue?"

When she opens her eyes, I look up so she sees just how much I'm willing to give her. "Do it then. Punish me."

Her legs immediately squeeze around my throat, but I don't waver as I cover her clit with my mouth and suck.

"Goddammit, you filthy fucker," she groans, gyrating her hips against my face. "Again, you roped me into this."

"Fuck yes, give it to me," I mutter as I suck on that little swollen clit.

She squeezes even harder until I can feel all the blood leaving my face, but still, I don't relent. I knew she'd be a sucker for hurting me. That's why I chose her, why I can't stay away, why I need to submit to a woman like her. The way she enjoys dishing out the pain makes me want to give her my all.

"I'm gonna come," she mewls. "Lick that pussy."

"Oh yes, drown me with your wetness," I groan, burying my tongue into her pussy before I roll it around her wetness.

Her fingers dig into my scalp, and I can feel her clit throb as a loud moan escapes her lips and a gush of wetness fills my mouth. I almost blow my load right then and there.

Suddenly, the doors in the back open, and she shoves me down so hard my face goes underwater.

I can hear someone talk, but I don't know who, and I can't fucking see shit as I thrash around in the water.

When she finally pulls me up again, I gulp in the breaths. "I didn't mean actually drown."

"Sorry!"

I smirk and press a kiss to her leg. "Not that I mind drowning for you."

"You two fucking around in the pool?"

I look up to see Nathan leaning against the door with his arms crossed.

*Oh boy. No wonder she panicked.*

A lopsided grin forms on my face. "It's not what it looks like."

He slams the pool door shut and walks over to the water. "Your face between her pussy lips? Yeah, I'd say that's exactly what it looks like."

She scrambles away from me and gets up. "What are you doing here?"

"Checking up on you after that asshole over there failed to report back," Nathan says, eyeing her up and down. "But it seems he's got you covered."

"Are you ...?" She frowns and folds her arms, a mischievous look on her face. "You're jealous."

His eyes widen, and he homes in on me as I lift myself out of the water, and both of their eyes immediately swipe over my wet shirt clinging to my abs along with that hard dick poking right through my pants. She swallows when I grin at her.

"I'll let you touch me any time you want."

When I glance at Nathan, he adjusts his package and grinds his teeth.

"Both of you, actually," I add with a wink.

She rushes out of the pool and pats down her wet clothes.

Nathan's nostrils flare. Turning, he waltzes to the sauna in the back, opens the door, and points inside. "In. Both of you."

She folds her arms right underneath those tits, and I can see her nipples protruding right through her dress, making me lick my lips. "Why would I?"

"Did you forget our agreement?" he retorts. "You do what I say."

She clenches her teeth, and it takes her a moment to process, but then she still marches over to that sauna. Right before she enters, she looks at him and says, "You're only doing this because you're jealous."

"I am *not* jealous," he spits back. Suddenly, his fingers wrap around my throat, and he pulls me close. "I *am* upset you chose to do this without me."

And he shoves us both in and closes the door behind him.

\*\*\*

## LANA

Wow. "So you *are* jealous," I say, turning around to face him.

"Milo," he says without even looking at him. "Block the door."

I swallow away the lump in my throat as Nathan approaches, my wet clothes quickly warming up from the heat inside this small sauna.

"I asked Milo to check on you, see if you needed anything, and then I find you both here, soaking wet and with his tongue stuck in your pussy?"

"We fell into the fucking pool," I retort, glancing at Milo over Nathan's shoulder. "Thanks to him."

"Doesn't matter." He grabs a strand of my hair, curling it between his fingers. "He gave you an orgasm, didn't he? Was it good? Did it make you want more?"

I try to ignore the throbbing between my legs. "How did you even find me here?"

He tilts his head. "Your friends were very eager to please."

My jaw drops. "You asked them?"

"No," he says with a smug smile as he slowly begins to peel away each button of his shirt. "I don't ask. They practically begged to tell me."

I don't even know how they knew we came in here.

Then again, I wouldn't put it past nosy Brooke to take a sneak peek.

He pulls away his shirt, leaving me breathless and completely confused as to why I can't look anywhere else but at those rock-hard abs and all the intricate tattoos like a Phantom logo that covers his very muscly chest.

Fuck. He's ripped in all the right places, and that's putting it lightly.

With each step Nathan takes toward me, I take one step back until I bump into the wooden seats. He clutches my arm to stop me from falling, his body mere inches away from mine. And I'm struck by how gorgeous he is up close, despite the bitterness in his eyes. It's the kind of pain that's all too familiar to me. Maybe that's why I hated looking at it so damn much.

His hand comes up to my face, and he tips up my chin to make me look at him. "And I want to hear you beg too."

His thumb grazes my lip, his gaze fluttering over my skin almost as if he's memorizing each pore. As he towers over me, he slowly opens my mouth and dips his thumb inside, pushing my tongue down. He spits into my mouth, forcing me to taste him.

"Swallow."

When I do, he moans, his finger still inside my mouth.

He pulls out and grips my hair, then slams his lips onto mine. His kiss is coarse, greedy, almost as though he's pouring every ounce of his rage into this one kiss. And as our lips unlatch, it feels like the air is knocked from my lungs.

"Fuck," he groans.

"Too late for you too?" Milo muses in the back.

"Shut up," Nathan growls at him without taking his eyes off me.

His hand slides down my neck, slipping down my body, my tits, almost like he's savoring every inch.

"I thought you hated me and my family," I say, confused by the reckless kiss he just gave me.

"Your family, yes... but you ... I'm fucking thirsty for you."

He slides his hand down my body, his fingers dipping between my legs as he pushes the dress up, and I try not to feel affected, but god-damn, the way he touches me makes it so hard.

"Milo played with you," he murmurs, sliding my panties aside. "Now it's my turn."

# 35

⚮

## NATHAN

I dip my middle finger into her pussy and watch her clench her teeth to prevent the moan from spilling out. She may be able to stop them now, but that won't last for long.

Before we're out of here, I'm going to hear her scream my name, and it won't be from the building heat inside this cubicle. It'll be from my cock ramming into her wet, aching pussy.

I grasp her by the hair and make her look at me as I shove another finger inside. Her o-shaped mouth tells me enough.

"You thought I couldn't please a woman with these fingers?" I roll them around inside her, touching her G-spot with ease. "Imagine what I could've done if I used all three."

"Fuck."

I lean in while fingering her and whisper into her ear, "Milo made you so fucking wet, didn't he?"

When she shudders, I pull out, and she breathes out a soft moan, quickly followed by a squeak when I fish the toy I've been waiting to use out of my pocket.

"What is that?"

"You don't need to know what it is." I push it underneath her dress and into her wet pussy. "Just know it'll make you fall to your knees and beg."

I push it inside, and she lets out another mewl as I turn it on and the buzzing begins. And fuck me, I can practically see her fall apart right in front of me.

I push her down, forcing her to sit. "Enjoy the vibes ..."

And I walk toward Milo, who stares at me sheepishly while I go to my knees in front of him and unzip him. "What are you doing?"

"Enjoying what belongs to me," I say as I pull out his hard-on. "Both of you."

I turn to look at her. "Now watch, and don't you dare look away."

I take Milo into my mouth and lick him off while he just stands there whimpering like the little simp he is. But I don't give a goddamn care in the world. If these fuckers are going to play, I'm playing with them. And I sure as hell won't allow him to have pleasure without me.

So I lick his cock while stroking my own through the fabric of my pants, sucking him off as hard as I can, all while making consistent eye contact with Lana who's having trouble breathing through it.

His knees buckle, and I have to bring his hand to my hair so he won't fall.

"Hold me," I growl.

"But you never—"

I slap his ass. "I do what I want with this cock. Now stay there until I bring you to the brink of madness."

"But she's here too," he mutters, gazing at Lana, who's writhing on the bench behind us.

"Don't look away, Lana," I order her.

And I zip down my pants and pull out my hard-on. Her eyes home in on it like the lusty whore she is, and I enjoy every secret glance she throws my way while trying her best not to be affected.

She's drenched in water and sweat as the heat in this sauna rises. She's on the verge of coming again. I can see it from the way she clenches her legs. A smile forms on my lips as I reach into my pocket and turn up the speed.

"F-fuck," Milo groans as my tongue rolls around his shaft. "Oh my God, this feels amazing."

I pull down his pants and shove a finger in his ass so he squeals. "That's more like it."

When he's throbbing in my mouth, I pull out, leaving him hanging on the edge.

"Oh fuck, I almost came," he murmurs.

So I slap him on the ass so hard he groans out and falls to his knees. "I didn't say you could."

I get up and focus on Lana, who swallows when she sees the hard-on hanging out of my pants. "Enjoyed the show?" When she doesn't answer, I march at her and grip her chin, making her look at me. "Answer me."

She licks her lips, delirious with need. "Yes."

I tip up her chin. "Did you just come?"

The little sucks of breath tell me enough, and a wicked grin spreads on my cheeks. "Such a horny little slut."

Her nostrils flare. "Fuck you."

I turn off the device and reach between her legs, pulling it out in one go.

"F-fuck!" she moans. "Why'd you have to—"

She shuts her mouth the second she realizes what she was about to say.

My brow rises, but she merely blushes and looks away.

I snap my fingers. "Milo, sit down on the bench beside her."

He does what I ask, and she looks up at him as he sits down, his tattooed cock fully erect and glistening with both pre-cum and spit.

I pull her up from the bench and flip her around so her back is turned to me, my hard-on poking her in the ass. I grip her tits, pinching both of them right through her dress until she practically gyrates against my hard-on, burying the tip right where I want it to be.

"Fuck! What is it with you and hurting me?"

"I don't enjoy hurting anyone I admire," I whisper, planting a kiss right underneath her ear. "And I admire you very much."

"Then why do you do it?"

I slide my length up and down her slit. "Because there's pleasure ... and then there's pleasure from pain."

I twist them even harder until she squeals out loud, and then I turn her face and cover her lips with mine, stealing away her sounds. Milo groans from excitement as I claim her mouth and make her mine right in front of him. When our lips unlatch, she murmurs, "Asshole."

I grin against her lips and kiss her again. "Yet you don't pull away."

"You're keeping me here in this sauna," she retorts.

"Am I?" My brow rises. "Or are you just telling yourself that so you don't have to bear the responsibility of your own needs?"

She sucks in a breath but still stays put as I plant kisses all over her neck. "I felt that key in your pocket, Lana. You can leave whenever you choose to do so ..." I slip my hand into her dress and fondle her bare nipples, pulling her tits out for Milo to enjoy. "But you won't ... because deep down you want this as much as we do."

And I thrust into her wet pussy, burying myself to the base. She moans out loud as I bend her over and fuck her hard and fast, not giving a shit that anyone could find us here at any moment.

I need to have this girl. Wherever, whenever ... it doesn't fucking matter.

I told myself it was all for the money, but now that I've dealt with the debt, I want more, so much fucking more.

I don't think I'll ever have enough of this pussy or this violent fucking kitty.

"Fuck, you're so tight and wet," I groan as I grip her throat to hold her steady. "Look at that pussy-whipped boy. Look at his cock begging for a chance at pleasuring this pussy. Look at how he yearns for you. How he'd worship the fucking ground you walk on if you let him."

"Fuck," she mewls, her wetness coating my shaft with every thrust.

"He belongs to you as much as he belongs to me," I say. "But I'm willing to fucking share him with you, just like I want to share you with him."

And I ram inside one last time before I pull out and whisper into her ear, "Now straddle him and give him what he craves so badly ... while I give you what you deserve."

\*\*\*

Lana

I walk up to Milo, my mind going blank as I crawl on top of him. I'm entranced, and I don't know whether it's from the rising heat in this sauna pushing us to our limits or the sheer amount of lust building inside my body and clouding my judgment.

Because right now, I want nothing more than for the two of them to fuck me into the next plane.

When the tip of Milo's curved length bounces up and down against my opening, I feel so much fucking power. The whimper that follows when I lower myself on top of him is nothing short of pure magic.

Just my pussy as it sinks deeper and deeper over his length is enough to bring this boy to his knees, and it is so fucking arousing I could come again. His curvy tip touches my G-spot, almost making me moan without any effort.

"Now ride him," Nathan whispers behind me, his fingers digging into my thighs as he guides me over his dick again and again.

Milo moans too, and his hands find their way to my breasts, fondling, squeezing, toying with my nipples like he's adoring every inch of me with his hands and his eyes.

"Fuck, your pussy feels divine," he groans, throbbing within me.

"Don't come yet, pussyboy," Nathan growls, and he slaps Milo's inner thigh so hard he jerks up and down.

After that toy Nathan used on me, I'm so overcome by need I start to use Milo like a dildo, but he doesn't even seem to mind. This boy is so smitten with me; the love is almost pouring out of his eyes alone, and it moves me so much I lean down to smash my lips on his.

It's crazy, stupid, and I'm probably drunk on lust, but fuck me, his lips feel so good while I'm riding him.

Nathan suddenly pushes something hot into the small of my back, and my body arches from the sizzle. My hand rises to turn and slap him. "What the f—"

He grabs my wrist and opens my hand to stuff a hot stone inside. "Now you know the pain ..." His eyes travel to Milo, who swallows, not from fear but from excitement. "Wield it. Make him beg for it."

I shouldn't do this. I shouldn't play these games, yet the heat, the pain, how it felt makes me want to dish it out too. So I bring the stone to Milo's chest and press it down hard.

I thought his whimpers would make me hate him, but it only makes me want to give him more.

"Fuck," I mutter as I pull back and watch the red mark appear on his chest.

It's a testament to my rage. My undying need to hurt people.

And he's a willing victim.

"Do it again," Nathan growls behind me.

"But it's hurting him—"

Out of nowhere, Milo grasps my wrist and shoves the stone onto his other chest out of his own volition, and his dick throbs inside me.

This ... turns him on. He *wants* this. And he wants *me* to do it to him. To hurt him and relinquish my anger by taking it out on him.

Nathan leans in and whispers, "Now you know why I don't like seeing him with others ..."

"He is your perfect victim," I mutter. "A willing, hungry participant." I turn to look at him. "And you're afraid I might take that away from you?"

He rolls one of the stones against my back, making me acutely aware of how much of a sadist he is ... and that I might grow to like this pain too.

"No one is ever going to take him away from me. I won't let them," he groans, and he pushes one of the hot stones into Milo's thigh, watching him writhe with desire. "But I'm more than willing to share."

Nathan suddenly perches himself behind me, and he pushes me down so my chest rests on Milo's.

"It's about time you learned what it felt like to be owned by us," Nathan murmurs.

My lips break away right as he pushes inside my pussy as well, and a loud moan escapes my mouth as he stretches me.

"That's it, slut. I know you can take it," Nathan groans, burying himself inside me too.

"Fuck, I can't take it," I mewl as he starts to move.

He fists my hair and tilts my head so far back I see the sauna's ceiling along with his penetrative eyes boring a hole into me. "Look at me." When I do, he buries in even farther. "You can do it because you're a good fucking girl, and you like to be used."

"Fuck! It's so full!" Milo moans beneath me.

When they both start to move in sync, my eyes almost roll out of my head.

"Yes, that's it, Lana, feel our cocks own this pussy now," Nathan growls as he thrusts in and out of me. "Now use the stones. Give him the pain I'm giving you."

I grab one of the stones he laid out on the bench and push it into Milo's shoulder, then watch as he bites his lip in agony. He shivers underneath me, his dick throbbing, hard, ready to blow. And I realize this is such a fucking turn-on for me that my own pussy begins to throb along with him.

"You can feel it, can't you? The need to explode all over my goddamn cock," Nathan groans, slamming into me with full force.

"Fuck, give it to me," I mutter, delirious from the lust and pain entwining inside me.

"Beg," he says. "Beg and I'll let you."

"Please, Nathan!" The word slips out without effort even though I once thought I would never say it.

But goddamn, these men have gotten me to my knees, willing, wanting so much fucking more that I'm prepared to beg for it.

Nathan shoves two stones into my hand. "Now fucking come."

And as I push them against Milo's nipples, I moan out loud from the sheer heaviness of the orgasm rolling over my body. Milo whimpers, and I can feel him explode inside me right when Nathan buries himself to the hilt, filling me up to the brim too.

"Fuck!" Nathan groans, pulling out of me swiftly, his dick still pumping.

When I realize the stones are still on Milo, I wipe them away as the burn marks appear on his nipples.

"Shit, I'm sor—"

Milo grips my face and kisses me so hard all the words I meant to say turn to drivel in my head. God, I never thought I could want three men as badly as I do right now, but apparently, even an icy cold queen's heart can melt after finding the right amount of heat.

When his lips unlatch, he murmurs, "Don't *ever* apologize for giving me your all."

My cheeks flush, and sweat drops roll down my forehead and onto his.

God, it's so fucking hot in here, and not just from the sauna.

Nathan grips my throat and pulls me to him, turning my head enough so our lips can touch. And my God, his kisses are nothing short of pure magic.

I never once believed I could fall for a trap so perfectly laid out for me, but I was wrong. So fucking wrong. All the lines are blurred. His kisses are like a much-needed calm after the high of the storm, and my lips return his eager kisses with as much enthusiasm.

His lips unlatch, only to plant kisses all over my neck. "Now you know what it feels like to hurt, that rush of endorphins coursing through your veins when you give in to what you need the most."

"And what's that?" I mutter.

"Us." He zips up again, leaving me feeling bereft.

I get off Milo, who just lies there, completely wasted.

"Wait ... are you saying it hurts you to want me?" I push my breasts and panties back into place, my dress still clinging to my body despite the heat steaming at least some of the water off. "Why?"

Nathan raises his hand again, showing me the missing finger, and finding the words is hard.

For some reason, a part of me almost feels ... guilty.

Even though I wasn't the one to cut it off, it still feels like I could've done something, stopped my brother from fighting with him, or at the very least show mercy.

Mercy Nathan never showed me.

My hand forms a fist. "I know what my brother is, how violent he can be when he perceives a threat. He protects what he loves."

"Just like I do," he says.

"Yet you couldn't get it across your goddamn heart to protect me," I grit.

His lips part as shock contorts his face, almost as if he didn't consider the possibility to think of me as anything other than a plaything. But then why does he keep looking at me like he wants more? Like he could almost give himself to me fully?

"Guys, can we not fight right after sex?" Milo grouses, leaning up on his elbows.

We both ignore him.

"Protect you from what?" Nathan tilts his head. "Is someone threatening you?"

I narrow my eyes. "You."

He gulps, visibly shaken by what I just said. "You know why I did that."

"Yet you continue to hold my pictures hostage to control me," I say.

He reaches for my face and softly caresses my cheek, eyes settling on my lips as though he wants nothing more than to kiss them. "I haven't shown them to anyone. And I don't intend to."

*He doesn't intend to?*

My pupils dilate. "So it was all an empty threat?" I shove him away. "You bastard!"

He snorts and shakes his head. "I told you ... I would do anything for Ro's safety."

"Anything ... including lying to me," I say, feeling like he just stabbed that knife of his straight into my heart.

*Why? Why do I even care?*

"Guys, please ..." Milo mutters. "Can't we just be together? Without all the fighting?"

Grumbling to myself, I turn around. "This was a mistake."

"A mistake?" Milo parrots, jumping off the bench to follow me. "No, no wait, please, Lana."

"Let her go," Nathan barks as I open the door. "She clearly doesn't want to be ours."

"You know, I almost, almost thought I could let you all ..."

I stop before I say something I won't be able to take back.

Both boys stare at me, wondering what that last word would be that could slip off my tongue.

But I won't give them the satisfaction of knowing.

"Never mind," I say, and I storm off.

"Let us what?" Milo calls from the sauna. "Please, Lana, don't leave."

But I stick up my middle finger despite the tears welling in my eyes.

But Sicklittlebitch13 wouldn't ever cry in front of the people she wants to murder, so I swallow them all back down and keep walking.

# 37

### KAI

I stare out the window at the snowflakes slowly falling. I can almost feel the cold right through the glass, the shivers reminding me of that night in the alley. When we ravaged that girl I can't fucking stop thinking about. I haven't heard from Lana in a couple of days, and it's starting to make me antsy. In the middle of class, I pull out my phone and text her.

*Me: Have you been up to some bad stuff again?*

It takes her a while to respond.

*Lana: What kind of stuff are you thinking of?*

*Me: Sex ... murder. Maybe both at the same time.*

*Lana: Wow. OTT.*

*Me: Not when it comes to you.*

*Lana: True.*

*Me: So you admit you're a kinky li'l kitty. I like it.*

*Lana: Why are you texting me?*

*Me: I told you ... when I call, you come.*

*Lana: So you want me to come now? Like a dog?*

*Me: Not like a dog, but if you want to get on all 4s for me, I won't deny you the opportunity.*

I smirk at the thought of watching her crawl to me. Good God, the hard-on I already have. I should definitely not be doing this in the middle of class, but I'm bored, so why the hell not.

*Lana: Ur just like your friends.*

*Me: Y?*

*Lana: All you do is use and destroy.*

I frown, confused. Where is this coming from?

*Me: Did something happen that I'm not aware of?*

*Lana: Ask your fucking friends.*

Okay, now I really need to know more, so I open my conversation with Nathan.

*Me: Did you talk with Lana?*

It takes him a while to respond.

*Nathan: Talk is a big word.*

My hand tightens around the phone.

*Me: WDYD?*

*Nathan: Milo and I had some fun with her.*

*Me: Without me?*

*Nathan: She's ours too.*

*Me: Would've been nice of you to tell me.*

Since when does he keep shit from me?

*Nathan: Now u know.*

*Me: She's angry. Why?*

*Nathan: Bcuz I told her I wasn't planning on sending those photos to her brother.*

I sigh out loud and rub my face.

God-fucking-dammit.

If he said that straight to her face, she's gonna go ballistic.

I get up from my seat and storm out in the middle of class.

"Excuse me, Mr. Torres, where are you going?" the teacher asks, but I ignore him. "Mr. Torres?"

I don't care that I'll miss important information. I need to find her. Now.

I bolt out of the building and call her on my phone.

"Where are you?"

The snooty voice on the other end makes me seethe. "Why do you care?"

"Don't play coy with me now, kitty," I growl. "Give me a location."

She makes a tsk sound. "I'm busy."

"With what?"

"Friends. You know what those are?"

God, I fucking hate when she's being difficult and icy because it makes me so goddamn hard, and I can't be hard in public. At least not when no one knows she belongs to me. Yet.

"You tell me where you are at right now, or I swear to God, I will tear down the entire fucking campus until I find you," I growl as I march across campus through the snow.

"Okay, okay, chill, I'm in the rose garden."

I frown, clutching my phone tightly. "The rose garden? No one takes their friends there. That's a make-out spot." Okay, now I'm really getting fucked up. "Lana, who the fuck is there with you?"

She just laughs and ends the call, so I pick up the pace as I head straight toward the garden in a small courtyard behind the school. It's more like a giant maze than an actual garden, surrounded by many trees and bushes large enough to overshadow the area and allow for plenty of privacy. Privacy to do things you shouldn't be doing when someone has already staked their claim on you.

And fuck me, if I find someone, *anyone*, touching *my* girl, the entire fucking earth will not be a safe place to hide from me.

\*\*\*

## LANA

God, I love riling those fuckers up.

I mean, they kind of deserve it after what they keep putting me through.

I'm not here with anyone except myself, trying to get my work done in peace. But he doesn't need to know that. Let him fucking fume.

They can play me, but I can play them just as well ...

I adjust in my seat underneath this big tree, which protects me from most of the snowfall. It's beautiful out here, and the serenity allows me to focus on my homework.

Suddenly, the bushes behind me rustle, and I look up, my heart racing, thinking it's Kai. But when Jason walks into the garden, my heart immediately sinks into my shoes.

"What are you doing here?"

"I could ask you the same thing. Expecting someone?"

I throw my books down on my bag and get up. "What the hell do you want?"

"I think we need to talk." He rubs his nose. "You've been avoiding me ever since that dinner."

"Yeah. I think I was clear enough, right?" I say.

He approaches, and I don't like it one bit. "Look, I fucked up. I get that, okay? Can't we talk?"

"No," I say.

"You won't even let me apologize?"

I fold my arms. "Not interested."

He comes even closer, holding out his hand. "C'mon, Lana, I just want one chance. I know now what I did wrong."

I step back, away from his grip. "Don't. Don't even fucking try after what you did."

"It was just a bunch of pictures," he says. "I get that now."

"No, I don't think you do," I say, shaking my head. "You tried to blame me."

"I don't want anyone to look at you like that. Please, Lana, you have to know I care." He attempts to grab my hand, but I jerk away. When he gets too close, I push him away.

"Ew, get off me."

"Why would you say that? I'm trying to make things right with you."

"I don't want you anymore," I say, my voice becoming unhinged.

"Not now, but maybe in the future. I'll wait for you," he says, gripping my arm. "Just tell me who they were."

"What?" I push him away and try to jerk my arm free, but he won't let me go. "No, let me go."

"Goddammit, Lana, you have to trust me!"

When I finally manage to wring free, I run off into the snowed-under maze to try to get away from him. Even though my knife pokes into my thigh from my pocket, I don't want to pull it on him. I don't want to hurt him.

But I can hear his footsteps behind me, cracking through the snow, and it strikes fear into my heart.

Not because I'm afraid of him, but afraid of what I'll have to do if he won't let me go.

"Leave me the fuck alone, Jason!" I yell, bumping into some snowed-under rose bushes on my way through the maze.

Thorny roses push into my skin, but I try to ignore it as I keep running.

"I need you to be safe, Lana! Please! Stop and talk to me!"

I come to a full stop in front of a dead-end.

*Shit.*

I turn around, and he's right there in the only exit out of this part of the maze.

*Fuck.*

I don't want to fight him.

Jason used to be here when I needed him. When I needed to lull that part inside me that screamed to be let out.

But now it's too late. Too late to put the genie back into the bottle.

"Stop," I tell him as he walks closer. "I *cannot* give you what you want."

"I'm just asking you to tell me who took those pictures," he says, approaching fast. "I want to protect you."

"Too late. I gave you a chance to help me, and you didn't take it," I say, tears welling up in my eyes. "I don't ever want to see you again."

His face contorts. He's mere inches away from me. "You're my girlfriend. I won't allow that. I need you."

My heart's beating in my throat when someone jumps out of the rose bush, skin cuts and snow all over, and thrusts a knife right to Jason's face.

*Kai.*

"One more inch. One touch. And your eye meets my blade."

I'm frozen to the ground.

His whole body is covered in an aura of violence, like a silent killer ready to strike. And the mere sight of him even makes Jason's knees weak.

"I'm ..."

"I know who you are," Kai says, an air of calm and collectedness surrounding him, like a ghost before it's about to haunt its victim's soul. "Jason Foley from the Skull & Serpent Society."

"Who the fuck are you?" Jason growls back.

"Kai," he hisses, tilting his head.

Jason's eyes widen. "Torres."

"So you do know me," Kai muses, smiling.

"Lana ..." Jason's eyes skitter between Kai and me like he's trying to warn me.

"Didn't you hear? She doesn't want you," Kai says, his voice low, commanding.

Jason looks over Kai's shoulder at me. "You know this dude?"

But Kai raises his knife again, pushing it into his forehead so deeply a bloodied mark appears. "Don't talk to her. Talk to me."

Wow. I've never been guarded like this.

It almost makes me feel ... protected.

Jason's lip quivers. "What the fuck is wrong with you?"

"You. I've got a problem with you trying to touch my girl."

"Your girl?" Jason's brows furrow.

*Oh fuck no. Now he's gone and done it.*

"No, no, she's my—"

"*Girlfriend?*" Kai mocks. "The girlfriend you can't even please?"

Jason's stammering. "Wha—"

"The girlfriend I gave the most amazing orgasms to when you couldn't even bother to look at her and see what she truly craved?"

Jason's eyes turn murderous. "*You* ... You're the one who's been toying with her?"

"Kai," I mutter, but he pushes me behind him.

"You're the one who took those fucking pictures of her?" Jason growls.

"I didn't do shit. But you sure as hell won't take one step closer," Kai warns. "She's not yours. She never was."

"Lana, if this is the guy you needed help from, tell me now or—"

"Or what? You want to fight me?" Kai pushes the knife even farther between Jason's eyes.

A droplet of blood rolls down his nose.

"Are you sure about that? There is a reason I lost one eye, and it wasn't an accident. Choose your battles carefully, Foley. I have very little to lose."

I swallow the lump in my throat while Jason's whole body quakes.

Kai leans in to whisper, "She belongs to me."

"Phantom scum," Jason says, making a fist. "You'll pay for this."

A wicked smile forms on Kai's face. "Bring. It."

Jason takes a step back, and he homes in on Lana. "You want this fucker?"

I don't answer, not because I don't want to but because I can't.

I don't even know what I want anymore.

But judging from the way Kai's protecting me, he's already chosen for me. And I don't think I have the will in me to resist.

"You're making a big mistake, Lana," Jason says.

"Speak one word to her brother about this, and I will put your head on a stake outside the Skull & Serpent Society," Kai warns.

Jason's face turns white as snow.

Kai tilts his head. "Now are we good?" He brings the knife to his lips and licks the blade, along with the droplets of blood. "Or do you need some convincing?"

Jason swiftly shakes his head and promptly runs off.

"Come talk to her again, and I'll be waiting to rip out your tongue," Kai yells after him.

When Jason's finally gone, I breathe a sigh of relief.

"Is that the *friend* you were talking to?" Kai grits, his back still toward me, probably to make sure Jason doesn't come back.

"No ... I was actually alone," I admit. "I just lied to you."

He throws me a glance over his shoulder. "Why?"

"Because I was angry."

"He was following you ... And you had a knife," Kai states, turning to face me. "Why didn't you use it?"

"I ..." I avert my eyes. I almost feel ashamed that I didn't. "I didn't want to hurt him. I couldn't, he's my brother's friend," I say as tears well up in my eyes. "But now he knows everything."

"Hey." He pulls me into his embrace, and I'm smashed against his chest, completely stunned. "I'm here. I will *always* be here."

I'm overwhelmed by the sudden affection and don't know what to do or say.

"I won't let him hurt you."

I push him away. "But you're the one who caused it." I point at his chest. "If you and your friends hadn't stalked and used me, he wouldn't have known a thing. You just told him everything."

"He won't tell your brother," he says, as his tongue darts out to wet his lips. "Unless he has a kink for dying."

"What if he does? Then what?" I'm panicking, pacing around to calm myself, but it's not working. "This is everything I wanted to avoid. If people find out we're fucking, I'll be ruined."

"You won't be."

"You're a Phantom," I shout. "I'm the sister of the goddamn leader of the Skull & Serpent Society. You two are literal enemies."

"I don't care," he says.

"Don't you understand?" I say. "My brother will kill me."

"You think I'd let him?" he scoffs. "He won't come anywhere near you, and neither will Jason." He grabs my arm and forces me to stop. "Lana. Look at me." When I don't, he cups my chin. "I'm not afraid to fight for you."

I swallow, the glimmer in his white eye drawing me in, making me feel things I'm not supposed to feel for my stalker, a killer.

"Now tell me how he knew about the pictures."

I sigh. So he heard. "At my father's dinner, he stole my phone and saw the picture Nathan tried to threaten me with." I frown at the memory. "But he tried to blame me for it. Said he couldn't support me so I told him to fuck off."

His eyes narrow and his hand tightens around his blade. "Do you want me to kill him?"

My eyes widen. "What?"

His jaw clenches. "That useless son of a bitch wasn't there when you needed him. I knew I should've just executed him."

I suck in a breath but no amount of breathing can ever draw in enough oxygen. "You'd kill him for me?"

He cups my face, caressing my cheek as tiny specks of snow fall all around us. "I would kill every goddamn fucking human on this fucking planet for you."

*Why is it suddenly so hard to breathe?*

His lips are so close to mine I can feel his breath on my chin. "No one's ever done that for me ..."

"All you have to do is point this knife at someone." He slips his knife into my hand. "And I will end them."

I rub my lips together, thinking about the idea of Jason dying at Kai's hands. Even though I'd love nothing more than for him to pay for not supporting me and scaring the shit out of me just now, it still wouldn't feel right to literally end his life.

"No. Let him live," I mutter.

"Fine, I won't kill him." He leans in to whisper, "But I will take great pleasure in knowing he could never pleasure you the way I can."

He smashes his lips onto mine, claiming my mouth with fervor. Even as cold snow showers down upon us, the heat in his kisses could scorch the entire sky dry. The kiss is intoxicating, completely overtaking every inch of doubt in my soul.

"What the ... oh my God."

I drag my lips away from Kai's as we both look in the direction of the voice...

Only to come face-to-face with Crystal, who literally drops her books onto the ground when she sees us. "Him too?"

*Oh fuck.*

# 38

## LANA

Panic seeps into my bones.

I shove Kai away, handing him back his knife.

She bolts off with widened eyes, so I chase her through the rose garden. "Wait!"

"No, I saw nothing!"

"Crystal, please!" When I catch up with her, I grasp her arm and force her to turn around. "Please, don't run away."

She's the only friend I have in common with Penelope, and I don't want to risk losing a friendship over this.

"You have to understand it's not what it looks like."

"That sure looked like you were kissing Kai fucking Torres," Crystal replies, whispering, "Do you know what your brother would do if he found out about this? I mean, Nathan's one thing, but Kai too?"

Kai comes running through the maze, but when she spots him, her face goes as pale as the snow falling around us.

"There's no need to run from me," Kai says from a distance. "I can find anyone, anywhere, anytime I want to. Ask Lana."

Her eyes widen, and she gulps down her nerves. "He's freaking me out."

"He won't come near you, promise."

"Why are you even with him? And what about Milo and Nathan? You're seeing all three of them?" she asks.

A blush creeps onto my cheeks. "It's not really seeing them, more like ... an arrangement."

"An arrangement to kiss?" She frowns. "You're not making any sense."

"It's not just—Never mind, what I'm trying to say is that I just want you to know it doesn't mean anything important."

"Yes, it does," Kai says with a threatening voice, and when I turn my head to throw him a snooty glance, he's simply staring at Crystal. "She means *everything* to me. And if you like her as your friend, you'd be wise to keep your mouth shut."

"Kai!" I warn.

God, I'm terrified of anyone finding out what I've been up to, and now this.

"I won't tell anyone," Crystal says.

"Good," Kai responds, finally tucking his knife back into his pocket. "Guess that's settled then."

"I'm sorry," I tell her and grab her hands. "Please don't be mad."

"I'm not mad. I'm just worried." She squeezes my hands. "I just want you to be safe. Even though you only see me as Penelope's best friend, I consider you a friend of mine."

I pull her in for a hug. "Thank you. And you *are* my friend. You always will be, even if that fucker over there doesn't like it."

I narrow my eyes at him, but the killer smile he gives me throws me off.

I pull away as Kai approaches. He holds out her books. "You dropped these."

We both stare at him sheepishly as she snatches them back and tucks them into her bag.

"I was just trying to find a quiet spot to study, and then I find you two kissing," she mutters.

I snort. "Ha, same, except ... I'm a boy magnet apparently."

*That came out a lot less funny than it sounded in my head.*

"So like ... what kind of arrangement do you guys have?" she asks, tilting her head to look at Kai.

"None of your business," he says.

"Be nice," I warn him.

He bristles. "Fine." And he sticks out his hand. "Nice to meet you."

She grabs his hand, but when she looks under his hoodie and sees his scar and the icy white eye underneath, she visibly recoils. His mouth twitches as she swiftly retracts her hand, and he pulls the hoodie farther over his face.

"I ... I'm sorry," she stammers.

He clearly doesn't like to be stared at. But he shouldn't have threatened her either.

I grab her by the shoulder and pull her away. "Let's just go."

"Where?" Kai asks briskly.

"To study," I respond.

"I wasn't finished yet," he says.

I throw him a warning glare. "I am. *Don't* follow us."

When I walk off with her, I half expected him to hunt me down and make me stop, but he doesn't. He just stays between the roses and lets the flakes fall onto his body, as though he intends to remain there as a watchful guardian, never swaying from his post, never tempted to go anywhere else but exactly where I left him.

Waiting.

For me.

And with every step I take through the crackling snow I can feel the ice that had frozen my heart crack with it.

\*\*\*


# NATHAN

**Later that day**

"Up!" Rory squeals when I lift her up from the ground and onto the stump. "Down!"

I grasp her and hold her like an airplane, zooming her through the air, and she squeals again with delight.

"Up!"

I put her back on the stump, ready for another takeoff, when someone behind me clears their throat.

"Reliving your childhood?" Crystal muses, making me turn my head.

"Oh, hey, didn't see you there," I reply. I turn to Ro and say, "Go play by yourself a little."

"Okay, but only if you promise to take me for another ride after," Ro bargains.

I roll my eyes and hold out my hand. "Deal."

With a gleeful smile on her face she shakes my hand before running off towards the nearest slide.

"You've got a handful with her," Crystal murmurs.

"Yeah, she's gonna be a wild one when she's grown, that's for sure," I reply.

"Cute."

I sit down on the bench and take a much needed breath. "Got a study break?"

"Yeah, but not because I wanted one." She laughs awkwardly. "I wanted to ask you something but I don't know how."

"What?"

"You and Lana ... you're a thing now?"

My pupils dilate and a blush creeps onto my cheeks. "Uh ... who told you that?"

"Well, she kinda gave it away." She snorts. "And then also because Milo was basically worshipping her in front of us and spilled the beans."

I slam my hand against my face and rub my eyes. "Oh God."

She giggles. "I just thought maybe you wanted to know she told us."

"Who else knows?"

"Her friends. Irina and Brooke."

I groan out loud, and it only makes her giggle more.

"That wasn't even the most awkward part. I actually caught her kissing Kai in the rose garden."

"Oh."

"Oh? So you know they're a thing too?"

I shrug. "We're a mess. I'm not gonna lie."

She looks at me like I've lost my mind. "But I thought you were into ... boys?"

"I am. I never said I wasn't. Lana just makes us crazy."

"Ahhh ..." She rubs her lips together. "That explains it."

"What?"

"Well, Kai almost looked like he wanted to kill me for intervening," she says, chuckling, but it's not an amused chuckle at all. More like she's surprised she's still alive after crossing his path, and I don't blame her at all.

"Sorry about that. He's very protective of her."

I feel the same way, but I trust Crystal.

"Yeah, I noticed."

"Are you upset I didn't tell you?" I ask her, curious what she thinks.

"No," she replies, smiling. "It's just that, of all the people you could've gone for, Lana Rivera is the one?"

Now I'm smiling too. "Yeah ... Fate is funny, isn't it?"

"You know Felix is going to kill you three if he finds out, right?" she says. "He's been trying to find a reason to start up the feud again according to Penelope."

I smirk, sliding my tongue along my teeth as my blood begins to curdle. "Oh I'm ready."

"I love being friends, but don't involve me in this madness, okay?" she asks.

"Don't worry." I wink. "I won't put you in danger."

"Good. Because I don't intend to stop being friends with Penelope and the Skull & Serpent guys either, just so you know."

"I know. I don't expect you to," I reply.

She gets off the bench. "Speaking of which, they're probably wondering where I am. We've agreed to have a little get-together with everyone at Fi's Cups and Cakes." She licks her lips. "And I am not passing up on the opportunity to eat more cupcakes."

"Nathan! Airplanes!" Ro calls from the other end of the playground.

"And that's my cue," I muse.

Crystal walks off. "See you around!"

"Have fun at your little get-together," I reply as I walk toward my sister. "And if you get the chance, throw one in Felix's face for me, will you?"

She laughs. "One day I'm gonna get you to do it yourself!"

"Not in a million years!" I retort, on my way to Ro.

She winks. "In a million and one, then."

# 39

## KAI

**That night**

Even though it's the middle of the night, plenty of Phantoms are still awake, playing games together, talking with each other, fucking in their rooms with their girlfriends or boyfriends. The place comes alive during the night.

But it all feels so empty when I don't have her.

After she left with her friend, I tried to go back to my classes, but I can't focus on my courses when all I can think about is kissing her. She's taken control of my mind, my cock, even my heart, and every fucking atom in my body screams to be near her.

So I put on my hoodie again and make my way over to her sorority house, climbing up the same staircase I used before. Her window is opened slightly, just enough for me to push it open and climb through.

She thought she was safe, destroying my camera. But I don't need a camera to enjoy what's mine.

When I'm inside, I put on my mask and close the window behind me. I don't intend to exit this time.

She's sleeping peacefully in her bed, blissfully unaware of my presence. But she will know soon enough I am always watching, waiting for her to finally realize the nature of our relationship.

I am not just a stalker, and she is not just an innocent victim. I don't merely exist in her nightmares; I exist in her dreams too.

I approach the bed and slowly slip the blanket aside. Her nipples peak in the cold, and I savor the way they look in that little beige top.

Crawling on top of her, I kiss her ankle, her knee, and her thigh until I reach her pussy still covered by a few inches of fabric and a thin layer of satin. I slowly circle her pussy with my fingers until she moans in her sleep, and the satin soaks through.

Even now, when she's asleep, she still craves my touch, despite her trying to fight me every step of the way.

I pull the fabric away and press a kiss to her pussy, my tongue dipping out to have a taste of this divine creature. And I lap her up, slowly applying more pressure, circling her slit until it grows wet.

She's writhing around on the bed, still completely oblivious to what's happening, but her cheeks are stained red with desire.

My tongue curls up, and I dip into her pussy, taking what's mine, licking up her wetness until she's practically oozing with lust. Her clit throbs underneath my tongue as I swirl it around and around. In her sleep, her fingers curl around the fabric of the satin, desperate for more, so I apply more pressure and watch her come undone.

Her face radiates with heat, her pussy thumping as I drive my tongue inside, and I moan against her before I lean back to appreciate the scene. She looks so pretty when she's asleep ... ripe for the taking.

So I zip down and pull out my cock, which drips with pre-cum, and I nudge her legs farther apart. I perch myself between her delicious thighs and slide my length across her slit, coating it with her wetness. Her moans spur me to go faster, and when her eyes start to open, I push in.

The second her lips form an o-shape, I cover her mouth with my hand and thrust in and out deeply, owning every atom in her body like she owns mine.

Her eyes grow wild with both surprise and arousal as I bury myself inside her. A muffled squeal slips through my fingers, so I grip a little tighter as I impale her, making sure she feels every inch of my cock possessing her very fucking soul.

"Be quiet for me, little kitty." I put a finger against my lips. "Don't let your friends hear you moan."

\*\*\*

## LANA

With muffled groans, I try to make sense of what's happening. I can feel him pounding inside me, and I grow wetter with every passing second. One minute I'm asleep, having the filthiest, raunchiest sex dream of my life, and the next, I'm being impaled on the cock of the very same man I dreamed about. And not just him, all three of them invaded my mind.

*It's him. That mask he's wearing ... It has to be him.*

The way he fucks me is out of this world, so insanely good that I can't help but writhe underneath him as he buries himself to the hilt, and a moan slips out of my mouth.

The grin on his face makes me want to bite his fingers off, though.

"That's the face, kitty. Show me how angry you are at the way I invaded not just your body but your thoughts too."

My eyes widen.

"You've been dreaming about me, haven't you?" he says, adding more pressure with each thrust. "Ever since the last time I snuck into your room, you've been dying for me to claim that pussy again while you were helpless to stop me." His breath lingers near my ear, coyly whispering, "Admit it."

But I can't respond since his hand still covers my mouth.

"Just nod."

When I do, the smirk that follows is unconscionably hot.

His hand slowly moves away from my lips, only to wrap around my throat instead, while the other firmly grips my thighs, and he pushes my leg up to go even deeper. "Then let me show this pussy who it belongs to."

He buries in to the hilt, and I almost see stars on the ceiling just from how good it feels.

"You like that, don't you?" I hiss. "Sneaking up on people when they're sleeping."

"Not people. *You,*" he groans, gripping me even tighter as he goes slow and steady so I feel every one of his piercings as they enter me. "I fucking *crave* you. Every hour of the day, especially at night. I will fucking make this pussy mine. Even if you hate me for it, even if your family doesn't approve, even if the whole fucking world is against it, I will make you mine, or so help me God, I will kill them all."

His words set me off, and my pussy begins to contract around his shaft, and as a stifled moan comes out of my mouth, he slams his lips onto mine. His tongue probes around my lips, coaxing them to open as I fall apart beneath him, desperate for more.

I don't know when my brain and heart had separated from reality so badly they decided to fall in love with evil personified. But damn, if this is pure evil, then I don't ever want to leave this fiery hell.

When his lips unlatch, he whispers, "I know you fucked around with Nathan and Milo ..."

I gasp. "They cornered me in the swimming pool." I don't know why I'm explaining this. "It wasn't my choice."

His eyes narrow as a devilish smirk spreads on his lips. "You're worried what I'll think."

My brows furrow. "What? Fuck no."

"I know they both want you. And I won't stop them. I like to see you being owned." His hand slowly dips down between my breasts. "But whenever you fuck with them, you remember I was the first. I was the first to lay waste to this fucking pussy."

He slaps my pussy, and I yelp in response, but those same fingers then roll around my clit, making my eyes want to roll back too. Good God, I never knew I needed something so dark to get off, but with him, all I want to do is come again and again and never let go of this feeling.

He dips his fingers into my mouth, and my tongue instinctively swirls around them. He throbs inside me, the animalistic groans that slip from his mouth with each thrust making me want to gyrate right up against him.

"That's it, kitty. I know how you break for me. How you yearn to fall apart from this cock just like you fell apart on my knee the day I snuck into your room. When Jason couldn't even fucking satisfy you the way I did. You don't want someone to make love to you ... you want to submit."

*Fuck.*

*What am I doing? Why am I letting him do this?*

*Why don't I fight back?*

Instinct takes over, and I kick him so hard he's pushed away and falls off the bed.

My breath is ragged, unhinged, as I grab my knife off my nightstand, yet I still crawl over the edge to look at him in that same hoodie and mask I first saw him in that day, when I didn't know who he was, but he knew exactly who I was.

What I did.

What I'm capable of.

And instead of fear and deterrence, it instilled a hunger in him that frightens me.

Not because I fear him.

But because I fear what will become of me if I give in to this same urge.

And I need to know *why*.

He leans up from the floor, staring at me through the mask, tempting me with that tempestuous grin of his that drives me closer and closer, so I crawl on top of him and peel away the mask he hides behind, casting it aside.

He looks so naked and vulnerable without it, his face marred by whoever decided to scar him for life. I used to see so much rage in those duplicitous eyes of his ... but now? Pure and utter obsession.

And it scares me.

"You three torture and kill for the money, but me? I'm a cold-blooded murderer, and you don't even know why."

"No," he murmurs. "I can wait until you're ready to tell me why. But it won't keep me away from you."

My teeth grind together, trying to fight off the shivers coursing through my body.

I point my knife at him. "WHY? Why would you *want* me?"

"Why do I want you?" he asks. "That's the same as asking me why I wouldn't want to breathe fucking air."

It's as if he just sucked the oxygen straight from my lungs and into his mouth.

*Fuck.*

I push the knife underneath his chin.

"You can stay away from me as much as I can stay away from you," he mutters as the blade inches closer and closer. "Even if you kill me, it's already too late. Our violent hearts have already been chained to each other." He grips my wrist and pushes the knife even farther in until a droplet of blood spills. "I will always be with you, even after death, because no fucking plane of existence could ever free me of the hold you have over me."

*Fuck.*

My hand quakes. I try. I try so hard to push that knife into his body, but no matter how badly I want this to end, I cannot.

I cannot fucking kill this son of a bitch because I want him.

I want him so badly I can't fucking breathe … because he's stolen my breath from me.

And I throw the knife aside and slam my lips onto his, kissing him with every inch of that fucked-up soul tethered to his.

# 40

## KAI

Finally, she's mine.

When her lips come to claim me, I let her explore my mouth just as I've explored hers, the first taste of many yet to come. I know she's wanted me from the day we first met, but it took her a while to come to terms with it. And I was willing to wait an eternity until she was ready to admit it.

We're ruthless, savage killers ... and killers belong together.

My fingers course through her hair, gripping her as I pull her close, my other hand snaking around her waist while my cock throbs against her stomach. But I don't care about any of that when I can taste her desire on her tongue as it swirls around mine, desperate for more.

When her lips unlatch, they're swollen and parted, searching for words she can't seem to find.

"I hate you," she murmurs as she leans back.

A smirk still forms on my face. "Is that a declaration of love, kitty?"

Pressing a flat hand on my chest, she pushes herself off me and slides down until my dick sits snuggly between her slit, making me swallow away the arousal building inside me.

"Love?" she muses, raising herself, only to lower herself onto my dick. "This isn't love. This is pure carnal desire."

I groan with delight as she takes me in fully and pulls out, so I grip her waist only to push her right back onto my tip again. "You keep telling yourself that. Now ride this cock like my good girl does."

"I'm. Not. Your. Good. Girl." Each word is followed by another thrust, but I don't fucking mind. I don't fucking mind whatever words she speaks as long as that pussy is mine. Because I know the words that spill from her mouth as lies ... her wet pussy speaks the truth.

When she leans in just a little, I grasp for her throat and force her down on my length. "No ... you're my bad fucking slut. Now sit."

Her eyes practically roll into the back of her head as I spear into her, hips bucking against each other.

"Jason never gave it to you like this, did he?" I groan, and I slap her tit until she squeals. "He didn't make you feel like his personal whore to be fucked and used." I force her down onto my cock again. "Because you didn't fucking let him. You didn't want him close because he would see the darkness inside you and shut you out."

I pinch her nipples until her words spill out. "Yes."

"And every time he even tried to touch you, you thought of me, didn't you?"

When she doesn't answer, I slap her tit again. "Answer me."

"Yes," she replies.

"I'm not afraid of what you are," I groan, pushing her over all my piercings until her eyes almost roll into the back of her head. "I won't let you shut me out. I *own* that fucking darkness thriving within you."

"Fuck," she moans, grinding away on top of me.

"How much did you quake with need the second you discovered it was me who gave you all that pleasure you so desperately craved?" The desperate look on her face reveals the truth, and I bury myself to the hilt inside her wet, aching pussy. "Did he ever even make you come?"

"No."

Fuck that loser. He can't ever get close to transcending the fucking devotion I'm offering her.

My hand slides down over her navel until I reach her slit. "When was the last time he touched you?"

"I didn't let him ... not after you pretended to be him ..." she says as I circle her clit with my thumb.

Fuck. She was already sold to my possessive fucking. "Good girl."

The proud lion in me roars with excitement as my cock begins to throb deep within this pussy of mine.

Slowly but surely, a wicked grin spreads on her face, and it looks so goddamn beautiful I wouldn't even mind if she killed me after we're done fucking because, dammit, even dying at her hands would be a privilege.

I flip her over so her back hits the floor, pull out for a second, and rip her blankets off the bed. "Lift your hips for me."

When she does, I push the blanket underneath and say, "See that fucking cabinet behind you?"

Her eyes rise to look at the wood.

"Hold it tight."

I lift her hips and ram into her pussy so deep her mouth forms an o-shape. And I lean over her and press kisses to her belly while thrusting in and out of her with slow but steady motions, allowing her to feel the depth of my possession over her.

My hand slides across her tits, and I squeeze them before I rip the fabric apart with my bare fucking hands, exposing her nipples. I cover them with my mouth and chuck the fabric aside as I drive inside her.

She mewls with delight while I fuck her so hard the cabinet starts to scoot across the floor just from her grip alone.

I fuck her harder and faster, and when she's about to climax, I pause, feeling her contract around my shaft.

"Why'd you stop?" she murmurs between ragged breaths.

I fish my gun from my pocket, and her eyes widen.

"You brought a gun?"

She shudders underneath me.

I've always had a gun on me. But just because I can use it doesn't mean I want to.

Until now.

"Open your mouth, Lana," I command.

"Are you going to shoot me?"

I tilt my head. "Do you trust me?"

It takes her a while to nod.

I point the gun at her. "Will you put your life in my hands?"

She looks me dead in the eyes, unafraid. "You won't kill me."

I shake my head.

She slowly does what I say, and I dip the gun into her mouth. "Roll your tongue around like you'd lick my cock."

When she does, I groan from how it looks, and it makes my cock throb inside her.

I pull out the gun and bring it between us, pushing the barrel against her ass.

"Fuck, are you really going to—?"

She can't finish the sentence, her mouth widening as I push it into her ass.

With each thrust, I drive it in farther until the entire barrel is inside along with me. And the look on her face is nothing short of majestic.

"What if it goes off?" she asks.

"We're connected, Lana," I say, slipping in and out of her slowly. "If you die, my dick gets blown to smithereens."

"Fuck," she says through gritted teeth, having trouble differentiating between danger and sexual tension.

But what she doesn't understand is that those two go hand in hand with us.

"It's you and I together, kitty," I say, alternating the speed of my strokes. "You are my fucking slut. Say it," I groan, taking her in both holes at the same time.

"I'm your slut," she murmurs, struggling to even form the words.

I lean in and hiss, "Louder."

"I'm your slut!" she moans when I bury myself inside her balls deep *and* drive the barrel in completely. "Fuck, I'm gonna come again."

"Yes, come all over my cock like a good fucking slut," I say. "Break for me."

Her orgasmic clenches as she lets out another giant moan tip me over the edge.

"Fuck me, Kai!"

I come undone with her, teetering on the brink of madness as I fill her up to the brim and then some.

Completely wasted and out of my mind in love with this woman, I lower myself on top of her and spread lavish kisses all over her body, taking good care of those perky nipples as I pull out my gun and let her come down from the high.

And as I come face-to-face with her, I press a gentle kiss just beside her lips. "Do you still hate me now?"

Her breath is ragged, her face contorted with confusion. "I ..."

"You don't have to answer. I already know the truth."

I crawl up, pick her naked body up from the floor, and carry her in my arms.

"Wait, what are you doing?" she asks, her feet thrashing in the air.

"Taking you to bed," I reply, ignoring her fight against any form of kindness so I can put her down on her pillow before I go back to grab the blanket. "You must be tired. I fucked you in your sleep."

She yawns as I crawl into the bed with her. I pull the blanket over and pull her closer to me, snuggling her. "So dream of me instead."

Her body is flushed with heat as I plant a hand on her waist, her skin covered in goose bumps when I softly caress her.

"Why are you doing this?"

My brow rises. "Can't I take care of my woman?"

Her cheeks turn red. "Take care of me? But ..."

"Do I have a reason not to?" I ask, softly pushing her hair aside so I can press a kiss to her neck. "Despite what you think, I'm not your enemy."

She breathes out in puffs after each of my kisses, clearly affected, yet she still won't let me into her heart.

"Who's your enemy, then?" she asks.

My fingers clench around her waist. "You know who."

"No, not the Skull & Serpent Society as a whole. I mean, who specifically? They can't all have done you wrong?"

"Your brother cut off Nathan's finger," I reply.

She turns around in my arms. "I know that, and I understand why Nathan's mad, but you have nothing to do with that."

"I protect my friends," I say, looking down at her from underneath my lashes. "So I came to get my revenge."

Her hand slowly rises to my face, and I fight the urge to inch back as she touches that part of me I've hated for so long.

"This scar ..." she murmurs as the tips of her fingers softly peruse my face.

It feels so strange, having a touch so soft on something so heinous and violent in nature.

"Felix gave it to you?"

"Dylan Caruso."

She pauses and leans back to look at me. "That's ..."

"Your brother's best friend," I fill in for her.

She swallows. "Can you still see?"

I grab her hand and press a kiss to her gentle fingertips. "Not through that eye. But I can see enough to know all I want is in front of me."

The left side of her lips briefly quirks up, but then she licks them to make it disappear.

But I definitely saw the smile.

Her hand slips out from underneath mine, and it trails around the tattoo underneath my heart.

"It looked red when I first saw it at the Shack. Was it new?"

I nod.

"It's a date ...isn't it?" she murmurs.

I nod again, wondering when she'll realize.

"Wait a second, this was the day I went to that house and—"

Her breathing stops. I look down at her at the same time her eyes widen and her lips part, and it's the most beautiful, bewildered face I've ever seen on her.

"The day I met you."

I cup her chin and pull her to me, pressing a gentle kiss onto her lips to melt that last inch of resistance in her heart. "I told you, our hearts were already chained to each other from the day we first met."

She smiles against my lips, her body zinging with heat, the mag-
netism between us undeniable. She rolls around again just as a blush
spreads on her cheeks, and I pull her closer.

"Enough talking. It's late, let's sleep."

"But—"

"Shh ..." I whisper into her ear. "Sleep."

"You're still here," she murmurs, tucking in her hair.

"Yes ... and I told you I'm not going anywhere."

"Even if I—"

I wrap my arm around her belly and pull her even tighter toward
me. "Hate me. Love me. Kill me. I don't care. I won't leave you."

I'm not like him.

I've seen her at her worst. At her most evil.

And it only made me fall that much harder.

I will never be like him. I will *never* abandon her.

She breathes a gentle sigh. "Good night."

So many hidden emotions behind that one word.

But we'll get there someday ...

I have all the time in the world.

\*\*\*

## NATHAN

I stumble down the steps in my red robe, rubbing the salt from my
eyes from a good night's rest as I make my way to Milo's room to check
on Rory. She hasn't wanted to sleep anywhere else since she came to the
house, so Milo's been bunking with me while she took his room.

"Ro! You awake yet?" I open the door, only to find it empty.

Except for that giant unicorn Milo bought her.

Weird.

She'd normally be up and running about around this time.

*Where could she be?*

I make my way across the house to the kitchen. Maybe he's making breakfast for her there.

But Milo's not there either. Nor is Rory.

*What the fuck?*

Another Phantom passes me by, so I grip his neck and make him stop. "Ezra. Where is Milo?"

He flips his long hair around. "Uh ... out?"

"Out where?"

"I don't know." He shrugs. "He didn't tell me. He just took that little girl with him."

My eyes narrow. "Rory."

"Can I go now?"

I release him from my grip, and he immediately walks to the fridge, taking out a carton of milk while keeping a keen eye on me.

I fish my phone from my sweatpants and check the text messages. There are none.

*Why would he just take her?*

**Me: Where tf r u? Y did u take Rory?**

There's no reply, not even three dots to signal some words incoming, and it pisses me off. My nostrils flare as I sit down behind the counter.

"Want some milk?" Ezra asks.

"No, had enough last night," I reply.

Ezra's face is that of pure and utter confusion, but I ignore it and send another text.

**Me: MILO! Answer me!**

Suddenly, my phone rings. It's him.

I swiftly pick up. "Where are you?"

"Nathan ..."

My pupils dilate.

*He sounds distressed.*

"I'm sorry." His voice cracks.

"What's going on?" I ask, pacing around. "Is Rory with you?"

"I just wanted to take her to the playground down the mountain ..."

He gurgles and coughs up in hacking ways. "I'm sorry, Nathan, there were too many of them—"

I jump off the stool. "What happened?"

I hear a hard flop as though something ... or someone ... just fell to the ground.

"Milo? Answer me, please!" I yell through the phone, but there's no reply.

*Fuck, fuck, fuck!*

I run out of the mansion, barefoot, jump into my car, and race off toward the scene.

I frantically dial Kai's number on the way. "C'mon, c'mon, c'mon! Pick up!"

But the phone just keeps ringing, and I end the call.

"Fuck!" I slam my hands onto the steering wheel. "Milo, Ro, I'm coming!"

I fish a gun from the glove compartment along with a magazine while I race down the mountain as fast as I can. But the second I reach the playground, I ram my foot into the brakes so hard the tires screech against the pavement.

I bump into a trash can and knock it over before I come to a halt.

Through the windshield, I see the bloodstains marking the rainbow paint on the floor, a piece of someone's tattooed skin lying on the grass next to the slide. All the hairs on the back of my neck stand up.

Grabbing the gun, I shove the magazine inside before I jump out of the car in my sweatpants and robe.

There's no one around. Not a single soul.

It's almost as if there was a bloodbath here, and all the bodies magically disappeared.

Until I spot one of them lying in the grass not far beyond the slide, one hand clutching a phone.

And my heart stops beating.

"MILO!"

I run toward him, checking my surroundings with my gun held at the ready, but no one is around except us.

I slide to my knees in front of him and grab his body, turning him over. There are gunshots in his abdomen and legs, and he's bleeding out fast.

"Fuck!" I yell.

"Nathan ..." He gurgles, coughing up blood.

I drag him into my lap. "Who did this to you? Are they still here?" I throw my robe off and rip off a piece to wrap around his leg, which is bleeding profusely.

He shakes his head as tears well up in his eyes. "I just wanted to give you some more time off, so I took her to play here," he says between breaths. "I'm sorry. I'm so sorry. I tried. I tried to fight them off, but I couldn't win. I didn't know they'd followed me all the way from the Phantom Society house." Tears roll down his cheeks. "I tried to protect her ..."

"Rory?"

He grips my arm, cuts all over his hands. "They took her."

# 41

## LANA

*The terrible sounds can be heard from across the hall.*
*Still, I move closer, sliding open the door when I know I shouldn't be in here.*
*Mommy told me never to come here at night.*
*But I want to know why I can hear my brother yelp.*
*I swallow as I see the two figures in bed, one on the bottom, arms flailing to the side, tears welling up in his eyes. I blink away mine and open my mouth, but when I try to scream, nothing comes out.*
*My hands shake violently.*
*And my eyes lower to look at them.*
*But my fingers have been replaced by bullets and my heart with death.*
*So I point my finger at the person lying on top.*
*BANG!*

My eyes open wide, sweat drops rolling down my back and neck as I try to adjust to my surroundings. Blinking a couple of times, I focus on the sights and sounds. I'm in my own bed, in my own room, and the sun is shining. But that smell ... it's musky and tropical, and unlike any perfumes I own.

Then I feel the hand creeping around my waist.

With widened eyes, I turn to come face-to-face with Kai, still lying in my bed, still cuddling me. And for a moment, I just simply stop existing.

"Good morning, kitty," he mumbles.

I can barely breathe when he's this close, his lips still as hot as I remember them being.

I thought he'd disappear in the middle of the night as he did before, but he's still here. Still holding me tight. Still invading every inch of my thoughts.

"You were groaning in your sleep," he murmurs.

"Oh ..." I lower my eyes.

He cups my face to make me look at him. "Did you have a bad dream?"

*Oh fuck. He noticed.*

"Tell me what it was," he says.

"I-I..." I'm never one to stammer, but I really don't know what to say. I don't know if I'll ever be ready to speak the words out loud.

His brows twitch. "Is this something that happens often?"

I nod and sit up. "I don't want to talk about it."

He leans up on his elbow, and the blanket that kept us warm slowly drops off both of us, revealing his naked tattooed body, and fuck me, my eyes can't stop perusing his thick slabs of muscle and that nine-inch dick like I'm shopping for a boy toy.

*What is wrong with me?*

I shake my head, but the smug grin on his face immediately makes me look down at my own chest. I forgot I was naked too. And he's definitely ogling my perky breasts, nipples peaking at the thought.

"Oh, I will never get used to the sight of those," he mumbles.

Grinding my teeth, I get up and march to my cabinet, fishing out some new panties, a fresh pair of jeans, and a short black top.

Kai licks his lips. "Cute. Matches your black soul."

"Are you getting up?" I ask, trying my best to put on the jeans under his scrutinizing gaze.

"I'd much rather watch you stumble around."

"Stop looking at me like that," I say as I put on the top.

"Like what?"

"Like you want to pounce on me," I reply.

Big mistake, because the shit-eating grin that follows makes my heart throb in a way I never asked for it to throb.

"Maybe I do."

Suddenly, his phone buzzes, and it breaks the spell between us as he picks it up. The look on his face darkens with every passing second.

"What's wrong?"

He jumps out of bed and immediately dials a number. "Nathan? Where is he?"

I have never heard his voice this unhinged.

\*\*\*

## KAI

"Who is it?" Lana asks, walking closer so she can hear.

"In the clinic? Okay, I'll be right there," I say, and I close the conversation and snatch my pants and underwear off the floor.

"What's wrong?" she asks, but I'm far too busy getting dressed as quickly as possible.

"Milo's been attacked while he was out with Rory."

Her eyes widen. "What?"

I can't explain this right now. "He's in the local clinic, Nathan's with him, waiting until he gets out of surgery. I have to go."

As I march past her, she latches onto my hand. "Let me come with you." Our eyes connect. "Please."

My Adam's apple moves up and down, the weight of her words not to be taken lightly.

Goddamn, that *please* nearly kills me.

I swallow again and nod. "C'mon."

She nods, and we bolt down the stairs, headed straight for the door. Several girls exit their bedrooms and look at me like they've seen a ghost walking, but I don't care or feel the need to explain. We'll deal with any fallout later. Right now, we need to get to Milo and Nathan.

He left so many messages and called me a million times, but

my phone was on silent because I didn't want anyone to disturb my precious time with Lana.

But fuck, I wish I'd at least kept it on buzz now.

I throw open the door and say, "My car's back at the society house. We gotta run."

"No," Lana says, and she picks up a helmet from a box in the yard in front of the house. "We'll take my bike. It's faster."

I frown as she hands the helmet to me. "I can't drive that thing."

She smirks as she puts on her own helmet. "No, but I can."

I watch her jump on the bike and rev the engine before she coaxes me with those claws of hers. "Jump on."

Gripping the helmet tight, I hesitate for a moment.

*It's just a bike. Jesus. How hard can it be?*

Clearing my throat, I jump on behind her and put on the helmet.

"Hold on tight," she says.

I'm surprised she knows where to go, but I guess that comes with the territory of being a Rivera. This clinic is only accessible to those on the criminal path.

When she races off, I'm not prepared for the speed, Jesus fucking Christ, the way she whizzes across the streets, zigzagging from left to right as if it's child's play to her. I hold on tight, her body tensing when my fingers splay against her belly, and I grumble into the helmet from how good it feels. Her delicious scent wafts into my nose, and I take in a breath to get high on her smell.

It doesn't even register with me when we finally arrive at the clinic. That's how obsessed I've become with being close to her.

She parks the bike, and I get off so I can hand her my helmet, but she throws them to the side and grabs my hand, dragging me along. "Where is he?"

"I don't know."

When I see Nathan in the hallway, I run over to him. "Is he alive?"

"He's in the recovery room," Nathan says, his eyes red and his face twisted with emotions. "He's alive, but no thanks to you."

"I'm sorry," I say, shaking my head.

"You weren't fucking there! I was the one who found him!" Nathan yells, shoving me away. "I called you, and you didn't fucking pick up!"

"That's my fault. He was with me," Lana says.

Nathan aims his ire at her. "Five fucking gunshots. FIVE!"

Despite his flaming rage, she pulls him in for a hug, tightening her grip around him while he fights her every step of the way until he finally caves in and grieves against her, wrapping his arms around her.

"I almost lost him," he mutters. "I almost lost Milo."

She blinks and glances my way before patting Nathan on the back. "It's going to be okay. He's strong. He can survive this."

"God, I wish I could've been there," Nathan says.

"What happened?" she asks.

"He tried to give me time off and took Rory to the playground when some fuckers ambushed him," he says, leaning away to look at me. "They took Rory."

My eyes widen. "Fuck."

Suddenly, a doctor comes into the waiting area. "Nathan Reed?"

"Yes!" Nathan turns around, all frazzled and running his fingers through his hair. "Is he awake?"

"Yes, you're free to visit him if you want. He's in room 15."

Nathan shoots past the doctor, racing up the stairs instead of taking the elevator, and we follow suit. He bursts into Milo's room, but the beeping machine immediately stops him.

"Milo …" Nathan mutters as he sinks into his bed and grips his hand. "I'm here."

Milo's eyes flutter open, and he coughs. "Hi …" His voice is all crackled from the tubes.

Lana approaches his bed too from the other side and grabs his hand to squeeze. "Hi, Milo."

"Am I dreaming?" Milo muses. "Or am I seeing angels now?"

She grins. "Still got your charms, I see."

"How are you feeling?" I ask.

"Well, for someone who just got shot five times … pretty good."

Both Lana and I snort from his comment. Always the jokester, even when he's on the brink of death.

"They sutured me up?" he asks, looking at the bandages.

"The doc said you were quite a mess to fix," Nathan says, pushing some of the bloodied hairs off Milo's face. "But he did a good job."

"I'm sorry, Nathan," Milo mutters. "I'm sorry, Rory—"

Nathan plants a finger on his lips. "No more. It's not your fault. I just wish I could've gotten there sooner."

"Did you see what they looked like?" I ask.

"I don't know. They were wearing long coats and skull-shaped masks." Milo points at his chest. "There was an emblem, there. I could only vaguely catch a word before the guy shot me ... Bones."

A shiver runs up and down my spine.

"Fuck." Nathan looks up at me and immediately fishes his phone from his pocket.

"What is it?" Lana asks.

"Bones can only mean one thing," I say.

"Bones Brotherhood," Nathan grits as he types into his phone. "And they've obviously been hired by someone to take care of my parents' debt, no matter the cost."

"Bones Brotherhood?" Lana chimes. "I've never heard of them."

"They work under the radar. Notorious for accepting only the dirtiest jobs for the richest among us. They do anything for money, and they operate in several cities. Our parents would never work with scum like that."

"So like assassins?"

"Not just that," Nathan says through gritted teeth, still holding Milo's hand for dear life. "Trafficking."

I swallow as I watch Lana's face go as white as snow.

"Fuck! No wonder I couldn't get rid of these fuckers," Nathan says.

"They don't play by the book," I say.

Nathan's messages land on deaf ears, so he opts to call the guy who extorted him instead. When he picks up, Nathan puts the phone on speaker and yells, "You son of a motherfucking bitch, give me back my sister!"

The guy on the other end laughs. "And you think that's going to work?"

Nathan clutches the phone so tight I can hear it crack. "Listen, you little bitch, I paid off my parents' debt. I gave you the money. Our deal is finished!"

"No, I don't think so. You see, we only got the money owed to our contractor," the voice mumbles, clearly amused. "But you failed to provide the added interest."

Nathan's pupils dilate. "Interest?"

"Yes ..." The voice on the phone is downright malicious. "But don't worry, we'll take care of it. You get to live. Your parents get to enjoy prison. And your sister? Well ... you'll never see her again."

"Oh God," Lana mutters, covering her mouth with her hand. "They intend to sell her."

Nathan's patience breaks. "I'LL FUCKING KILL YOU!"

But the conversation is cut off before he can finish his tirade, and Nathan throws his phone.

I catch it just before it hits the wall. We need the information more than he needs an outlet for his rage.

"FUCK!" Nathan yells, almost ripping his hair out of his head. "Rory, I can't leave her there. They're going to hurt her. Sell her off to God knows what kind of pervert. Oh God."

Lana fishes her phone from her pocket and texts someone.

"I'm sorry," Milo says, coughing again. "I wish I could go out there and fight them."

"What are you doing?" I ask Lana.

"Shh," she mutters, still texting.

"You're staying here. You need to rest," Nathan tells Milo.

"Do you even know their location?" I ask.

Nathan shakes his head. "All I had was a phone number. That's it."

"I do." Lana holds up her phone, showing an address.

"How'd you get that?" I ask.

She shrugs. "Penelope's parents are notorious for hunting criminal groups like these. I just asked her if she knew anything about it, and she gave me one of their hideouts in the city." A smug smile forms on her face. "Along with a warning of course, which I intend to ignore."

She walks to the door.

Milo asks with a raspy voice, "Where are you going?"

"To save Rory," she says, her face cold-hearted, vindictive. "And to kill those sons of bitches." Then she focuses on both me and Nathan. "Now are you two coming with me or not?"

Nathan's eyes grow big as if he can't believe his own damn ears.

A girl we extorted, used for our own pleasure ... offering us her help.

"Wait," Milo says, and he tries to lean up from the bed. "Don't go alone. If I can't come with you ... call Blaine. He's a friend. He'll help you out."

"Blaine?" Nathan furrows his brows at him. "You still talk with him—"

"Please don't worry about it. Not now." Milo coughs a few more times and groans with pain from his wounds.

"We don't have time for talking if we're gonna save your sister," Lana says, and she grasps Nathan's hand and drags him out the door. "Let's go."

# 42

## LANA

"What's the plan?" Kai asks as we hide behind the dumpster and gape over it to the entrance of the grimy-looking club.

I grab my bag and fish out some knives along with a mini gun and stuff it all into my sky-high boots.

"You do *have* a plan, right?" Nathan asks.

"Nope."

"Wait, what?" Kai frowns.

They both look at me like I've lost my marbles.

"We can't just barge in there," Nathan says. "They know my fucking face. They'll be expecting me."

"You can't, but I can," I say.

Kai grabs my coat and pulls me close. "If they find out you're in there, they'll kill you. I won't allow it."

"Well, fancy meeting y'all here."

The sudden unfamiliar voice makes us all look up. A tall as fuck guy stands right in front of our hideout behind the dumpster, clutching an umbrella to stop the snowflakes from falling onto his long black hair, some strands covering the gentle smile on his face.

He sticks out his hand. "Blaine Navarro."

I shake his hand, but Kai and Nathan don't want to.

"*Blaine* ..." Kai says, looking him up and down like he recognizes him from somewhere. "You're one of Milo's friends. But wait, you're from the Tartarus House, aren't you?"

"Yup. Your girlfriend here called me to come and help you guys out." He stretches out. "So here I am."

Nathan snarls, "You told him about—"

"That girl?" Blaine interjects, throwing a glance at Nathan. "Yes, I know your Rory is missing."

"I had to tell him, or he wouldn't come," I say when Nathan's nostrils flare.

"This guy's dangerous," he says.

Blaine goes to his knees behind the dumpster, barely able to crouch far enough to hide because of his height. I dare say he's even taller than Milo. "More dangerous than what you three are trying to attempt?"

Nathan makes a tsk sound.

"So you want my help or not?" Blaine asks.

"Fine," Nathan barks. "But don't get in our way."

"Jesus, what's his problem?" I whisper to Kai.

"Milo's got a history with a bunch of guys. He's one of them." Kai winks.

My jaw dropped. "Milo hooked up with this dude?"

"Not anymore," Blaine says, lurching over our shoulders.

I shove him away. "Don't get up in my face like that."

"Sorry, I was just curious what you guys were talking about, but I see I've already made quite the impression," Blaine says, smiling. "So is there a reason you're trying to infiltrate an actual trafficking ring by yourself instead of going to the police like normal people do?"

"You think the police can be trusted?" Nathan grits. "My parents are in jail because of them. You think they'll help us?"

"Fine, fine, you've got a point there," Blaine says, rolling his eyes.

"Here." Nathan slaps a mask into his chest. "Put this on."

Blaine scowls. "What is this plastic thing? It'll ruin my face."

"Good," Nathan quips, and I snort in response.

"Put it on," Kai tells Blaine. "Or you'll be recognized."

Blaine sighs out loud. "Fine, but you owe me a new bottle of cream if I break out." And he puts it on, almost looking like a Phantom too now.

The guards at the back entrance walk off for a smoke break, and I hiss, "Now's our shot."

"Lana, wait!" Nathan hisses. "You can't just bust in there."

I just throw them a look and march on, right at the back entrance, and I knock a few times while the boys hide again. "Hello?"

The door opens up just a sliver, and some grumpy guy peers through. "What do you want?"

"I'm here for work."

He narrows his eyes at me and looks me up and down, then shuts the door. My heart throbs in my throat. Within a few seconds, the door opens up fully, and I barge right past him, pretending I've been there a million times before.

The music blasts into my ear the second I step one foot inside. It's dark and hot here as I go to the changing room and throw my coat onto a hanger. I steal a sticker from one of the girls' tables and paste it over my heart-shaped top, pushing up my breasts to make them look even perkier before I step out into the strip club.

There's a stage in the middle of the room with girls dancing and twerking, showing off their skills, while men watch with hunger in their eyes. Champagne and expensive liquor is poured left and right, while some of the more important guests get private treatment in the back.

If there's ever a place nasty deals would take place, this would be it.

I make my way around the room in my high heels and grab a tray filled with shots off the bar, seamlessly blending in with the servers as I look around. Several curtains all over the place lead to more private rooms, but one curtain draws my attention because a guard is stationed in front of a door behind it.

I pass by it and serve a customer a drink on the house while I sneak a glance.

Someone important must be in there. It's worth investigating, but there's no way I'm getting in there with that guard blocking the way.

"Hey, bring me something else," a customer suddenly says, pushing a shot glass onto the tray. "This didn't even come close to a good drink."

"Of course," I say, smiling as I hurry off toward the bar. On my way there, I pass the curtain again and sneak another peek. There's not just one door, but two, and one of them has an exit sign.

An entry for the boys.

I fish my phone from my pocket and send a text.

**Me:** *Wait @ southern exit entrance.*

**Nathan:** *Wth are you planning???*

**Me:** *Just do it.*

I shove my phone down the small pocket in these tiny leather pants and put my tray on the bar. "I need a spicier version of whatever you gave table 5 just now."

The bartender squints at me. "Always the demanding ones those." He makes a new drink and places it on my tray. "Tell him to come to the bar if that's not good enough."

"Thanks, will do." I wink at him and pick up my drinks, but I don't intend to bring them anywhere close to table five.

Right as I pass the curtains, I pretend my heel is broken and fall, the glass shattering into a million pieces. The guard exits the curtains and asks, "Are you okay? I saw you fall."

"Ow, I hurt my leg," I mumble, rolling around through the glass.

He inspects me and pushes the tray aside. "Can you stand?"

"I don't know," I say in my best cutesy voice. I lift it and hiss when I see the blood drops. "I'm bleeding."

"Oh crap. Let me get you a towel," he says, walking off.

Away from the door.

A dirty smile forms on my lips as I crawl to my feet and slip behind the curtain when no one is looking. I close it and run to the emergency exit, pushing it open. Kai, Nathan, and Blaine wait for me there with their masks on, but the looks in their eyes are anything but amused when they see my outfit.

"What the—" Kai pushes me inside and corners me. "*This* was your plan?"

"Do I blend in well?" I wink at Nathan, who's getting all flustered.

"Spicy outfit," Blaine says, licking his lips.

"Tell me no one touched you," Kai growls.

"I was only pretending to be a server," I reply. "No need to get jealous."

"Jealous?" Kai frowns. "I'm not jealous—"

"Yeah, you are," Blaine retorts as he moves around the room to check if there's anyone here.

"No time to argue. If they find us here, we're screwed," I say.

"Let's move," Kai says.

I push myself off the wall. "There was a guard at this door—"

"Hey! What are you doing in here?"

*Oh shit. He's back.*

We all stare at him, and the air is thick with tension.

When he pulls out his gun, I whip out my knife from my panties and chuck it at his eyeball.

He drops dead right into the curtain.

"Quick!" I say, beckoning them.

Kai and Nathan drag the body inside and shut the curtain again. "This was your grand plan?" Nathan asks.

"I don't have a plan. We improvise," I reply, stepping over the corpse.

"They're gonna look for him," Kai says.

"We'll be gone before they find us."

"How do you even know she's in there?" Nathan asks.

"Penelope said her dad hunts these fuckers, so he knows all of their locations," I reply, and I jerk open the door.

Behind it is a staircase and a corridor beyond with several doors.

"Let's go," I say as I make my way down.

"Fuck, we're going down into the belly of the beast," Nathan growls.

"Catch," Blaine says, and he throws Nathan a gun with a silencer. "Always come prepared."

Nathan throws out another tsk sound. "I have my knives."

"Knives are cool, but guns are faster," Blaine says with a wink.

In the back, I hear the cries of a girl, and my eyes widen. "Rory."

Nathan immediately loses his cool and shoves past me, running straight toward the door.

"Wait, Nathan!" Kai yells.

Too late. He barges into the door and throws it open with his weight alone, but behind it are several guards, two of them playing a game, while two others watch the cameras in the club above. None of them seem too happy with our arrival.

"Shit," I mutter.

"Who the fuck are you?" one of them roars at Nathan.

Beyond the door, I spot a cage in the back, and in it is a figure hidden in the dark, whimpering quietly. *Rory.*

"I'm coming for you, Ro!" Nathan yells at her.

Suddenly, one of the guards whisks out a gun.

"Nathan, duck!" I yell.

*BANG!*

# 43

## LANA

The bullet ricochets off the wall behind us.

Kai fires his gun too as bullets fly through the room.

*BANG! BANG!*

"You really like making a grand entry, don't you?" Blaine says, and he runs toward the fighting too.

Nathan's exchanging fists with a guard who's got him cornered, and another guard comes at him from behind. I fling my knives at the guard rushing toward Nathan and save him from a chokehold.

He briefly glances at me, shouting, "Thanks!"

Another guard runs out of the room and into the hallway, and I fling my last knife straight at his throat. Blood pours out as his hand wrings around his neck in an attempt to pull it out while he sinks to the floor.

The other doors open too, and two more Bonesmen step out to see what's happening. "Motherf—"

Blaine pulls out an actual goddamn sword from his umbrella and shoves it into his belly.

"Don't waste precious words," he mumbles as the guard sinks to the floor.

"You gave me your gun and start fighting with a motherfucking sword instead?" Nathan growls from the other end of the hallway.

"It's not a sword, it's a katana," Blaine argues. "But of course you wouldn't know."

"Jesus, can we not right now?" Kai growls at both of them.

Suddenly, one of those Bonesmen jumps me from behind, wrapping his arms around my neck.

*BANG!*

Kai fires his gun all the way from the other end of the hall, hitting the guy in the temple, and he sinks to the floor.

Right then, an alarm goes off, and we all exchange panicked glances.

"Fuck," I mutter.

I run toward the room the boys are in while guards from all sides of the corridor pour in.

"Run, Lana!" Kai barks.

I glance over my shoulder, and a bunch more Bonesmen come in via the stair entrance. It's like the whole club was infested with them.

We're cornered.

"C'mon, c'mon, c'mon!" Nathan growls.

Right when Blaine enters, Nathan shuts the door while Kai pushes a chair underneath the door handle.

"Fuck, we barely made it." Blaine takes a minute to breathe.

"Wish you fucking hadn't," Nathan mumbles under his breath.

Blaine side-eyes him as he wipes his katana on his pants. "I heard that."

Nathan immediately runs over to Rory's cage. "Ro, I'm here." He unlocks it and pulls her out into his embrace. "Are you okay? Are you hurt? Did they touch you anywhere?"

She shakes her head.

"I'm just scared," she says, crying her eyes out as she holds on to him for dear life.

"I'm here; you don't have to be scared anymore," Nathan says. "I'll take care of you."

"What happened to Uncle Milo? Those guys hurt him when I tried to run," she says, shivering.

I approach her and pat her little hand. "He's okay. He's in the hospital, but he'll be all right. Don't you worry about him."

"Are you here to save me?" she asks me.

I nod. "We're not leaving here without you."

Nathan holds her tight while he directs his attention on Blaine, who's casually eating one of the apple slices the guards left in their hurry to attack.

"Jesus Christ, an umbrella, katana? Really?" Nathan growls at Blaine. "You brought some nunchucks too while you're out here trying to cosplay as Jackie Chan? No wonder Milo left you."

"Yet you know about the nunchucks," Blaine muses. "Who do you think taught him?"

They go head-to-head, seemingly forgetting all about the reason we came here.

"Guys, we need to look for a way out," I say.

"Stop fighting," Kai barks at them both.

Banging on the doors makes me step back. "Guys, we gotta hurry."

"Open this fucking door!"

"I'm scared," Rory murmurs, hiding in Nathan's neck.

I check the room, but there's no other doors except the one we came through. "Fuck, we're stuck."

"There has to be another way out of here," Nathan says.

Kai holds down the door, shoving another chair underneath. "This won't hold for long."

"We can just face them head-on if you like," Blaine says, chomping on some more apple slices like he's having the time of his life. "I mean, we were already charging into it without thinking twice. Might as well finish the job."

"Of course you'd suggest that," Nathan scoffs. "You forgot we've got a kid we're trying to keep safe."

"Who the fuck are you?" a voice yells from behind the door.

We all look at each other.

"I don't want to die." Rory hides her face in Nathan's shirt, shaking terribly.

*We can't subject her to all this violence. She has to get out of here unharmed, but how?*

"What do you want to do?" Blaine asks, clutching his katana. "I'm ready to plow through them if needed."

"And risk everyone in the club knowing what we look like?" Nathan grits. "If one of them rips off these masks, it's game over."

More banging on the door ensues.

"We have to make a decision," Kai says.

I look around the room and spot a vent in the back big enough for a kid like her, and maybe just big enough for someone like me ...

"No, give her to me," I say, holding out my hands.

"What do you want to do?" Nathan asks as he hands Rory over.

I hold her tight as I point at the shaft.

"No way that'll fit," Kai says. "Except for Ro."

"No, we can't let her go alone!" Nathan growls.

"I'll go with her," I say.

Kai swallows. "You're leaving us here."

"We came here to get Rory. She needs to be safe. We can't get her through that hallway with those men waiting out there for us."

Nathan takes in a deep breath. "You want to save her first."

I nod. "It's the only shot we have. We have to take it."

"Nathan? I don't want to leave," Rory mumbles, reaching for him.

He watches me with a concerned look on his face. "Okay. I trust you."

I don't know if he's just saying that to make her feel safe or if he really means it, but it's enough for me to immediately move.

"C'mon, Ro," I say as I push her up to the shaft. "Push the lid aside."

She does what I ask, and I lift her over my shoulder and into the shaft.

"I need help," I say when it's my turn.

Kai approaches. "This better work," he warns. "If you die out there, I'm coming to haunt you."

"I won't, don't worry," I say, winking.

"Lana!" Nathan says, drawing my attention. "Save her. Get her out of here. No matter the cost."

I swallow, realizing the gravity of his words. "I will."

"We'll take care of these fuckers once they break in," Blaine says, whipping his katana around. "This blade is hungry for blood."

Kai lowers his hands and puts them underneath my foot. "Got you."

Right as he pushes me up, the door cracks.

We all turn our heads toward the sound.

*BANG!*

My eyes widen as I see them barge in.

Right then, I lift myself into the shaft. "Rory, go! Crawl as fast as you can!"

Her panicked little body shifts from side to side as we make our way through the dusty shaft. Below us, the fighting breaks out. The sound of gunshots fills the shaft, and each one makes her flinch.

"Don't listen to any of the sounds; just keep moving," I tell her as the shaft tilts upward.

"I'm scared," she says.

"I'm here," I reply, going around a corner. "We're almost there."

I slide across the metal, headed for the opening in the far back where light pours in.

"I can see the floor," Rory mutters.

"Okay, now jump down carefully," I tell her. "You can turn around, right?"

She nods when she looks at me, and then she curls her body up into a ball and switches her legs to the front.

"Just like on the playground, you just jump down."

"But what if there are people there?"

"Don't worry about them. If they even see you, they'll be far too busy with Nathan, Kai, and Blaine to care," I reply.

She hesitates but still pushes farther, dangling her little legs over before she makes the jump.

It's not far down, and when I crawl ahead, I can see her.

"Hide!" I tell her.

She moves away from the shaft and remains out of sight for a second as I lower myself face-first and hang onto the ledge to let my feet drop first.

But as I come to a stand, I feel the weight of my own blood coming down on me.

Because in front of me is a hoard of Bonesmen, their tattoos giving away their allegiance. They're sporting butcher knives and gnarly-looking grimaces.

"Please don't hurt me," Rory murmurs from underneath the table to my left.

I step to the side to block them from looking at her.

"Don't worry, Ro," I say, with a smug grin as I pull my tiny gun from my boot while the Bonesmen approach. "I won't let them touch you. Now close your eyes and don't open them until I say so."

# 44

## KAI

When they burst into the room, I brace myself and wait until they've run over the door before I shoot. Bullets ricochet across the room, zooming past my ears as I shoot them down one after the other. Nathan storms at one of the Bonesmen who comes too close and rams his knife into his throat, then roars when he pulls it out. His eyes almost blaze with fire after every kill he makes, vengeance turning him into a psycho killer. And it puts a goddamn smile on my face.

"I'm gonna kill you all!" Nathan screams, shoving his knife into someone's eye.

"Please..." my victim mutters, but I shoot a bullet straight between his eyes.

They should've thought of mercy before they tried to attack us.

Blaine skewers the Bonesmen on his katana like he's counting bodies in his head, trying to beat Nathan at the killing game.

I guess Milo really picks his friends with care.

When one of them attacks Blaine from behind, Nathan shoots him down. "You're welcome."

"I didn't ask for help," Blaine retorts. "But thanks."

"Behind you!" I yell when Nathan's too distracted by Blaine's words, and I shoot another Bonesmen down before he can put a butcher's knife into Nathan's belly.

More gunshots follow, and I lift the table and hide behind it for cover, rising only to shoot. Meanwhile, Blaine and Nathan are having a knife match in the hallway beyond.

"Don't get carried away!" I yell.

A bullet grazes my face and tears off my mask.

I duck behind the table.

Fuck.

If even one of them sees my face, it's over.

Those Bonesmen will come hunt me for the rest of my life. Maybe not the ones from this establishment, but the others surely will. These fuckers are the worst of the worst, and they won't stop until they have what they want—revenge.

"You think your little game will work?" one of the Bonesmen yells. "We'll fucking rip you to pieces! Your bodies will never leave this fucking club!"

When I look over the table again, I can see Nathan and Blaine being pushed back into the room by the sheer volume of enemies. *Shit. We're losing. Fast.*

"Focus on weakening them!" I yell, taking another shot. "We don't need to kill to get through!"

"The fuck I'm leaving any of these bastards alive!" Nathan yells back as he thrusts his knife into another one's heart.

Suddenly, I hear more gunshots up ahead, but they're not focused at this room. As I shoot down more Bonesmen, it appears some of them are turning around. But why?

"Fuck, they're pushing us back," Blaine calls at me. "Kai, shoot down the one in charge!"

"Trying!" I yell back, shooting my shots, but the fucker is fast on his feet.

"Where is Romeo?" Nathan growls at the Bonesmen.

Fuck, they don't know who we are, and now he's going to reveal us.

"Nathan, don't!" I yell back, but he's incensed, and he pulls out the silencer Blaine gave him, saving it for last to shoot three to four guys at once until the silencer runs out of bullets.

"SHOW YOUR FUCKING FACE, ROMEO!"

"He's not fucking here, you dimwit," a bald one yells. "But I'll be sure to let him know you came looking ... and give him your head."

More Bonesmen push their way inside the room, so I push the table forward and shove it up against the door to keep them out. "Help me lift it!"

Blaine jumps into action and helps me push the table into place to seal the door. It won't keep them away forever, but it's enough to give us some time to catch our breaths.

"There're too fucking many of them," Blaine says.

"I don't fucking care!" Nathan growls at him. "I'll kill every last one of them for daring to take Ro."

"I'm not fucking dying on your behalf," Blaine growls back.

Nathan pushes against the table with all his strength. "Then why the fuck did you come?"

"None of us are fucking dying today," I retort.

"We're outnumbered," Blaine responds.

More gunshots can be heard, but they're not aimed at the table.

Suddenly, I hear cries and groans from behind it. Then loud thumps, like bags of potatoes dropping to the floor.

"Do you hear that?" Blaine says as he peeks over the table.

"Wait, it's not safe," I growl.

But all the gunshots have ceased, and I don't hear a peep from beyond this room.

"It is," he says, his fingers clenching around the top.

I slowly rise above the table, and my eyes widen the second I spot the bodies littered across the hallway. All of them, dead.

"Quick," I bark at Nathan as we drag the table away.

But as I stop and stare, my whole body feels as though it's turned into dust.

Lana stands in the hallway, a severed head in her hand. She chucks it through the hallway, and when it's done rolling, the ghostly eyes make me do a double take.

It's the fucker who was leading the charge.

And all of them are dead.

She's breathing wildly, clutching a knife in one hand, a gun in the other, and has blood spatters all over her clothes. I swallow in awe at the sheer destruction in front of me. None of us knows what to even say.

She did all of this ... on her own.

I thought she'd take Rory and flee, that she'd let us fight it out until our last dying breaths.

"You came back," I murmur.

"You were overrun," she replies. "I wasn't going to let them kill you."

And here I was, thinking there was still a slight chance she hated us enough to leave us here to die.

Not a chance in hell.

A smug grin spreads on my lips. "No... that privilege belongs to you."

She smiles back and steps into a side room. "You can come out now, Ro. It's safe. But don't open your eyes."

Little Rory steps out, shivering and all.

Nathan's face visibly relaxes when he sees her alive and well, and he immediately runs toward her to pick her up and wrap his arms around her. "I'm here, Ro. You're safe now."

"Are you coming or what?" Lana asks us.

Blaine winks at me, and we both run through the hallway, hopping over the bodies as we make our way to the exit near the curtains. Everywhere I look, blood cakes the walls and floors, Bonesmen bodies covering the area. It's like a giant massacre took place. Only one girl responsible for nearly half the dead.

And when I look at her, confidently striding through the building, I realize I have fallen madly in love with this cutthroat god of a woman.

"Where the fuck do you think you're going?"

We all look over our shoulders, but Lana pushes us farther out the door. "Go!"

*BANG!*

She shoots her shot, but after fighting so long, she misses the vital points, and the bullet hits the Bones Brotherhood guy in the shoulder instead.

"*You* ... What the fuck is a Rivera doing here?" the guy yells before she seals the door shut.

"RUN!" she yells, and we all bolt through the street, Nathan with Rory in his arms while Blaine offers backup. Adrenaline shoots through my veins, sweat rolling down my back, my lungs dragging in the oxygen as I run as fast as I can.

The guy slams open the door behind us, but we've already jumped into the vehicle, Blaine beside me on the passenger's seat, and I start the engine and race off. He runs out onto the street, and with ragged breaths, both Lana and Nathan look out the rear window from the back seat to see him swear and raise his fist.

But we've made it out alive, and he's not fast enough to catch up.

"Can I open my eyes yet?" Rory asks.

Nathan slowly pulls away his shielding arms and says, "Yes. You're safe now."

She opens her eyes and blinks as she looks around.

Lana's blood-smeared face strikes fear into her eyes.

"Don't be afraid," Lana says, holding out her hand. "I'm still me. I won't hurt you. I promise."

She rubs her lips together but still lets Lana touch her shoulder. Rory begins to smile. "You saved me."

Rory jumps into her arms, and Lana stays frozen to her seat for a moment like she doesn't know what to do with all that love.

"Cute," Blaine muses. "If we forget all the dead bodies she left."

"Hey," Nathan warns, making a gesture near his lips. "Zip it."

"I'm just saying." Blaine shrugs. "She's a force to be reckoned with."

"True," I say, glancing at them through the rearview mirror.

"I heard so many bangs. I was so scared," Rory mutters.

"But you got through it," Lana replies. "You're a big girl."

"Because I had you," Rory replies. "Will you be my new Auntie?"

Nathan bursts out into laughter. "Whoa, hold your horses, Ro."

"What? Can't she be? Can I have more than one?"

"If you want to call me Auntie, I'll be Auntie for you," Lana says. "But my name is Lana. Lana Rivera."

"That's a beautiful name," Rory says, making Lana blush as she tucks her bloodied hair behind her ear.

But something gnaws in the back of my mind that I just can't let go.

"That guy back there ... he said it too." I look at them all through the rearview mirror, but in particular Lana. "He knew who you were."

She swallows. "We all knew the risks when we came here."

"You should've run with Rory when you could," I say.

"And leave you all to die?" she retorts, her eyes as stern as her voice.

My lips part, but I don't know how to respond.

Something about the idea alone that she killed all those people without a single scratch on her gives me chills.

"You killed all of them yourself?" I ask after a while, curious if she had any help.

She looks right back at me. "You've only seen me kill for sport. But this? This was personal. And I don't take that lightly."

Nathan glances at her, his neck turning red as his eyes slide over her bloodied clothes and face, inspecting every inch as though it's the first time he's really seeing her for the enthralling, powerful woman she is.

"But that guy ... he saw your face," I say.

Nathan glances at me through the mirror too now along with Lana.

"We destroyed their chance of getting more money," I add. "And they'll put the blame on her."

"Let's worry about that later," Lana says, clearing her throat. "I just want to get home and have a nice, warm shower."

Blaine laughs as he shows off his bloodied outfit. "You and me both."

# 45

NATHAN

When we get back to Spine Ridge, I check Rory for any marks and blemishes before I give her a bath, after which I put her back in Milo's bed because she was already used to sleeping there, and she was tired as hell after what happened to her.

Milo's room is awfully empty without him, though, and it's a tough pill to swallow. It'll take him a few days more to get back on his feet.

I pull out my phone and text him back after he sent a couple of frantic texts asking about her.

Me: We got her.

Milo: Thank fk.

Me: How r u?

Milo: Better. I just wanna know if Ro's safe.

Me: She's in one piece.

Milo: I was so gdamn worried they hurt her.

Me: No. Just scared.

Milo: Won't they keep coming after her?

Me: We killed almost all those Bonesmen.

Milo: Almost?

I swallow away the lump in my throat. That guy who followed us outside definitely saw Lana. And while we were wearing masks, she pretended to be a server and couldn't, so her identity got exposed the second she decided to fight back instead of run with my sister.

I don't understand why she would risk her own life to help us.

**Me: Don't worry bout it. U just rest.**

**Milo: Don't gimme a reason to come back early.**

**Me: If you don't focus on gettin better first, I'm gonna kick your ass back into the clinic.**

**Milo: Oh, don't fkn tempt me with a good time, or I might just do it.**

I roll my eyes and grin.

**Me: I'll c u soon.**

I put my phone back into my pocket and check on Ro to make sure she's sleeping, then tell the other Phantoms to stay vigilant and keep watch to make sure the Bonesmen don't come here.

Though I doubt they'd be able to enter the university grounds that easily.

Ever since Dean Rivera took over, the place has become locked down and tightly guarded.

I head upstairs, my blond hair sticking to my cheeks from a mixture of sweat and blood, but all the hardship was worth it because I got Ro back, and no amount of pain could ever stop me from finding my way back to her. Ro is all I have left, and as her big brother, I need to keep her safe.

When I head to my room, the steam emanating from the bathroom makes my brows twitch.

I walk inside and watch as Lana clutches her arms close to her naked body, rivulets of water mixing with blood as it slowly washes off her hair and back.

I swallow as my eyes glide over her smooth body and ass, every curve making my mouth water and my dick twitch.

I once thought I was all that stood between Ro and the cruel outside world, and I tried so hard to shield her from the tough reality of living without parents or money. Tried so hard to keep her out of harm's way, and none of it worked because they still went after her.

But she...

She came to help me without prejudice, risking her own life to save a girl she barely even knew, a girl who was the sister of her enemy.

When push came to shove, there was no hesitation ... she simply annihilated her enemies like it was child's play to her. As though she was waiting for a chance to unleash her wrath.

And I am in so much goddamn awe of her that I'm drawn closer, like a moth fluttering to a flame, knowing full well it will burn like the brightest fire, but it won't dissuade me.

All this time, I thought we were the ones destroying her, but it turns out reality was quite the opposite.

*She* ... has ruined me.

Her ruthless brown eyes connect with mine in a flurry of emotions as she glances at me over her shoulder when I come to stand in front of her.

But no amount of rage could ever convince me to stay away.

\*\*\*

## LANA

"Do you always watch girls shower?" I jest as Nathan comes to stand behind me.

He's looking at me like he's never seen me before.

"No," he says with a low voice. "Just you."

The smile disappears off my face. I feel like I just got caught masturbating even though I wasn't. But the way he's looking at me ... like he's completely infatuated with me, makes me swallow. Hard.

"You're in my room," he says, putting one hand on the wall beside me.

"Sorry, I just wanted to shower to get all this blood off, and this was the first one I found."

His eyes narrow. "You chose my room, and you're not afraid?"

I look around the open room, the metallic wallpaper so crude and emotionless, while the man who lives here is filled with so many of them. I gaze at the furniture in his room—the long, black couch, the metal cage in the back, the bed with poles, the rigging and entrapment items used to keep someone in place, along with all the whips hanging from the wall.

I know whose room this is. I've known for a very long time.

But I'm not afraid of him.

"No—"

Suddenly, he grips my face with his one free hand and smashes his lips onto mine. And I'm too stunned to even react as his lips roam around mine, taking me in greedily, hungrily, like he's never wanted anything more than me. Not even the water pouring down on him, drenching his black shirt and pants, stops him from claiming me.

Even though I'm covered in another man's blood, and the kiss tastes like poison seeping straight into my veins, I still feel consumed. Hot water mixed with blood and sweat all roll down into my mouth, but when his salty tears blend in, my lips unlatch from his. His reddened eyes catch me off guard.

"Thank you," he mutters.

"For what?"

"For saving my sister." He holds my face like he never wants to let go. "For saving us."

But then his knees cave in on him, and he sinks to the floor on hands and knees.

"What are you doing?"

"I treated you like shit," he says, his voice gritty, confused. And it unfurls all kinds of emotions in my heart I didn't know I had. "Bullied you, extorted you, fucked you like I didn't care what you felt."

Tears roll down his cheeks as he looks up at me, and I'm utterly shocked.

"And after all that, you still helped us when we needed it the most." He leans over to press a kiss to my bloodied foot, and the simple gesture moves me. "I was wrong. So wrong to despise you," he says, pressing more and more kisses against my ankles like he's desperate to right his wrongs. "I owe you my fucking life."

As the water pours onto my head, I stare down at him and his attempt to apologize for all his past behavior, and a part of me is almost ready to cry along with him. But the other part of me ... it burns with rage.

And I grasp my knife from between the shampoo and shove him to the floor, knocking him down as I kneel on top of him and push the blade underneath his chin.

He looks up, unafraid, meeting my anger head-on.

"You tried to take *everything* from me," I say through gritted teeth. "For her."

His Adam's apple rises and falls against the blade. "Do you want my life?"

My eyes widen, and I'm stunned. "What?"

He grasps my wrist and pushes the blade even farther into his neck. "Take it."

I can't even move as I try to fight his grip. "You *want* to die?"

"It's what I deserve," he says.

"I saved your fucking life!"

"Yes," he replies, not even looking mad that I have a blade to his neck. "And now my life belongs to you."

He pushes the blade even farther into his skin until his skin cracks and blood seeps out. And a part of me really wants to push through and make him pay for all the pain he caused me, end things once and for all so no one will ever find out about the pictures he took, and my killer secret stays hidden.

But he looks at me like I've beguiled him, and the sheer gaze of adoration suddenly makes it hard to breathe. I was here before not too long ago, and it feels as though history is repeating itself, but I can't stop it either.

No matter how much I hated him for using me for his own devious plans and pleasure, I can't bring myself to actually kill him.

"I deserve every inch of your wrath," he says, his hand rising to touch my face, the caress so sweet I practically melt into his hand. "But if you let me ... I will beg for your forgiveness every single day until eternity."

His hand guides me closer until we're separated by mere inches, and I can feel his warm breath on my skin. "All this time, I thought I didn't want to share Milo with you ... but I'm just so fucking jealous of the bond you two have ... because I *want* you. I want you more than my own goddamn life."

And fuck me, even with the blade perched right underneath his chin, my lips still land right back on his. The way he kisses me is nothing short of pure magic and delicious desperation all wrapped into a cruel package.

His hand snakes through my hair while I maintain a tight grip on the knife, afraid of what'll happen when I let go. When I finally let myself long for these evil boys that have thrown themselves at my feet.

He groans into my mouth, his lips parting mine as his tongue drives inside and licks at the roof of my mouth while I'm desperate to put a stop to the madness that has become me.

But it's too late. Too late to resist, too late to fight, too late to even flee from the inevitable fall.

So I give in and release the knife, letting it clatter to the stone floor as he kisses me with so much fire I can feel it burn in my soul.

When his lips unlatch from mine, we stare at each other for a moment. His eyes roam my face like he's seeing me for who I am for the first time in his life.

"You ..." His hand travels down my face, the tips of his fingers leaving an electrical current in their wake as they slowly make their way down my neck and chest, tickling my nipples until they peak, a devilish smirk appearing on his face. "You are a fucking goddess."

A blush spreads on my cheeks. No one's ever called me that.

Suddenly, his hands grip my ass, and he drags me over his hard, wet body until my pussy is right in front of his face.

"And I want nothing more than to devote myself to this fucking pussy."

My lips part, but I can't even say another word because his tongue drives into me with full fervor, leaving me fighting for a breath. He buries his tongue inside me and curls it, licking me from the inside out, and my knees start to quake from sheer need.

"Fuck," I mutter.

"Sit on my face," he groans, lapping me up.

My jaw drops. "What?"

He slaps my ass. Hard.

And I'm forced down on top of him because of it.

"Did I stutter?" When I do what he says, he groans like a man succumbing to a long-ignored lust. "Sit and let me lose my breath on your pussy."

His tongue circles around so good it makes me moan out loud, and I don't even mind anymore. Hot water pours down on both of us, and the blood of my enemies still covers my body, but all I can think of is rolling my hips around his mouth and letting myself enjoy his sinful tongue.

Because good God, does he know how to use it.

Even though he must be having a hard time breathing, his tongue does not relent. And slowly, I begin to gyrate on top of him as his tongue bores into me.

"That's it, my little slut, use me, fuck my tongue like a good girl," he murmurs between licks and kisses, driving me insane.

I grip his hair and roll around on top of him, enjoying every inch of the wickedness that's become us.

His thumb drives into my ass, and I don't even mind as he starts moving back and forth, adding even more pleasure, bringing me to the brink of destruction.

"Let me taste you," he murmurs, slapping my ass with his free hand. "Come for me. Come all over my face."

And the mixture of pain, delicious licks, and his devilish voice pushes me into the pit of ecstasy. The orgasm is so good I moan his name loudly, "Nathan!"

His eyes open wide, and he suddenly stands with me still in his arms, carrying me back inside the shower, only to press me against the wall, and he smashes his lips onto mine with so much force I'm lost for words.

The kiss numbs every doubt I had in my mind; these boys have captured my soul and ruined me for anyone else.

"You called my name when you came..." he murmurs when his lips unlatch, and his piercing blue eyes bore into mine. "Does that mean you'll forgive me?"

I bite my lip. "No, but I might if you work for it hard enough."

A slow, dirty grin forms on his face. "Hard ... I can do that."

And he pushes up against me with his thighs, pushing my legs up so I can feel his length bouncing up and down, piercings tingling my skin. Grumbling sounds emanate from deep within his chest as he presses filthy kisses all over my neck, his tongue darting out to lick up the blood of our enemies.

"You taste like a heavenly package wrapped in sin," he murmurs. "Sent straight from the gods into my lap."

"Yet you were convinced you hated me because of my brother," I mutter as his lips roam across my breasts.

He takes my nipple into his mouth and tugs at it when I speak, making me bite my lip. "Make no mistake, I still hate him with every fiber of my being." He looks up at me from underneath his lashes as he zips down and pulls out his hard cock. "But the need I feel for you burns harder than that kind of hatred ever could."

When he thrusts in deep, my mouth forms an o-shape, stars in my eyes.

And as we connect, I realize his thoughts mirror my own.

\*\*\*

## NATHAN

I bury myself deep inside her and watch her face unravel, wishing I hadn't been such a fucking fool. I was too blinded by rage to see what was right in front of me, to see the beauty in her violence and make it mine.

I wanted to. I wanted to so badly it made me hate her with every fiber of my being.

How was I attracted to the one girl who almost destroyed me?

The girl who carries the same name as the guy who ruined my life?

But Lana fucking Rivera has me fucking hooked, and I just can't get enough.

Despite all the hatred I spewed at her, she persisted. Fought back and owned the darkness hiding within her soul, wielding it like a weapon to save my sister from a terrible fate.

And the second I saw her emerge when Kai and I pulled the table away, I finally realized the truth.

I need this woman.

I need her more than I need my fucking life and am willing to die for it.

I hover in front of her, still deep inside her, throbbing with need.

But I need to hear her say it.

"Please ... forgive me," I whisper, my lips aching for hers. "I won't stop until you do."

"Kiss me," she murmurs, rivulets of water rolling down her face. "And maybe I will."

I kiss her with everything I have to give, taking her mouth as though it always belonged to me, even though I'm not the only one to stake this claim. I'm more than willing to share as long as I can have this.

This mouth, this pussy, this goddamn divine body, and that killer brain of hers.

*Mine.*

I drive into her, whispering into her ear, "You're mine, even if you hate me for making you, for wanting you so desperately neither of us can stop, but fuck me, you're mine, Lana, and I *will* make it up to you, even if it costs me the rest of my fucking life."

"Yes, fuck, yes," she moans, and it's all I need to hear to roar out loud and explode deep inside her, coating her pussy with cum.

Suddenly, the door closes, and I tilt my head to see Kai standing in the doorway, his arm hooked underneath Milo's shoulder to help him stand.

"Milo," I mutter.

And with my cock still inside her, their eyes widen in front of me.

"What are you doing with my girl?" Kai growls.

# 46

⌘

## MILO

Nathan swiftly pulls out of her, but it won't hide the fact that we obviously saw them fuck.

They've just gotten home and already going at it?

Jesus.

"*Your* girl?" Nathan zips up and narrows his eyes at Kai. "I thought you'd—"

"Relax." Kai smirks at Nathan. "I'm not mad. Just surprised she'd let you."

Lana's brows furrow. "He jumped me."

Nathan turns to look at her. "Is that what you call riding my face until you come?"

Lana shoves him with her elbow.

"Oh, fuck me, don't get me hard already," I murmur. "I've only just gotten home."

Kai sets me down on a chair near the door, and I adjust my pants with difficulty due to the bandages all over my body.

Lana turns off the shower and wipes some remaining blood on a towel before she wraps it around her body while Nathan zips up again. "Milo ... are you okay? Why aren't you at the clinic?"

"I'm done lying around. I hate that place," I say, coughing, but it hurts so much I cringe.

"Are you sure that's a smart idea?" she asks.

"I told you to rest," Nathan growls, annoyed.

"I know," I reply. "I just ... missed you guys."

Nathan's face visibly relaxes as he approaches me, and he goes down on his knees in front of me. "Are you sure you're okay?"

I nod. "Good enough to sit."

He eyes the bandages.

"It'll heal. Or so I've been told by the nurses. They took out quite a few bullets." I fish a tiny bag from my pocket and show it to them with a grin. "Look. Souvenirs."

Suddenly, Nathan lunges at me and wraps his arms around me, smothering me.

"Thank you. Thank you for protecting her."

"But ... I failed," I mutter.

"No." He grips my chin and makes me look at him. "You almost gave your life. And for that I'll be eternally grateful."

"You sure are throwing around a lot of eternities lately," Lana muses, putting her hand against her side.

Kai looks her up and down. "Looks like you've got three problems on your hands now instead of just one."

She snorts. "If that's my biggest problem, it's not so bad."

"I'm not a problem for anyone," I say.

Nathan leans back. "Oh really? Then what do you call showing up here while you should be in a bed being taken care of?"

I shrug. "You know I can't resist the urge to be with you all."

\*\*\*

## LANA

I scoff and fold my arms. "Yeah, right."

"What?" Milo says, confused. "I mean it."

"Y'all are only with me to get some free pussy," I retort.

All the boys frown, but they know I'm right. We had an agreement, and that's why they all keep coming back. But if it wasn't for that deal ...

Kai tilts up my chin. "You think that's the only reason, or are you just telling yourself that so you don't have to feel like we destroyed that icy barrier you kept your heart locked up in?"

But that's not just it.

I raise my hands and show some of the blood still caked on there. Guess that shower didn't work out after all, thanks to Nathan.

"Look at me. This is who I am. A natural born killer."

Kai lowers his eyes at me, his green eye smoldering with desire. "I *am* looking at you."

"We see you for who you are," Milo says as he gets up from the chair.

I shake my head. "No. None of you truly know me."

"Then let us get to know you," Nathan says, approaching too.

I take a step back. "You don't fucking understand. I don't just kill for fun. I don't kill like you guys. I kill to—"

"Satiate the hunger inside you," Kai interjects. When my eyes widen, he adds, "Yeah, I see the way you look at your victims." He curls my still bloodied hair around his finger. "I see how you revel in the power and enjoy the taste of their blood."

I shudder with both fear and delight. My secret is now out in the open for them to use whenever they feel like it. We will never, ever be equals as long as they hold that power over me.

A hint of a smile tugs at his lips. "I told you, I'm not afraid of you."

I look down at the floor, but my own bloodied footprints make it hard to stay sane now that I've come down from the high of all those killings. I have only ever killed one or two people in a single night, but this? This was a murder spree, and it felt so fucking riveting that I was almost afraid I'd be unable to stop.

I shiver in place, and when Nathan touches my arm, I pull back. "Don't."

"Tell me what's wrong," he asks.

I look at my hands, but they're becoming blurrier by the second, the image of a gun appearing in my mind's eye. It feels like I'm dreaming. Everywhere I go, I see blood—red stains on the wall, on the floor, on the bed. I'm unsteady on my feet as I see two images merge into one, the here and now mixing with the past as the blanket on the bed rises, the room darkening as two figures move in the bed. Groans and cries emanate from down below, and a single tear rolls down my cheeks.

Because when I look at my hands, I see a gun.

A gun that doesn't belong to me.

A gun I was never supposed to take.

"Lana!"

Hands shake me until I finally realize I'm not asleep or dreaming. Kai's firm hands pull me back into the now, and I stare up into his green eye, which flicks from side to side to decipher what's going on.

They don't know the horrors that lie awake inside me, devouring my very soul.

"Tell me what you saw," Kai barks, staring down at me.

*How does he know? Was I that out of it?*

I swallow away the lump in my throat.

If I tell him, I'll have exposed my last secret. Free for them to use against me.

But if I don't ... I don't know how much longer I can survive.

"I saw my mother," I mutter. "She was in that bed, covered in blood."

I look at Nathan's bed, but it's completely normal now. There's no one in there, not even a bump.

"Your mother ..." Milo mutters as he comes close too. "Is that why you've been killing people?"

My eyes dart to his, and I feel like my world is spinning out of control.

"Please tell us, kitty," Kai says, tipping up my chin. "We *want* to understand you."

A single tear rolls down my cheek. "My mother ... assaulted my brother when we were younger. Used him in the middle of the night for months on end." The words stream out of me like an endless river washing away my sins as I stare into his emerald eye. "And I was the one who discovered it. I told my father, and he killed her."

Nathan's face contorts with disgust while Milo's brows furrow as he slowly shakes his head. But Kai remains focused on me and my story so I can say the words I have been dying to say.

"My mother was a monster," I say through gritted teeth. "And that monster visits my nightmares every single goddamn night of my life because I was the one who caught her." I'm screaming now, but I don't care. I need to let this go. "Because I was the one who told my father. I'm the reason she died. The reason behind my father's misery."

Tears pour down my cheeks, but I don't care anymore. It's out now, along with all the emotions I've kept bottled up for so long. And if they use this secret to destroy me, then so be it.

*  *  *

## KAI

Out of all the reasons I could come up with as to why Lana Rivera was such a ruthless killer, this was the least expected.

But fuck me, does it explain so goddamn much ... About her and her brother.

"Sicklittlebitch13... that's why you put that thirteen there," Milo says.

"All those predators, you kill them because of her," Nathan mutters. "They're an outlet."

I grab her chin. "You did not cause your father's misery, Lana." When her eyes drift, I say, "Look at me. You are not responsible for what other people do. Not your brother, not your father, not your mother."

"But I am my mother's child," she whispers.

And there it is.

The fucking bullet that's been boring its way deeper into her skin until it almost fractured her heart and mine along with it.

Fuck.

I wrap my arms around her and pull her into my embrace, almost crying along with her just because of the pain she's feeling, and I wish more than anything I could swallow all of her anguish and make it mine just so she wouldn't have to feel it anymore.

All this time, she has been killing men who turned into monsters just to repent.

A girl with all that agony left to fight her own demons that follow her wherever she goes.

She sniffs. "When I look in the mirror, I see her."

I lean back and grasp her face with both hands, my forehead against hers as I gaze into her soul. "You are not your mother. You will *never* be like her. Do you hear me? She was the foulest creature on this planet, and you are a living, walking angel."

She tries to shake her head, but I won't let her.

"Yes, you are," I reiterate. "You kill to save people from pain. There is nothing more angelic than that."

"But I'm a murderer," she says, her bloodied hands trembling. "And I can't stop. I can't stop the killing. I can't stop wanting more blood, more pain, more suffering. I can't make it stop."

"Then don't stop," Nathan says, drawing her attention away. "Don't ever fucking stop."

"What ...?" she mutters.

He looks at her like he's in awe of her self-control. "Kill whoever you need to kill, but don't you ever hate yourself. You don't deserve it."

She blinks a couple of times and brushes the tears away.

"I understand now why you were so adamant on protecting your secrets," Milo says. "And why you're so obsessed with protecting people. Your brother. Us. His sister. You're trying to erase their pain."

She smiles gently. "I don't understand; I thought you'd all—"

"What? Laugh? Be mad?" Nathan says, caressing her cheek. "I used to want to hate you so damn much, but now that I know the truth, how could I?"

"But you hate my brother," she says.

He nods several times. "Yeah, well, we all know what he did to me was unfair." He holds up his missing finger. "But I get why he's a vicious bastard now."

She snorts and laughs it off, but when he cups her face, she still leans into it.

"So you're not going to tell anyone?" she asks.

He shakes his head. "Why would I?"

"Because I took your deal and—"

"Fuck the deal," he says, smashing his lips onto hers. He holds her face like he's afraid she might disappear if he doesn't, and this is his last shot. And I'd be lying if I said it didn't make me jealous just a little bit, but I know the connection we share is just as important.

Milo pushes his way through both of us and suddenly grabs her towel, shoving his lips onto hers, kissing her no-holds-barred. And when their lips unlatch, I steal her away from him to claim her mouth as mine, rolling my tongue around hers in a greedy attempt to get so much more from this divine little kitty of mine.

She is nothing short of pure perfection. A rough-cut diamond.

And because of us, she almost turned to dust.

My lips briefly unlatch so I can tell her what I've been meaning to say, "There is no deal; there never was."

She looks up at me with confusion.

"I just needed a reason to have you," I say.

"But those pictures and my username," she mutters as I peck another kiss onto the side of her lips.

"I have way too much fun watching you kill, and if we'd revealed them, you would've stopped," Milo adds.

"I just used those pictures to get what I needed, and I needed money to save my sister from those Bonesmen. But then I had you ..." Nathan grabs her hand and presses a kiss on top. "And you proved to be far more valuable than money."

"I don't want you to just be with us because we'll reveal your secrets," I say, curling my fingers through hers as I bring them to my neck. "I want you to be with us because you *want* to."

"I ..." she murmurs.

"Could you?" Milo asks. "Be with us?"

She looks conflicted, and rightfully so. After everything we put her through, this is a lot to put on her plate. But my God, I can't let this woman walk. I just fucking can't.

She raises her brow, her lips parting.

*BANG!*

A loud explosion down below, coupled with the whole house shaking, makes us all look at the door, and whatever she wanted to say disappears along with our safety.

Because if I heard that right ...

"The Phantom building is under attack," Nathan says, and he immediately bolts off.

We follow suit as he opens the door, but come to a halt in front of the big banister overlooking the hallway down below.

Because none other than Felix fucking Rivera is standing in the door opening ... and he's got his gun pointed right at my face.

"WHERE IS SHE?"

# 47

<br>

## LANA

I can't even focus on what's going on because when I hear my brother's voice, I'm completely overcome by shock.

"GIVE ME MY FUCKING SISTER!" his voice blasts through the hallway.

But before I can shout his name, the gunfire erupts.

"Milo! Get back in there!" Nathan roars at him.

Nathan and Kai each duck and roll to a different side of the two main staircases while Milo crawls back into the room and closes the door.

"Lana, Felix is worried about you!" Dylan's voice calls. "Can you please come out here? Thanks, girl!" But his chipper voice does nothing to calm my nerves.

I can see Kai's face twisting with rage the second he hears his voice, and he jumps down the stairs where Dylan's standing and engages with him. "You motherfucker, I've been waiting for a chance to kill you."

Dylan laughs.

*BANG!*

The bullet narrowly avoids his head.

"Oh, I remember you," Dylan muses. "How's the eye?"

Kai roars and shoots all the bullets left in his gun, missing all of the shots because of his rage, and then he charges at him with his knife.

"Fucking Skull & Serpents in our fucking house? No fucking way, you're gonna die today!" Ezra yells as he shoots at both Dylan and Felix.

Alistair jumps out from behind a pillar and shoots him in the arm, and Ezra groans as he slumps against the banister near the stairs. "Don't fucking shoot at my friends," Alistair growls.

Gunshots fill the hall from left and right as more Phantoms emerge from their rooms, ready to kill whoever set foot in their domain. And I'm in the middle of it all.

*What the fuck do I do?*

*I have to put a stop to this.*

"I'LL KILL EVERY LAST ONE OF YOU!" Felix yells.

"Felix!" I shout, but he can't hear me over the gunshots ricocheting off the walls and floors.

A bullet flies into the door through which Milo just fled, and when I look around to see who shot at him, it's none other than Penelope Ricci, my brother's girlfriend. Or rather, all of their fucking girlfriends.

"Penelope?" I yell.

When her eyes connect with mine, she mouths, "Oops," but she continues shooting at the other Phantoms like she's hell-bent on making them pay for something they didn't actually do.

Paintings on the walls are left with holes as I run down the steps on my bare feet, wearing only a towel. Behind me, Phantoms shoot at Skull & Serpent guys and vice versa, none of them giving a shit who gets hurt. It's like an all-out war in the Phantom house.

Nathan rushes down the stairs and heads into Milo's room, yelling at one of his Phantoms to protect the door at all costs before he leaves again and focuses on the intruders.

"Motherfucker." He storms toward Felix to face him head-on.

Felix tries to shoot him, but his gun empties swiftly, and he chucks it aside, only to pull out a knife instead.

"I've been waiting for this," Nathan growls.

"Well, come and get it, then!" Felix shouts back. "You touch my sister, you deserve to fucking die!"

"Nathan, don't!" Kai yells from the top of the stairs, but Nathan's too consumed by hatred to listen.

So I rush down the last few steps in my towel. Nathan almost has his knife in Felix's shoulder when I bolt between them and spread my arms. "STOP!"

"Lana?" His eyes widen. "You're here ... in a fucking towel?"

"I was showering," I reply, incensed. "Pull back your guys."

"Fuck no, those Phantoms fucking stole you, and now they're gonna pay for it!" Felix barks, and he tries to shove me aside, but I stand my ground and push him back.

"They didn't steal shit. I came here out of my own accord," I retort.

He blinks a couple of times, his face contorting with confusion. "What the—"

"Come on and kill me then, motherfucker!" Nathan roars from behind me. "Or I swear to God, I'll chop off all your remaining fingers for daring to take one of mine!"

Felix's nostrils flare. "You motherf—"

"STOP!" I yell at Felix, and then I direct my attention at all of them, including Kai, Dylan, Alistair, and Ezra. "Stop! All of you!"

Dylan's got Kai by the collar, with his knife pointed at his leftover eye while Kai's knife is pointed at Dylan's heart. Both of them are unwilling to let go, but they both focus on me.

Even Penelope stops shooting and homes in on me.

"Stop fighting!" I scream. "Enough!"

"Give me one good fucking reason, Lana," Felix says through gritted teeth, throwing every ounce of his rage into his voice. "They extorted you!"

My eyes widen.

*How does he know?*

Jason swiftly hides behind a pillar at which Kai just shot, and my pupils dilate at the sight of him.

"You ..." I grit when our eyes briefly connect. "You *told* him?"

"He did his fucking job," Felix replies. "Jason cares about you." Felix narrows his eyes at Nathan. "Unlike those fuckers."

Nathan still points his knife at Felix. "I'd be real careful about your words if I were you. You don't fucking know us."

"You're Phantom scum who hurt Penelope and her sister, and now you're trying to hurt my sister for revenge," Felix says.

"This isn't fucking revenge," I explain. "It's more than that."

Penelope approaches and places a hand on Felix's shoulder. "Felix, maybe we should listen to her?"

"You're delirious," he tells me, ignoring her.

And I'm so goddamn tired of this that I just give him a hard slap.

He stares at me in disbelief while Penelope steps back to let us fight it out.

"Listen to me! I *want* to be here."

He just stares at me for a moment before his hand slowly rises to touch his cheek.

"I'm sorry," I say. "I don't want to hurt my own damn brother. But for once in your life, can you please listen to me instead of what *you* think is supposed to happen?"

"Lana," he mutters.

"All of you, stop and come here," I bark at Dylan, Kai, Alistair, and Ezra.

After a few seconds, they all stop pointing their knives at each other and make their way to their friends, keeping a keen eye on their enemies, like they're ready to be at each other's throats again.

Phantoms on one side, Skull & Serpents on the other.

What a mess.

Nathan and Kai clutch their knives tightly as if they're ready to strike, but I hold up my arm, and they finally back down. "Let me take care of this."

"I trust you," Nathan says.

"You *trust* her?" Felix parrots like he can't believe his ears. "What the hell is this? You'd better explain fast."

"Jason didn't tell you the full truth," I say, setting my gaze on him. "Or did he not tell you he literally told me to my face that he believed it was my fault I was being extorted?"

Felix's brows furrow, and he snaps his fingers. A Skull & Serpent grabs Jason and drags him to the front.

"Is that true, Jason?" Felix asks.

Jason stammers, "It's not like that. I tried to tell her, but—"

"No, you didn't want to support me, you made that very clear." I interrupt. "And then as icing on the cake, you literally came at me when I told you to leave me alone. You kept running after me and cornering me, forcing Kai to intervene."

Penelope's jaw drops. "Jason? What the fuck, is that true?"

"*Kai*?" Felix says through gritted teeth. "So you're on first-name basis with them now?"

"Oh ..." Penelope folds her arms. "So this is why you asked me about those boys."

"She asked you about them?" Felix snarls at her.

She raises her brow at him. "*You* made her a list."

"Because I didn't want her to even *talk* with them!"

"Talking isn't all we've done," Kai muses.

Felix raises his fist, but I grab it and lower it. "Don't. He's baiting you."

"So what? I don't care. He deserves a fist to the jaw for that comment," he growls back.

"I get that you're protective of me. You care about me, just like I care about you," I say, looking him in the eyes. "But I don't need your protection. Not on this one."

"So what, you're just hanging out here with these Phantoms?"

"Hanging out is an understatement." I turn my head as Milo casually strolls down the stairs. "We've been having a lot of fun with her."

"Fun?" Felix reiterates, his face almost turning red with rage. "You've had sex with *my* sister?"

Felix raises his gun again, pointing it straight at Milo's face.

# 48

## LANA

"Not just him," Nathan grits.

Felix takes off the safety, but I still grasp the barrel and shove it away.

"It was my choice, Felix," I reply.

"You can't be serious," he says. "They're the fucking enemy."

"Yours," I retort. "Not mine."

His jaw tightens, but Penelope drags his arm farther down. "Felix, stop, please. She asked you to for a reason."

"I told you not to associate with them, and you're going behind my back?"

"It's complicated," I answer, swallowing away the lump in my throat. "But they understand me, unlike Jason." I throw him another wicked glance, and he looks away in shame.

"Jason scared the living shit out of her," Kai says. "I would've put a knife in his brain if it wasn't for the fact that Lana wants him to live."

"I tried to make it right!" Jason exclaims.

"By making her feel threatened?" Kai retorts.

Jason points at Kai, Nathan, and Milo. "You're the one who sent those pictures!"

"So it's true?" Felix's grip on his gun tightens so harshly I can hear the metal crack. "They took lewd pictures of you and tried to shake you for money?"

"They did, but it was for a good reason," I say.

"What good reason can anyone have? Tell me now, or I swear to God, I will put a bullet in all three."

"They needed the money to save his sister from being taken by traffickers," I explain.

Nathan grips my arm. "Hey."

"I'm sorry, but I need to tell him the truth if you want him to leave without killing you all," I say, and Nathan grinds his teeth, then nods and backs off again.

"All that is over now," Kai says.

"Shut your damn mouth," Felix quips.

"Hey, can't we all relax?" Dylan muses. "Take a chill pill."

"Don't you even fucking start," Kai retorts.

"Don't start fighting again now," I warn. "Or I'll punch all of you back into your fucking rooms."

Penelope sniggers behind her hand.

"So what is this, then? Some kind of relationship?" Alistair asks. "Like ours?"

My eyes narrow, and I look away as I softly mouth, "Um ... I guess."

"You guess?" Felix's eye twitches.

Kai places a hand on my shoulder. "She's ours."

"Take your hands off my sis—"

"Felix." Penelope interrupts him and places her hand on his shoulder too. "Don't you see? They're in love."

The whole room goes quiet, and I feel like all the blood just drained from my body.

"What?" he says under his breath.

"Don't you remember what it was like for us in the beginning?" Penelope muses. "The tension, the heat, the rage."

"True, she's like a fiery goddess," Milo says with a big grin. "And I'm smitten."

"Oh God," I mutter, burying my face in my hands.

"Fuck me," Felix grits. "You're having sex with all of these dudes? Is that why they made those pictures?"

"Not all of them. Just Kai, Nathan, and Milo," I reply, trying not to make it sound awkward.

"I actually intended to send the pictures to you," Nathan quips with a smirk on his face.

Felix looks like he wants to bite his head off. "Swear to God, if you show those to anyone, you're dead."

"He hasn't," I say, lowering his hand. "And he wasn't planning to," I say, glaring at Nathan. "Right?"

"I won't. Because all those delicious pictures are meant only for us," he replies with a wink.

Felix snarls, "You motherf—"

"Ah. Stop." I interrupt. "*Enough.* You've done enough. I'm not in trouble. I'm safe here."

"Safe? This is your definition of safe?" he retorts.

"They care about me," I say, swallowing away my apprehension to tell him the truth. "And I care about them."

"Do you even know what they did?" he says through gritted teeth. "They bullied Penelope's sister and then tried to attack her too."

"Hey, I didn't have a fucking choice, and you know that," Nathan spits out. He glances at Dylan.

"Thanks to your father, who tried to extort my fucking parents by sending information to the police."

"Let me know when you're all done," Alistair murmurs as he sinks down against a pillar and casually lights a cigarette.

"Hey, I've got nothing to do with this," Dylan says, raising his hands. "Leave me out of it."

"Oh, is that why you took my fucking eye?" Kai growls at him.

"You attempted to go after Penelope," Dylan retorts, getting up in his face.

"It's because of *her* Nathan lost his finger and got his legs broken. Of course I did. He's a Phantom, and Phantoms protect each other," Kai says as their foreheads collide.

"Stop it, all of you," Penelope says. "I hate those boys as much as you do, but all this fighting is getting us nowhere."

"She's right," I say. "Besides, did you forget Dad told us we'd get in trouble if he caught us again?"

"Right," Dylan says in a long-drawn-out manner. "I forgot about that."

"Why are we even fighting?" Alistair asks all of a sudden, taking another drag of his smoke. "If this is what she chose, isn't it up to her to decide?"

Everyone looks at him, even Felix, even though he's not amused by the concept of letting me decide for myself what I do.

So I cup his face and make him focus on me. "I know you want to protect me. But I can protect myself."

"How, when you choose them?"

"You don't know us the way she does," Kai retorts.

"And I don't fucking want to," Felix replies, but then he sighs out loud when he looks at Lana. "But if you want to fucking be with them, that's on you."

I take a breath. "Thank you."

"Soooo ... no one's going to shoot me, right?" Milo mutters.

I snort. "No, Milo, no one's going to kill you today."

"Not me," Alistair murmurs from the pillar he's seated against.

"Cool, cool, because I've taken enough bullets for a whole damn year."

"Unless you want me to," Nathan muses, winking at him.

"Wow, what's this all?" Dylan laughs, pointing at both of them. "Are you guys like ... fruity?"

"It's complicated," Milo says.

"Eh, I dig it," Dylan says with a wink. "The more, the merrier, right?"

And he bumps elbows with Felix, who still does not seem at all amused.

"So ... You three are fucking my sister." Felix makes it sound like a statement instead of a question.

"You could put it like that," Kai replies.

"Rather blunt if you ask me, but sure," Milo muses.

Felix makes a *tsk* sound.

"Hey, I don't like it either. They fucking hurt me and my sister," Penelope says, "but if this is what Lana wants ..."

"It's not right," Felix says.

"We weren't either," Penelope says, looking at Felix, Dylan, and Alistair. "Remember how we all started."

"So you're copying us now, huh?" Dylan muses. "Aight, I dig it."

"We're not copying anyone, bitch," Kai growls at him. "We do it better."

"Don't insult us," Alistair responds, chucking his cig on the floor like he doesn't give a shit.

"Okay, everyone shut up," I say. "I don't want y'all to fight over me. I'm fine. I can make my own decisions."

"Yeah, she's a big girl," Milo muses, winking at me.

I roll my eyes. "My point is, thank you, Felix, for being concerned. But I am fine."

"What about the extortion, then?" Jason rebukes.

"That's none of your concern," Nathan retorts.

"They already apologized," I say. "It's not up to you to decide whether that's good. I don't want to be involved with you any longer."

Jason's jaw drops, but I don't care if he's embarrassed. He deserves it after what he tried to do.

"Jason, you fucked up big time," Penelope says.

Jason's face turns red. "Look, I'm sorry, okay?"

"Save it," Kai says. "She's not interested." He steps forward and blocks Jason from trying to get closer. "Get out of my house."

"*Your* house?"

"Yes." Kai has so much of an aggressive aura surrounding him that I'm not even sure I'd fight against him if push came to shove. "Mine. Just like her. And if you don't get out of my face within five minutes, your bones will be mine too."

Fuck. I didn't think I could get flushed in front of Felix, but here we are.

"Believe him, he'll hang them to dry right above our logo," Milo says with a grin.

Kai narrows his eyes. "Now leave."

"Jason ..." Alistair gets up from the floor. "Listen to him."

Jason slowly steps away. "Fine. Because *she* asked. Not because of you."

"You didn't even fucking support me when I told you what happened!" I shout at him. "You don't even have a right to be here."

Felix suddenly turns on him and points his gun at Jason's face. "You'd better get out of here now. In fact, get off this goddamn campus."

"What?" Jason's eyes widen. "But I'm a Skull & Serpent member."

Alistair marches up to him and tears the emblem straight off his shirt, leaving him with an exposed nipple. "No, you're not."

Jason shakes his head. "Please ..."

"I believe my sister ... and if she says you didn't help her, you're dead to me," Felix growls. "Now get out of here."

Jason starts walking backward and then turns around and runs off like a coward with his tail between his legs. Which is probably a good thing, or I would've stolen Felix's gun and shot him in the knees.

"Glad we got rid of that one," Dylan mutters.

Penelope frowns at him.

"What?" Dylan shrugs. "I don't like him, and I'm just saying what everyone's thinking."

I sigh out loud. "Whatever. Can we stop this? I'm really tired of fighting. Today's been a lot."

Penelope looks around the house. "We left a lot of holes ..."

"Yeah," Kai says. "You gonna fork up the funds to fix it?"

Dylan makes a wide-eyed weird-looking face. "Well, I think it's about time I leave."

When he tries to run off, Alistair grabs him by the collar and stops him. "Nope. You're staying."

"But this shit is uncomfortable as fuck!" Dylan complains.

"Yeah, so that's why this is the moment when you pay them off," Alistair hints, throwing glances.

"We don't owe them shit. They're lucky they get to keep their fucking fingers after touching my sister," Felix growls.

"Felix," I mutter. "Please. Can you just ... go back to the Skull &
Serpent Society? Pretend Jason never told you anything?"

"No," he answers, but he still comes closer and cups my face. "Come
home with me."

I smile and lean into his hand. "I can't."

"Because they won't let you?"

"Because I want to stay here," I add, tears welling up in my eyes, but
I push them away.

He looks up at Kai. "You'd better fucking keep her safe. If she's
harmed in any way, I'll fucking gut you in your sleep. You understand?"

"Thank you for coming. But I'm okay. Please, guys ... go home," I say.
"We'll talk later, okay?"

Dylan and Alistair nod, but it takes Felix physical convincing as
they have to drag him away from me.

"We'll send the bill for the house," Nathan yells from behind me.

"I'll shred it along with your finger," Felix growls back.

Nathan sticks up his middle finger. "Fuck you, I'm fucking your
sister!"

Felix wrings free from Dylan's and Alistair's grip, but Penelope's
strong gaze keeps him grounded. "C'mon. Let's go home. We'll figure
this out later."

Felix gestures at Nathan, Kai, and Milo, pointing his fingers at his
eyes first before he points at them. And then they all leave the building,
like a rescinding flood leaving chaos in its wake.

"Jesus fucking Christ, that was intense," Milo mutters.

"Tell me about it," I say, breathing out another sigh.

Kai rubs his face, his knife still firmly lodged in his hands. "I just
renovated this fucking place. Fuck. It's gonna take forever to fix this
place back up."

As the adrenaline finally starts leaving my body, I feel so dizzy my
knees begin to quake, and before I know it, my vision grows blurry, and
I sink to the floor.

# 49

⟨⟨⟨∽⟩⟩⟩

## KAI

I rush to her and catch her just before her head hits the floor.

"Fuck," Nathan says as he jumps to the floor with me. "What happened?"

"I don't know," I reply, looking around at the other Phantoms as they come out of their hiding spot. "Clear the area. Call the cleaners to come clean this shit up and give them some extra hush money. Call the renovator, Ezra. The walls will need a new coat of paint." He nods at me and walks off with his phone in his hands. "We'll take care of Lana."

I touch her wrist, and I definitely still feel a pulse. Her breathing is shallow, though.

She must've exhausted herself after all that fighting at the Bones Brotherhood club and then with her brother here too.

I lift her in my arms and carry her back up the stairs, with both Nathan and Milo following me. I take her to my room upstairs and lie her down on the triple king-sized bed.

"Are you sure she's okay?" Milo asks, cringing from the pain in his stomach, but he still follows us inside. "Is there anything I can do?"

"She needs to rest," I say. "I'll stay with her."

Nathan swallows and glances at her body, grinding his teeth. "Fine. I'll go check on Ro, make sure she's safe."

I nod as he leaves the room, but Milo tentatively stays behind.

"You should rest too," I tell him.

"I'm too agitated to sleep," he replies.

Always the worried soul.

He really does care a lot about her.

I lie down beside her and clutch her hand as she gently begins to snore.

"Focus on healing," I tell Milo. "I'll watch over her while she sleeps."

He nods. "If you need anything, just call."

He throws me my phone from my bedside stand, and I catch it just before it hits me in the face. "Thanks."

"You're welcome," he says with a wink. "Don't go ravage her like a somno while we're not here, okay?"

"Don't worry, none of you will ever find out," I reply, winking back.

And he walks out of the room, struggling to fight the pain. But I know he'll be all right.

He's not the only one worried about her.

My hand slowly reaches for her face as I caress her cheek. Looking at her beauty while she sleeps calms my nerves and makes me forget about the outside world. It's as though there's no one left but us. And even though she's not responding to my touch, my heart still pounds in my chest at the thought that she can feel me.

I truly have fallen ...

But I don't regret a single moment of the dark descent.

\*\*\*

## NATHAN

When Ro sees me, she runs over and hugs me tight. "I was so scared. There was so much noise."

"I know, Ro. But you don't have to worry about that."

"Has it stopped?"

I lower myself to her level and nod. "And it's not coming back. I'll make sure of that."

She looks at my arm and touches it, her finger retreating with a lick of blood on it, her eyes widening at the sight. "Are you bleeding?"

I hadn't even realized. "Must've been a scrape. Don't worry about it. I'm not hurt."

"When can I come out?" she asks.

I pat her on the head. "Soon, Ro, soon. They need to clean up the place first."

"Clean? Did someone make a mess?"

I laugh. "You could say that, yeah."

She runs to the play corner Milo installed and pulls out a small broom. "I can sweep!"

"No, no," I say, holding her back. "This is a mess only grown-ups can clean."

"Aw ..." She pouts. "But I want to help."

"I know," I reply, smiling. "Tell you what, I'll tell them to leave some of the rubble for you to clean up after they finish, okay?"

She grins. "Yes."

"Good, now go play." I push her to her play corner. "I'll bring you some drinks and food in an hour."

But she's not listening anymore, so I slowly back out of the room and breathe a sigh of relief. She's safe, and that's all that matters.

I walk up the staircase and check out the walls littered with bullets. It's gonna take a ton of work and money to fix the holes. Fuck. We're gonna have to beg Kai's mom again, aren't we?

Sighing, I walk into my room but stop when I spot Milo standing in the cage.

"What are you doing in here?"

He touches the bars. "I miss this." He glances at me over his shoulder. "I miss you."

I close the door behind me and step forward. "You miss me taking my rage out on you?"

He smirks. "How do you know me so well?"

"I can't," I say, folding my arms. "And you know why."

He looks down at the wounds on his body. "It's nothing. Just a wound."

"You almost died," I respond. "I'm not going to touch you and be the reason you actually die."

"Aw ..." he jokes, but he knows as well as I do that I'm serious.

"You know I can't control myself," I say.

He swallows and bites his lip. "I know."

I walk toward the bed and lie down. "Then why are you here?"

"I just wanted to remember what it was like ... uncomplicated ... messy," he murmurs. "But now that those Bonesmen have been taken care of, I feel like there's nothing left for you to latch onto."

I frown. "You're scared I'll lose my sting."

"They were what made you angry," he says, exiting the cage. "Obsessed."

I get up and walk up to him, stopping him from walking any farther, and I push him right back into the cage and onto a chair in the middle. "Sit."

He obeys me like a puppy dog with smoldering eyes.

"I took out my rage on you over what they did to my family, but now that they're gone, it doesn't mean I don't still feel rage." I grab a rope hanging from the wall and wrap it around his body, leaving out one hand. "And it definitely doesn't mean I don't feel the need to hurt people."

I press my lips to his, taking a kiss, whether he wants me to or not. But he doesn't seem to mind.

"You really are yearning for a punishment, aren't you?" I murmur.

My cock throbs as his words come out in a half mewl. "Oh fuck, yes."

A wicked smile spreads as I tie him up to the chair. Not too tight to touch his wounds, but tight enough to keep him in place. "I can't hurt you when you're this fragile."

"Fragile?" He scoffs.

My tongue darts out to lick my top lip. "But I can still give you pain."

I stand back and admire my work with a tilted head. "Does it hurt?"

He shakes his head as I step back even farther.

My dick pulsates with need. "It will."

I fish my key from my pocket and lock the door.

"You want my cage? My punishment? Fine, you can have it," I say, leaning between the metal bars. "But I won't lay a single finger on you until your wounds are fully healed."

"What?" He gasps.

"You came out of the clinic against my orders, so this is your punishment. You can stay on that chair until I feel like you're ready," I say, a grin forming on my lips. "And until then ... all you can do is watch."

And I take off my shirt that still clings to my chest from the shower I took with Lana and let him feast his eyes as I unzip and take out my already half-hard shaft, stroking it with glee.

He licks his lips, inching closer, fingers prying through the bars as he whimpers. "Oh God, don't do this to me."

"You're a naughty boy, Milo. And if I can't punish you physically, then it'll have to be mental torment," I say as I begin stroking my cock. "Now enjoy the view."

*** 

# LANA

**The next day**

*I'm running through the complex, throwing my knife and ending another life.*

*BANG!*

*More gunshots emanate from the hallway up ahead, but I push on and shoot too, hitting them right in the head.*

*The more bodies drop, the more I'm lost in adrenaline until nothing is left but me and the blood caking my skin. Each kill brings me closer to that high, closer to insanity.*

*But when I look at my hands, the bodies begin to disappear in the dark of the night, and at the end of the hallway, a bed appears.*

*In it are two people, one crying, softly pleading for help, while the other bounces on top.*

*And the horror that settles in my stomach is too much to take.*

*BANG!*

*Blood stains the sheets.*

*The intense scream that follows rings in my ear.*

*Dark eyes boring a hole into my skull, dragging my soul out with it until nothing is left but a hollow mess of me.*

*Eyes I recognize.*

*Hands that feel familiar.*

*"It's gonna be okay," the voice says.*

*But all I hear is the ringing of the gunshot like a memory being seared into my brain.*

Screaming, I awaken to someone lying beside me. I grasp the nearest knife I can find on the bedside table and roll on top of the person, pushing the knife under their neck. Hands raised, completely at my mercy. But it isn't until my eyes find his that I realize what I'm doing.

"Lana, it's me," Kai says.

It takes me a while to calm the panic raging through my heart.

"Where am I?" I mutter.

The last thing I remember, I was in the hallway in my towel.

I look down, but the towel is gone. I'm completely naked, sitting on top of him.

"It was wet, so I had to take it off to make you warm again," he says. "I haven't touched you. I was just watching over you."

I shiver in place from the cold draft passing by my nipples.

The last thing I know is that I was arguing with my brother, and he'd just left when I ... collapsed onto the floor.

"You're in my room now. You're safe," he says. His hand reaches for my face, and he caresses my cheek so gently I almost break under his touch. "I'm not here to hurt you."

"I ..." I mutter, slowly retracting the knife.

"You were dreaming again ... weren't you?"

I nod and roll off him, pulling my knees up to my chin as I sit in the bed. "The nightmares are intensifying."

"Nightmares ... about your mother?" he asks.

I swallow away my pride and nod.

He sits up too, intently listening to me even though I just held a knife to his throat.

"They've never been this bad before," I say, sniffing. "Usually the killing keeps them at bay."

"So revenge on predators wasn't your only reason," he says.

I shake my head. "I need it to stay sane." When I look at him, he doesn't seem the least bit afraid. "I'm sorry. I almost killed you there. I wasn't trying to."

"I'm fine," he says, touching his neck to make sure there's no blood, then he shows me his hand. "See?"

I smile. "Good."

"*Good*?" His brow rises. "Lana fucking Rivera not trying to kill me? That's a first."

I snort and bump into him. "Stop, you know why I am the way I am." I think about my nightmare, trying to decipher what I saw. Something just doesn't sit right with me. The memories I have of that time are so blurry that I don't know what part is real and what part isn't. My brain prevents me from accessing them and has stored them away for my own safety, but they still creep out in my sleep.

When I shiver again, he places a hand on my back. "What do you usually do when you have those dreams?"

I gulp and tuck my hair behind my ear. "The thing you guys have been holding over my head..."

"Murder," he fills in.

I nod. "It's an outlet. The killing keeps me sane."

"And since your victims deserve their fate, you don't feel guilty," he says.

I sigh out loud. "I wonder if it'll ever be enough." My fist balls. "But killing is the only thing that douses the fire burning in my heart."

"Be right back." He hops off the bed and exits the room, leaving me confused.

What is he planning?

I wait until he eventually returns with something that looks like leather.

"What is that?" I ask.

"An outfit. Stole it from Nathan's room."

I narrow my eyes as he approaches and tosses it my way. "Put it on."

"You think I'll fit into this?"

"It fits Milo snugly, so I'm confident," he says.

Suddenly, he grabs my hand, and he pulls me out of the bed. "C'mon."

"What are we doing?" I ask as I put on the outfit, which fits surprisingly well.

But he doesn't answer as he continues rummaging in his closet.

So I go and check myself out in the mirror. It's like a wetsuit with pants, but much softer and more flexible, with a zipper that goes to the top. Slick.

"What's this been used for?" I ask. "I hope it isn't what I think it is."

"It is," he replies.

"Ew."

He snorts. "It's been washed." He's still going through his closet until he finally finds what he's looking for. "Perfect."

He comes up behind me. "Close your eyes." When he gets too close to my neck with whatever he has in his hands, I grip his wrist. He leans in to whisper, "Trust me."

I throw him another glare through the mirror, but I still do what he says, and I release his wrist.

Something brushes past my cheeks, pressing against my forehead, as two ribbons are tied behind my head. And I can feel his breath near my ear, drawing me closer to him as he whispers, "Open your eyes."

My eyes flutter open to a mask covering my face, a black cat mask similar to mine, but with lace and little kitty ears, gems studded all over the eyes, along with a cute crystal button for a nose, complete with whiskers and all.

My lips part, but I don't know what to say.

His glinting green eye and pearly whites find mine in the mirror. "You said only killing makes you feel better ... So let's kill."

A bright grin forms on my lips, rivaling his. "What a sweet, sinful proposal. I'm in."

# 50

MILO

**That night**

I close the buttons on my shirt and pull up my pants, zipping up before I put on my bulletproof vest. Can't risk getting shot a second time.

When I'm done strapping in, I grab my white mask and march out the door with my bag. The car out front is being loaded up with equipment and stuff, and when I hop down the steps, they all look at me like they're seeing a walking corpse.

"Hey, guys," I say, waving as I casually place my gear into the trunk.

Nathan glares at me while clutching the passenger's seat door. "What do you think you're doing?"

"Coming with you," I say with a beaming smile.

"I think the fuck not." He slams the door shut. "You should be upstairs, resting."

Kai closes the trunk door. "It's not safe for you."

"If it's not safe for me, it's not safe for you. So why are you going?" I raise a brow.

"Because she needs a kill," Kai says, pointing at Lana, who sticks her head out the window.

"Are you sure you want to say that out loud?" she asks.

"It's the middle of the night. No one's listening," Kai responds without looking at her.

Nathan's gaze remains fixated on me, and he doesn't seem too pleased.

"I don't like it when you guys go without me," I say.

"Milo, I don't want you dying on me again," Nathan says.

"I've got this vest." I pluck at it to show it to him. "Won't be dying anytime soon."

Nathan makes a tsk sound. "That won't keep the bullets out of your brain."

"What bullets?" I retort, sporting my nunchucks. "Hit 'em in the head before they even try. Pow." I flick them around.

Kai snorts. "You're ridiculous."

I resort to pouting. "Please."

Kai rolls his eyes. "Fine."

"What?" Nathan throws up his hand. "You can't be serious."

"Dead serious. He's not gonna let this slide," Kai says.

"Nope," I add.

"It's late, and we've already wasted enough time. Now get in." Kai beckons me.

"Yes," I say, and I grab his hand and high-five myself because I'm a hundred percent certain he wouldn't do it, but I don't mind. "Thank you!"

I hop into the back seat before Nathan can stop me even though he gets in on the other end of the vehicle. He folds his arms and throws me judgmental glances every once in a while.

"That went well," Lana says, looking at us through the rearview mirror.

"Yes."

"No."

We both say in tandem.

And it makes her snort, hiding her laughter behind her hand.

Kai steps in too and shuts the door. "Let's go." He starts the car and races off the campus grounds within no time.

"So where are we going?" I ask casually.

Nathan looks out the window, agitated. "Nowhere."

"Found an address on the site," Kai says. "One of our old sock-puppets had bait."

"One?" Lana parrots. "You mean to tell me you had multiple accounts?"

"You do what you have to if you need the money badly enough," Nathan says.

"You just have one?" I ask Lana.

She shrugs. "I didn't think I'd ever need another one. The requests just kept rolling in."

"This is the place," Nathan says, pointing at the old apartment building at the end of the street.

My heart rate is already picking up from excitement as Kai parks the car, and we all jump out.

I fish my bag from the trunk, and Lana puts on her mask, which looks awfully familiar. She takes off her coat, revealing the wetsuit underneath, which looks suspiciously like one of mine.

"Wait a damn minute," I mutter, looking at Kai. "You raided my closet?"

He grins. "Had to give her something to wear while her clothes were wet."

"You could've asked," I quip.

"How could I when you were roped down in Nathan's cage?" he retorts, making my cheeks flush with heat and my balls blue with the memory of unspent cum.

"Holy shit," Lana says, her jaw dropped.

Nathan tips her chin up as he walks past her. "It's not nice for ladies to stare."

"Well, excuse me," she scoffs.

"Granted," Nathan says, a big old smile on his face when he sees her steam up behind him.

"Let's go, guys," Kai says, throwing his bag over his shoulder.

"Ready to murder some bitches," Nathan says, raking his fingers through his blond hair, and he zips open his bag to take out his bat.

I grin as I follow them all inside. "Oh yeah, that's what I'm talking about."

The doors can't even open fully, and they squeak like hell. Inside, the walls have chips, and the carpet smells like dirt. The whole place seems like it's falling apart, but we still go up the stairs. The hallway at the top of the stairs is filled with doors.

"Which one is it?" I ask.

"Fifteen," Nathan replies, swaying a bat in his hand.

"Here," Kai says, grinning as he knocks on the door. "Ready?"

"More than ever," Lana muses, fishing out her knives.

The second the dude opens the door, Lana stabs him in the arm and blocks him from closing the door by shoving a foot inside.

"FU—"

Kai shoves him inside, and we all barge in. "Hey, prick. You asked for a hookup? Here we are."

"What the fuck?" the guy yelps when Lana rips her knife out.

I shut the door behind me.

"You thought I'd be a young girl?" Lana flips her hair over her shoulder. "Do I look convincing enough to play the part?"

In shock, the guy tumbles backward into his own sofa, screaming wildly.

God, I love watching her put up a cold-hearted show and destroying people with just a few words.

Kai snatches one of the towels off the kitchen rack and smothers his mouth. "Don't want to wake the neighbors now, do we?"

I smile at him like a motherfucker before both Nathan and I knock out his knees in tandem.

*CRACK!*

The guy screams so harshly into the cloth that his eyeballs almost pop out.

"Pwease, pwease!" the guy begs. "It hurts!"

Lana rips his head up by his hair. "How many other girls did you convince to come here?"

"I don't know," he whimpers. "I've never—"

Kai shoves a knife underneath his throat. "Don't. Lie."

"It's only been a couple. Five. Maybe six."

Six girls. All used by this monster.

Kai's jaw tightens, and he glances at Lana for a second before suddenly pushing the guy back. "We need something better than this."

Nathan swings his bat over his shoulder. "Wait, are you going to—"

"Backpack." Kai interrupts.

I hand it over to him, and he fishes out the syringe.

The guy's eyes widen. "Oh God."

"This will hurt," Kai warns, and he shoves the needle into the guy's neck before he can even so much as blink.

The scream that follows dies out in a few seconds.

"What are you doing?" Lana asks. "I thought we were gonna kill him. Not spare him the pain by knocking him out."

"Oh no, I'm not going to spare this guy. Not for a single second," Kai responds as he takes the syringe out, and we all watch this guy's lights go out. "But this place won't do for what I have in store for a fucker like him."

He snaps his fingers at me and Nathan. "Take him downstairs and put him in the trunk. It's time we had some old-fashioned fun."

*** 

## KAI

Fuckers like him don't deserve to go in the comfort of their own house.

He needs to feel the pain in his fucking soul before I'll let him go into the nether beyond. And I know the perfect way.

We haul him into Nathan's room after driving back with him sleeping off the drugs in the trunk. By the time I've snapped my fingers, he's groggily waking up. Too late.

Nathan and Milo ram one of Nathan's hooks through his back and hang him from the rod in the back of his room, next to the cage.

The guy wakes screaming in agony, blood dripping down his back, but the sounds are like a song to my soul.

"Wakey, wakey." Milo pokes him in the belly.

When he doesn't respond, he whacks him with the nunchucks.

"Fuck! What are you doing to me?"

"Giving you all the pain you deserve and more," Nathan muses, and he grabs one of the whips off his walls with the metal tips attached. "We told you this was going to hurt ..."

Nathan holds the whip out to Lana. "You do the honors."

She grabs the whip, and the power that takes hold of her when she clutches the leather is magnificent.

She whacks the whip into his belly, and the cries that follow are a perfect melancholy filling the room.

"Milo." I snap my fingers. "Go wake one of the other Phantoms and tell them to guard the door. No one comes in without my explicit permission."

Milo nods and heads outside while Lana whips the guy hanging from the hook.

"How much blood will it take to make you regret you ever laid a finger on those girls?" she growls, snapping the whip.

He whimpers. "Please, I didn't want to hurt them. I just can't help it."

WHACK!

She strikes him again, this time in the groin, blood pouring onto the floor.

"Lift him higher," I growl. "Make him dangle."

Nathan turns the wheel in the back of the room, causing the hook to embed farther into his back as it hoists him up into the air. He's hanging by his own flesh now, and the sight of him in pure agony is fucking glorious.

Milo returns, grabbing a chair and casually sitting to watch her from a distance while she goes wild on the guy.

She whips him again from all sides, not stopping until blood rains down on the floor and on top of her. She doesn't care how much is spoiled or how much she's covered with, and when she's done, her breathing comes out in ragged breaths, blood staining her wetsuit.

She drops the whip and fishes out her knife, jabbing it into his thigh.

"Please! Stop!" the guy keeps begging, but she ignores him.

"Holy fuck ..." Nathan mutters, admiring her from a distance as she keeps going, boring holes into every inch of his body.

Yet he's still breathing, still existing in the most painful corner of human existence.

She allows us all to experience the depth of her depravity. Every once in a while, her eyes connect with all three of us as though she's begging us to see her for what she truly is. A beautiful, frenzied monster of justice and destruction. To look at the darkness sweeping through the room, taking us all over in a storm of retribution.

I'm in awe and enraptured by this homicidal kitty of mine.

She thrusts her knife into his body until nothing remains but holes, blood spraying from all sides, covering her too.

For a second, she glances my way, almost as if she's wondering when I'll stop being enamored and start being terrified.

But I will never, ever reach that point.

If this is her worst moment ... I want to live inside it with every atom in my body.

"Make it stop, make it stop," he begs, his voice soft, practically a peep.

He can barely stay conscious.

"Please ..."

Lana slowly drags out her knife and holds it out to me.

"Do any of you still want a chance?" she asks.

A smile forms on my face as I take the knife from her and jab it underneath his rib cage. Blood pours from the wound, though not as fast as before, but the droplets still stain my face and chest.

He cries again and vomits all over himself, but then his eyes slowly roll back into his head.

"He's done for," Milo mutters.

"Lana?" I offer her the knife back.

Instead, she hands it to Nathan. He stabs him in the legs, but the guy no longer responds to any of the jabs we give him.

"Told you," Milo adds.

Nathan makes a tsk sound as he pulls out the knife again. "Pathetic fucker."

He hands it back to Lana and then lowers the guy from the hook. "Lana, do you want to do the honors?"

She frowns at him. "Didn't you need his money?"

Nathan shakes his head. "Not this time."

Her lips part, confusion settling on her face. "But why else would you do this?"

I step forward and grip the hand holding the knife. "For you."

Nathan grabs the guy's hair, tilting his head back, while I bring her hand along with the knife to his throat. My body presses up against hers, the sheer amount of violence irrevocably chaining my soul to hers.

"Now kill him."

And as the blade punctures his skin, I plant a kiss onto her bloodied neck, savoring the taste of her savagery, her pulse quickening with every kiss, every stroke of the blade while it cuts through his flesh.

Blood streams out of his neck, spouting onto us, but I don't give a care in the world as I take her mouth and claim her while she kills him. Nothing is sweeter than the taste of murder on the lips of the girl I love.

She leans back for a second, blood rolling down her face. "Are you still not scared?"

I let my fingers travel across her bloodied face, appreciating every drop of blood before I tip up her chin to make her look at me. "The only thing I'm frightened of is losing you."

The knife clatters to the floor, and she kisses me back just as desperately. Her body comes to life in my hands as they snake around her waist and back. I zip down her wetsuit, desperate to touch her naked skin and remind it of its only master.

Me.

I am the only one she bends to. The only one who can make a girl like her yield. Other men can only dream of that kind of power.

I slip the wetsuit off her shoulders and down her tits as her hands wrap around my neck and mine cup her tits. With every squeeze, her moans become louder, and my dick twitches with excitement.

As our lips unlatch, I murmur, "Good little kitty. Now purr for me."

I dip my blood-soaked hand down into the bottom half of the wetsuit, rubbing her pussy until she moans.

"All that violence got you so wet," I whisper into her ear as I dip a finger inside. "I gave you what you craved so badly, and now I will take what I hunger for."

She gasps as I dip another finger inside, her wetness mixing with the blood, causing orgasmic looks on her face.

I take a fistful of her hair, force her head back, and lick her neck, suckling off all the blood before I bite down. She whimpers against me, but instead of pushing me away, she fingers my shirt and tugs me closer.

Fuck.

I withdraw my teeth and growl, "Nathan. Grab whatever you need. Now. Before I destroy her right here, right now on this very fucking floor."

"What?" Her eyes widen. "What do you mean?"

"You've had your fun. Now it's our turn," I say, smiling against her ear. "And you're going to be a good fucking kitty and take all of us."

# 51

⟨⟩⟩⟩⟩

## LANA

Before I know it, Kai's dragged me all the way to the back, inside the cage, where Nathan has hung a bar along with a bunch of rope. And he ties the rope around my body and arms, sealing me in. Then he places a second rope underneath me.

"Kneel," he says.

For a second, I contemplate running, but then I remember all the things they said to me, all the things we shared, and all the doubt washes off me.

*They can't hurt me.*

I drop to my knees right on top of the rope.

He wraps it around each of my ankles, keeping my legs separated as my ankle is forcefully kept in a kneeled position and tied to my thighs. Without being able to support myself, I fall face-down onto the floor, but Kai catches me just in time.

"Wouldn't want to damage that pretty face before we ruin it," he says with a wicked grin.

And I can't deny that my heart thumps in my throat as wildly as my clit does.

They hoist me up from the floor like a rag doll. I couldn't move, even if I wanted to, with my arms tied behind my back and both legs secured like I'm the roast they intend to eat.

Nathan secures the rope from my back to the bar at the top of the cage, suspending me. The bar twists with ease, and when he presses his finger into my knee, I start to spin around.

"Perfect," he says, his voice low, heady.

Kai fishes his own knife from his pocket, and with a leisure stroke, he slides it down my legs. "Now tell me ... are you afraid, kitty?"

I swallow away the nerves, which are quickly replaced with excitement. "No."

A devilish glint in his eyes makes my pussy throb. "A natural born killer without a single shred of fear ... now that's perfection. Yet you're defenseless. We could easily kill you right here, and no one would ever find your body."

"You won't kill me," I say boldly. "You want me."

His eyes narrow, and he grips my face. "You know me too well. I can't kill you because I want you so bad it would kill me too. But I can always make you scream."

He twists my nipples so roughly I bite down on my lip, and he smashes his lips onto mine, claiming the pain for himself. His kiss is rough and greedy and all things unholy, driving me insane with lust.

Two hands clasp around my ankles, pulling me closer, and suddenly, I feel a tongue dive into me.

"Fuck!" I moan.

"Pussy and blood ...a delicious combination," Nathan murmurs as his tongue drives inside.

But I can't focus as Kai zips down right in front of me and pulls out his long, hard cock, the piercings gleaming in the harsh light.

He grabs my hair. "You took his life, but your wicked soul belongs to me. Remember that as we use your body until we're spent."

And he shoves my mouth over his hard-on, salty pre-cum rolling across my tongue. I cough as he hits my uvula, thrusting even farther until the tip hits the back of my throat.

"You can take it; you're a wild cat," he groans, his length throbbing deep inside me.

Nathan's tongue spears my pussy, driving me wild with lust, and my whole body begins to zing.

I never knew being tied up could feel so freeing.

My blood was boiling before, but I want to submit after relinquishing all that hatred.

Let them ravage me, body and soul.

They can take what they want and leave nothing but crumbs of me.

"Fuck, she looks so pretty all tied up like that," Milo murmurs as he goes down underneath me and grips my tits. "I just want to lick her entire body."

He lifts his head and takes my nipple into his mouth, sucking so hard I mewl against Kai's shaft. And he shoves it even farther into my throat just from the sounds I'm making.

Suddenly, Nathan retracts his tongue, and I hear a zipper going down.

"Fuck, I need to have her again," he groans, and he plunges into me, every thick ridge, every glinting barbell, until I'm filled on both ends.

And my brain is entirely overridden by the lust coursing through me.

Milo moves away from my nipples, and when his tongue dips out, my eyes almost roll back into my head. He's actually licking both me and Nathan. I can feel it every time he enters me.

"Fuck!" I groan as Kai pulls out to watch me writhe in the ropes.

He clutches my face. "Too much already, slut?"

"No," I reply.

He grins. "Your entire body will be covered in our cum before we're done with you."

And he hovers my mouth over his tip again, claiming me once more. But I no longer have any fiber of resistance left in my body.

This is it.

These three boys ... they're my undoing.

Not just now, but for the rest of my life.

Because I don't think anything will ever be able to make me forget them.

Or that I'll ever even want to.

\*\*\*

## KAI

I plunge into her mouth, taking her sweet tongue like it belongs to me as it wraps around my length and licks off the salty pre-cum. When she gargles, I only go in deeper. "That's it. Choke on my greedy cock."

Her moans are like music to my ears as she dangles in the air, completely helpless and submitting to our every whim. When I pull out, I drag her saliva across her face, mixing it with the blood, and dip right back into her mouth.

"Taste your own kill, Lana, taste the fucking sweetness of murder," I groan, fucking her little throat while I squeeze the life out of her.

She gasps when I pull out again, but Nathan thrusting into her pussy makes her bump right back into my dick, and she gleefully swallows me up like the vixen she is.

I can see from the way she's tightening her muscles she's about to come.

"Falling apart already?" Nathan muses. "Fine then, Milo, give her the first orgasm."

"The first?" she exclaims, but I fill her mouth again before she can say anything else.

She writhes in the ropes as Milo rolls his tongue around her needy little clit so well she's consumed by the orgasm that swiftly overtakes her body.

"That's it; there's no fucking escaping us, little kitty," I say. "But you don't mind, do you?"

She doesn't answer me, so I choke her a little more until her eyes almost close, and then I release her.

"Answer me."

She sucks in a breath. "Use me."

Nathan pulls out and slaps his dick against her pussy. "Beg for it."

"Fuck," she groans. "Please. Give it to me."

"Good little slut," he says, and he thrusts in so deep she mewls with delight.

I push her lips together, forcing them open. "You'll accept my cum like a good girl, won't you?"

She nods and looks up at me as I bury deep inside her, and I arch my back and release all my pent-up need, coating the back of her throat. I moan out loud when she starts swallowing with me still lodged deep within.

"Fuck, lick me like that while I claim this pussy," Nathan grunts, thrusting in wildly as Milo goes to town on the both of them.

When I pull out, my dick is still hard as fuck, and I grasp the rope. "My pussy. My turn." I glare at Nathan directly in the eye.

His nostrils flare, but he still pulls out and lets me spin her around so her pussy is right up in my face, and I bend over to take a soft little lick. Her whole body hums to my tongue as I circle it around her sensitive, swollen clit, and as I dip a thumb into her wetness, she squirms from my touch.

"Do you even understand the kind of willpower it takes not to make this pussy come so many times you'd be begging me to stop?"

She gulps and turns her head to look at me. "Please ..."

Fuck.

Just that one word can make my knees buckle.

For her, I would just about do anything.

Even bend the fucking knee.

And I thrust my tongue into this willing pussy, giving it all the lavish attention it deserves.

"I will have you begging on your knees like that before I ever stop making you come."

She moans out loud as Milo licks her tits, but Nathan quiets her with his dick.

I pull out my tongue, only to replace it with my hard-on, thrusting in to the base. And the sound from her mouth is nothing short of pure perfection.

This pussy, the way it fits so snugly around my throbbing cock, it's almost like it was sculpted by God himself just for me.

And I growl, "Tell me. Say the name of the person who owns this pussy until your last dying breath."

"Kai," she mutters, shivering from a mixture of satisfaction and burning pain.

"Louder!"

"Kai, please!" she begs, her voice unraveling me completely.

And I lean over and lick all the beads of sweat off her back, marking her as mine until we both perish. From this moment on, every part of her, her wrecked heart, her decrepit soul, all of it belongs to me just as I belong to her.

"*Mine.*"

\*\*\*

## NATHAN

The way she looks at him over her shoulder, so full of complete and utter devotion, has me going crazy with jealousy. "Ours," I grit, smashing my lips onto hers. Claiming her mouth and tongue with every fiber of my being, I pour every ounce of my affection into this one kiss.

She doesn't struggle and practically melts in my hands as I cup her face and caress her cheeks, letting her know Kai is not the only one who desires her more than anything.

Lana Rivera is my downfall, my absolute ruination, and not a single part of me ever wants to stop kissing her and fucking her. And when my lips unlatch to allow her a breath, I whisper, "You're *mine* too."

"Is that possible?" she mutters.

Milo pinches her nipples until she squeals. "Of course it's possible. You're ours just as much as we are yours."

"Fuck," she mewls, retracting from my lips to look at him.

But Milo swiftly claims her mouth when I'm not looking, smashing his lips onto hers with a passion I've only seen him kiss me with.

"You know I can't resist your cries," Milo says, kissing her greedily. "I want to fucking worship you every fucking day for the rest of my life. Please. Say the words, and I'm fucking yours."

"Yes," she murmurs against his lips.

I can see that rotten smile on his face that he always gives me, now handing it to her on a silver platter. And fuck me, it makes me want to shove my dick into both their mouths.

"It's all I'll ever want," Milo mutters. "Well, and him, of course." He looks up at me and winks.

"Good. Then you can both lick the cum off my cock," I groan, and I thrust into her mouth as he perches underneath her and opens his mouth too, allowing me to swap between them.

And fuck me, their tongues are the best thing in the entire fucking world.

"Lick me," I growl at them as I switch between their mouths. "Good fucking sluts."

I bury myself into her throat first before I pull out and take his next, alternating between the two as the pressure builds in my balls. Right before I explode, I pull out and howl as I come all over their faces, spreading my seed equally as they lap me up.

Then I grasp their faces and bring them together. "Now fucking kiss."

Their lips collide, mixing my salty cum with their sweet saliva, exchanging my cum between their mouths, spit-balling it around.

All while Kai's thrusting away into her pussy like a madman, relentlessly pounding into her.

He roars again and spends himself inside her once more, filling her to the brim.

"Fuck," he murmurs as he pulls out and slaps her ass.

She squeals against Milo's mouth and bites his lip.

He retracts, touching his lip, blood spilling out, but he sucks it all up along with the cum still on his lips.

"Ouch ... do it again," he says, leaning closer.

But I'm not nearly finished with her.

"Swap again," I growl, twisting the rope before Kai can even say another word.

I don't care if he agrees or not. I'm taking every hole she has because they all belong to me.

So I swipe my length across her slit, dipping in and out of her pussy before I push up against her ass.

"This is gonna hurt ..." I groan. "And you're going to enjoy and thank me for every inch of pain I give you."

# 52

## MILO

Kai steps away for a second, and I crawl out from underneath her, grasp her body, and lift her in my arms.

"What are you doing?" Nathan growls at me as I step closer so her tits press up against my chest.

"Taking what I want," I say as I zip down and push my cock up against her pussy.

Nathan grits, "I didn't say you could."

But as I push inside, I lean over and grab his face, kissing him over her shoulder, and his resistance practically melts away.

"Fuck," he says through gritted teeth. "Kiss me like that, and I'll have you on your knees next."

"And I'll be begging for it," I murmur, smiling against his lips.

I plunge into her pussy as he buries himself into her ass, and her cries almost make me fall apart right then and there.

"Fuck!" She bites into my shoulder, the feel of her teeth against my flesh making my cock throb inside her.

"Oh, yes, harder," I groan, feeling Nathan through the thin wall that separates us.

With each of my thrusts, her teeth dig deeper into my skin, and I savor the pain as much as I savor this godlike pussy.

As her teeth withdraw, I grasp her face and smash my lips onto hers, the taste of my own blood on her tongue almost sending me to heaven and back.

"Fuck, I'm yours, forever and always," I groan. "I need your fucking pussy so badly. I can't fucking take it anymore."

And I bury myself inside her, taking her even though no one compelled me to. But not even Nathan can keep me away from obeying this greedy little pussy begging for more cum.

Spearing her, I hold her tight and kiss her on the lips before I lean over to kiss Nathan as we fill her up.

Her mewls make me kiss him even harder, desperate to hear more of these delicious cries. And I fall apart right then, spending my seed deep inside her while I whimper with desire for more.

But my orgasm is cut short by Kai dragging me away from her. He throws me into a chair in the back and says, "You. Stay and fucking watch like the simp you are."

I gulp as he walks back to her and lifts her thighs with ease, lowering her onto his big, hard cock like a stallion mounting his woman, and fuck me, I could just about kiss him too for being that stern with me.

"Look at us fuck this little slut while you're not allowed, Milo," Nathan groans, and I do. My eyes are practically glued to their bodies as they grind away.

Both her holes are filled, and she moans wildly as they thrust into her one after the other and both at the same time. I'm still dripping, but it's so hot I could just come again from looking at them.

There is nothing in this world I enjoy more than watching the people I would die for enjoy each other. And I don't think it'll take much longer for her to figure out she wants us all the same.

\*\*\*

## LANA

I can barely focus as the two of them rail me together, salty sweat and dirty kisses all mingling into one. Bloodied bodies against bodies, grinding away in a grimy cell.

My eyes briefly find Milo in the chaos of it all, his body rigid on the chair as he jerks himself off to the sight of us.

"Fuck," he groans, his voice making me clench my thighs.

Being watched like this adds another layer of pleasure I never thought I'd enjoy, but fuck me, I could fuck like this for days and still not have enough of them.

It's so tight with both of them inside me. It feels like my guts are being rearranged, but I love every second of it. Every thrust, Kai's piercings sensitize my pussy to the point where it throbs just from him entering, so much that I don't even need anything else to fall apart.

The moans become louder, less constrained until I can't control myself any longer.

"I'm coming!" I squeal as they both bore into me.

My body convulses against Kai, shocks rippling through me.

Suddenly, Milo moans along with me, spurting out more cum onto the floor.

"Couldn't hold it together?" Nathan muses, grasping my hips as he plows into my ass. "Clean up after yourself. Lick it all up."

I watch as Milo bends over and runs his fingers through his juices before licking it all off his body and the floor.

And fuck me, I didn't know it was this sexy to watch someone eat their own cum. It makes me want to shove his face down in it ... and the best part about it is that he'd actually beg me to do just that.

Kai grabs my face. "Look at me. Open your mouth." He spits inside. "Swallow." When I do, he murmurs, "Good girl." And he claims my lips with his, spearing his tongue into my mouth just like he buries it into my pussy.

"Fuck, your pussy is so tight," Kai moans against my lips, coaxing out more moans. "I'm gonna fill you up and watch it drip out of you. And then you're going to lick all of it up."

His dirty words almost send me over the edge again.

One, two, three more pumps and he jets all of his seed into me with a big moan.

"Fuck, I'm coming too," Nathan roars, and he fills me up to the brim.

I'm panting, completely wasted, but Kai isn't done with me yet as he pulls out and starts circling my clit with the pad of his thumb.

"One more."

"I can't," I stammer.

"Give me what I want," he growls, flicking my clit until I almost faint from all the pleasure they're giving me. "This body is mine, and I want your fucking orgasm. Now."

I shiver in the restraints, my whole body straining to reach the climax once again, but when I finally do tumble over that cliff, it's as if I'm ascending to heaven itself.

I don't even remember them hoisting me down from the bar.

Or Kai pushing my face down into the puddle of cum beneath me.

All I know is that my tongue dips out to lap it all up.

"Lick. Clean all of it like a good fucking kitty," he murmurs, clenching my hair tightly until I've swallowed every last drop. "Good girl."

I used to hate these boys for making me submit, but now I crave it more than anything.

The release that comes after the fall is unparalleled.

I sink to the floor, completely wasted on ecstasy, but goddamn, it was worth every second.

When I look up, Milo kneels in front of me. He cups my face and presses a kiss to my lips, and I can taste his salty cum.

"You're my fucking goddess, you know that?" he murmurs.

I smile. "You already said that."

"How many times do you want me to say it? A hundred? A million?" He presses another sweet kiss to the side of my lips that has me flying that high. "Because I'll do it."

"Every day?" I reply.

He grins against my lips. "Every day it is then, my goddess."

Kai and Nathan untie the ropes that bind me, and Nathan lifts me from the floor, carrying me back to his bed. "What are you doing?"

"You think I only hang and whip people or something?" he jests with a grin. "Aftercare is important too."

"Aftercare?" I joke back as he places me down in the middle of his bed. "Really?"

"He may be a sadist, but he's not a complete savage," Milo muses while he grabs a bottle of lotion off a shelf.

"Hey, watch your mouth," Nathan warns.

Milo throws him the bottle, and both Kai and Nathan lie down beside me.

"But what about the dead body?" I ask.

"We'll get some of the guys to get rid of it later," Kai says. "At our usual spot."

"Usual spot?" I joke.

"Yeah, there's a whole graveyard in the city down below, remember?" Nathan says.

Nathan opens the bottle and rubs my wrists with the warm gel while Kai rubs it into my thighs, casually brushing past my pussy every once in a while to remind me of how good it feels. And the added smirk definitely doesn't help to keep me from feeling all hot inside.

"There," Nathan murmurs as he puts the bottle on his nightstand.

Kai pulls me toward him, wrapping me in his arms like he wants to protect me from something. Nathan rolls up behind me and wraps his arm around my waist, spooning me. And I've never felt safer or more cocooned than I do now.

Almost enough to make me want to fall into a deep, soothing sleep.

Suddenly, Milo clears his throat as he stands at the edge of the bed, pouting.

Nathan grumbles, "Fine, come here."

Milo grins and crawls up the bed between Nathan and I, almost smothering me as I'm pushed farther into Kai's muscular chest while Milo wriggles in. But when he wraps his arm around me too, my heart practically explodes.

*Is this what it's supposed to feel like?*

*Is this why Felix and his friends couldn't stay away from Penelope?*

*Am I falling for these boys?*

I swallow, feeling like the lump that was stuck in my throat came straight from my clogged-up heart.

"Milo ..." Kai grumbles with his eyes closed.

"Yes?"

"Take your hand off my dick."

I snort when I see Milo's hand move sneakily.

"I thought ... after you started commandeering me around, you—"

"I know," Kai responds, his eyes still closed, but brows furrowed. "We're close. But not that close."

I bite my lip, laughing a little. "Yet."

Kai opens his good eye and stares down at me with judgment, and it makes me giggle. "What?"

Even Nathan chuckles.

He sighs out loud. "Good night, my little violent kitty."

I used to hate that word.

Kitty.

It reminded me of being a weak, helpless little furry pet.

But now, when he says that word, it makes me want to purr.

# 53

LANA

**Days later**

After everything that went down inside the Phantom Society building, Nathan decided it would be a good idea to bring Rory back to her aunt, just for safety reasons. I agreed and helped him drive her back. He could've done it by himself, but the emotional toll it took on him was too much, so I hugged him tight and drove us back after we dropped her off.

But my first class is starting soon, so I can't dwell on difficult decisions. Even though I know Ro's home is a temporary one and we'll need to find a permanent solution.

I grab my bag off the table and open the front door of the sorority building, but I come to a full stop the second I lay eyes on all three boys standing outside with a wide smile on their faces.

"Um, what's going on here?" I ask.

"Starting your first class for the day?" Kai asks.

"Yeah ..." I reply with furrowed brows. "How'd you know?"

"I keep track of your class schedule," he says like it's the most normal thing on earth.

"Hey, Lana!" Milo says with a cheery voice, waving at me from behind both of them.

"Hey, you're here," I mutter. "You feeling better yet?"

"Yeah, the stitches don't hurt as much anymore, and the wound is healing quite nicely," he replies with a big smile. "So I figured, why not go to school?"

"So what are you all doing here?" I ask.

"We're taking you to school," Milo says, running his fingers through his red hair.

Nathan smacks him in the arm. "You were not supposed to say that out loud."

"Wow, wow, wow, absolutely not." I fold my arms, staring them down.

"Why else would we come here?" Nathan says.

"Yeah, why?"

"To protect you," Kai replies. "In case those Bones Brotherhood fuckers show up on the campus grounds."

I snort. "You think they would?"

"Definitely," Nathan answers, showing off his knives before tucking them into his pocket. "It's better if you're not alone."

"I'm not letting you go to class by yourself," Kai says, gripping the doorjamb.

I don't think I'll win an argument against these guys, let alone a fight. They've already made that point clear.

I roll my eyes. "Fine."

"Yay." Milo jumps forward and steals my bag, stuffing an extra mystery box inside.

"Hey, what are you doing?"

"Food. You need more; I got it." He winks. "Sushi."

"Thanks, I guess?"

"If you tell me your favorite, I'll make it for you every day," he muses, handing me back my bag.

Now it's really hard to say no to all this pampering.

Behind me, two girls gasp in shock, and when I look over my shoulder, both Irina and Brooke are giggling their asses off like they're seeing celebrities.

I sigh out loud and march out the front door. "All right, fine. Let's go."

They follow me around campus as I head to my first class, hovering behind me like some kind of bodyguards, scaring away anyone who even dares to throw a glance at me, and it kind of freaks me out.

So I stop midway there and spin on my heels. "Stop."

Nathan's brow rises. "What?"

"Stop glaring at everyone I pass. I'm not trying to make more enemies."

"They might be," Nathan retorts.

"Not everyone is out there to get us," I say.

"He's just protective." Kai interjects.

"Oh, so another clone of you," I spit, throwing him a narrowed-eye glare.

Which he throws right back at me.

"Lana. Be nice."

*That motherfucker ... using my own words against me?*

I lift my top lip, showing off my teeth like a goddamn hissy cat.

But all it does is make him smile in such a deadly way, and I mean the heart-murdering kind. "You're cute when you're angry."

"And after throwing me *my* words, you should be happy I let you keep your dick."

He smiles even harder. "Wouldn't be of much use to you if it wasn't on me, now would it?"

"I could make a mold out of it and turn it into a nice dildo," I retort, getting up in his face.

He grabs my chin a little too tightly as he leans in to whisper, "You could, but it would be no different from the simple fuck Jason offered you. And it would never satisfy you like I do."

He presses his lips onto mine, stealing my breath away with a deep, sensual kiss.

Right in front of everyone.

"Everyone can see us," I whisper when his lips unlatch.

"Good. I need them to know you're *mine* so they don't get any ideas."

Why does that make me bite my lip and smile like a crazy girl?

"Now are you happy to let us escort you?" he murmurs.

"If you behave and don't scare away everyone who walks by," I reply. He smiles against my lips. "Deal."

"We'll be good fucking boys," Milo muses, throwing his arm around Nathan.

Kai throws his arm around my shoulders as the other two come to walk beside me too. "Let's get you to class. You're almost late."

"You don't have to escort me," I mutter.

"Yeah, we do," Nathan says. "Those Bonesmen are still out there."

"You think they already infiltrated Spine Ridge?" Milo asks, tilting his head.

"They could," Kai answers, tightening his grip around my shoulders. "But we'll be ready if they show their faces."

People are still looking at us, even when they're not eye-killing everyone in sight, and I just know they're all wondering "*what is a Rivera girl doing with the Phantoms?*" And the truth is, I don't know either. All I know is that I can't say no anymore.

So I let them escort me into the school building while we bump into a couple of Skull & Serpent Society guys on the way, and the looks they exchange are anything but pleasant.

"Fuck. My brother is going to kill me for this when he finds out," I mutter under my breath.

"I doubt it," Nathan says. "You made your choice. He doesn't control you."

"No, but he's my brother. I don't want him to be mad at me."

When we get to class, Nathan stops me and pushes me against the wall near the door. "Listen to me. He's your brother. If he loves you as much as you say he does, he has to let you do what you want." He tips up my chin. "He won't get in our way."

"How do you know?"

"I'm a big brother too. I know how it feels," he says with a smug grin. "But I'm not gonna let that stop me."

He grabs my face and smashes his lips onto mine in the middle of the hallway while people are walking past us, some of which I saw outside too.

Fuck, now everyone knows I'm not just involved with one of them but multiple Phantoms.

When his lips unlatch from mine, I'm dizzy with lust.

"The point is, your heart should matter too," Milo adds, leaning in too so he can place a tiny kiss onto my cheek so soft it melts my heart. "And if he can't see that, that's his problem, not yours."

"What if he never wants to talk to me again?" I say.

"That's his choice," Kai says, folding his arms.

"It's not that simple."

"He's your brother," Kai retorts. "It is simple."

"You *know* our history," I say, and they all rub their lips together like it's hard to talk about. "If I don't have my brother, everything we've been through, everything I did, will have been for nothing."

Milo gently caresses my cheek with his thumb. "I'll talk to him if you want."

"Do you think he'd listen to you?"

"Well, he's the least angry with me." He shrugs. "It's worth a shot."

I sigh. "I don't know."

"Hey, worst-case scenario, he hurts me, I enjoy it, the end."

"Hey," Nathan barks. "No enjoying torture without me giving it to you."

"I'm just saying, I doubt he'll kill me," Milo says.

"That would be an all-out war," Kai points out.

I bury my face in my hands. "Fuck. What have I done?"

Kai grabs my wrist so my hand yields away from my face, and he forces me to look at him. "Listen to me. It's going to be fine. We'll make it work."

"And what if it doesn't? What if both sides try to kill each other?"

"I won't let that happen," Kai says. "And if I have to choose between having you and my life ... you already know which one I'm going to pick."

I swallow at the intensity he looks at me with when he says those words.

"I already told you I'm not afraid of anything, and that includes him," Kai says.

"Neither am I," Nathan says, tilting his head.

"You already know nothing terrifies me," Milo muses, casually putting his hands behind his head as he winks. "Except maybe you."

I snort, but it swiftly turns into laughter. "You should be."

"Hey, Lana." Brooke casually bumps into me from behind. "I see you've kept yourself busy."

"Oh yeah, we definitely keep her busy, all right." Milo winks.

A blush manages to creep onto my cheeks.

"Wow, I did not peg you to be the three-on-one type, but you go girl," Brooke says, and she grabs my hand and high-fives herself before she heads into the same room I'm supposed to be in.

"Your class is starting," Nathan says as he peeks into the room.

Kai gives me a gentle push. "Go on."

They're in the door opening, and everyone's glaring at them, but none of the boys seem to care about it. "They're definitely looking at all of us," I mutter.

"Good. Tell them the sex is wicked." Kai winks before he shuts the door behind me.

# 54

NATHAN

After all that shit with the Bones Brotherhood went down, I have so much of my studies to catch up on now, it's ridiculous.

I sift through the book in front of me, trying to make sense of it, but economics is really getting the best of me. Maybe I shouldn't have chosen this fucking course, but I wanted to make my parents proud.

I snort to myself. If only I'd known how things would play out. Maybe I would've made a different choice.

I glance to my right and spot a bunch of Lana's friends near the window, chatting away. Irina and Brooke, I think. When they spot me, their eyes widen, and they look away, almost like they're afraid I might come their way.

I smirk to myself.

"Hey, Nathan."

I almost fall over in my chair when I hear that voice.

"Sorry, didn't mean to scare you," Caleb says, gripping my shoulders as he looks down at me.

"What the—What are you doing here?" I hiss, staring right into his coal eyes.

He chucks his bag on the same table and scoots back a chair. "Studying. What else? It's a fucking library."

He casually throws himself down on the chair, and he rolls up his white shirt to reveal even more tattoos added since the last time I saw him.

"I thought you said you were done," I say.

"I know; I just couldn't resist," he muses, slapping his books onto the table like he owns the place. "Guess that's what you get when you go through heartbreak."

Grinding my jaws, I look the other way and focus on my laptop.

"What are you doing?" he asks.

"Homework."

"Okay ... what course?"

"Economics."

"You're awfully direct today," he says, eyeing me down.

I throw him a look. "Because I told Milo I wouldn't talk to you anymore."

The cheeky smirk that appears on his face, pulling his lips from pierced ear to pierced ear, makes me want to roll my eyes. "And I thought he wasn't the jealous type."

"He's not. It was my choice," I say.

He grabs his heart. "Ouch. Don't stab me."

"Why are you sitting here?" I ask. "You could choose any seat in the room, yet you choose to sit here next to me."

"Can't I just sit? I'm not doing anything," he says.

"Yet," I reply.

His eyes narrow. "You don't trust me anymore?"

"Have I ever?"

He snorts and opens his book, shaking his head. "Wow. Becoming a Phantom really has changed you."

I put my hand under my temple to support my face while I stare at him because it's fucking on now. "What's that supposed to mean?"

He licks his pierced lips. "I'm just saying ... you used to be so much more fun and easygoing."

"You're only saying that because you're angry with me," I muse.

"I miss you, okay?" he says, clutching his book while throwing me a casual glance with his dark eyes every now and then. "Isn't that enough?"

I take in a breath and scroll down on my laptop to pretend I'm working. "Nope."

"Look, I tried to ignore whatever it is you've got going on with that Milo dude, but I need my friend back. Okay?" He glances over my shoulder at my phone, on which I have a picture of all four of us, so I turn it away.

"Who was that?"

I frown. "Just my friends."

"No, there was a girl on your phone."

*Fuck.*

I put the phone down. "It's none of your business."

"Is that why you don't want to hang out with us anymore? You're too busy with Milo and that girl, whoever she is?"

"What I do with my time is my choice," I retort.

He sighs drearily. "Oh, c'mon. The Tartarus parties are no fun without you. You don't miss it? At all?"

"I don't miss being betrayed," I say.

He frowns. "What do you mean?"

Like he doesn't know *exactly* what Ares did.

"You weren't there when we needed you guys," I quip. "When Phantoms were being attacked by Skull & Serpent Society, and the previous dean threatened to close down our society, you didn't step in and help us."

"What were we supposed to do?" he quips.

"Offer weapons? Men? Money?" I retort. "Hell, anything would've been fine."

"You know it doesn't work like that," he says, shaking his head. "I don't make the decisions, and I couldn't convince Ares to ..."

"No, but you could've supported us. You could've supported *me*."

He sighs out loud. "I know. I'm sorry. I just wish things would've been different. Can we please be friends again?"

"Whatever. I have to think about it," I say, averting my eyes. "Let's just focus on our studies."

I tap the pen vigorously against the paper, trying to write down this essay I have due, but I can practically feel Caleb's eyes boring a hole into my back. I open a folder on my laptop, but I accidentally click on the wrong one, which holds all the photos of Lana, so I quickly tap away before he sees and starts asking questions I don't want to answer.

Suddenly, my phone rings, the name appearing on the screen making my heart palpitate.

"Fuck."

"Who is it?" Caleb asks.

Crescent Vale City Penitentiary is calling.

I jump up from my seat. "I gotta take this one. Watch my stuff."

I run off to take the call in private.

"Mom," I mutter as I close the door to the bathroom behind me. "How are you?"

"I'm doing good. I just wanted to call and ask if you've been taking care of Rory."

"Of course," I reply. "But it wasn't easy."

"Don't let them get to her, you hear me?" she grits. "I cannot lose my little girl to those sons of bitches."

"Mom, I'm trying, okay?"

"Try harder!"

"Is that why you're calling me? To badger me? I'm already taking care of it; don't fucking worry about it."

"Yes, no, my point is, take care of her because she's all you got."

I frown, clutching the phone tightly. "What do you mean?"

"We're not getting out."

I swallow away the lump in my throat. "How long?"

"Life."

The phone cracks.

"Without parole."

It feels like I got struck by lightning just now.

"That has to be a mistake," I say. "There's no way—"

"They know about everything, Nathan. All the money, it's gone. They took it. And since our businesses got hounded by that Bones Brotherhood, the feds assumed we were part of them too."

"What? That's bullshit!"

"I know, but you have to stay away from them," she says.

"I'm trying, but you left us with a giant fucking debt they wanted paid," I say through gritted teeth.

"I know, and I'm sorry, Nathan. I wish I could undo what we did, but I can't."

"Why did you do it?" I yell.

"Because we wanted to give you two a good life!"

My fists ball so hard my nails dig into my skin.

"A good life doesn't mean shit when Ro has to live the rest of her life without her parents," I grit. "Because of *you*, I'm all she has left."

"Nathan, I—"

I disconnect the call.

I'm done with them.

I'm done talking with them for the rest of our lives.

They made a mistake, and we're the ones paying the price.

*But how am I going to tell Ro she'll never see her mom and dad again?*

I punch the door as hard as I can before I tuck the phone back into my pocket and storm out the door.

When I bust back into the library, Caleb's already gone.

I snatch my laptop and my books off the table, marching out of this library that requires silence when my heart wants nothing more than to roar.

\*\*\*

# LANA

I take lots of notes in class, making sure I'm all ears to the teacher as I've already missed too many classes. But as the time goes by, more and more buzzing on the phones of the people in my class distracts me from what the teacher is trying to explain, and by the time his class is almost finished, it's really starting to grind my gears.

"Lana," Brooke mutters next to me, but I'm far too busy staring angrily at other people in the class.

"Am I missing out on some group chat or something?" I mutter. "Why is everyone's phones buzzing?"

"Lana. I think you need to see this," she says, and she holds out her phone.

There's an email that got sent to almost the entire school, and all the students are going wild over a picture.

All the blood slowly drains from my face.

It's a picture of me without my mask, strapped to a chair, being taken from all sides by Kai, Nathan, and Milo.

Right next to the dead body in the Shack.

My whole body goes numb, and I don't think I have a heart anymore ... because it stopped beating.

Everyone saw me getting railed.

Everyone knows I'm a killer now.

Everything I ever wanted to avoid has happened.

I scoot my chair back.

Everyone's looking at me like they're seeing a living corpse.

I take out my phone and open the email to see for myself, but I can't even stop my hands from shaking so vigorously I almost lose control.

The sender was anonymous.

But I know an *anonymous*.

The only anonymous who had access to those pictures along with his friends.

"Lana Rivera, can you please sit back down?" the teacher says.

Instead, I grab my bag and storm out of class, hell-bent on revenge.

If they're going to drag me down into my own personal hell, I'm taking those fuckers with me.

# 55

KAI

"I'm gonna have to look for a permanent alternative for Ro," Nathan says as he takes a huge drag.

I lean against the fountain, and Milo hands me a cig too, which he lights up as I put it in my mouth. "How come?"

"Mom called. Said she and Dad got life with no parole."

I almost choke on the drag I take, and I swiftly take the cig out of my mouth. "What the f—That's bullshit!"

"It is what it is. All I know is they ruined our fucking lives." He takes another deep drag.

I don't think he wants to talk about them.

Poor Ro, though. To never see your parents again that young has gotta be tough.

"Did you tell her yet?" Milo asks.

Nathan shakes his head.

He must still be gathering the courage.

"What are you going to do now?" I ask. "Leave her with your aunt?"

"No, she's the only family I have left," he says, glaring at me. "I have to think of something else."

"She can't live with us at the Phantom Society," Milo says. "I mean, she's cute, but it's too dangerous there with us and our murder sprees."

I shush him. "We're on public grounds. Not everyone needs to know."

*WHACK!*

437

I feel something swoop past me before I turn to see a knife lying on the bottom of the fountain.

*What the ...?*

*WHACK!*

A second one lands on the stones right beside Nathan's hand, which he quickly lifts to avoid getting scratched. "What the fuck—"

"YOU LIED TO ME!"

The scream makes all our heads turn collectively as none other than Lana Rivera marches toward us, pointing her knives right at us in broad daylight.

"What's going on?" Nathan asks.

She chucks another knife his way. "You did this!"

"Did what? What is happening?" Milo asks.

"Don't play dumb with me!" she shrieks, chucking another knife until she's all out. "I deserve better than that!"

"Let's talk about this, little kitty," I tell her as she approaches.

Suddenly, she dropkicks me out of nowhere, hitting me in the nuts. "Don't fucking *Kitty* me!"

I'm bent over, coughing and heaving from the pain. "Jesus, fuck, I thought we were over this?"

"If you want to hit someone, hit me," Milo practically begs, opening his arms, but she ignores him and steps over me to punch Nathan in the face so hard he's bleeding from the nose. "What the fuck, Lana?!"

"Don't pretend you don't know," she says, and she kicks him in the gut, knocking him to the ground.

"No, I don't know!"

Then she pulls out her phone. "This!"

She turns the phone around to show me too, and my jaw drops the second I see us all in masks and her strapped to that chair the night at the Shack.

A picture sent straight to everyone's email.

*Fuck.*

"You sent this! This was your picture! And now the whole fucking school knows!"

"What the f—I didn't send this," Nathan says.

She kicks him again. "Bullshit!!" She's turning red with rage. "You promised me you wouldn't send them!"

"No, I swear, I didn't," he says, holding up his hands.

She steps off him and snatches the knives out of the fountain.

"Lana," I mutter.

She points the knife at me now. "NO. Stay back."

"Nathan says he didn't do it," I say.

"And you believe him?" she retorts. "He had every reason. You just wanted to use me, and you got your wish," she snarls. "After everything I gave to you three ..."

It hurts to see her in this much fucking pain.

"I trusted you!"

Her voice is in as much shambles as my own fucking heart.

"*Everyone* saw *me*!" Tears well up in her eyes.

"Is it so bad everyone knows we're a thing?" I ask.

"You don't understand," she says with a hushed voice. "That dead body is in the picture. They know I'm a killer now."

I swallow. "We can fix this."

"NO, YOU CAN'T!"

Everyone's looking at us, but I don't care.

They already know we've fucked with her in a disturbing way.

There's no hiding anymore.

"Everything I worked so damn hard for, my reputation, my life, my family ... it's all destroyed because of you."

"Don't say that," Milo mutters. "Your brother doesn't know yet, does he?"

"He will," she says. "It's only a matter of minutes until someone shows him." She sniffs, raising her murderous eyes up at me. "And then he'll come for you."

"I didn't share that picture," Nathan says as he crawls up from the ground.

"I don't care. It's your fault it got out," she says, pointing the other knife at him too now. "I made a deal with you, and you broke your end."

"Lana ..." I warn, feeling my blood curdle.

"Don't. That deal we had, it's over."

I raise a hand, trying to control my own emotions as well as hers. "Lana, think hard about the words you're saying." I look her deep in the eyes as her lip twitches with rage, but she doesn't look away. "I think you know as well as I do there is no escaping us. Deal or no deal."

"I should've left you all to die in that club," she hisses.

Her words sting like a knife thrust straight into my heart.

"Don't do this, Lana," Milo pleads. "Please."

"Too late," she says.

"You won't kill us," I say, tilting my head as she pushes the knife underneath my chin. "You *can't*."

She grinds her teeth, clearly getting more enraged by the second.

Still, she retracts her blades and tucks them back into her pocket, then turns around and marches off.

"Where are you going?" Nathan balks.

"Away from you. And don't even think of following me," she yells back.

"It doesn't matter where you go, Lana. I'll always be there," I say.

But instead of saying another word, she merely sticks up two middle fingers and struts off, right through the crowd of people who part just for her like she's motherfucking Moses splitting the Red Sea in half.

\*\*\*

## LANA

I bury my face in my pillow and scream so loudly my voice box cracks from the sheer weight of my emotions.

I wish I could kill them.

I want to. So badly.

But I know I physically *can't*. And it breaks me.

How could I let them get to me like that? How could I let them into my world, my life, my fucking heart, and crush it all up like it meant nothing?

That deal we made meant nothing.

I gave my body to those fuckers, and they betrayed me by throwing my secret out into the world.

"Fuck!" I yell, punching the pillow.

Someone knocks on my door, and I pause. "Lana? Brooke called and said you wouldn't let anyone into your room so I thought I'd come over. Are you okay in there?"

It's Crystal.

"Yeah, I'm fine."

I wipe away the tears and sit up straight.

She gently opens the door and peeks inside before stepping in and closing the door behind her. In her hair is that same rose from before.

"She told you about the picture?" I clutch the pillow against my chest.

She swallows and nods. "I saw it. I'm sorry. Can I sit down next to you?"

When I nod, she gently sits down and wraps her arm around my shoulders.

"It's okay."

"I'm mortified," I mutter.

"It's not your fault," she says, sucking in a breath.

I glance her way. "Please promise me you won't tell my dad or my brother."

She places a hand on my knee. "I won't. I promise, but I can't guarantee other people won't." Her eyes travel off. "Most of the students at school already saw it."

My nostrils flare. "I hope the one who spread it dies a miserable death."

She rubs her lips and shivers a little. "You know what? I think you need some ice cream to cheer you up."

"Ice cream?" I parrot as she gets up.

She pulls me off my bed and drags me out the door. "Yeah, let's go. Before you turn into a pile of mush."

\*\*\*

Crystal takes me to Ice, Cookies, & Cream down in Crescent Vale City in her car and gets me two flavors on her. Chocolate and strawberry, my favorite. We sit on a park bench and watch the animals casually stroll by, looking for a nibble.

I take a bite and almost moan. "God, it's so good!"

"I know, right? This shop's my fav."

"I get why you wanted to come here now," I muse, taking another bite.

"Yeah, they're far better than the one on campus. I mean, no offense if that's your fav."

"None taken. I don't have a fav, but this one might just be it," I reply, and we both smile.

"You know what? We should grab some food after," she says, winking.

I snort. "We're literally eating ice cream, and you want more?"

"Yeah, it's almost dinnertime." She points at the large outdoor clock hanging from the park entry. "I'm more of a 'have dessert first, then food' girl."

"That's actually a great idea," I reply. I guess we could. I mean, it's not like I have anything else to do now that the boys are out of the picture. "All right, let's do it."

"If you want, you can invite over those boys you've been seeing."

I almost choke on some of my ice cream. "Ah..."

"What? You four are an item, right?" she says, taking a bite out of her ice cream.

I take another bite from my ice cream, determined to get brainfreeze before I have to answer, but a peculiar van outside the park catches my attention and I forget what I was about to say. I don't know why, but it feels familiar, somehow. I just can't put my finger on it. It definitely doesn't belong to Kai, Milo, or Nathan, though.

"Hi, ladies," someone behind us says.

I turn my head.

*CLICK.*

I know that sound.

The safety has been pulled off a gun aimed directly at my back.

"Don't turn. Don't make a sound."

"Lana ..." Crystal peeps.

I shush her.

"That's right, you're gonna be real quiet, and you're gonna get up and walk to that van," a voice growls behind me.

"And what if I don't?" I say.

From the corner of my eye, I see the gun being pushed into Crystal's head instead. "You really wanna try me out?"

*Fuck.*

I gulp and look at Crystal as a tear trickles down her cheek.

I would've fought him off if he only threatened me.

But now that Crystal's involved, I don't want to risk her life too.

"Move," the voice behind me growls.

I get up and grab her hand, mouthing, "It's gonna be okay."

We walk stiffly toward the park gates, the guy tailing us, his gun hidden behind his coat as it pushes into my back.

He pushes me, and my ice cream drops to the ground.

The van pulls up to the gates, and the back doors open. Two guys wearing a hat and fake hair grab us by the arms and drag us inside, sealing us in.

"Please, don't kill us," Crystal mutters as the men hold us down.

"Shut up," one of them tells her, and he directs his attention toward the guy in front of the wheel. "Drive."

The van's engine roars as it races off, veering from side to side like they're in a hurry.

In the dark, Crystal's fingers find mine, and I squeeze and hold on tight to the last semblance of hope I can offer her in this nightmare. A nightmare she got dragged into because of me.

# 56

NATHAN

"This whole thing with Lana is your fucking fault," Kai grits while I throw my bag on the first table I find inside the Phantom Society building. "If you hadn't taken those pictures, no one would've ever seen them."

"I didn't fucking share them," I say, my voice booming through the hallway.

"Bullshit, who else could've done it? You?" Kai points his finger at Milo now, who just stares at him sheepishly.

"Who me? Of course not, why would I?" he replies.

Kai marches at him and grabs him by the shirt. "Did you share them with *anyone*?"

Milo shakes his head. "No. They're on Nathan's laptop, that's it."

"I haven't kept them anywhere else. I swear," I say.

Kai's eyes narrow. "How the fuck did those pictures get out then?"

I rub my forehead. "I don't fucking know."

"Was it even safe? What if someone broke in, huh?" Kai growls. "This is all on you." He paces around. "If I lose her because of this, I swear to God ..."

"You'll what?" I retort, standing my ground. "Kill me?"

He marches to me but stops mere inches away from my face. "Don't give me a reason, Nathan."

"I never thought a girl would get between us," I say under my breath.

"And I never thought you'd be so careless about the only thing that kept her bound to us."

"What do you mean?" Milo asks.

"We made a deal with her to safeguard her secret, and now it's all out in the open." He grinds his teeth. "There's nothing left to stop her from running."

"Yes, there is," Milo says, making a fist. "Us."

"She hates me now," I say. "There is no us."

"No, you're right," Kai says. "There is no us. But there is *me*."

He narrows his eyes, staring me down like he means to tell me I no longer matter.

That I've forfeited my spot in this society over this mishap.

My fists ball. "I didn't fucking do it."

"Then who the fuck did because they were only on your fucking laptop?" Kai retorts, getting up in my face.

"Guys, don't fight. Please." Milo tries to squeeze between us, to no avail.

"Did you take the laptop out of this house?" Kai grits.

"It's my school laptop, but I always take it wherever I go," I say. "I just brought it to the library, and ..." My eyes travel away from his as terror slowly sinks into me. "Oh God."

Kai grips my collar. "What?"

I avert my eyes, lost in my memories, drowning in the hatred bubbling to the surface. "Caleb was there. When I got the phone call from my mom, I told him to watch my stuff."

Kai's nostrils flare. "Caleb? From that Tartarus House?"

"His ex," Milo mutters, putting his hand in front of his mouth.

"He was chatting me up. I thought he was just trying to be friends again," I say between thoughts.

Kai's jaw tenses before he finally releases me. "You think he stole them and shared them with everyone?"

"Who else could it have been?" Milo asks. "I would never share those pictures myself. I treasure them. And I know Nathan does too."

But I'm not listening to anything they're saying anymore because of the fire raging in my body. "I'm gonna kill him."

\*\*\*

I slam both fists onto the Tartarus House. "CALEB. SHOW YOUR FUCKING FACE!"

"Maybe it'd help if you ring the doorbell?" Milo says, casually pushing the button.

I keep ramming my fists onto the wood until the pain reverberates in my arms. But it's still not enough to quell the rage inside my heart.

He did this. It has to have been him. No one else had access to my laptop. I carry it with me everywhere I go. The only exception was that one fucking phone call.

When I stop, Milo rings the doorbell again.

After a few seconds, someone finally opens the door.

"See?" Milo muses.

But I just ram my fist into the guy's face instead, hurling him to the floor.

"Where the fuck is Caleb?" I yell as I grab him by the shirt and lift him from the floor to meet my fist for a second time.

"Wow, chill, dude. I don't know," the guy says. "Hey, aren't you ...?"

"Phantoms, yes," Kai says with his hands in his pocket.

"What the fuck do you want from Caleb?" the guy asks.

"No worries, I'm here."

I release the guy from my grip at the sound of Caleb's voice. He approaches from behind us with a bag slung over his shoulder.

"*You* ..." I grit as I turn to face him. "You motherfucking asshole!" I yell, grasping him by the collar. "You stole my pictures, didn't you?"

"I didn't steal shit," he retorts. "Are you accusing me?"

My teeth almost break from the amount of grinding I'm doing.

For a split second, I contemplate biting into his flesh instead.

"Nathan." Kai's warning voice pulls me back from the violent beyond. "Don't."

Fuck.

We can't risk getting even more enemies. The Skull & Serpent Society is already enough to have on our plate. We don't need the fucking Tartarus House on top of that too.

"Go on. Ask me what you wanna ask," Caleb murmurs.

I can barely speak without sounding like a mad man. "Did you send my picture of Lana to everyone's email?"

"No."

My nails dig into my skin. "Don't. Fucking. Lie."

"It wasn't me," he growls. "I already tried to tell you that, but you won't believe me."

"No shit!" I spit back. "You were the only one in the library with me."

"There were a ton of other people," he quips.

"Yet you were the one watching my laptop."

"Was I?" He lifts a brow. "Or did you just tell me to?"

*Fuck.*

I probably did, but I'd assume he'd do it.

My teeth grind together.

"We weren't the only ones there," he adds.

*He's the only one with a motive, though.*

"You're the only one to hate me enough to send that picture to the whole goddamn school." Fury makes me lash out, and I roar before I raise another fist. "You motherf—"

"Enough."

A stern voice coming from the front door makes me stop midair.

Blaine's standing there, gripping the doorjamb, glaring at both of us.

"I won't allow you to soil this ground with blood," Blaine says, smiling when he sees me looking. "You're all better than that. C'mon. You were lovers once, right?"

"True," Milo muses.

"Shut up," I bark at him.

"Your boy Caleb over here decided to put some very private pictures of Lana and us on the group chat," Kai growls at Blaine.

"I did not," Caleb retorts. "And I keep telling them that, but they refuse to believe me."

Blaine walks out of the Tartarus House and approaches us. "Interesting." He stops when he reaches me while I still have Caleb in a death grip, ready to pound his head in. "Caleb, you'll fix this."

"What? But I didn't do shi—"

Blaine interrupts him with a single finger. "Just do it."

"How is he gonna fix this?" I retort. "Everyone's already seen the picture. Fuck knows the entire internet by now."

"Turn it into a story," Blaine says, waving his hand. "Make her look like a victim."

"What ... you mean turn us into predators?" Kai folds his arms and tilts his head. "You think I'm going to agree to that?"

"Your girlfriend must hate you right now, no?" Blaine retorts.

Kai's eye twitches, but he doesn't respond.

"Then I guess this is the only chance you've got to make it right."

"Um ... is everyone forgetting the dead body in the picture?" Milo pulls out his phone to show it to both Caleb and Blaine.

Kai snatches the phone out of his hand. "Great job, Milo. Now even more people saw it."

"They already did." He shrugs.

"Yes, I'm aware of the dead body," Blaine says. "I've seen the picture."

"People will assume she's a killer now," Kai says.

"Not if we make people believe the three masked men in the photo were responsible," he says, a hint of a smile forming at the left corner of his lip.

"Go on," Kai says.

"Take your guy off Caleb first."

Kai throws me a glance, and I hesitantly move off Caleb, lifting him to his feet.

He pats down his shirt and pants and brushes off the remaining dirt. "Asshole."

"You'll probably have to pose for another kill with those masks on for it to work, though," Blaine says.

"Caleb can help with that," I snarl at him. "I can turn you into a corpse in no time."

"Fine. I don't care how, just make it happen," Kai says. "We have to make the school believe she's innocent."

Suddenly, my phone buzzes.

I fish it from my pocket, but when I see the message, all the anger I felt for Caleb is redirected at the phone.

*Romeo: You really, really, shouldn't have come to our club, Nathan ... Your girlfriend left quite the mess.*

I snap as the phone screen cracks under the weight of a cruel frenzy to tear him from limb to limb.

*Romeo: I'm so glad one of my guys managed to catch a glimpse of her face, though. It was easy to find her. Come with money, and I might give her back. If you don't ... I'll sell her to the highest bidder.*

# 57

MILO

Nathan's body is shaking. He howls out loud in front of everyone and sinks to his knees, staring at the words in the chat.

Holy fuck, I have never seen him collapse like that.

"What the fuck happened?" I ask.

"Nathan?" Kai approaches and tries to touch his shoulder, but Nathan grips his wrist and yells, "Romeo took Lana!"

My eyes widen. "What?"

"Oh fuck no," Kai grits, stealing Nathan's phone from his hand to check the message himself.

Then he pulls out his own phone. "I'm calling her."

"It's no use. Romeo wouldn't send this if it weren't true." Nathan's hands touch down on the ground, his nails digging into the concrete. "They took her because she saved Ro."

Little droplets darken the pavement beneath him.

"It's all my fault. If my parents hadn't committed fraud, if I'd just saved Ro by myself, if we'd never taken those fucking pictures—"

I grip him by the shoulders and make him look at me. "Don't blame yourself."

"She got taken because of *me*!" he screams.

"We couldn't protect her because we were too busy arguing over some stupid fucking pictures!" I yell back.

He stares blankly at me for a moment, realizing the fault lies within all of us for not sticking with her even when she hated us the most.

And I wrap my arms around him, hugging him tightly. He molds into my embrace, burying his face into my neck.

"We'll get her back," I say.

I've never seen him this distraught before.

When shit breaks out, he's always the strong one, the one who wields his rage as a weapon.

But if he can't gather his anger and use it against them, I'll be his rock for him.

"I promise."

***

# KAI

Every beep on the phone makes my heart rate pick up. "She's not answering. Dammit."

She's never not picked up when I called, which means she really is in trouble.

*Fuck.*

My fist balls at the thought of someone snatching my little kitty. If there's one thing you don't do, it's mess with a guy's kitty cat.

My Lana ... stolen from me.

Someone's going to bleed empty today.

"Wait ... are you telling me the same guys we saved your sister from now went after your girlfriend?" Blaine asks with narrowed eyes.

"Yes," I reply through gritted teeth. "Except she wouldn't have been fucking taken if we'd been able to keep an eye on her, which we fucking couldn't because of that picture Caleb shared, which made her hate us."

"Which I didn't," Caleb interjects, and I scowl at him.

"I see ..." Blaine mutters under his breath, and he turns to look at the guys watching us from the door opening to the Tartarus House.

"All right, Caleb, you go with them to save her."

"What?" Caleb rasps.

"You heard me," Blaine says.

He runs his fingers through his hair. "I'm not even responsible for this fucking mess, and now I get to shoulder the blame?"

"Caleb. It's settled. You're going with them," Blaine commands.

"Fuck no, I'm not going anywhere with those three—"

"You wanna take it up with Ares?" Blaine raises a single brow.

It immediately shuts Caleb up.

"Good. Then it's settled," Blaine says.

"We're gonna need more help, though," Milo says, looking up at Blaine. "Please?"

Blaine makes a face and rubs his lips together. "I really have to stay out of this one. I already came along the last time. I can't keep risking—"

"Yeah, yeah, we get it," Nathan interjects, and he grabs Milo's arm and drags him away. "Let's go."

We walk back across campus with Caleb veering to the side of the group, staying as far away as possible from us as he can. I don't mind as long as he sticks around and fights when we need him to. Whether he is or isn't responsible remains a point of dispute, but if he helps us get her out of there, it might clear him of the blame.

"Wait ..." Milo pauses midway past the Skull & Serpent House. He points at his chest, and my eyes widen when I spot the red dot. "Why is there a marker on me?"

"Take another step and I'll put you all down," someone growls from the top window.

"What the—Have you gone insane?" Nathan yells at the sniper.

He lifts his head above the rifle, and my eyes widen when I see it's Alistair. "Might want to check your back."

As he turns around, Felix pummels him in the face. "You motherfucker! You're the one who took those pictures of my sister, aren't you?"

Caleb snorts.

Nathan growls at him, "Ow, fuck! What's so funny?"

"You punch, you get punched. We've gone full circle now," Caleb says.

A metal barrel prods into my back. "Make one wrong move and I'll make you crawl for the rest of your life."

I raise my hands, not wanting to get shot. "Wow, calm down. We're just passing through."

"Like hell you are," Dylan grits. "You three were in that picture that got shared all around campus. You involving Lana in murder now?"

I snort and let out a big sigh.

"You think this is funny?" Felix asks, punching Nathan in the gut before turning his attention to me.

"Yes, considering she was the one who killed him," I say.

His eyes widen in surprise. I guess he didn't know his sister as well as he thought.

But it's all out now anyway, might as well get rid of the last secret still standing.

"No fucking way," Felix says.

"You think she's all sweet and innocent?" I say. "She's been killing longer than you can imagine."

"Fuck no, my sister would never—"

"She likes it." I lick my lips at the sight of his rage.

He grips my collar and looks me dead in the eyes. "Give me one good reason not to shoot you point blank right now."

"You won't because she'll hate you for it," I say, tilting my head.

"You're a liar," Felix says through gritted teeth.

"Ask her yourself," I say.

"Where is she?" he seethes.

"Gone."

"What the fuck do you mean gone?"

"Pull back your men, and I'll tell you," I say.

His nostrils twitch, but after a while, he throws a single look at Dylan and Alistair, who was still trying to snipe us down from the window. The red dot disappears, and Dylan's gun is removed from my back.

"Thank you," I say.

"Tell me where my sister is," Felix says with a stern voice.

"She was taken," Nathan fills in for me, his face full of worry. "Bones Brotherhood."

Felix's pupils dilate, and he releases me from his grasp to march right over to Nathan. "You let her get taken by those fuckers?!" he screams. "FUCK! What the fuck do they want with her?"

"Revenge," Nathan replies. "She went into their club and killed a bunch of them."

"Why? Why the fuck would she?" Felix growls. "She wouldn't fucking do that."

"She would ... to save my sister," Nathan says, averting his eyes.

"That sounds out of character," Dylan mutters.

"Is it, though?" I reply. I tilt my head at Felix when he glances at me. "Or is she just good at hiding it?"

"She saved my sister, and Romeo found her, and he's taken her fuck knows where," Nathan says.

Penelope barges out the front door in a simple bathrobe. "What the hell is going on here? I was trying to take a shower, and then I hear you all screaming." She looks at all three of us and sighs out loud. "What are you doing here?"

"We just collected our little helper over here," Milo says, placing his hand on Caleb's shoulder.

Alistair calls out from the window, "Is that a Tartarus guy?"

"Yep. He's gonna help us free Lana, aren't you, Caleb?" Nathan says, folding his arms. "I'm sure you don't want to disappoint these three Skull & Serpent Society guys. Felix here is Lana's brother."

Caleb's eyes narrow, his muscles tightening. He knows it's a threat.

Nathan makes a tsk sound, but I throw him a glare, and he keeps his mouth shut.

"Free Lana?" Penelope mutters. "What do you mean? Where is she?"

"The Bonesmen took her," Dylan says.

"Oh God." Penelope plants her hand against her mouth. "I told her about their location."

"You did what?" Felix snarls at her.

She folds her arms and sneers, "She asked for my help, so I gave it to her."

"To save my sister," Nathan fills in.

"She'd really go through all that trouble for you?" Dylan mutters.

Nathan raises his brow. "Does it sound so hard to believe?"

"Yes, yes, it does," Alistair yells from the top window.

Felix balls his fists. "I knew I shouldn't have let her get close to you three. She's in this shit because of you!" He tries to hit me again, but Penelope stops him.

"Don't! Not again! She asked you not to fight!"

"Can we go now?" Caleb says impatiently. "My blade is itching, and if I don't shove it into one of those Bones Brotherhood fuckers soon, it might want a taste of your blood first."

"Shut it," Nathan grits. "We're working on it."

"Look, I hate them as much as you do for what they did to my sister," Penelope says to Felix.

"For your information, we didn't *want* to do any of it. You know we were forced. My parents would be reported to the feds if I didn't oblige," Nathan says.

"So much for that because they're still in jail," Dylan quips, and the remark almost makes Nathan snap.

"And you? What's your excuse?" Penelope rasps at me.

"I owe his family a lot," I say, swallowing. "I did what I had to for my friend."

"If she's really in trouble, there's no time for random chitchat," Alistair calls from the window.

Penelope makes a tsk sound but keeps her mouth shut. "Fine. If Lana's in trouble, we gotta save her first."

"Wait, what?" Milo mutters. "*We?*"

"You didn't think we'd let you go out there by yourself, did you?" Penelope quips, and she rushes back into the house. "Wait here."

"Wait, you're not thinking of inviting them to come with us, are you?" Nathan growls at me.

"No one's inviting anyone," Felix retorts, flashing his knife. "I'm coming to save my fucking sister."

A lopsided smirk forms on my face. The protectiveness runs in the family, I see.

"All right," I say. "As long as you keep your boys away from us."

"You stay in your lane; I'll stay in mine," Felix snarls, going back inside with Penelope. "You stay."

"There's no way I'd ever step one foot into the Skull & Serpent Society building," Nathan says.

"I would," Milo muses, shrugging.

Nathan throws him a look. "You just want them to hurt you."

"How do you know me so well?" Milo winks.

Caleb makes a gag motion. "Sorry, I just threw up a little."

"And there's a reason I left your ass for his," Nathan retorts.

"No time for being petty," I tell them. "We have a job to do. Let's do it properly."

"Do you even know where we're supposed to go?" I turn my head to see Alistair casually strolling out of their door.

I shrug. "We'll go to the same club and see if they're hiding out there. If not, I'll find someone and make them tell."

"No need." Penelope throws a giant bag on the ground in front of us. "I already know where they're keeping her."

I bend over and zip it open, marveling at the number of guns and weapons inside.

Felix pushes a magazine into his gun. "For where we're going, you'd better pray that's enough."

# 58

## LANA

The drive through the city feels like it takes an eternity, my heart rate picking up with every bump on the road. Crystal's palm is sweaty, and she shivers beside me.

"It'll be okay," I tell her.

"I'm so scared," she murmurs.

"I know," I whisper back.

Slowly, she begins to cry, so I squeeze her hand.

"I won't let them hurt you," I say.

"I'm sorry," she murmurs. "I'm so sorry."

"It's not your fault—"

"Yes, it is," she says, her tone fluctuating. "I took you to the park for some ice cream."

"Oh, girl ..." I lean closer to her, despite being unable to hug. "You don't need to apologize."

"Yes, I do." She shudders. "When I heard about the fight from Brooke, I got too scared to tell you the truth. I was afraid you never wanted to talk to me again."

She swallows while I narrow my eyes to see in the dark because I really want to look into her eyes.

"That picture that got shared around ... it's my fault."

My heart practically stops beating.

"Nathan gave me his passcode once, so when I saw he left his laptop at the library, I figured he wouldn't mind if I used it to look something up for my course. But then I saw that picture of you and them. I thought he'd taken that picture without your permission, and I wanted to send it to you so you'd know about it. But I didn't understand how his email worked and then I accidentally sent it to the entire school." She cries again. "It was too late to un-send it. The damage was already done."

I don't even know how to respond, but my fingers still instinctively unlace from hers, disgusted by the mere idea that someone I consider a friend would do this to me.

Out of all the people I suspected of sharing the picture ... Crystal was last on the list.

"I'm sorry, Lana. I'm so sorry," she says, whimpering from fear. "I didn't mean to. It was an accident. Please, don't be mad at me."

If it's true what she says, if it really was an accident, if she really intended on sending it to me alone ...

Then I accused the boys without merit.

"Shut it!" someone yells from the front of the van.

*Fuck.*

I look at Crystal, but I can barely see her in the dark.

I wish more than anything I knew what to say, but my heart is so full of hurt that I opt for nothing at all.

I don't want to give these bastards more reasons to hurt us.

When the van comes to a stop, I'm jerked harshly against the chains that hold us down. I groan in frustration and wait until they finally come and get us so I can kick their asses.

The van doors open, and some guy steps inside to unlock the chains around our wrists.

The moment I'm released, I punch him in the jaw and knock out some teeth, then ram my other fist into his belly. He bucks and heaves while I kick him aside, fighting my way through the men as they try to subdue me.

I look back at Crystal, who's frozen to the van's floor, desperate for help.

And I realize then that I can't stay mad forever.

It was an accident. She didn't mean to do it and tried to help me get through it.

Despite it all, she's still my friend, and I don't want her to get hurt.

The nefarious plans these men have aren't something I'd wish upon my worst enemy.

I have to get her out of here.

"Jump! Now!" I yell at Crystal.

Crystal's eyes burst open, and she bolts out of the van, but she's captured within seconds.

"No! Let her go!" I scream.

One of them smashes his hand in front of my mouth to silence me. "Give it to her."

I shake my head and bite him in the fingers while another stabs a needle into my neck.

All the energy flows out of my body like a faucet that has been turned on, and I lose both the will and the strength to fight them off.

"Bring them inside," one of them snarls.

They put my arms over their shoulders as they drag me inside, my feet scraping across the pavement. I try to scream, but no sound escapes my mouth. It's already dark outside, and no one can even see me, let alone hear me.

Crystal tries to shriek, but her mouth is stuffed with something to keep her quiet.

I don't know what happens next.

One second, we're going through a door, and the next, I'm shoved into a tiny cell. The time between is a blur, and it all happens so fast. I don't know what they put in that syringe, but it's overpowering and taking away all my sense of time.

"Make sure she doesn't try to escape," one of them says.

Cold metal wraps around my wrists.

*CLICK.*

I'm strapped into place against the wall.

Instinct kicks in, and I fight the two men trying to chain me as best

I can, throwing kicks into the air with all my strength. One of them grabs my leg and pushes it to the wall. "No!"

"Stay down, you bitch!"

I manage to kick one in the cheek, and he makes an *oompf* sound before grasping my other leg as well and pinning it to the wall.

*CLICK.*

My ankles are bound by the same metal clasps as my wrists, stopping me from kicking and punching anyone in my vicinity and forcing me to stay upright. The men in front of me laugh. One of them smothers my face between his thumb and index finger.

"Not so catty now, are we?"

My eyes burst open. "Catty? Fuck you, I'll fucking skin you for this."

They both laugh. "What a fucking joke. You know, I think we're going to have lots of fun with you."

He slaps me harshly, and then they both walk out the door.

"Wait!" I yell with the little energy I have left after whatever concoction they gave me. "Where's Crystal?" When both of them laugh again, my blood begins to boil. "Don't you fucking lay a finger on her! I'll kill you!"

The door shuts tightly, sealing me into a tiny prison.

It's so quiet in here.

Deathly quiet.

Except for that one scream that penetrates the walls.

"CRYSTAL!" I yell, but no matter how many times I raise my voice, every call I make falls on deaf ears.

If they hurt her, I'll never forgive myself.

I have to get their attention somehow. But what do I do?

They'd only bring me here because they want something from me. Which means I'm an asset they don't want to lose.

I bang my head against the wall hard enough to make myself bleed.

Over and over again.

Until finally the two come storming back in. "What the fuck are you doing?"

Blood pours down the back of my head. "You want me alive? Don't fucking hurt Crystal."

The one in the front snorts. "You think you can make demands now?"

The other one approaches me. "This cell is soundproof. His grimy hand touches my face, and I lean away as his filthy fingers slide down my neck. "I could do anything I wanted to you, and no one would hear you scream."

"But that wouldn't make me a valuable sell anymore, now would it?" I retort with one eye closed.

He grinds his teeth, angered by my comment.

He knows I'm fucking right.

"No one will want me," I mutter.

"You're just scared one of those fuckers will bid a million on you just to torture you," he retorts.

"No ... I just know they'll see in my eyes I'll rip off their balls and feed it to them in the night if they ever so much as blink in my direction."

The guy leans away, his finger shaking as he swallows away the bile.

I smile at him. "You think I fear them? No. They should fear *me*."

The guy backs away slowly.

"This bitch is mad," the other one says.

"Seal her in. Tell Romeo to come handle it," the guy who touched me says, and they run out and shut the door tightly.

But I don't think they'll lay a single finger on Crystal now.

Not until that Romeo guy has talked with me. And I'll make sure he understands what he's dealing with too.

"Hey, motherfuckers!" I yell, pushing through the fatigue from the shot I got. "I'm still here!"

I bang my head against the wall again, but it hurts like hell.

Finally, someone comes into my cell again. His black hoodie is stained with blood, but the syringe in his hand catches my attention.

"Oh no, fuck no," I say, shaking my head.

"You won't behave? We'll make you," the guy says, spritzing out some of the fluid.

"Stay away from me!" I yell. "Let me go!"

"You should be happy we're trying to sell you," he says, approaching slowly.

"Fuck you!" I spit, fighting the chains that hold me down.

He pinches my cheeks and makes me look at him. "If you're going to fuck someone, you should at least know their name."

My eyes narrow. "*You* ... you're the reason I'm here, aren't you?" I swallow back the unsettling fear. This man is responsible for all the trafficking this group does. "Romeo."

"Bingo." He smiles the most wretched smile, showing off his golden teeth.

I spit in his face.

He wipes it away and smears it on my clothes. "Bad girl."

Suddenly, he flicks out a knife and cuts me in the cheek.

It stings enough to wake me the fuck up. "Where did you take Crystal?"

"She's safe ... for now."

"Fuck you," I growl again, straining against the metal clasps that keep me down. "You're not even man enough to face me. I'd kill you with just one hand."

"Sure you will," he muses. "But if you don't start behaving soon, no one will want to buy you. And that's a problem, even for you."

*What the fuck is he going on about?*

He taps my chest with his filthy fingers. "Because then we'll be forced to keep you and make you our personal toy." His hand travels down across my chest, touching my breasts. "So what's it going to be? Us or them?"

When his finger reaches my face, I bite and miss, but I think I got my point across.

"Bad choice."

He rams the syringe into my neck, and I scream out loud from the burning pain searing its way through my veins again.

"One way or another, you're going to break for me. And I'll be ready to pick up the pieces and crush them with my bare hands," he hisses into my ear, but his voice sounds off as I begin to fade. "You murdered my men ... and in return, I will destroy your soul."

The drugs are too strong to fight, and I feel myself slipping away, regardless of my will to fight.

I don't want to lose. I don't want to be trapped. I don't want to succumb to the will of these monsters. But I'm all alone in this cell, and there's no way I can win.

*What if I never get out?*

Terror seeps into my heart as, one by one, my senses all shut down until nothing is left but me and my thoughts and that demonic voice laughing like a goddamn devil taking me to hell.

# 59

NATHAN

We park the cars near a giant warehouse in the outskirts of Crescent Vale City. Everyone jumps out and hides behind our vehicles while Alistair removes all the weapons.

"So how do you know this is the place?" Milo asks Penelope.

"My dad hunts these fuckers," she says casually like it means nothing.

"Hunt?" I parrot.

"He has a thing for punishing criminals," she muses. "Though, normally, he'd take them out one by one in secret. Not a big-scale operation like this." She fishes a gun from the bag and fills it with a full magazine. "Grab your weapons of choice, boys. We're going hunting."

We all pull out our guns and knives, tucking plenty of them into the belts Felix brought. I don't like using his equipment, but it's worth the annoyance if I can use it to save Lana.

"You go first," Felix barks as he inspects the back door. "We'll guard the back."

"So you can shoot us?" I grit.

Felix narrows his eyes at me. "I might if you keep complaining."

Penelope shoves her elbow into his side, and he coughs from the sheer force. "Stop fighting. We'll need everyone alive to get her out of there."

Felix pushes a magazine into his gun and preps it so he's ready to shoot. "You want to stay alive? Stay out of my way."

He gets up and walks away from the car, then signals for us to move.

"Okay, guess it's time for our little showdown," Caleb muses, following suit.

Dylan holds out two canisters with a mystery liquid along with a lighter.

"What the fuck is that?" Kai asks him.

"You'll find out soon enough," he muses, grinning like a motherfucker before following Felix as they head toward the building in the darkness.

"Let's go," I say, pulling Milo up from the ground just as he's tucking his weapons into the belt.

"Are we just gonna attack them? Or are we going to sneak inside?" Milo asks as we reach the back door to the building.

*BANG!*

Felix kicks the door in with his foot, causing it to fall over.

"Okay ... guess that's an answer," I say.

"Go," he growls at us.

Kai nods and heads inside with Nathan and Caleb, so I follow them into the grimy building.

There are rows and rows of halls, each leading to more halls, all filled with doors. In the back is a giant hall, where half the floor is lined with chairs, and in the far back is a stage.

"What the fuck is that for?" Milo asks.

"Auctions," Penelope answers.

"I don't see the valuables."

Felix knocks on the doors, and one girl screams.

"They don't sell things," Alistair says. "They sell *people*."

A chill runs up and down my spine.

*What if they've sold her already? I'll never forgive myself.*

"We should hurry," Kai grits.

"Who's there?" a voice in the back yells.

*BANG!*

"Fuck," I hiss as the bullet narrowly misses me and lodges into the wall.

"They found us," Kai says.

I pull out my gun as adrenaline rushes through my body.

I'm fucking ready to murder these sons of bitches for daring to take her.

"Lana!" I scream. "We're coming!"

\*\*\*

## LANA

I'm still so woozy from the drugs I can't see straight, and I don't know where I am or what I'm supposed to feel like. All I know is that I can barely stay awake.

*How long have I been here?*

*It feels like ages.*

I blink a couple of times, trying to focus, but my vision is blurry. My wrists and ankles burn into the metal, the upright position straining my body to its limit. I don't know if I can hold on much longer.

Tears well up in my eyes, but I push them away.

*Don't let those fuckers see you cry.*

I know they're watching. There must be cameras everywhere, even in this tiny cell.

My lungs drag in a breath, but it doesn't help calm my raging soul.

I'm here because they came looking for me. They knew what I looked like, who I was, where I'd be.

And now the only ones who could ever have the balls to come in here to rescue me hate me because I accused them of something they didn't do.

I sigh out loud. They won't come for me. I made it very clear I never wanted to see them again.

*Do they even know I'm missing?*

I swallow back the fear and focus on the metal keeping me in place, but no matter how much strength I put into it, I can't free myself.

It's hopeless.

Completely and utterly hopeless.

*What the fuck do I do?*

\*\*\*

## MILO

*BANG!*

More bullets ricochet against the wall behind us.

"Look who's come into our den," some guy in the back growls. "Boys, get them!"

A bunch of men pour into the hallways from all sides, sporting all sorts of guns and rifles, and my heart rate picks up while my body remembers what it felt like to be sieved with bullets.

Nathan shoves me aside and shoots at the people near the auction area while Felix flanks us and shoots at the men in the back.

"They've got us cornered," Penelope grits, shooting at them too.

"We'll fight our way through," Kai replies.

"I'll take the side. Caleb, you come with me," Nathan growls. "Fuck all of them up."

"Don't forget why we're here," Penelope says. "Find Lana and get out."

"Yeah, yeah, we got it," Dylan replies, waving his gun around before he shoots a bunch of shots at the guys in the back.

When only one of them goes down, he throws the gun to the side. "Fuck it. It's time for the big stuff."

He pulls out his canister along with his lighter and sprays it all over his knives before he runs at them and lights them at the last second, setting the knives on fire.

"Yee-haw! Taste my flames, bitches!" he screams like a madman before stabbing some guy in the eye.

Alistair is behind him, jumping the victims so they can't move while Dylan guts them.

To my left, Kai tries to fight off a Bonesmen who got too close and grabbed his arm, stopping him from shooting.

But no matter how hard I try, I can't seem to raise my gun and shoot.

My whole body shakes, and I can't shrug off this fear I'm going to die. Because I almost did.

And the guy who shot me stands in the hallway, staring me down with a challenging gaze.

"Milo!" Nathan's voice pulls me from my thoughts. "Fight!"

*Fight. That's right. I came here to fight. To protect my friends.*

"If you won't fucking do it for yourself, do it for your fucking queen!" he yells.

My eyes open wide.

*Lana. She's in here somewhere.*

"Queen?" Felix repeats, his face looking like he just got struck by lightning.

He chucks a knife at a guy in front of him and turns to face Nathan. "You'd better not be referring to Lana as a goddamn queen."

"You don't fucking know what she's capable of," Nathan growls back. "Milo, focus on saving her. Lana needs you."

*That's right. She needs me.*

My body stops shaking as my muscles tighten while I take a deep breath. And I push the gun back into my holster and grip my nunchucks instead. I storm at that fucking Bonesman who's aiming to shoot and knock his gun from his hand, then hit him in the balls and the face in a triple knockout.

I steal his gun from him and tuck that into my holster too.

With a smirk, I tell Nathan, "Ready to kill some sons of bitches?"

He grins back and yells from across the hall, "Glad you're back. Let's fuck some Bonesmen up."

# 60

## KAI

I aim and shoot at one of the men in our way, but he jumps to the side right before it hits him.

*BANG!*

A bullet hits me right in the shoulder, and I hiss in pain.

"You're in Bones Brotherhood territory now, boy. You want to join these girls in the auction?" He laughs in a sinister way.

"WHERE IS LANA?" I growl back.

He laughs. "You'll never see her again."

"Did you sell her?" I scream and shoot at him again, the bullet hitting him in the thigh.

He grunts and stumbles but still shoots.

*BANG!*

Miss.

"There's a ton more just like me waiting here for you. We'll fuck you up and make you beg for mercy. You'll never win this, boy!"

"I'll fucking die trying," I growl back, and I bolt toward him, avoiding every shot before I chuck my gun right at his face.

He looks shocked as the gun knocks him back, and I pull out my knife and jab it straight into his heart.

"You mess with my girl, you mess with me," I say through gritted teeth before pulling the knife out of his chest and watching the blood spray out.

Another one runs up to me from behind with a knife in his hand,

470 - CLARISSA WILD

and I shove it into his belly before he can even get close. The gurgle that follows only makes my bloodlust grow.

"Where is she?" I roar through the hallways.

Alistair tugs at each door, starting in the back of the hallway, so I take the ones in the front, shooting open the locks before ripping the doors open. Most cells are empty, save for a few filled with boxes of weapons and drugs. In a few others, women shriek and rush past me toward the exit.

"Run for your life!" Alistair beckons them.

They would probably be sold just as Lana would be if I don't get to her in time.

*Where the fuck are they keeping her?*

*Am I already too late?*

My heart almost cracks under the weight of that predicament, and I grunt out loud as I rip the next door off its hinges. Inside are two Bonesmen casually counting money.

*BANG. BANG.*

Two shots are enough to put them out of their misery. They deserve more than a second of pain, but I don't have time to waste on torture. I've opened all the doors here and still no sign of her.

Fuck.

"There's a staircase here," Milo yells from the other end of the hallway, so I run toward him.

"Is she there?"

"I don't hear anything, but it's worth a shot," he replies.

*BANG! BANG!*

Shots come from behind us, and I look to see more men pouring in, separating us two from the flank group and Alistair.

"I'll fight off these fuckers! Focus on finding Lana!" Alistair calls at me. "I'll fight my way to the rest!"

"Nathan's on his own," Milo mutters.

"Go!" Nathan yells over one of those fuckers' shoulders before he engages in another fight.

*BANG!*

"You check the other hallway with Felix's group and Caleb!" I yell back at Nathan.

"Don't mind me; I'm just killing some Bones Brotherhood bastards!" Caleb yells back.

We run down the stairs as fast as we can. Nathan's the only one left behind, but I trust him not to die on me.

We run down into the basement, where there are a ton more men, and I immediately shoot while Milo charges at them. We work in tandem, alternating fists with knives and gunshots until I'm all out of bullets and knock one of them out with my gun. I don't need weapons to win this; all I need is determination, and I am *not* fucking leaving here without my little kitty.

"C'mon, boy, hit me with your best shot," the fucker says, so I sucker punch him in the chin, knocking him down to the floor.

"Don't ask for what you can't take," I retort, while Milo bashes his head in with his nunchucks.

I hear faint moaning behind the third door, so I yell at Milo, "Here!"

He knocks the lock out with his nunchucks, and I kick open the door with every inch of rage I have inside me, knocking it off its hinges.

But when my eyes find Lana hanging on a wall, blood rolling down her face, all the anger that flooded my body suddenly dissipates into thin air.

And all that's left in the madness of bullets and violence is silence.

# 61

## LANA

I hazily see the figure standing in the doorway, and I inch back into the wall, worried they might be here for reasons other than drugging me more. These men are foul, and I don't doubt they've used the girls they capture for far more nefarious reasons than merely selling them. After all, who's ever going to find out about it?

My body feels so weak against the metal that I can barely move, let alone react, when he steps inside.

*Is it my turn now to scream? Fuck.*

Sweat drops roll down my back as I try to focus, but my brain refuses to cooperate.

"Lana?"

*That voice ...*

My eyes burst open, and I home in on the way it sounded.

*Could it be ...*

No, he can't be here. My imagination must be fooling me.

Something hard clatters to the ground, and the figure rushes at me.

I close my eyes.

Only for two arms to wrap around my body so fiercely I almost melt away.

"Lana, you're alive."

I suck in a hampered breath. "Kai?"

"Yes, kitty, I'm here."

The tears welling up in my eyes refuse to back down, sheer disbelief dripping into my voice. "You came ..."

"Of course I came for you," he says, his voice so soothing I just let the tears flow freely. "Why do you sound surprised?"

I suck in another breath. "I just thought, after my outburst about those pictures, you guys would never—"

"I would scour the world for you and burn it all down just to rescue the only woman I love."

*He ... loves me?*

He smashes his lips onto mine for just a second, but that one second is enough to snap me back into reality. And for the first time in what feels like forever, I can see clearly again, his marred face shining like an angel coming straight from the heavens. And I have never in my life been happier to see someone.

He leans back and grips my face, his thumb caressing the wound on my cheek. "That's not a scrape ... Who did this to you?"

"Romeo," I mutter.

He bares his teeth. "That bastard will pay for touching what's mine."

I swallow as I brace while he grasps the metal clasps that keep me a prisoner in this cell. "I'm getting you out of here," he growls.

Someone else approaches, and I blink a couple of times when I notice the red hair. "Milo?"

"In the flesh," he muses. "You didn't think we'd leave you here to rot, did you?"

I smile through the tears as he comes close and pecks me on the cheeks. "You look like you're about to fall asleep, though."

"They drugged me."

He looks at me with half-mast eyes. "Is it getting stronger or wearing off?"

"Wearing off, I think," I mutter.

He nods before ramming his nunchucks into the clasps. With a few more hits, my wrists are released, and Kai and Milo focus on my ankles next while I rub my painful wrists.

My body leans forward the second I'm freed, my feet still wobbly from the drugs, but Kai catches me before I fall.

"Whoa. I've got you," he murmurs, clutching me tightly.

I can feel myself growing weak in his arms, lulled by the safety he offers me.

"Can you walk?" he asks.

I nod softly. "If I focus."

But I'm still stuck in this hellhole, and a million of those Bonesmen are swarming this compound.

*BANG!*

A gunshot makes me look up at the door.

I grasp Kai's arm in shock. "Wait. Crystal. We have to find her."

"What? Who?" Milo asks.

"My friend, she was taken and brought here with me." My fingers dig into Kai's skin. "It's my fault. They'll sell her. We have to save her."

Kai puts his arm underneath my shoulder to support me. "We'll try our best, but you're my main priority. We have to get you to safety."

"I can't leave here without her," I reply starkly.

"If we must, we must," he grits back as he drags me to the door. "C'mon. We'll look for her on our way back."

A guard runs down the steps, but Milo throws his nunchucks at him before he can even reach us.

"Thanks," Kai says.

"I've got your back." Milo winks, grasping his nunchucks before beating the life out of the guard.

"Check the doors," I say, pointing at the other ones. "I heard a scream coming from one of them."

Milo hits the locks with his nunchucks, and they fall apart with ease, but each time he opens the doors, the cell behind it is empty.

"Shit," I mutter, pushing myself off Kai's shoulder so I can wobble to the cells and have a look myself. "Where is she?"

*BANG! BANG!*

"We don't have time for this," Kai says.

More screams from upstairs catch my attention, and I jerk free from Kai's grip and bolt toward it.

"Lana! Be careful!" Kai yells as he runs after me, but I'm fixated on the noise.

Upstairs, I pause and stare at the scene in front of me. Bodies litter the hallways, blood and remains splattered across the floors everywhere I look. When I take another step, I spot the guards coming from the main hall to our left, guns at the ready.

Just before he pulls the trigger, Kai drags me back behind a wall.

*BANG!*

"Get down!" Kai barks, shielding me from the gunfire with his own body.

Milo jumps out only to shoot right back at them.

"Lana. Focus. We need to get out of here."

"But we haven't checked all the doors," I say.

"There's no time. We've already been through most of those cells. Most were empty."

"But she has to be here!" My voice sounds as desperate as my heart feels.

Kai grips my shoulders and shakes me a little. "Look at me! I'm not losing you after just getting you back. Do you hear me?"

I'm shocked and overwhelmed at the same time because my body is still trying to fight the drugs while my brain is overloaded with fear.

Fear for losing someone dear to me, who's stuck here because of me.

*BANG!*

The last gunshot ricochets through the corridor before a gun is thrown across the hall. I hear fighting and lean around the corner to watch Milo kick the guy's ass, pummeling him to the floor with ease before smashing his face in with a chair.

Milo's face is covered in blood as he turns to look at us. "Go!"

Kai grabs my hand, lacing his fingers through mine as we run through the hallway with Milo on our tail to cover us.

I stop in front of another door and pull at the lock, but it won't budge.

Grunting, Kai yells, "Move."

And he slams the lock open with an empty gun snatched off the floor.

I open the door, but no one is inside.

More tears well up in my eyes.

*We're too late.*

"We have to go. Now." Kai leans around the corner to watch more Bonesmen pour in.

"What about Crystal?" I ask.

"No more time," Milo says as he pushes us forward.

We run down the hallway, but then I bump into someone and lose my balance, falling ass first onto the floor.

*BANG!*

Someone right in front of me holds up a smoking gun, the frame and blond hair familiar, and when he turns his head to look at me, I almost want to burst into tears again.

I lean up on my elbows. "Nathan?"

*He came here too?*

He turns around and goes to his knees in front of me, wrapping his arms around me.

"You're safe," he mutters, burying his face in my neck. "I was so fuckin' worried they'd already sold you. I'm sorry. I'm so sorry."

I'm momentarily too stunned to even speak.

"Where's Felix and the rest?" Kai asks. "And what about Caleb?"

"They're killing everyone who's trying to block our only way out," Nathan replies, and he returns his attention to me. "I'm sorry, Lana, I should've been more careful with those pictures. If I had, you wouldn't have gotten so angry, and we could've kept you out of their claws."

"Yeah, this is kind of your fault," Milo says, and Nathan throws him a seething look.

"I didn't share those pictures." Nathan focuses his attention back on me. "I swear on my goddamn sister's life, it wasn't me."

*His ... sister?*

*She's all he's wanted to protect, and he swears it on her?*

I suck in a breath. "I believe you."

"I don't know who did it, but I will find them and punish them." He grips my face. "I don't want you to hate me. I can't bear to lose you too."

His words strike my heart and gut it open, forcing me to come face-to-face with my own anguish and infatuation.

Because those pictures forced us together.

Bound us in a way that was inescapable.

And then those binds were suddenly released.

"I know who—"

"Talk later." Kai interjects as he runs at a guard and engages in a fight.

Out of nowhere, a guy covered in tattoos and piercings shoots at the guards. "I've got you covered. Don't worry."

"Who is that?" I mutter.

"Caleb. Long story," Milo says. "We should run."

Nathan pulls back and caresses my cheek. "Even if you despise me, I will keep you safe. I promise."

He presses a gentle kiss onto my hand before helping me stand.

But as I stand, I briefly glance over my shoulder at the others and notice one Bones Brotherhood guy with a hoodie and a ton of tattoos, making my blood run cold.

*Romeo.*

He's aimed his gun right at me.

My eyes widen.

Nathan's eyes follow mine, and when he sees the guy, he jumps right in front of me, shielding me.

The gun goes off.

*BANG!*

The bullet lodges into Nathan's back, and his knees buckle and he falls into me while I scream, "Nathan!"

# 62

## NATHAN

Blood spurts out of my wound as I collapse onto her. She sinks to the ground with me, clutching my body close to her as the blood begins to drain from my veins. My back stings with pain, electricity shooting out into my legs.

"Oh God, oh God, oh God!" Milo yelps as he runs to my side and cradles me too. "He hit your back! Fuck!"

I try to move, but it hurts so damn badly that I just stay here in Lana's arms. Above me, gunshots fly left and right, and Kai and Caleb are the only ones left fighting to keep the Bonesmen at bay.

"Fuck! There are too many," Kai grits, directing his attention toward Caleb. "You take the left; I'll take the right!"

"We have to do something," Milo begs Lana.

She rips a part of her shirt from her waistline and binds it around me, sealing my wound. "It's soaking right through. Dammit."

"We have to get him out of here," Milo says.

*BANG!*

They duck for cover, hovering over me to protect me.

"Why did you do it?" Lana whispers into my ear. "Why did you protect me?"

"Because I love you. And I protect the people I love."

I can feel the tears falling down onto my hair, the cold droplets soothing the pain just a little, taking the edge off things.

"Please ..." she murmurs.

Her whole body begins to quake against me, and she leans over to grasp my knives and tucks them into her own pocket. Then she slips out from underneath me and tells Milo, "Keep watch over him. Don't let him die."

Milo nods.

"What are you going to do?" I mutter and lean up to look at her march straight toward Romeo, her head held high, knives at the ready. Like a goddamn motherfucking angel of revenge.

"Protect the people *I* love."

***

# LANA

I shake off all of the drugs and focus on the adrenaline coursing through my veins. Pure hatred drives me as I run toward Romeo.

Shots fire past my head, and I bolt from left to right to avoid all of them.

A knife whips past me, and I glance over my shoulder to see Caleb covering for me. I focus on getting to Romeo, ignoring the other guards headed in my direction.

"Stay away from me!" Romeo yells.

"You messed with the wrong bitch," I growl as I run right at him. "You touch my friends, you fucking die!"

I chuck two knives at his face, and he dodges them, so I chuck the third at his knee. He groans when it lodges into his flesh, and he collapses from the pain. Just in time for my knee to hit his nose.

*CRACK!*

Blood pours from his face, and I ram my fourth knife straight into his back.

He yelps and cries out in pain.

"Get away from me, you bitch!" He attacks me with his own knife, swiping it from left to right like a madman.

One cut slices through my arm, but I ignore the pain and grasp his wrist instead, bending it until it snaps and breaks.

"FUCK!"

The knife falls to the floor, and I pick it up and jam it into his belly, pulling it through.

He falls to the floor, bleeding everywhere, and I perch myself on top of him.

A knife comes out of nowhere, and he tries to ram it into my thigh, but I grasp that arm too and slowly bring his own knife back to his face.

"You thought you could take me? I murder men like you in my spare time," I hiss. Leaning in close, I whisper, "Now fear me."

He whimpers, the cries slowly becoming more agonizing as the blade pierces his eye. Blood sprays onto my face and body, but it only makes me smile harder. I take my time, making sure he's alive to feel all the pain he deserves. And I don't stop until his body stops writhing entirely.

When his body goes limp, I get off and pull out all the knives, looking around the auction room. The chairs are upended and the floor's caked in blood, but in the back a rose with half its petals lies on the floor, and my eyes follow the trail of blood leading up to it.

A door is wide open. Behind it, a van is parked out on the street ... Crystal's eyes boring into mine.

"Crystal?" Caleb yells.

*He knows her?*

He bolts right past me, headed straight for the door through which they disappear.

But he's no match for their speed.

The van doors slam shut right before it races away in front of Caleb.

"FUCK!" he growls out loud.

Too late.

She's gone.

I clutch the knife tighter, fury overcoming me, and I roar out loud and rush toward the rest of the guards.

"LOOK AT ME!" I scream.

Slowly but surely, all the Bonesmen stop firing at my friends and home in on the blood caking my skin.

"Your leader is dead," I say, pointing at Romeo's dead body. "His blood is on my skin."

Even Kai and Milo gaze at me in awe.

"And this will be your fate too if you don't let us go. Now."

The men swallow, fear settling in their bones.

The first one drops his gun.

Then the next.

And soon, all of them drops whatever they are carrying.

I walk through the hallway and chuck a knife at the last remaining guard still trying to keep us here.

He drops to the floor like a fly.

I walk past, blood smeared all over my body, but the second I lay eyes on my own damn brother along with his friends and Penelope, I stop moving entirely.

Felix's eyes widen at the sight of me. Or rather, the violence I've inflicted upon these monsters.

I swallow back the lump in my throat. The secret I've been holding feels awfully heavy on my shoulders. Each step I take leaves a trail of blood on the floor.

"Lana?" he mutters, almost as if he doesn't recognize me.

But his voice soothes my soul.

All of the years of suffering ... all that bloodshed and the frenzy to murder ...

It was all for him.

If he hates me now, so be it. I wouldn't want to touch someone as violent as me with a ten-foot pole. Let alone the fact that I'm covered in someone else's blood.

Instead, he runs at me, chucking his gun to the side, and wraps both arms around me.

I'm stunned to even react, blinking rapidly.

But I eventually cave to his safe arms, burying my face into his chest.

My body feels so heavy I can barely stand. Now that the adrenaline has worn off, the drugs have the upper hand again, and they're draining all my remaining energy.

"You murdered him in cold blood," Felix mutters.

"Do you despise me?" I ask.

"No," he says, and I can hear him smile. "I'm proud of you."

I grin against his chest and take in a breath.

"We should go," Caleb says, clearing his throat. "This truce won't last long."

I lean away and watch the men stare us out.

Kai and Milo have helped Nathan up. "Can you walk?" Milo asks him.

Nathan nods. "I can try."

"Let's get out of here," Alistair says as he approaches us from behind and places a hand on Felix's shoulder. "Y'all can have a family reunion later."

Felix supports me while we run toward the exit, with Kai and Milo keeping Nathan on his feet. At the back entrance, a blazing fire stops us. In front of it is Dylan, chucking random guards on top of a pile of bodies burning to a crisp.

"Hey, guys! Back already? I cleared out this area!" he says cheerfully. "Roasted them like sautéed chicken."

I'm both mildly disgusted and impressed at the same time.

"We're done," Penelope tells him. "Let's go."

Alistair runs ahead of us and gets the car, driving it toward us so we can easily get in.

"Fuck, it's gonna take forever to get those stains out," Dylan mutters when he sees all the blood his friends drip onto his leather seat.

"Worry about the cleaning later!" Penelope yells at him.

"I'll take our car back with Nathan and Milo," Kai says. "You go with your brother. Caleb, you go with her too."

I nod and jump in with them while Milo and Kai help Nathan into the back seat of their car. Both cars race off together, leaving behind a bloodied, crippled Bones Brotherhood.

But the longer we drive, the bigger the hole in my heart becomes.

Crystal.

Tears well up in my eyes.

"What's wrong?" Penelope asks.

"Crystal got taken with me."

Penelope's eyes widen, her face turning white as snow.

"She was here too?" She grasps my shoulders. "Why didn't you tell me?"

"I thought there was still time to save her," I reply. "But when I finally found her, she was getting shoved into a van, and it raced off before I could get to her. I couldn't see the license plate. And now they've taken her to God knows where."

"I'll ask the Tartarus boys to check with their connections and see if they can find her whereabouts," Caleb says.

"Thank you," I mutter, still overcome with emotions.

"Felix," Penelope growls.

He stares at her through the rearview mirror. "No."

"Felix, we have to go back."

He only hits the gas harder. "No."

"She'll be sold!" Penelope yells in terror.

"We'll go back for her later. We have to get Lana to safety first."

"But Crystal—"

"Will be saved too," Felix interrupts. "You can count on it."

Penelope sits back, still antsy as she glances through the window behind her. "Crystal ..."

"I'm sorry, Pen," I say.

She swallows back the tears. "It's not your fault."

"She came to my room to talk and get ice cream, but then we got taken by the Bones Brotherhood because they were shadowing me. It's because of me that she's—"

"Stop," Penelope interjects. "Stop feeling guilty, and promise me you'll help me find her."

I nod a few times. "I won't stop looking for her. Promise."

Alistair rubs my back. "We'll get her back."

I know he's only saying that to ease the aching in my heart.

The truth is, no one knows how far the Bones Brotherhood's connections span. She could be anywhere by now, on her way to be sold to the highest bidder.

Poor Crystal ...

We may have lost her forever.

# 63

KAI

When we return to campus, Milo and I haul Nathan into the nurse's office through the school's back entrance.

She shrieks when she enters the room in her nightgown, carrying a gun. "Jesus Christ, I thought you were burglars!"

"Please help us," I say, breathing ragged breaths.

"What the ... you're students, aren't you?"

I nod.

"What happened to you?" she asks, putting down the gun. "It's the middle of the night!"

"Does it matter?" Milo asks.

She sighs out loud and waves her hand around. "Put him on the bed."

We do as she asks, dragging him all the way to the bed.

"Turn him over," she says, grabbing her supplies.

He groans from the pain as we flip him over. "Fuck."

"You want my help? No swearing," the old lady grumbles.

He groans again. "A little hard when you've been shot in the back."

"Is he going to be okay?" Milo asks.

"Let me check," she says, rolling his way on her little chair.

She grabs her tools and starts digging into his wound. He roars from agony.

"That's a bullet," she says, and she eyes us both suspiciously. "Yours?"

I shake my head. "We've made enemies."

"So it seems." She narrows her eyes.

"Can you take it out?" Milo asks.

"I'll try," she replies, grabbing a syringe.

She shoves it into his side, and he hisses from the pain. "Jesus, did you have to get a needle that big?"

"Stop whining, boy," she says. "It's a sedative."

"Oh ..." Nathan sighs, and Milo hides a little bit of laughter.

"It'll still hurt a little, though," the nurse says as she digs into his back.

Suddenly, the door bursts open, and Lana storms in, completely covered in blood. "Is he alive?"

The nurse looks up, her tool still stuck in Nathan's back, and her eyes widen in shock at the sight of all that blood. "Oh my God."

"It's not mine," Lana says swiftly, laughing it off.

"What happened to you?"

"Good question," she says, grasping a few paper towels to wipe herself off, but it's no use. "I'm fine. I just want to know if Nathan's okay?"

"Working on it," Nathan groans back.

She immediately walks to him and grabs his hand. "I was worried."

"Worried? About me?" he retorts, coughing, then cringing from the pain. "I'll be fine. It's just a flesh wound."

I laugh. "You're only saying that because she's here."

"Shut up," Nathan retorts.

The nurse plucks out the bullet, and he grunts in pain again, gripping the bedding with his free hand. "Goddammit."

The nurse smashes a cotton soaked with alcohol into the wound, making him hiss even harder. "What did I say about swearing?"

"So is he going to be okay?" Lana asks.

The nurse sews him up. "He'll be fine."

We all breathe a collective sigh of relief.

When she's done, he rolls over again on his back. "Thank you."

"You're welcome," she replies, then turns her attention to Lana. "Now let me look at you." She pulls Lana's face toward her. "That's a big cut. Where'd you get that?"

"Nowhere," Lana mutters, looking anxious.

She inspects her arm next. "And that stab wound?"

She shrugs and eyes Nathan. "I protected him."

He smiles. "You did."

The nurse cleans her wounds with an alcohol pad and sutures her cuts too. "There. Finished. Here's a towel too." The nurse chucks a wet one her way. "To clean up the blood."

"Thank you," she replies.

"Are you two good?" the nurse asks Milo and me.

I nod. "No wounds, other than a couple of scratches."

"Same," Milo adds.

She narrows her eyes at us like she doesn't believe us.

"What about Nathan? What do we do with him now?" Lana asks.

"He needs rest."

"That's it?" I ask.

She shrugs. "That's it. If it starts to fester, you call me."

Suddenly, the door smacks open again and in step Felix, Penelope, Alistair, and Dylan.

The nurse's eyes widen. "Oh God. Not you three."

"What?" Dylan says.

"I'm not going to do this again," the nurse says, sighing as she waves them away. "Whatever your business is, you can do it on your own. I don't care if you stay here. Just don't touch my stuff. I'm going back to sleep."

She waltzes past them and throws the door shut.

"Well, that was interesting," Penelope mutters, laughing a little.

"She really hates our guts," Alistair says.

"We didn't even do anything," Dylan adds.

Penelope folds her arms and stares at him. "Really?"

Dylan just shrugs and walks off whistling.

Felix approaches us and focuses on Lana. "You okay?"

She nods. "Better now that I'm here."

Caleb comes in too, clearing his throat. "I see you all made it out alive."

Nathan tries to sit up, but it's tough. "Thank you for helping."

"Sure. So we're done here?" Caleb asks.

Nathan nods. "Sorry I blamed you."

"Yeah." He runs his fingers through his hair. "It's all good. Keep this on the rain check for when I need y'all, okay?" he says, winking. "See ya."

And he walks off again, closing the door behind him.

"Thanks, I guess?" Lana mutters.

"I thought he was the one who shared your picture," Nathan says, reaching for her.

"Yeah, about that ..." She grabs his hand. "Crystal did it."

Nathan's eyes widen. "Crystal? No, she wouldn't—"

"It was an accident. She didn't mean to do it." She interjects, swallowing back the tears. "I wanted to forgive her, but I never had the chance to tell her. And now she's gone."

I swallow back the anger and take her into my embrace, hugging her tight.

"Crystal ..." Nathan grinds his teeth together as he looks at me. "We have to go look for her. She's my friend too."

I nod, still hugging Lana tight. "We'll do our best."

"Hey ..." Felix growls.

When he sees how Lana leans into me, he backs off again.

"I'm sorry," she murmurs at all three of us. "For yelling and not believing you."

"We understand why you had to," I answer, tilting her chin up. "You don't have to apologize. You did nothing wrong."

She swallows. "But I hurt you guys."

"True," Nathan says.

"And got yourself into some nasty trouble," Milo says, snorting.

"But we saved you," Penelope says, winking.

"I'd get hit by ten more bullets if it meant I could keep you safe," Nathan brags, groaning when he moves too much. "Okay, maybe nine."

"Thank you, everyone," Lana says, smiling at us. "I can't believe you all worked together."

"You think I'd just abandon my sister?" Felix scoffs, making a tsk sound.

I grab her shoulder and whisper into her ear, "I'll stay here. Go talk with him."

"He knows everything now, doesn't he?" she whispers back.

I nod. "Everyone saw the picture. We can spin a story for the rest of the students, but it'll take a bigger lie to convince him ..."

"No, it's all right. I want him to know the truth," she answers, looking at me intently before heading toward Felix.

"You think she'll come back?" Milo asks. "You know, since the deal we had no longer exists."

A devilish smirk forms on my face. "What do you know about cats?"

He frowns, confused. "I don't know? They have nine lives?"

I lick my lips as I watch her walk into the hallway together with Felix, but before she disappears, she throws one last glance at me. "A cat will always know the way back home."

# 64

LANA

"So," Felix mutters.

"So," I retort, awkwardly biting my cheek.

"You're covered in blood," he says.

"You noticed, huh?" I laugh.

"Hard to miss."

The light above our heads flickers, casting an eerie glow.

He leans in to touch the bandage around my arm. "Does it hurt?"

"Not that badly," I reply.

"Alistair told me you got drugged," he says.

I nod, tucking my hair behind my ear. "They tried to subdue me. To make it easier for them to sell me." I tap my feet around, uncomfortable that I have to talk about this with my brother. "And Crystal."

"I'm sorry about that. I'll get my guys to scour the area around the compound in search for clues to her whereabouts. She's our friend too, so I'm not gonna let them get away with this."

"Thank you," I reply. "I appreciate that."

He shakes his head. "I know it's not enough. If I'd known—"

"It's not your fault." I interrupt. "She would've never been taken in the first place if I hadn't ..." I gulp away the fear. "If I'd just told everyone I love the truth."

"That picture?" he asks, his jaw tensing.

A blush creeps onto my cheeks.

His fist balls. "Did those fuckers force you to do it?"

I shake my head. "We had a deal. I'd give myself to them in exchange for them to keep quiet about my ... other cravings."

"A deal ..." He squints. "What other cravings?"

"That body you saw in the photo wasn't their kill," I explain. "It was mine."

He swallows, visibly worried, and it makes me avert my eyes.

"I... kill people."

"Like what, daily?"

I don't like the judgment, but he's already seen me holding someone's head in my hands. What point is it to lie?

"No. Just when I feel like I need to."

His eyes twitch. "Random people."

"No, mostly predators I find online," I reply.

He frowns. "How long has this been going on?"

"Years."

God, it feels like I'm opening a very old wound.

"Why?"

I draw in a breath, unable to look him in the eyes. "Because ... it hurt to watch you suffer. To see Mother in your bed."

His whole body tightens when I mention her, and it unravels my heart.

"I keep seeing it over and over while I sleep, every nightmare waking me up to the point where I just want to kill people who try to do the same to others."

He just stares at me for a good few seconds, the look on his face anything but pleased.

I may have said too much.

But my God, the burden on my shoulders finally feels a little less heavy.

"I'm sorry," I mutter. "I'm sorry I can't be the sister you think I am. I'm not perfect. I date the wrong people. I'm a murderous girl. I—"

Suddenly, he wraps his arms around me and pulls me in for a hug so tight I can't even breathe.

"Don't ever apologize," he says, shaking me to my core.

"What? But I'm a—"

"Killer?" He snorts. "Yeah, it runs in the family."

"But—"

"No. I am not ashamed of you." He pulls away and grabs my shoulders. "Do you hear me? You're my little sister, and I love you. That's the last time you'll ever hear me say those words, so remember them."

I smile and wrap my arms right back around his body. "Thank you. And thank you for coming to save me."

His hand caresses my back, and it's the first time in ages that I don't feel like I want to push him away.

"You're the reason I'm here today," he says, his voice soft, unlike his usual self. "If you hadn't screamed when you saw our mother ..." His voice is hampered by his emotions. "I wouldn't be alive without you." I shudder against him, and he takes in a big breath. "I'm the only one who should be saying thank you."

Our hug is so deep and warm it feels like both of us are pouring out all our feelings into each other.

"I was so goddamn worried about you," he grumbles. "When those fuckers told me you'd been taken by that Bones Brotherhood, I nearly snapped their necks."

"It's not their fault," I say.

"They should've kept you safe," he growls. "I will never allow them to get—"

I push myself away from him. "Don't. Don't finish that sentence. Please."

The muscles in his jaw tense up. "Those bastards took that photo of you."

"And I let them," I reply. "Don't blame them for my own struggles, please. They didn't share it."

"Who did?" he grits.

"It was an accident. That's it." I shrug, and I grab his hand. "You have to stop fighting them."

"But they—"

"They *love* me," I say.

His eyes burst open and his lips part, but no words spill out.

I've never seen him this speechless.

"And you believe them?" he asks.

I nod.

"You're not being forced to say this?"

I shake my head, smiling.

He rubs his lips together and points at the door. "Those fuckers hurt you."

"Like you hurt Penelope?"

His lips slam together, and he grinds his teeth, looking irritated as hell that I'd point this out to him.

"But you love her too," I say, trying to find his eyes while all he's trying to do is avert his from mine. "Admit it."

"Yes."

"Someone called my name?" Penelope comes walking out of the waiting room.

"No," Felix says. While I say, "Yes."

"What's up?"

"Nothing," Felix swiftly replies.

"I'm just trying to determine if he sees his own hypocrisy."

Penelope smiles and crosses her arms. "Oh, this should be interesting."

"You're dating three guys, right?" I ask her.

"What about it?"

Felix rubs his forehead. "Fuck me."

"Answer me, please."

"Fine. Yes, she is."

"Then you know what it feels like," I say.

His brow twitches. "But all three of them?"

"Oh ... so it's about those boys," Penelope muses. "I figured as much."

I grab Felix's other hand too. "If you love me as much as you say you do ... you'll let me decide."

His jaw tenses again, but he doesn't move away.

After a while, he nods. "All right. I trust you."

I smile and hug him again, his arms slowly wrapping around my body to return the warmth.

He sighs out loud. "But don't ever forget you're a Rivera first."

"I won't," I reply, leaning back. "Oops. I smeared blood all over your shirt."

"Eh, I've had worse," he retorts, shrugging.

"How's it going out here?"

I turn my head to see Milo's happy face peeking out the door, his upside-down cross dangling from his ear.

"We're finished," I reply.

"Nosy bastard," Felix growls.

So I step on his foot like any good sister would.

"Ow, fuck!" he grits.

Milo snorts. "I see he's as nice as ever."

"Oh, fuck off," Felix growls back, so I slap him on the chest.

"Felix will be nice to you from now on. Won't you, Felix?"

"Sure," he replies stoically. "As long as you don't try to take any other lewd pictures of my sister."

Milo laughs awkwardly and rubs the back of his head. "Yeah, about that ..."

Felix's eyebrow twitches. "Don't tell me ..."

"We have like a ton." Milo puts his fingers together. "But we won't share them with anyone, promise."

I blush. "Oh boy."

"TMI," Felix grits.

"Did either of you hear anything from other students yet?" I ask.

"Well, from what I've noticed, they all seem to think you got used and that it wasn't your choice," Milo mutters.

"Okay ..." I breathe out a sigh. "Could be worse."

"At least no one thinks you murdered the other dude in the picture," he muses.

"Do you think my dad saw the picture?" I ask.

Felix closes his eyes and rubs his forehead. "Maybe."

"Fuck. That's gonna be embarrassing," Milo mutters.

"You should talk to him," Felix says.

"And tell him what?"

"We can explain it was an accident." Milo shrugs.

"What about the body?" I retort, folding my arms.

"Tell him the truth," Felix says.

"Are you kidding? Really?" I say.

"Why not?" Milo asks. "He sounds like a nice guy."

"He killed our mother," Felix growls.

Milo's face turns white.

I cringe. "Bringing this kind of news to my dad isn't gonna be easy."

"We'll figure it out," Felix says, placing a hand on my shoulder. "I've got your back."

I place my hand over his. "Thank you."

Kai's face appears behind Milo too now, and I struggle to hide my smile.

Even though I was so convinced I hated these boys for what they did ...

None of it seems to matter anymore.

My heart's already made its choice.

"Nathan is up. We're bringing him home," he says, winking.

Then he turns around and drags Milo with him.

I'm almost tempted to go with them, but Felix's hand on my shoulder keeps me from moving.

"Have you decided yet?" Felix asks.

A pause follows.

"I won't stop you. But I'm just one call away if you ever need me."

I swallow away the last bit of restraint I still had left.

Felix leans over and whispers into my ear, "Go on then. Follow your fucked-up heart."

And he pushes me away from his strong grip and toward the door that signifies my demise. But oh, the fall into oblivion has been so fucking sweet.

And as a fucked-up masochist, I don't think I'd have it any other way.

I look back one more time just to grin, and Felix grins right back at me in that signature Rivera way.

"Don't let them treat you badly, or I'll kill them," he says.

"They won't," I retort.

"How do you know for sure?"

"Haven't you heard?" I wink. "I'm their motherfucking queen."

# 65

## NATHAN

Kai and Milo help me out of the nurse's office and out of the building, praying we don't see anyone while we're walking here with bloodied clothes and stitched-up wounds.

I get into the car parked near the fountain and sit in the back seat while Milo jumps into the passenger's seat and Kai hops in front of the steering wheel.

But right as he reverses the car, someone knocks on our window.

And the sight of the black-haired beauty staring right back at me makes my heart race.

Kai lowers my window.

"Got room for one more?" Lana asks.

A mischievous smile forms on my face. "I don't know ... there might be room in the trunk, though."

Her jaw drops, and she leans in to grasp me by the collar. "You fucking wouldn't!"

My brow rises. "Is that a challenge?"

"He'll do it," Milo muses.

"True," Kai adds. "But I'll make sure you can breathe ... after sucking my dick." He winks.

She gasps but then bites her lip. "You filthy motherfuckers."

"Damn right we are, and you love it, admit it," I say while she still holds me in her grasp.

But I'm not afraid. None of us ever were. And I think that's why she likes us so damn much.

"Take that back," she says, leaning in.

A devilish smile forms on my lips. "Make me."

An equally dirty smile slowly creeps onto her face before she smashes her lips onto mine, claiming my mouth like she no longer hates me for ruining her life. And you know what? I think she might even forgive me for my sins.

She bites down onto my lip, and I moan into her mouth while she laps up the blood with her tongue, leaving me desperate for more.

"I'll make you pay dearly for that, you know," she murmurs.

"Bring it," I say, my voice husky and so goddamn ready for whatever she wants from me. "I'll take all you have to give."

Her brow rises. "Really? You sure you're ready to grovel for me?"

"Kitty, I'll let you chain me to the ceiling and whip me until all my scars belong to you," I say, completely smitten.

"Wow," Milo mutters, looking at us through the rearview mirror. "He never offered any of that to me. Lucky girl."

She laughs. "I didn't think you were a pain-lover too."

"I'm not, but if that's what it takes to earn your forgiveness for those pictures leaking out ... I'll do anything." I swallow as she holds my face like she's seeing it for the very first time.

She plants a delicate kiss on my lips that takes my breath away. "I'll hold you to that."

I smile against her lips. "Good. I'm ready whenever you are."

\*\*\*

# LANA

"Scoot over." I open the car door, and as Nathan scoots over, I sit in his spot.

"Are you sure you want to do that, kitty?" Kai asks, gazing at me through the rearview mirror with intense eyes. "The deal we had is gone. Your secret's out. You're free to do whatever you please."

"What I *please* ..." I repeat, gawking right back at him. "And what if I want you to please *me*?"

His tongue darts out to wet his lips, and my whole body zings with excitement at the feral look he gives me. "I won't let you walk away. Not this time."

I push the button to raise the window in defiance, showing him I mean it.

"You all said you loved me ... prove it, then," I quip.

*CLICK!*

The door lock snaps into place as a wretched grin forms on his face. "Now that's a deal I'm willing to accept."

And he hits the gas and drives off back to the Phantom Society building, where he parks the car and unlocks the doors.

But before I can even step out, he leans to the back and crawls over the middle to grasp my face and smash his lips onto mine. It's a kiss so greedy it takes my breath away as he undoes my belt buckle. But then he wraps it around my throat instead, and my eyes burst open. His mouth is still on mine, tongue swirling around, and I'm helpless against the onslaught of lust coursing through my body.

"You want this?" he murmurs, his lips dragging a line all the way down to my chin as the belt buckle tightens like a noose.

I nod, shivering from his delicious licks, and my hand instinctively reaches for Nathan's dick, desperate to hold something. He's already hard and groans with excitement when I touch him.

"Last chance, little kitty," Kai groans, running his tongue all along my neck and across the belt. "Or you'll be mine until you take your very last breath."

I don't hesitate to nod, despite feeling the constriction in my neck suffocating me.

"Say it. Say the words I want to hear," he whispers into my ear. "You *know* what they are."

If these boys will be the death of me, then so be it.

I'd rather live a life filled with ecstasy and pain than not to have lived at all.

"I love you," I whisper.

The belt suddenly unwraps from around my neck, and I suck in a breath as his lips come to claim mine again in a ravenous frenzy. "Good girl."

He crawls over me and opens the door, then swoops me out from the back seat.

"Milo, help Nathan inside," he commands as he carries me to the door.

"I can walk, you know," I reply.

"I know you can," he says. "But these feet have felt enough concrete for the rest of this goddamn year."

My cheeks flush a little as he storms inside with me in his arms.

Ezra comes up to us, spluttering, "You're back. Whoa. That's ... a lot of blood."

"Our bedrooms are off-limits," Kai tells him.

"How long?" he asks. "And what about the cleaners?"

"Cancel them for the rest of the week," he answers.

"A whole week?" I say as he carries me up the stairs.

"I warned you." There's a hint of danger in his eye. "Regretting your choice already?"

I grin. "No."

"Trust us when we say you'll beg for another week once we're through with you," Nathan adds, winking as they come up the steps too.

His words send chills up my spine, definitely the good kind.

Kai carries me all the way to his bedroom, and I take a curious look around. I don't think I've been here before. The place is a good mixture of black and brown furniture, and it has a gothic feel to it, with a wooden king-size bed with embellishments carved into them and a canopy on top. The whole place kind of has a rustic feel to it, but at the same time, everything looks quite ... pointy. But the bear rug on the floor feels awfully soft to my toes.

"Hmm ... interesting."

"You like my room?"

"Like is a strong word," I muse. "It could do with a little makeover."

He circles me. "A makeover?"

"Yeah, but I could get used to this."

A filthy smirk forms on his lips as he stops behind me, wrapping his arms around my waist. "Are you implying you're moving in?"

"I don't hear you opposing me."

He leans over and places a kiss on my shoulder. "You didn't ask."

The kiss swiftly turns into a piercing bite, and I moan to let out the pain. He tilts my head and absorbs the moan with a kiss, letting me taste my own blood. "Go ahead then ... ask."

"Please ..." I whimper from the way he lavishly kisses me.

"Please what?" He bites down again, and I shudder in place.

"Can I stay?" I mutter.

"Hmm ..." He groans, licking up the bloodied wound. "I have to think about it."

Gasping, I turn in shock and attempt to slap him, but he catches my wrist midair, a smirk following quickly. "Ah, ah, kitty. First, I'll have to declaw you."

He pushes me all the way to the wall, spinning me around, and we slam into it together. While his hands cup my face, his mouth covers mine within an instant. And I don't even fight him off, my body desperate to get closer to his.

"Shouldn't we shower first?" I mutter between kisses.

"Fuck no," he growls. "Every fucking drop of blood on your body is a mark of honor that I want to praise with my tongue."

His lips roam freely across my neck.

"You undo me, Lana. You've chained me. Turned me into a blood-thirsty monster."

His lips drag all along my jawline, making my heart rate shoot up.

"And I've fallen in love with every single violent inch of your soul."

Someone behind us clears their throat. "Still going at it?"

Nathan sits on the bed.

Milo closes the door. "Are we doing this here?"

"The first part," Kai responds.

"First?" I parrot, my tone fluctuating.

"Yeah, you didn't think once would be enough, did you?" Nathan muses, planting his hands on the bed to show off his raging hard-on. "You caused this. Now you get to deal with it."

I swallow. "I can take it."

"Can you?" Milo asks, and he unbuckles his belt, dropping all the weapons along with it to the floor. "Because now that the deal is gone, nothing holds back any of us."

"You've got me all fucked up, kitty," Kai groans as his hand travels down my cheek and slithers down my chest. "I want to destroy you and leave nothing left."

I suck in a breath as his fingers travel across my nipples. "Then destroy me."

\*\*\*

## KAI

God, how long have I waited to hear her say those words?

Love me.

Own me.

Destroy me.

It's all I've ever wanted to do to her, but a heart can't be devoured unless it's offered willingly. And now she's finally handing it to me on a platter, all mine to consume.

I grab her by the throat, but she doesn't cower, doesn't claw at my fingers. And I lean over to lick her bloodied skin before I rip her shirt to pieces and take her nipple into my mouth, sucking hard.

She moans wildly, so I dip my free hand between her legs, her thighs drenched from my kisses. "So fucking wet for me. God, I want to devour this pussy whole."

I drag her away from the wall and set her down on the bed right beside Nathan.

He takes the opportunity to grab her face and kiss her on the lips while I go back to my closet and fish out all the stuff I'll need.

"What's that?" she asks when I return with a bag full of stuff, which I dump out onto the floor.

"Wow, is that a strap-on?" Her eyes widen.

"You didn't think Nathan was the only one with toys, did you?" I wink as I fish the dildo used in the strap-on off the floor and rub it along her pussy, right through the fabric of her panties. "I was actually planning on using this on your ass while I fucked your pussy. But looks like I won't need it with these boys around to plug all your holes."

She mewls when I rip her panties apart with one hand and slide the dildo across her wet slit.

"You're already so fucking wet, little kitty ..." I groan as I slowly shove the dildo into her. "You're just waiting to be fucked like a good little slut, aren't you?"

She nods as her eyes close from all the sensations, so I bury the dildo in deep.

Then I go to my knees in front of her.

"What are you doing?" she asks.

I split open her knees, pushing myself between them. "Having a taste of this pussy that belongs to me."

# 66

## LANA

"Us," Nathan says as he waltzes to the cabinet and takes out something.

He stands in front of me, an actual leather whip in his hands.

My eyes widen at the sight of the five strands, and my heart palpitates.

Until he places it in my hands and sinks to his knees too.

"I once told you I would let you whip me ... now do it. Punish me."

I inhale a sharp breath. Not just from Kai's tongue still swirling around but also from Nathan's commitment. "But you're still healing."

He plants a finger onto my lips while he parts my legs even farther, placing himself beside Kai between my legs.

"Let me beg this pussy for forgiveness too," he groans, leaning in to lick me too. "Now give me all you've got."

My fingers tighten around the whip, and I strike his back.

He hisses from the pain, arching his back, but still kisses my pussy.

I'm torn between the pleasure I'm receiving and the pain I'm dishing out.

"I don't want to hu—"

"Hit. Me." His stern eyes pull me over the edge.

*WHACK!*

The whip comes down again, and he groans against my pussy, his tongue still swiveling back and forth like he refuses to give up, despite the whip cracking open the skin on his shoulder.

Kai's tongue still swirls around as he shoves the dildo in with every strike I apply to Nathan's back, almost encouraging me to push on.

"Let it all out," Kai says.

I hit him again, pouring all my fury over what happened to me into these strikes.

*WHACK! WHACK!*

I strike Nathan again and again, creating a pattern on his back. And I don't stop until I'm screaming and crying with pleasure at the same time. Until his entire back is covered with red marks, a testament to my anger, now belonging to him.

He's made me wield my bottled up rage and turn it into something deliciously dark and so incredibly powerful.

"Good girl," he murmurs against my skin.

The praise makes me drop the whip, and I grasp his face and bring my lips to his, claiming his mouth like he claimed mine.

And I couldn't be more grateful than I am right now.

"Thank you," I whisper between kisses.

He licks the seam of my lips and whispers back, "Now you know why we're one and the same. Sadists with an unquenchable thirst."

I nod even though I would've cussed him out weeks ago.

But that version of me saw a girl in the mirror she didn't recognize, one she loathed and hated with every fiber of her being just because she was vicious.

But these boys have made me see the beauty behind this wretched soul.

Made me fall in love with the wicked sinner I am.

So I push his head back down between my legs and moan, "Now lick like a good boy."

\*\*\*

# KAI

My tongue rolls around that swollen clit of hers, applying ample pressure while I pause only to blow hot air against her sensitive spot. Nathan and I both alternate our tongue strokes to drive her mad, all while I keep dipping the dildo in and out of her.

"Fuck, this is hot," Milo groans behind us.

"Come help us then," Nathan mutters between kisses.

"Fuck, yes," she moans, running her fingers through Nathan's hair. "Milo. Come here."

"Yes, my queen," he says like a puppy dog, kneeling on the bed beside her.

"Kiss me like it's your last chan—"

She can't even finish her sentence before he grabs her face and plants his lips onto hers, making her moans his. Her hand immediately reaches for his hard-on, and she begins to stroke it right through the fabric of his pants.

I swivel my tongue around her clit while Nathan licks her sensitive slit around the dildo, driving her wild with lust.

"F-fuck," she mutters between the dirty kisses she exchanges with Milo.

When I look up, he bites her lip and tugs at it with his teeth, drawing in until our eyes connect. And fuck me, even *my* cock throbs.

She zips him down and jerks him off right in front of me, driving me wild too, because I can already imagine those fingers curling around my shaft instead of his. My tongue increases the pace at the mere thought.

"Don't stop," she murmurs at all of us.

I swivel back and forth across her pussy, thrusting the dildo in and out, coating it with her juices.

"Yes, come for us," Nathan says.

"No." She suddenly closes her legs, pushing us back. An evil smirk on her face follows. "You haven't earned it yet." She grabs Milo's neck and pushes him down too. "You all need to grovel for forgiveness, remember? On your fucking knees."

He goes down onto the floor with us, and now we're all here, clutching her legs, waiting for her.

"Kiss."

I frown. "What? This?" I lean in to press a kiss to her thigh, but she pushes me back again.

"No ... You want to prove your love? Then kiss."

"Kiss ... him?" Nathan mutters, looking at me.

"Yes. Kiss each other."

My jaw drops as I look at the two of them.

"I kissed all of you, too. You've already kissed each other through me. Now I want to see you do it in front of me."

"Wow," Milo mutters, excited. "I'm ready."

"I'm not," I say. "I'm not—"

"Have you tried?" She raises a brow.

"No," I retort.

"Then how do you know?"

I turn to look at Nathan who just stares at me all flustered, and fuck me, I don't know what to do.

"You want to make up with me? Then kiss."

"That's it?" Milo muses, biting his bottom lip as he looks me up and down. "I'll do it."

But she keeps her eyes locked on me, tempting me with that feverish look of hers.

Guess I'll have to fuck that audacity out of her after this.

"Go on, then ... do it." She leans in, licking her lips as she gazes at each one of us. "Or are you afraid?"

*Me? Afraid? Fuck no.*

"Is that a dare?" I ask, grinding my teeth because she's challenging me.

"You can't do it, can you?" she quips.

Fuck that. Now she's gone and done it.

I grab Nathan's face and kiss him right on the lips.

"Whooo!" Milo yells in shock.

The kiss only lasts a few seconds, but it's enough to let me taste her on his lips. When our mouths unlatch, he looks at me all flustered and shit, his cheeks reddening with every passing second. When my eyes lower, I clearly spot a hard-on in his pants.

Even Lana's looking at it, and Milo's gone real quiet.

And then my cock begins to throb too.
Oh fuck.

# 67

NATHAN

I can't believe it.

Kai's lips were just on mine.

And he didn't even gag.

*Am I dreaming?*

My whole face is turning beet red, and I can't look away from those goddamn lips, not even if I forced myself to.

Instinct suddenly takes over as I smash my lips back onto his, desperate for another taste of whatever the fuck that was. I don't care if he pushes me away, and I don't care if he doesn't want it. Just this once, I want to feel what it was he wanted to give to me for her.

But he doesn't push me away, doesn't spit in disgust as I part his lips with mine and let my tongue roam freely across before I dive in.

And our tongues swirl around each other as I probe inside, consumed by the idea of having him too.

*Could all three of them be mine?*

I groan, hungry for more, but he immediately pulls back and blinks a couple of times, staring at me like he doesn't know what's happening.

Suddenly, Lana sinks to the floor with us, the dildo flopping out of her as she grips his face and kisses him right in front of me. The sight is so fucking hot, my cock bobs up and down in response, but then she turns around and kisses me too.

Her tongue hastily curls around mine, desperate for attention, and I can taste all of us on her like a perfect blend of possessive love.

Milo sinks to the floor beside her, and she unlatches her lips only to capture his instead. I lean in closer, gripping her body so I can intervene and kiss her at the same time, our mouths colliding in a three-way before Kai says, "Fuck it."

And he dives in too, kissing all of us, our tongues diving into each other's mouths with greed and a hunger that's never been satiated before.

In my delirium, my hand dives down between her legs, and I coat my fingers with her juices as I rub her, kissing her, Milo, and Kai. But when Kai unzips, I reach for his cock instead.

He flexes and freezes from my touch but doesn't pull back as I rub her juices all over him.

"Fuck," Lana moans as her eyes look down.

"I want you so badly," I murmur into her mouth. "All of you."

Milo reaches for my pants, unzipping me before taking out my dick too.

"Yes, stroke my cock," I groan, watching him jerk me off while Kai's shaft bobs up and down against my fingers.

"Oh fuck," Kai groans, almost thrusting into my hand.

Maybe, just fucking maybe, Lana wasn't the only one hiding something.

I smash my lips onto his, not giving a shit about the consequences or the fact that he always told us he wasn't interested. Because this hard dick sure tells a different story, and I'm all here for it.

"Go on then, make her come," I whisper into his mouth.

He grabs the dildo and shoves it into her pussy, thrusting it in at the same pace as my hand jerking him off. She moans loudly, her eyes connecting with us one after the other until her body quakes with desire. And I can see her fall apart right in front of me.

Her body is covered in red splotches as Milo leaves hickeys all over, and I'm overwhelmed by the desire to come all over his hand.

*Not so fast, not so fast.*

"I can't hold it," I groan.

"Not yet," Lana says after she's come down from the high. "Milo. Lick."

He immediately lets go of me and bends over to eagerly lick her pussy. I writhe in agony from blue balls while Kai grows closer to the edge.

Suddenly, he grabs my face and kisses me again, harder and faster than the previous time, almost as if he's consumed with lust while thrusting that dildo into her.

I grow meek in his hands, his tongue prying open a side of me I thought no longer existed. Because fuck me, I am a sadistic bastard who enjoys dominating people, but for him, I'd go to my knees.

When he unlatches, he looks into my eyes with intent, searching for answers I can't give him.

Suddenly, he pulls away and grabs Lana's body, lifting her back onto the bed.

"Lie on the bed and lick her," he tells me.

I swallow and do what he says.

"You too," he barks at Milo.

But as I perch myself on top and dip my tongue into her, he pulls out the dildo and thrusts into her pussy instead. Watching him bore into her pussy while both Milo and I lick her has got to be the hottest thing we ever did together. It probably beats even murder.

*** 

# MILO

I lick her pussy fervently, applying ample pressure to her clit while Kai fucks her raw. His face is pure feral rage, an unending lust to drive into her and mark her as his, and I adore every second of watching both her and him knot together as they build into ecstasy.

I glance at Nathan who's kissing and lapping her up all the same, hungry for more, desperate for Kai to release himself inside her.

"Look at me," he groans. "All of you."

We obey his command like it comes naturally.

"Whose pussy is this?" he growls at her.

"Yours," Lana says, and we follow her lead.

He thrusts into her like he can't get enough. "*Mine*. Forever fucking *mine*."

"Fuck!" she yelps as he spears her.

"Yes, come all over my cock," he growls, gripping her thighs while he buries himself to the hilt inside her.

Her eyes roll into the back of her head, and it's the most amazing thing to watch, knowing we're causing all these delicious orgasms.

"Oh fuck, I'm coming too," Kai groans, and he pulls out.

Just in time for me and Nathan to catch his cum with our tongues, lapping up all the juices that spurt out of him.

"Fuck, you taste delicious," Nathan murmurs, licking his lips.

Kai grips his hair and tilts his head up. "You're next."

*Wait, what?*

Nathan's eyes widen and so do mine.

Kai gets off her, his dick still hard and bobbing up and down, and he throws the strap-on in front of her feet.

"You like punishment, don't you?" he asks me.

I nod gleefully.

"Spread your ass for her then," he says.

I swallow and crawl into the bed, leaning down onto the pillow.

"I've never used this before," Lana mutters as she picks it up and puts it on.

"Here." Kai puts the dildo inside for her, his fingers sliding past her swollen clit to make her all flushed again. "Now fuck all of your rage out into him just like Nathan does."

"Wait, but that's my job," Nathan says as he gets up.

But Kai grabs his shoulders and forces him down onto the bed so he faces me.

*Wait, is he going to ...*

Kai rips down what's left of Nathan's pants in one go.

*Holy shit.*

Kai's going to fuck him.

"What?" Nathan turns his head, but Kai pushes him forward until our lips almost touch.

"Stay down and take it."

He perches himself behind him and pushes the tip inside.

"Fuck!" Nathan groans as Kai slowly dips in, using her wetness as lube.

I brace myself against the mattress as Lana perches herself behind me. After she squirts on the lube, I can feel her entering me so slowly I bite down into the fabric. "Fuck, I need it."

She pushes in even farther until it begins to hurt real good.

"Oh my God," Nathan grunts, scrunching up the blanket. "You never told me it feels this good."

"You hurt my little kitty ... so now you'll take all the pain you deserve," Kai growls, burying himself to the hilt inside Nathan.

And from the look on his face, he's completely overtaken by lust. "FUCK!"

At the height of it, I lean forward and kiss him hard, drinking in the pain I adore so much.

"That's it, ride him, Lana," Kai growls at her, and she goes to town on me, slapping my ass.

"Fuck, this feels good," she murmurs.

"Push the button on the bottom of the dildo," Kai says.

It takes her a while to find it, but when she does, I almost come right then and there.

"Oh God, I can feel the vibrations too," she yelps, thrusting into me.

"Double the pleasure, double the fun," Kai says, slapping Nathan's ass. "Now ride me."

Nathan backs up into him, shivering with delight. "I can feel all of your piercings."

Kai leans over to kiss his lips. "Doesn't it feel good?"

The sound of dicks clapping against asses, along with moans, fills the room with so much noise I'm worried someone might come check on us. Sweat drops roll down my back as the pressure begins to build.

And I can feel Lana shiver up against me, her whole body quaking with the mounting orgasm that's about to unleash.

"Fuck," she murmurs, putting her whole weight behind thrusting as she rubs herself against the vibrations. "I just came again."

"Oh God, what is this? Why is my cock throbbing?" Nathan moans, looking over his shoulder at Kai. "Am I ...?"

Kai thrusts in so hard Nathan actually whimpers. I've never heard him whimper in my life.

And when I look underneath him, I see cum spurting out of his dick. *He's had a prostate orgasm, oh my God.*

I'm turned on so much I can't stop my own dick from releasing. He smashes his lips onto mine, and we both come together, rolling our tongues around each other in a match of who can moan the loudest.

I've only ever had him at his darkest, but this is a whole other side of him. And I don't think once was enough now that I've seen what it does to him.

# 68

## KAI

When I'm about to combust again, I pull out of him and lick the salty droplets of sweat off his body. I push him over until he's facing me, and I take a good look at his spent cock before my gaze settles on his flushed face. "You came from me."

"I ..." he mutters. "I've never had that happen before."

"You've never been fucked before?"

He shakes his head. "I do the fucking."

"Not with me, you don't," I say.

I don't know what's gotten into me. One moment, I'm dead set on pleasing my girl, and the next, I'm kissing Nathan. A guy. Fucking him like I want him too.

And the strangest part is ... maybe I do.

Maybe I do want them both.

He blushes as my hand caresses his cheek. "I thought you weren't—"

"Guess there's a first for everything." Lana interjects, giggling.

She pulls out of Milo, who mewls and falls down onto the bed, curling up to Nathan to peck him on the cheeks.

And I lean in to give him another kiss just because I can, because I want to, because why the fuck not?

Maybe I'm not as straight as I thought I was.

"Fuck," he whispers.

"What?"

"I've fantasized about it, but I never thought it'd be this sexy."

I laugh as I crawl off him with a half-hard dick and grab his hand, pulling him up too. "C'mon. Time to make it even sexier."

Lana takes off the strap and gets off the bed, so I swiftly grab her and throw her over my shoulder.

She squeals. "Hey! What are you doing?"

"You gave us our punishment," I say, slapping her ass so hard she squeals again. "Now it's time for yours."

"What? I didn't do anything!" she huffs as I take her across the corridor half naked, but I don't give a fuck that everyone can see us.

"You accused us of something we didn't do, then got yourself into big fucking trouble because of it," I growl as I carry her into Nathan's room.

The boys follow inside, and Milo locks the door as I put her onto the floor while Nathan grabs the stockade.

She grumbles, "Fine. I did. I'm sorry."

"Too late," I growl as I grasp her wrists and pin them to the stockade. "This slutty body is going to pay the price now."

I push her head down before sealing her inside.

It's our turn to play.

\*\*\*

## LANA

"What?" I gasp as he puts on the locks so I can't get out.

Fuck. I hadn't anticipated this after just having fun fucking Milo. First, Kai has his bi-awakening, and now they put me in an actual fucking stockade to have their way with me.

"Grab the lube," Kai barks at Nathan, who immediately does what he asks. "We're going to give her a taste of her own medicine."

He approaches me and tips up my chin as far as possible. "You liked fucking him a little too much, didn't you?"

When I don't answer, he forces my lips open and spits inside.

"Answer me."

I lick my lips. "Yes."

He smiles. "Good ... you'll enjoy this even more."

Kai walks to my back and leans over behind me, licking me. Just one lick is enough to send me into the next plane.

"So fucking wet." He snaps his fingers at Milo. "Get me a plug."

I try to look, but it's impossible with these restraints.

I hear something squirting and then feel something cold and hard push into my ass.

I gasp and grind my teeth. "Fuck!"

"You can take it. You've taken my big cock, so you can easily take this plug, kitty," he says, pushing it until it's all the way inside.

"And now you'll take my cock along with it too," he says.

"What?" I yelp, but before I know it, he's already pushed into my pussy, slowly dipping in deeper, stretching me to the limit.

Nathan grabs the whip and stands before me, then parts my lips with his thumb. "My cock isn't satiated yet, little slut. Are you going to fix that?"

I almost want to bite him for that comment, but I'll behave. For now.

Especially with that whip looming in my face.

He slowly dips into my mouth, coating my tongue with his juices. I can still taste the salty cum from before as he pushes in deeper. But it's hard to even focus with so many things going on all at once.

"That's it," he moans. "Lick it all off."

*WHACK!*

When the whip comes down onto my back, I cry out in both agony and bliss. "Remember this pain," he tells me, and he strikes again. "Feel it. Let it own your soul."

*WHACK!*

I cry out with the next hit. "Why?"

"Because you need to feel the pain first before you can dish it out."

He strikes me again, and I let the wave of pain wash over me, adding to the pleasure of feeling him slip deeper into my throat.

Milo comes to stand beside him, gleefully watching over his shoulder. But then Nathan steps aside and pushes him forward. "You too."

I spit. "Wait, both?"

*WHACK!*

Kai slaps my ass so hard I squeal.

"I gave you a way out. You didn't take it. So now you'll be a good little fucking kitty and let us stretch your mouth, pussy, and ass. Understood?"

Fuck. That made the wetness practically drip out of me.

I nod and part my lips again, and both boys immediately dip their cocks into my mouth. It's so much I can barely take it, and my eyes begin to water when they try to push farther.

"See how good you take all of our cocks?" Kai groans, thrusting in to the base. "That's my little kitty, always ready to accept everything we give her like a good little whore."

I'm lost in ecstasy, my brain overridden by lust, and I don't even care.

I want nothing more than these boys—these boys who drive me crazy and have me obsessed. Kai's plowing into me, the plug adding extra pressure to an already pleasurable experience, and my whole body begins to zing.

When Milo hesitates, Nathan whips him instead, and he mewls with arousal.

"Fuck her mouth," Nathan orders.

Milo goes in even deeper despite the resistance from my teeth.

"Fuck, rub your dick against mine, just like that," Nathan groans, and he whips him again and again until his skin becomes red and his moans come out in yelps.

But Milo never stops going deeper, and with each strike, he throbs inside me.

With one hand, Nathan grips Milo's chin and French-kisses him right in front of me, all while they're both still inside my mouth.

"Fill her up, boys," Kai says, burying himself inside me.

Nathan and Milo come in sync as their shafts rub against each other while swiveling across my tongue, and I practically choke on all the cum they shoot into the back of my throat.

"Don't swallow. Hold it," Nathan orders.

Kai suddenly pulls out of me and marches to the front, waving Nathan and Milo to step aside. He tips open my mouth only to bury himself inside too.

"That's it, kitty. Drown in us."

He roars out loud as he jets into me, filling up my throat with a mixture of the three of them, all salty and sticky in a different way.

And with his dick still lodged in my throat, he groans, "Now swallow."

When I do, his eyes practically roll into the back of his head.

I gasp and heave as he pulls out again, but then he bends over to kiss me so passionately I melt into the restraints that hold me down.

No man has ever been able to subdue me and chain me down, heart and soul.

But these boys ... they aren't just any men at all.

They're devils in disguise, evil incarnate, demons that have stolen my soul.

And they are *mine*.

"Now what do you say we leave her here until our cocks are hard again?" Kai muses.

"What?" I bark, thrashing against the stockade. "You wouldn't!"

He grins.

*POP!*

The lock comes undone.

"You're right. But I do like you when you hate me so damn much."

"God, I hate you all so damn much," I mutter as he lifts the stockade to free me.

He grips my cheeks and makes me look at him. "Say that again."

"I hate—"

He smashes his lips onto mine, stealing my breath, even if just for a second.

"Now say it again," he mutters.

"I ha—"

Another kiss has me moaning in response.

"You're not even trying," he whispers.

"I—"

"Now say what you really mean," he says.

"I ... love you," I mutter, and I almost hate that I have to admit that, but I know it's the truth. "All of you."

Kai rewards me with another kiss, placing them all over the corners of my mouth so gently I almost melt away right then and there. He steps aside for a moment, only so Nathan and Milo can kiss me too, their mouths setting my heart ablaze.

"I've never not wanted to bow beneath your feet," Milo hums, lowering himself so he can kiss my hands.

"Love," Nathan groans. "Do you understand what you've done when you said those words out loud, kitty?"

When I nod, he lifts me from the floor and sets me in the shower, all three boys joining me.

"You belong to us. And not even the devil himself will take you from us." Kai grips my chin while Milo turns on the shower. "You're ours from now until forever. Yes?"

I nod as the water rushes over our bodies, and I'm overtaken by their commanding smiles, forcing me to submit my heart.

I used to be so goddamn angry they'd attempt to take it.

But now all I feel is a rush of fear ... fear for the excitement my future holds.

"You're not scared of soap like an actual kitty, are you?" Nathan muses.

When I shake my head, Milo grabs a loofah and empties a bottle of soap onto it. "Lean back and relax while we clean, your royal highness."

# 69

## LANA

**A few days later**

"You called?" I close the door to my father's office.

His eyes immediately home in on the wound on my arm, so I rub it with my hand to try to hide it.

"You're hurt," he says.

"It was just a fall. No biggie."

He steps away from his desk. "How are you doing?"

I frown, not knowing how to answer. "Good, I guess."

"I saw the picture."

*Oh God.*

"It was an accident," I say, mortified. "I—"

"If those three boys hurt you, tell me now, and I will end them." He grips my face tightly. "No expulsion. No trial. Death."

His words resonate in my soul. I've never heard him say he'd actually murder someone out loud, and it makes me admire him even more.

"No," I say, shaking my head. "They didn't. It was a private picture that accidentally got shared."

"Who else has seen it?"

"Probably the entire school," I say, biting my lip.

He closes his eyes and rubs them. "It's okay. We'll fix this."

"The boys are already telling everyone it was a staged scene at an escape room and that none of it was real."

"Clever." He frowns. "Wait. *The boys?*" His eyes flash with concern. "So it was real? You are having sex with these boys?"

My cheeks heat as I blush. Admitting this to my father is a big deal to me.

"But what about Jason?"

"He wasn't there for me when I needed him, so I ended it, and then he tried to hurt me," I explain.

His nostrils flare. "I will have him expelled."

I shake my head. "That'll only anger his parents, and I don't want anyone else coming for Spine Ridge or the Rivera family. Let him stay, and I'll ignore him as best as I can. He's out of the Skull & Serpents anyway."

My father caresses my cheek with his thumb. "I just want to protect my little girl."

Tears well up in my eyes. "I know."

"That picture was not easy to see," he says.

I'm embarrassed, but maybe I'll survive this.

"I'm sorry." I avert my eyes. "I didn't want it to end up in the wrong hands, let alone yours. I never wanted you to see me like that."

"What about that body? Is that—"

I inhale sharply. "That was a guy who hurt young girls. Consistently. And I couldn't let it slide."

My father's eyes twitch with curiosity.

"Maria?"

An assistant steps in.

"Bring in Nathan, Kai, and Milo."

My eyes widen. "You already brought them here?"

"You think I haven't watched you while you were here on these campus grounds?" He smiles. "You underestimate your own father's obsessive need to keep track of the dangers his kids put themselves in."

I snort and hide my laughter behind my hand.

Of course, he'd be just as deranged as me.

A knock on the door follows, and in step all three boys ... along with my brother.

The assistant peers over their shoulders and says, "Your son is here too."

"Felix?" I mutter as they all step inside. "What are you doing here?"

"Dad asked me to come." He closes the door behind him. "What's this about? Why are they here too?"

"I'd wanted to ask if you knew anything about that picture." He eyes all of the boys as his hands dive into his pockets. "I don't want any of you hiding things from me."

Felix leans back against the wood with his arms crossed. "I'm not hiding anything."

"And you ..." My father narrows his eyes at Kai, Nathan, and Milo. "You took a picture of my daughter in a precarious position and shared it with the world?"

"It was a mistake," Nathan mutters.

"An accident," Kai adds. "It wasn't on purpose."

"Right. But it did happen."

"I'm sorry, it's my fault," Nathan says. "I was careless."

"Yes, you were."

*CLICK!*

The noise alerts me.

*He's got a gun.*

I immediately step in front of the three boys, unafraid of the bullets he's threatening them with. "Don't."

"Lana!" Felix growls. "Don't do it!"

"Tell me why you choose to protect them," my father grits, incensed.

Seconds feel like hours.

"Because I love them!" I've never felt something so fiercely in my heart.

But now that it's finally out in the open, I feel relieved.

"And we love her," Kai says, stepping forward to grasp my hand and lace his fingers through mine. "And if you want to kill me for loving your daughter, then fucking kill me now because I will never, *ever*, stop loving her harder than the day before."

My heart almost jumps from my chest because of his unabashed devotion.

"I'll take a bullet for you. I already did so once, and I'd do it again and again," Nathan says, stepping up to grasp my other hand. "I'm the one responsible. Kill me if you must."

"No," Milo says, stepping in front of all of us. "I will not let you hurt the people I love."

My father's jaw tenses, but his body relaxes just a little bit. "*Love* ..."

"Yes. Do you remember what that felt like?" I ask.

His lip rises in disgust. "No. I've not felt the love of a woman or for a woman since your mother destroyed it with her bare hands."

The pause that follows feels like it lasts an eternity.

*CLICK!*

The gun's safety is put back on, the sound making me feel like I can breathe again.

He puts his gun away. "But I love my kids, and I'd do anything to protect you." Tears well up in my eyes as he approaches. "If you still want these boys, despite the fact they hurt you ... then I'll accept your choice."

My father places a hand on Milo's shoulder. "You're a brave guy."

"Thanks," he gulps.

"That body in that picture, did you clean it up?" he asks like it's no big deal.

The boys all nod in silence, all stupefied by how easy he makes it sound.

"Good."

"Wait, you're not mad?" Nathan asks.

"Of course, I'm mad. But that doesn't stop the killings because if it did, you wouldn't be doing it in the first place," he retorts.

"I thought you summoned us here to expel us," Milo mutters.

"I was going to kill you, actually."

Milo's face turns ghostly white.

"But seeing as how that would upset my little girl, I opted not to," he muses like it's the most normal thing on earth.

"How many more have you killed?" he asks.

"Plenty," Kai responds. "More than I can count on two hands."

"And was she there?"

I blush again. "That kill was actually mine. Along with a bunch of others."

He sighs softly, shaking his head, and rubs his forehead with his fingers. "I should've known it wouldn't skip a generation."

"Wait ... What?" Felix mutters. "You knew? All this time? And you didn't say anything?"

"You think I don't know what you're both capable of?" my father retorts, tilting his head. "You're my flesh and blood. I *know* that insatiable hunger. Why do you think I told you to stop fighting? I knew you two would be dragged to that dark side if you didn't."

"Wow," Milo mutters, snorting. "This is a turn of events."

"Dad," I mutter. "I ..."

"You don't have to explain yourself."

He places his hand on my shoulder, and memories flash through my mind like a movie running at two-hundred times the normal pace. My tiny self, searching for the bathroom, finding a light on in my brother's room, seeing my mother in his bed ...

The gun from the cabinet ... and a firm hand on my shoulder.

A sharp breath follows.

"Dad ..."

"What is it?" Dad says.

Tears well up in my eyes. "You didn't kill Mother, did you?"

I look up into his eyes, which yield to my gaze like only a father's eyes would when he's tried so hard to protect his daughter from reality.

My lips part. "I did, didn't I?"

This truth has haunted my soul for years.

It takes him a few seconds to reply. "Yes."

His face contorts with a pain unlike any other, and he pulls me away from the boys only to hug me so tightly all the waterworks begin to flow.

"I'm sorry," I say.

"Don't. Don't apologize." His hand wraps firmly around my hair, stroking me. "You have nothing to be sorry for. You did the right thing."

"I killed her," I say.

Felix stands in the corner, silently watching us, but the pained look in his eyes makes me cry even harder.

"You saw something unforgivable, and when I found you in his room with that gun, I took it from you."

"You told me you were the one who shot her," I murmur against his chest.

"I didn't want you to live with that guilt," he says. "So I lied to shield you from the truth."

"Lana ..." Felix murmurs, and he approaches, wrapping his arms around us too. "I'm sorry, I didn't know."

I wail loudly, crying out the tears I've kept buried deep down with those memories for so long.

"All those nightmares," I whisper. "They were true. I'm a monster."

"You're not a monster," Felix responds. "You saved me."

My father leans back and cups my face, forcing me to look at him. "You are loyal. Honest. Smart. Ruthless. And your heart is full of so much love. You are *my* daughter. And I am proud of you."

More tears well up in my eyes, but they're not tears of despair but tears of pride and joy. And we hug again, harder than we ever have before.

"Well, I don't think I've ever seen a more loving family than this," Milo says, chuckling as he blinks away a few tears of his own.

"I'm jealous," Nathan says.

"Hey, we make a pretty good family," Kai replies, winking. "But it's not complete without her."

I turn to look at them and smile at my dad, waiting for him to nod before joining Kai, Nathan, and Milo and embracing them too.

"Are you okay?" Milo asks.

I nod. "Yeah. It was heavy. But I'm glad it's finally out of my system."

"You really killed your own mother, huh?" Kai says. "Savage. I like it."

I snort and playfully punch him in the shoulder.

"So you're gonna live with them now?" Felix asks.

"If it's okay with Dad," I respond, looking at my father, who just shrugs.

"The sororities and fraternities are normally separated ... but I don't see why I couldn't make an exception for my own daughter." He winks. "As long as you don't go screaming it off the roofs so other students come begging me for the same privilege."

I laugh. "I won't. Promise."

"And I need you to keep your grades up," he adds, raising a brow. "No more slacking off. You want to go on a killing spree? Fine, but if you start to fail, you answer to me."

"Okay, I get it," I reply.

"No worries, sir. We'll keep her on track," Nathan says, saluting him.

"I doubt you will," my father responds.

Kai laughs and pats a defeated Nathan on the back. "You tried."

"I'll make sure you keep your word, don't worry," Felix says, throwing them a warning look.

"Oh, I'm so scared," Milo says, winking, which makes Felix growl out loud.

"All right, out of my office. All of you," my father says with a sigh. "I've got work to do and messes to clean up."

When we all exit the door, he adds, "Oh, and don't kill anyone here at school, please. For your own sakes."

"Not even them?" Felix says, pointing at Kai, Nathan, and Milo with his thumb.

Kai's eyes become half-mast. "You wouldn't stand a chance."

"Wanna bet on that?"

"Boys ..." I sigh out loud. "I thought we were over this."

"You're still my little sister." Felix grabs me and rubs my hair with his fist just like he used to, messing up my look. "Didn't I tell you not to talk to those fuckers?"

"Too late," Kai scoffs, snorting after.

"Yeah, our dicks have already been in there. We're way past the talking stage," Nathan muses, watching Felix combust with rage.

I physically have to stop him from acting out, and the boys laugh in unison.

"You motherf—"

I plant a finger onto Felix's lips. "Ah. Zip it. I don't want to hear it."

"But—"

I throw him a stern look, just like our dad just did.

"I get it. You're my big bro. You wanna protect me." I glance at Kai, Milo, and Nathan over my shoulder. "But I have them too now. So you'll just need to get along for me. Okay?"

His eyes twitch with annoyance, and he folds his arms. Then he sighs out loud. "Fine."

I hug him tight. "Thank you."

"Yeah, yeah. Go. Before I change my mind," he says, pushing me in their direction.

And the boys welcome me with open arms, kissing me on the cheek right in front of the entire damn school.

And you know what?

I don't give a care in the world.

# Epilogue

⟨⟨⟨

## NATHAN

**Months later**

"Okay, now close your eyes."

I sigh and roll my eyes at Lana.

"C'mon," she eggs me on from next to me.

I do what she says, and she wraps a red ribbon around my eyes. "Just to be sure."

"What is this all about?" I ask as the car door next to me opens.

"You'll see," Kai responds, holding out his hand.

I take his hand, and he hoists me out of the car while Lana scoots out behind me.

Milo closes the door. "Lead the way."

"Am I the only one blindfolded?" I ask.

"Shhhh, don't ask so many questions," Milo responds. "You'll ruin the secret."

"What secret?" I ask, nearly tripping over a ledge.

"Whoa, be careful," Lana mutters.

"I've got him," Kai says.

They guide me in somewhere. I can hear a door creaking, and when my feet land on wood, I tap the floor a few times.

"Okay, can we cut the crap now," I growl, getting impatient.

"Nathan?"

Rory's voice makes me rip the blindfold off immediately.

She's standing in the middle of a furnished living room, in a place I don't recognize, with a flower in her hands.

I run to her and go to my knees to hug her tight. "I missed you."

"I plucked this for you," she says, holding out the flower to me.

"For me?" I smile, and she nods. "You're too sweet, Ro."

She giggles as I hug her again, then I turn my gaze toward Kai, Milo, and Lana, who stare at me with mischievous looks. "What is this place?"

"Yours," Kai says.

I frown as I get up, confused by what he means.

"Well, hers too, technically," Milo muses, raising his brow.

"What do you mean yours?"

Lana dangles a key in her hands. "This house belongs to you and Ro now."

My eyes widen as they home in on the key, my whole body feeling numb to the core.

She steps forward and grabs my hand, tucking the key inside.

"But ... how?" I mutter in disbelief.

"Let's just say we all saved up some cash," Kai answers, winking.

"We thought you and your sister deserved a safe spot after everything you've been through," Milo adds, smiling gently.

"Are you all for real?" I mutter.

Lana laughs. "As real as can be."

I'm overwhelmed by pure gratitude, and I jump into Lana's arms, hugging her so tightly she can barely breathe. "Come here, all of you," I tell the boys, and they come to hug us too, my arms wrapping around all three of them.

Ro's little hands curl around my thighs as she mutters, "Me too."

"Aw," Lana murmurs.

"Thank you," I mutter, blinking away the tears. "Thank you all so much."

"We just want the best for you," Kai says.

"Is this our home now?" Ro asks, and I let go of everyone else to answer her.

But Lana already beats me to it. "Yep. And your room is upstairs to the left, so go check it out."

She squeals and jumps up and down before she runs up the steps.

"Don't fall!" I yell.

Someone knocks on the front door, distracting me from Ro, and I go to open it.

A lady with a hat stands on the doorstep, a big smile adorning her face.

"Who are you?" I mutter in confusion.

"Ro's nanny!" Milo muses, welcoming the woman inside. "Come in, come in."

"Nanny?" I parrot.

"Who else will take care of her while you're studying?" Lana winks.

Kai throws his arm around my shoulders. "You didn't think we'd let you out of the Phantom Society, did you? Once a Phantom, always a Phantom."

"Where is the little girl?" the nanny asks. "I've been told we're all going to go out for—"

"Ice cream!" Milo interjects.

"What?" I'm too flabbergasted to speak.

He pats me on the back and says, "It's what you promised her, remember?"

A devious grin spreads on my lips, and I grab his face and kiss him on the lips. "Perfect."

I march to Lana and Kai and grab their faces, kissing them too. I don't care that the nanny is watching us and practically fainting at the sight. "Good heavens."

"Thank you both," I tell them.

Lana chuckles. "Don't scare the nanny on her first day."

"EEEK! There's a unicorn!" Ro screams from the top of the stairs.

I narrow my eyes at Milo. "Don't look at me. Kai's the one who dragged it all the way here."

"You shouldn't have," I say.

"No, I shouldn't. But I did." Kai winks. "Now go get Ro."

"Ro! Come downstairs!"

"But I wanna play here!" she squeals back.

I put on my tempting voice. "How about some ice cream?"

Her curious face peeks around the corner. "Can I have strawberry?"

I nod. "As many scoops as you can count."

The biggest smile forms on her lips before she rushes down the stairs. "Yippee!"

\*\*\*

## LANA

**Weeks later**

I run through Priory Forest, the wind chasing after me as I bolt from tree to tree, firmly clutching the knife. Snowflakes fall all around me, but the cold only spurs me to run faster. The woman running away from me loses one of her shoes halfway across the small stream in the middle of the clearing, but she keeps going, and it fires up the adrenaline coursing through my veins.

*THWACK!*

A knife flies right past my ears, brushing along my skin before it lodges into the tree right next to me.

I look behind me to see a masked guy licking his lips. "Not this time, Lana!"

Those blond hairs waving in the wind give him away, and I wink through my kitty mask before I continue my hunt.

The woman screams as I catch up with her.

Nathan's on my heels, but before he can get close, I've jabbed my knife straight into her heart.

"Please ..." she murmurs.

"That's what your victims said too when they begged you not to sell them to the Bones Brotherhood. Too fucking late."

I twist the knife around, blood spurting out all over me.

"Bad kitty," Nathan groans as he comes up behind me. "Killing our prey already?"

"I told you I'd win," I muse, ripping the knife out of her body before I adjust the red ribbon in my hair.

He tilts his head. "And I think we told you what would happen if you attempted to steal this one too." He licks his lips, and I can feel the terror sink into my heart.

The kind of terror that makes my pussy throb and my brain spring to life.

More rustling up ahead makes me turn my head. A redheaded masked guy appears from behind a tree, flicking his nunchucks around like a toy. "You messed with our kill again ... tsk. I guess you'll never learn."

"Then we'll have to teach her." A low, smoky voice from atop the hill makes me spin on my heels. My heart beats in my throat when Kai runs his fingers through his dark hair and puts on his mask again. "The hard way."

A devilish smile meets mine, my whole body zinging at the thought of another chase.

But instead of the predator, I now become the prey.

Willingly.

"If I catch your ribbon, your body will be mine."

Kai lifts his fingers, sporting a rope in his other hand. And I'm already excited at the thought of them tying me to a tree and having their way with me.

*But first ...*

"Three."

One finger goes down.

"Two."

I brace myself against the soil.

"One."

His voice sets me free.

"Run."

# Thank you for Reading!

**Thank you so much for reading Evil Boys. Please leave a review if you enjoyed!**

Make sure to also read Sick Boys, Penelope, Felix, Dylan, and Alistair's story, also available in paperback and hardback!

Crystal, Blaine, Caleb, and Ares will also get their own story soon in Vile Boys. Sign up for my newsletter to know exactly when it releases: www.clarissawild.com/newsletter

You can also find me on Instagram:
https://www.instagram.com/clarissa.wild/
Or you can join the Fan Club group on Facebook: www.facebook.com/groups/FanClubClarissaWild and talk with other readers!

# ALSO BY CLARISSA WILD

**Dark Romance**
Sick Boys
Beast & Beauty Duet
Debts & Vengeance Series
Dellucci Mafia Duet
The Debt Duet
Savage Men Series
Delirious Series
Indecent Games Series
The Company Series
FATHER

**New Adult Romance**
Fierce Series
Blissful Series
Ruin
Cruel Boy & Rowdy Boy

**Erotic Romance**
The Billionaire's Bet Series
Enflamed Series
Unprofessional Bad Boys Series

*Visit Clarissa Wild's website for current titles: www.clarissawild.com*

# ABOUT THE AUTHOR

Clarissa Wild is a New York Times & USA Today Bestselling author of Dark Romance and Contemporary Romance novels. She is an avid reader and writer of swoony stories about dangerous men and feisty women. Her other loves include her hilarious husband, her cutie pie son, her two crazy but cute dogs, and her adorable kitties. In her free time, she enjoys watching all sorts of movies, playing video games, reading tons of books, and cooking her favorite meals.

Want to be informed of new releases and special offers? Sign up for Clarissa Wild's newsletter on her website www.clarissawild.com.

Visit Clarissa Wild on Amazon for current titles.

Printed in the USA
CPSIA information can be obtained
at www.ICGtesting.com
LVHW040727030624
782098LV00002B/21